T·E·R·R·A!

STEFANO BENNI

TERRA!

TRANSLATED FROM THE ITALIAN BY
ANNAPAOLA CANCOGNI

PANTHEON
BOOKS

NEW YORK

LIBRARY OF CONGRESS CATALOGING IN PUBLICATION DATA
Benni, Stefano, 1947–
Terra!
I. Title.
PQ4862.E565T413   1985   853'.914   84-22600
ISBN 0-394-54353-X

Manufactured in the United States of America
First American Edition
Designed by Beth Tondreau

CHARACTERS

○ ○

CARLOS PHILDYS PLASSEY—General and Prime Minister of the Sinoeuropean Federation

PYK SHOWSPOTSHOW—Secretary of the Interior and Show Business (Sinoeuropean Federation) and great busybody

LEONARDUS CHRISTOPHORUS KOOK—a somewhat troubled scientist

BOZA CU CHULAIN—a space pilot of dubious morality

MEI HO LI—a bewitching telepath

CARUSO RAIMONDI—chief mechanic on the Sinoeuropean spaceship *Proteus Tien*

SARA—Caruso's helper

LEPORELLO TENZO E-ATARI, ALIAS LeO—an intrepid biped

FANG—an old Chinese man, specialist in one-liners

FRANK EINSTEIN—child prodigy

GENIUS 5—the most intelligent computer in the world

KING AKRAB, SADALMELIK TEMUGIN—the Great Scorpion, king of the Aramerussian Empire, an alliance of Arab, American, and Russian sheiks

ALYA—a slimy royal counselor

AL-DABIH—a soothsayer

COYLLUR—leader of the rock group Dzunum

ALICE, LAUREEN, EDITH—other members of Dzunum

JOHN VASSILIBOYD AND IGOR DYLANIEV—space pilots on the spaceship *Calalbakrab*

SMITSKY, ZUKOV, SHAULA—sheiks

SAITO—Technogeneral of the Sam (Samurai) Military Empire, consisting of military men from all over the world

HITACHI—Saito's helper

YAMAMOTO—Sam general, captain of the spaceship *Zuikaku*

HARADA—Yamamoto's right arm

PI—spiritual head of the gray soldiers

VAN CRAM THE VIKING—a space explorer

PINTECABORU—the giant of Mellonta, the forgotten planet

GALINA PERKOVAIA—an astronaut witch

COYA—a young Indian woman

HUATUC—a mysterious old man in Kouzok

CATUILLA, AUCAYOC, NANKI—Indians

and: *Deggu N'Gombo, the king of videogames; Paul McCartney and Mick Jagger, industrialists; Captain Quixote, meteorite hunter; Garcia, the shark; Geber, space journalist; Charos, physician in the White City; Johnny Carlson III, TV news jockey; Father Mapple, space missionary; Flamingosapiens, the flamingo man; Gienah, chief of the Scorpion's guards; Munkal and Nakir, torturers; Cherry, a sexy pornorobot; Big Chief Eagle Drumstick; a few swinish scientists; Laika's descendants; a rock-loving crocodile; the Texan billionaire ibn-Hunt; Martians, Incas, and numerous spaceships.*

T·E·R·R·A !

PROLOGUE

● ●

On the night of August 30, 2039, an extraordinary heat wave swept over the United States. In New York, the temperature hit 42°C. At midnight Western Hemisphere Standard Time, all the showers of the city let out a long howl of agony, and the croak of the pipes heralded a shut-down of the water supply till eight in the morning. Half of the inhabitants poured into the streets and streamed seaward in search of relief. That night alone, Coca-Cola sold over forty million quarts—enough black, sugary liquid to float the entire U.S. Navy. Ice cubes were suddenly worth more than diamonds: some say there were families who drank their swimming pools.

In the middle of the California desert, inside a bunker code-named Mothell, sat the Pentagon's Secret Operations Head-quarters. General Kingwen, the President's right-hand man, and two technicians were monitoring the control panel in the Global Nuclear Strike Command Center. At exactly 12:20 a.m., the bunker's air-conditioning system broke down: some-thing had clogged the air vents. One hour later, the hundred or so men in the fortification were nearly dying from heat ex-haustion, their shirts clinging to their backs, their beer cans popping like machine guns.

At 1:30, General Kingwen gave orders to open the armored windows and let some air in. The desert moon washed the white walls of the bunker with its light, and contemplated its electronic image reproduced on all the antimissile defense monitors.

At 2:02, everything was in order again. After downing a tall glass of Cuba Libre and joking about the summer football scores with his soldiers, General Kingwen decided to turn in. The desert was perfectly silent; even the coyotes seemed to have given up on their nightly serenade.

At 3:10, the technician who was left to monitor the control panel heard a faint noise outside the window above his head. He called a guard, who immediately turned on the exterior spotlights, but they couldn't see a thing. The bunker was lo-cated in the middle of a hundred miles of mined terrain, fenced in and guarded by sixty thousand men. No one could have approached it. In the meantime, the team fixing the air-condi-tioning system discovered that the vents were filled with mice. They had gathered there mysteriously to die, as if fleeing some danger. It would take a good two hours to clear up the mess, they announced.

At 3:30, in the middle of New York's Central Park, thou-sands and thousands of people had gathered for a rock concert. Bands of young black musicians were improvising on street corners and on the roofs of cars. "Dance and sweat," they yelled. TV stations had sent camera crews to cover the events.

At 3:32, the disk-jockey of KCUA (California Über Alles), the Voice of the Desert, aired "Whoom," the new hit of the War Heroes, the hottest group on the singles chart. The guards of the Mothell bunker, all wearing transistorized helmets, began nodding their heads and tapping their guns in time with the music. The full moon was all hazed over.

At 3:38 in California, the pointy snout of a mouse poked through the window of the control room. The animal tried to slither down the long wall, but lost its footing and fell right on top of key 15, the red alarm button that propelled missiles out of their underground silos. And suddenly, in the pale light of dawn, the desert stirred with new life as dozens of white missiles, Coyote 104s, sprouted out of the sand and cast their shadows along those of the cacti. No sooner did the technician realize what had happened than, with a screech of horror, he reached for key CC, Cancel Command. But his scream scared the mouse which, beating him to the punch, darted from key 15 to key 12—the button that would launch an immediate and irreversible attack on the Soviet Union. Before the technicians could get to the door of the control room to sound the alarm, the first missiles were already streaking through the desert sky.

At 3:40, in his mountain retreat, the President of the United States was awakened by an insistent ring on the hot-line. He picked up the phone and said: "I hope you have one helluva good reason for waking me up at this ungodly hour." At 3:41, Soviet radar detected the American missiles and automatically launched a counterattack with ninety SMS 203s.

At 3:43, on Fifth Avenue, in New York, thousands of people were clapping their hands in time with the band's music when they heard a strange, distant rumble. A few windowpanes fell out of the nearest skyscrapers and shattered at their feet. From the stage, the singer yelled: "No sweat, folks. Just a few technical problems with the mikes." But the rumble grew louder and nearer. Somebody screamed.

In the KCUA studio, the disk-jockey announced: "And now,

my friends, after the War Heroes' latest hit, here's a new single that will really blow your minds!'' It was 3:45. The single was an instant smash, but no one heard it. The first Soviet missile reached California just as the bass guitarist hit his first chord.

And this is how World War III started. Three more followed.

1

ONE HUNDRED (AND MORE) YEARS LATER

A monstrous white creature was trudging through the icy waste. All one could make out in that blizzard was a huge, fuzzy worm, some twenty yards of it, crawling on several pairs of legs. It had four red eyes and a humped back. Suddenly it stopped, raised its tiny head for a second, and then changed direction. Impossible to figure out what it really was till it got much closer, when it turned into four white bears, harnessed together, one behind the other, like the cars of a train. Each wore a red headlight, and bore two men on its back: a sherpa, wearing the yellow uniform of thalarctic cabbies, and a passenger. The lead bear, with the registration plate Hawaii 8, stopped again in its tracks and nervously sniffed the air.

"Move it, Bayard," the sherpa yelled, "we're almost there!" And, in fact, after just a few feet, the bear nuzzled a large red knob, half-buried in the snow, and pressed it down with the full weight of its paw. The white expanse quaked and split as a hatch opened with a loud creak, revealing an underground tunnel.

The sign PARIS METRO stood out above the frosty entrance. Braking their descent with their claws, the four bears disappeared inside the tunnel. The hatch closed, and everything outside was again white and still.

○ ○

PARIS: AN INCREDIBLE ADVENTURE THAT BEGINS IN THE COLD

○ ○ ○

On July 29, 2157, the temperature in Paris was −11°C. It had been snowing for exactly one month and six days, and almost all the buildings of the old city stood buried. Nevertheless, life went on as usual underground, in the subways, along the tunnels, in the botanic gardens, and in the forums, where the temperature was stable at +8°C.

From the highest floor of the immense icebound pyramid, a shivering man was staring at the frozen, barren waste that stretched for miles and miles of utter blankness, only occasionally broken by the light of a sled. Within the town walls, few buildings rose above the thirty meters of accumulated snow. The laser flightways issuing from the tall cylinder of Mitterrand Spaceport cast an intricate technicolored video-game against the gray sky. From the space control tower of Fort Montmartre, the new Police Headquarters, the cables of flying TV cameras wound all over the city like the tentacles of an immense aerial squid. Further down, the Eiffel Tower stood capped in its bell jar, like an old souvenir. Above it floated the teleprism of the Entertainment Center, broadcasting round-the-clock commercials, old Riviera documentaries, and, live from the subway, a variety of casual murders and other acts of violence.

The man on the pyramid had removed his fur coat, an old mouse jacket, and was trying to patch one of its sleeves. But his hands so shook with the cold that he couldn't even thread his needle. At that point, he raised his eyes and spotted four red dots on the conveyor belt leading into the pyramid, a hundred and fifty floors below; he immediately recognized the color of the astronauts' uniforms.

Laying aside thread and needle, he pushed the button of the videocom. The bespectacled face of a secretary, with a solitary red tuft of hair on her forehead, appeared on the screen.

"Well there, Miss Minnie," he smiled. "Like your new hairdo. Nice and trim! Who's your stylist?"

"Radiation," the young woman hissed. "May I help you with something?"

"Yes, you may. First of all, I need a larger needle. And then I would like to know if the bipeds at the door are the ones I have been waiting for."

"Yes, your excellency," the young woman answered. "Your secret mission seems to have arrived."

The four bipeds were walking with their heads tilted back so they could take in the huge building bristling with icicles that loomed over them. A three-tiered pyramid five hundred and twelve meters high, the Headquarters of the Sinoeuropean Federation was the third tallest building in the world, after the nearly eight hundred meters of the Atari Tower, in the Japanese Empire, and the one thousand and thirty meters of the Nabo building, seat of the seven Aramerussian sheiks.

These huge buildings had been built immediately after WW VI, when it became dramatically clear that the Great Cloud, which had deprived the Earth of its sun, was there to stay. Thousands of gigatons of dust, gas, and radioactive fallout, churned up by numerous explosions, had precipitated a process of irreversible glaciation that in turn brought on a worldwide energy crisis. As if this were not enough, seas and oceans were frozen over and completely toxic, surface radioactivity was extraordinarily high, and, as a daily treat, one could always count on the sudden return of a few "hoboes," fragments of the three thousand satellites and missiles, launched during the wars, which had long been traveling out of control. Some of them, like sensor rockets, were still programmed to hit cities long since razed, and were wandering around the earth looking for an enemy that no longer existed.

The entrance of the Federation Building was guarded by two tall cuirassiers, whose immobility was due more to freezing than to discipline. At their feet dozed two ichthyolures, a kind of catfish weighing about a hundred kilograms each, with long, grim whiskers. Having escaped from their frozen rivers some fifty years earlier, they had gradually adjusted to life on land. Their tail-propelled walk was clumsy, but their bite was elegantly effective.

The bipeds passed by the watchfish with utmost respect and proceeded into the large hallway. At one end shone a large marble slab, entirely covered with colored postcards, a monument to the cities of yore. The bipeds filed in front of the long list of names, which began as follows: "Amsterdam, despite innumerable wounds inflicted on its dikes, and the overwhelming power of the surrounding enemy army, resisted valiantly till it was razed to the ground on July 24, 2130."

A couple of Soda Cops were waiting for them behind a blue crystal pane at the other end of the hallway—massive soda machines with wheels for feet. (During WW V, all coin-operated machines had been militarized and robotized.) The first cop, specializing in hot drinks and provided with a photoelectric eye and a popgun, barred their way, and warned them in its creaky voice: "Stop where you are or I'll shoot!"

"Gee, thanks," joked one of the bipeds. "I'll have a volley of coffee with a shot of sugar."

The machine stepped forward threateningly.

"Keep your jokes to yourselves, please. Now, proceed in single file and speak up so I can verify your voiceprints."

The first biped to pass was the jokester, a huge black with scars all over his face. His uniform bore the flying-tiger insignia of a space pilot.

"My name is Boza Cu Chulain," he said. "I was born in the space station of New Africa. My mother was African. As for my father, I can give you a list of three hundred candidates—"

"That's enough," the cop cut him short. "Next?"

A thin man with a heavy beard stepped in front of the photoelectric eye. "My name is Leonardus Christophorus Kook. I am forty, I am a scientist, and I work on a solar capsule. It's bitching cold down here! Why don't you tear this mausoleum down if you can't keep it warm?"

"Political decorum, Dr. Kook," was the cop's prompt reply. "Next, please."

The next visitor, still wearing his flight helmet, was an odd biped—round and barely one meter tall. "My name is Leporello Tenzo E-Atari, and I cannot tell you where I was born because—"

"I know, I know," the cop interrupted him. "Next!"

The last, an old Chinese man, bowed. "My name is Fang. I was born in a mountain village whose roofs shone in the sun like—" He was interrupted by a sudden clanking noise. With a powerful sneeze, the other Soda Cop had unwittingly ejected a few cans.

"Never mind him," the Coffee Cop said. "His circuits tend to freeze in this temperature, and then . . . he sort of regresses."

"Well, bless you," the Chinese man said. "Today it's snowing, but I am sure that Dr. Kook will soon recapture the sun, wherever it's gone, and will bring its warmth back to Earth."

"I hope you're right, Mr. Fang," the cop replied. "You may

go now. The elevators are located at the end of hallway 4. You'd better roll up your trousers. That green rug on the floor is mold."

"Damn decorum," Chulain grumbled after a few steps, as a couple of fat rats darted between his feet.

"The Federation is doing its utmost," Kook sighed, "and that's all we can expect these days." As they reached the elevators, an old-fashioned robot, all decked out in trigonometric formulas, came toward them and bowed graciously.

"See," Kook said, "even though it might be a little worn-out, everything is in perfect working order, like this kind elevator robot."

"All too kind," Chulain allowed. "He's still bent over."

"Please excuse me," the robot apologized with a feeble voice. "I'm afraid the joints in my back have gotten stuck. Would you be so kind as to help me straighten up?"

The four bipeds helped the robot, who, after an uneasy creak, found himself upright again. Kook and Chulain threw each other a perplexed look.

"Gentlemen, if you'd follow me," said the robot, "this is the elevator. It is operated by an old two-horsepower outboard motor, so it'll take us about four minutes to get to where we are going. In the meantime, I'll be glad to provide you with some useful data about the city. To begin with—over there, where I'm pointing—"

"Over there, where?" Kook inquired.

"Oh, I'm awfully sorry," the robot apologized again. "I forget, my right forearm is missing—minor surgery . . . Well, if you would be so kind as to turn to your right, you'll see the ruins of Defense sticking out of the snow. A little above them, you can see the dirigible of the Folies-Bergère and the Montparnasse Shelter. The entrance is on the last floor of the skyscraper. From that point, one can ski down a series of internal ramps all the way to the center of the new Paris. Do you have any questions?"

"Yes," Chulain answered. "When are we going to get there? It's bloody cold in here!"

"Sixty more floors, sir," the robot, somewhat irritated, answered. "The temperature is still within the limits of endurance."

"Speak for yourself," Chulain replied. "I've never heard of a frozen robot."

"You're quite wrong, Chulain," the short biped intervened. "A thermal clot in the silicon circuit, accompanied by the progressive freezing of the neuroterminals, or a draft through the logical doors, causes very unpleasant sensations, which I would not hesitate to compare to what you humans call bronchopneumonia."

"Are you interested in robotics, sir?" the elevator robot kindly inquired.

"Yes," the small biped answered, removing his helmet to reveal a huge metallic head and a beak like a parrot's. "I love my neighbors."

"Oh!" the robot exclaimed. "I'm sorry, brother!" And the two greeted each other with a typical robotic knock of their heads. "Anyway, gentlemen, we aren't the only ones with energy problems. The Aramerussians and the Japanese had to cut their interplanetary flights by half."

"I know, I know," Kook sighed. "Space travel has become impossible. Just think of this: five days ago I received the order to get down to Earth by today. I was thousands of leagues away, in my lab, in solar orbit. I barely had time to zip up my uniform before they were at my door with an ore ship. Sixteen hours in space to make the connection with the astroferry from Jupiter. Then, after three days of flight, I find out that because of some strike or other, the ferry isn't going to land on Earth, but rather at Clavius Spaceport, on the Moon. And there, of course, the line for a shuttle cab is two kilometers long. Finally, I find a madman, totally illegit, who manages to sneak into the flight lanes of the large spaceships and proceeds to pass them, one by one, at three thousand kilometers per hour, singing 'Leader of the Pack.' I cling to my seat without knowing which makes me sicker, his driving or his voice. Finally, at five in the morning, he drops me off at New York-grad Spaceport and rips me off to the tune of one thousand two hundred ingots. I catch the last flight to Paris, an Air Albania dirigible, by a hair. What a nightmare: limp seaweed for lunch, seaweed pie for dinner, *Son of E.T. III* for the movie, cold drafts blowing all over the place, and for stewardesses a bunch of old Monohag robots who slap all the passengers who refuse to drink coffee. After I don't know how many hours and seventy cups of coffee, I land at Paris-Mitterrand, where they tell me that the snowcats are out of service and that they've been replaced by larger cats; and, let me tell you, the swaying of those bears was more than I could take: it did to me what no spaceship had ever been able to do; it made me throw up my guts. Nevertheless, here I am, miraculously punctual after five days with hardly any sleep. I wonder what else can happen to me!"

Suddenly, the elevator lights went off. From the slight rocking motion, Kook judged that they were no longer moving.

"What's going on?" he asked.

"I'm afraid, sir," the robot explained, "it must be the usual blackout. Don't worry; it shouldn't last more than ten hours. What a shame! We were only two floors away from our destination!"

△ The Sinoeuropean Pyramid ▽

After six fairly monotonous hours, energy was restored and the elevator proceeded past the last two floors. Its doors opened on an enormous room, evenly divided by blue glass walls. A man, wearing a mouse fur and insignia identifying him as a general of the Sinoeuropean Federation, was waiting with a ceremonious smile. Prime Minister Carlos Phildys Plassey's mechanical hand and uncertain gait bespoke his lively participation in WW V and VI. Next to him stood a policerobot with a multijointed detector arm, which he immediately waved in front of the new visitors, a kind of blessing.

"I welcome you, my friends," Phildys greeted them. "I hope you won't let these petty formalities bother you, but for quite some time now, the Sams have been unusually active with their mechanical toys. Only yesterday we discovered that all the elevator buttons had been bugged. I wouldn't be surprised if they'd managed to do the same to you."

But at that very moment, the low, satisfied moan of the policerobot told him that the bipeds were clean.

"Please follow me," Phildys said. "I apologize for the disruption in elevator service. Of late we have had energy troubles. But, tell me, Kook, how is your research coming along up in your solar cap? To judge from your tan, I'd say it's going well."

"Not bad, not bad," Kook answered. "I am currently studying how solar flares and their radiations can contribute to the growth of certain plants."

"I know, I know everything about the Operation Basil Jungle," Phildys remarked with an ambiguous smile. "Even though I haven't seen you since the last war, my dear Kook, I have followed your . . . transformation with great interest."

Kook made no comment, and the group proceeded across the room to a section furnished with nothing but a dozen or so airplane seats.

"Please sit down and fasten your seat belts as tightly as you can," Phildys instructed them. "And if your head starts spinning, be patient."

He had barely finished saying this when the pyramidal room tipped over, pivoted on its apex, and then swung upright again. Now there was no longer a wall to the right but another huge room where a team of white-frocked technicians was working away at an immense computer panel.

"Now you may unfasten your seat belts. This is section 26, a very private room," Phildys explained. "We have reached it by spinning our own section on its joints, if I may so call them. This whole building is a Pyraminx, a pyramid made up of smaller pyramids that can move, spin, and interlock in a variety of combinations. It's a toy with great potential. Of course, occasionally there are a few problems. For instance, two days ago, the mechanism went berserk and the Cabinet found itself meeting in the toilets. And then, of course, there are those days when suddenly everything starts flying around—desks, files, penholders . . . And to avert a strike, we had to grant our employees a generous rotation bonus. Now we enter the section devoted to special research, and I'll introduce you to our chief. I warn you: don't let appearances fool you!"

Once inside the section, Phildys walked toward a bespectacled child who was stretched out under a computer, engrossed in a comic book entitled *The Kinkiest Games on Saturn.* Phildys coughed discreetly. "Ahem, Dr. Einstein? Mission Terra is here."

Blushing, the boy hid the magazine behind his back and said, "Just a moment, please. If you don't mind, I'd like to finish fixing this computer—minor data trouble—and then I'll be with you."

"He's a little gruff, but a true genius," Phildys whispered. "He is twelve years old, and was born *in vitro* at the Genetic Center for Scientists in Berlin. At nine, he was already running the mining department, and though he was out for a year with mumps, now he is heading up energy research. He's got brains, no doubt about that! But he's still only a boy."

"I understand," Kook nodded. "At his age I had data troubles, too."

In the meantime, the boy had reemerged, now sporting a fluorescent bow tie, a sign of high rank in the Federation. He was accompanied by a man with a sparkling toupee and vibrating plastic antennas.

"Doctor Frank Einstein," the boy introduced himself smugly. "I'm very pleased to meet you. This is Dr. Pyk Show-

spotshow, former TV host and current Secretary of the Interior
and Show Business."

"You may call me Pyk," said the man with the antennas.
"Have you heard the one about the kid who finds his mother
in bed with a Martian? He—"

"Mr. Showspotshow," Phildys interrupted, "I'm sure there
will be plenty of time for jokes. Right now, I'd like to finish
the introductions. Where were we? Dr. Leonardus Kook,
scholar of preglacial civilization. The honorable Mr. Fang, Professor of Science and Philosophy at the Sinic Academy, and
Telepath Emeritus. Captain Chulain, space pilot. Biped Leporello Tenzo, model A, E-Atari, otherwise known as LeO, robot
Friday, specializing in math and gastronomy."

"Let's start, then," the boy said. "Top secret!" At these
words, the doors closed, the glass walls became black and im-
penetrable, and the view of the snowy world outside gradually
darkened. As soon as everybody was seated, a slide was pro-
jected on a screen. It showed a metal stake, as tall as a man,
stuck into a block of ice.

"This object is the reason you were summoned," Phildys
explained. "It is MY-DBS, a property-claim vector. It was discovered a few days ago on a South American mountain in an
area inhabited by Eskimos and Mestengo Indians. The name
of that region is Kouzok, and it corresponds roughly to the city
of Cuzco in Peru on the preglacial map. Some mining technicians on a dig found it. For those who do not know it, these
'dibs,' as they are commonly called, are earthbound vectors
granted to the space hounds of the Mine Belt and to the sun
hunters—in short, to space explorers."

"Explorers, my ass!" Chulain grinned. "They're a bunch of
gallows birds in search of Uranium 235, who bump each other
off like animals!"

"I think you may be a little extreme," observed the boy,
unperturbed. "They are pilots to whom the Federation gives
free fuel and the permission to pursue their research on the

farthest and most dangerous planets, in exchange for fifty percent of their finds."

"Self-serving crooks!" Chulain grunted in spite. "I know
their kind!"

"We know, we know," Einstein nodded. "You've had a very
. . . adventurous past along those same routes. This is precisely
why the computer has chosen you—"

"You must know," Phildys intervened, "that whenever
these . . . explorers find some exploitable mineral on a planet,
they send this vector back to earth. Actually, it is recalled via
a Lassie impulse by the central computer in Kouzok. This way,
the space hounds can send us a tape containing precise information about the spatial location of their find, so that no new-
comer will steal it from them, as often happened in the past."

"And what did this particular explorer find?" Kook asked.

"Something rather . . . peculiar," Phildys answered pensively. "Now I'm going to let you listen to the first of his
messages, which he enclosed in the MY-DBS vector found in
Kouzok. Please don't let his language bother you. The pilot in
question is an old space sailor."

For a second, everything was silent; then a hoarse, metallic
voice resounded through the room.

♈ Van Cram, the Viking ♈

"Dear governmental flatasses. Today, July 4, 2157, I,
Captain Eric Van Cram, the Viking, commander in chief
of Spaceship *Langrebort*, claim the discovery of a natural
planet. But I can't tell you where the fucker is, 'cause all
my fucking computers are busted. My button-pusher says
he ain't never seen anything like it. It's as if somebody
had greased my instruments with rum; the needles
dance, the lights hiccup, and the central computer apes a
parakeet that can only croak, 'Data absurd, stop. Data
absurd, stop. Data absurd, stop.' Nevertheless, I stake the

claim and reserve the right to communicate all the data required by your bureaucratic flatassed law as soon as possible. My intergalactic-research license number is 43677; my ID number is ERC VCR 211 VKG; the size of my boots is seventeen. I am not going to tell you about my return course, either, since my acquisition is not yet in order and I wouldn't want any government lackey to get the idea of stealing it from me. As the spaceman's song goes:

> If Saturn's still got its outermost ring
> It's 'cause the government ain't done a thing.

Over and out. Hope you all freeze your butts."

The voice ceased, and the ruddy face of a large blond man with a patch over his right eye appeared on the screen.

"Is that Van Cram, the Viking?" Kook inquired.

"The devil himself," Einstein answered. "He's actually a very capable explorer. He has already found two satellites for Agenor, both rich in osmium."

"I still can't figure out what we're supposed to do with all this," Chulain nervously admitted.

"Patience, patience," General Phildys continued. "This is only the first part of the message. All these vectors contain a secret compartment we call 'the confessional.' This is where you'd put a message for the secret services, if you thought it particularly important. This is Van Cram's 'confessional.' "

"Type S message; I repeat, type S message," the familiar voice boomed. "I've been here for two days now. Folks, the little planet I've discovered belongs to the N1 series, absolutely natural. You can live here without a helmet, and no need for bioadaptation, either. It's chockfull of mountains, meadows, water, flowers, and greedy insects. There is no fallout, no radiation to speak of, and there's even a star that gives light and heat, and wanders up and down in the sky, just like our ex-sun. This big star can put on the prettiest petticoat dawns and the juiciest catsup sunsets! At the very sight of them, my crew, a bunch of kids who'd make gorillas look like fairies, stretch out on the grass and bawl like babies. And I hate to admit it, but even I can feel a big lump in my throat, because this planet—we've dubbed it Terra—is a perfect copy of our old Earth, the way the documentaries show it, before it was all frozen up by the bombs."

There was a brief pause. The listeners in the Federation room were visibly moved.

"Folks," the voice went on. "During my intergalactic travels, I've seen many wonderful things: Diurnus, the flower planet whose petals close at dusk, and Pollux, the heavenly hitchhiker that likes to cling to the orbit of larger planets. I've seen the flight of Myron, the stadium with a million seats, where the last Galactic Olympiad took place. I've bathed in the sea of Arutas and contemplated its variegated bottom, seven thousand meters down, and watched the frolics of transparent whales with luminous hearts. I've crossed the jungle of the giant cigars of Reemstma, with its pestilential smoke, and witnessed the duels of comets and the wedding of colossal myrtles. I've seen the pornomushrooms of Transpluto mate in forty different ways, and I've captured and caged four small rainbows from Tramuntium. I've drunk the four-flavored clouds of the sky of Freshko, and have smoked the grass of the satellite Aptenodytes with twelve penguins—at least, that's what I remembered afterward. But never, and I mean *never*, have I seen such a beautiful place. On this planet I've found all the things my grandfather Burz used to tell me about on those long wintry evenings while we were waiting for somebody to rob. There are flowers of all shapes and sizes, the tallest trees, flocks of black birds with twenty-meter wingspans, plants with golden fruit, and butterflies with polka-dot, technicolor, or litmus wings. I swear I'm not drunk. It's all true—this is paradise. My robots are making holes all over the place, and they tell me that the subsoil is crammed with minerals. If only I knew where the fuck we are! See if you can figure it out. I left Meskorska on June 2. After passing the satellite Ariel, I gave free rein to my old *Langrebort* until I found the entry into the Universal Sea, as it was marked on an old map that had belonged to the Boojum brothers, the ones who disappeared last January. Well, after three days, suddenly, all the instruments get roaring drunk, and we drop into a cloud of rarefied plasma, similar to the one around Saturn, and something makes us spin along like a drunken duck on an orbit with an elliptical cusp, and the temperature rises to seventy thousand degrees Kelvin. Just when we think we're going to fry, we enter the gravitational field of the natural planet. We landed on a very high mountain. I want to reconfirm the fact that not one of our instruments, including our central computer, is functioning. I can't make head or tail of it. Can you? Our last recorded position, before dropping into the cloud, was T-466-Aldebaran. Over and out."

"And here we are," Phildys said, as the lights in the room came on again. "This is the end of the second message. I think you've heard enough to understand why we called you and why we are ready to spend a third of the energy we have left on this mission. We've been looking for a planet like this for years. Do you know what it means?"

"Charter flights," Pyk chuckled with shining eyes. "Grand cruises! Huge hotels!"

"Oxygen, sun, sea!" said the general, paying no attention to him.

"Yes! Sea! Waves! Windsurf!" Pyk yelled with excitement. "Waterfalls! Postcards! Waterfall postcards! Panoramic restaurants! Sun! Sunscreens! Tanning lotions! Our children could play and chase after snails and deer. They could run, jump, sweat, buy cold drinks, and get sick! Aspirins! Thermometers!"

"Mr. Pyk, sir," Einstein brusquely interrupted him. "Do you think, maybe, between a cool drink and a deer, that we could also look for a few incidentals like uranium and a source for solar power, and try to mend our energy deficit, and cure a few subterrestrial diseases?"

"True!" Pyk agreed. "We'll have great hospitals! Spas! I've already got the slogan, 'Come up and see us sometime.' "

"But, aside from all these . . . slightly premature projects," Phildys intervened politely, "do you understand why we want to keep this mission totally secret?"

"So secret that you had to get a telepath to monitor us here?" Fang inquired with a sly smile.

"A mere precaution to make sure you were not hypnocontrolled," Phildys explained without the least embarrassment. "We knew you would soon find us out. Miss Mei, you may come in now." A young Oriental with long black hair entered from a side door and, advancing a few steps, bowed to our friends.

"Please excuse me for having to spy on your honorable minds. My name is Mei Ho Li, and I will accompany you on your expedition. I am twenty-two, and I am not the mistress of any government official, Mr. Chulain."

"Just curious," Chulain muttered, embarrassed.

"And now that you know what you're going to be looking for in that remote quadrant," Einstein said, "it might be time to talk about the third part of the message, and—"

"Just a sec," LeO interrupted. "My ears itch."

"That's awesome news, Mr. LeO," Einstein remarked. "But I would like you to give priority to our petty concerns."

In the meantime, Chulain had jumped to his feet and was scouring the room with his eyes.

"Look here, boy," he said, turning to Einstein, "if LeO's ears itch, it means that his radio receiver is getting tickled by interference nearby. In other words, there's a bug around somewhere."

"Impossible! We inspected the whole place only yesterday!" Phildys exclaimed, also jumping to his feet. "I don't see how there could be a single bug left."

"I do," Fang said with complete calm. "Your ashtray is trying to run away."

Phildys screamed as he saw the metal ashtray spin off his desk, dash for the window, throw itself against the panes, and then knock around the room like a crazed bat.

"Help! Call the janitors! Catch the damn thing! Shit, they have tricked us again!" Einstein screamed, quite forgetting himself. Four men with long metal brooms rushed into the room and, at one fell swoop, knocked the ashtray down. One of the janitors examined it briefly.

"A Sam receiver, Haiashi simulator."

"Take it to the lab and interrogate it," Pyk screamed, furious.

"You won't get anything out if it," Phildys said. "Besides, by now, both Arabs and Japanese have picked up all they wanted. Which they would have done anyway, sooner or later. But they won't be able to find the right course without our code. And there is a third part to the message which Miss Mei has just communicated telepathically to Fang. As she mentioned, she will be going with you, and in the course of the flight, she will remain in constant contact with us."

An intergalactic brain hookup? At that distance? Kook wondered. Can thought travel that fast?

Mei turned to him with a smile. "Does it take you very long to think of a star?"

"You'll be leaving tomorrow afternoon," Einstein broke in,

as he got up. "The computers are calling for maximum celerity. Do you have any other questions, gentlemen?"

"Just a small one," Kook said. "I understand why we might want to run from one galaxy to the next, looking for some crazy space explorer. But, even assuming we find that planet, where in the world will we find the energy we need to fly spaceships over there, set up a colony, and start mining those resources?"

"We've thought about that, Doctor," Einstein answered, slightly annoyed. "But I don't think this is the proper time to discuss it. Our computers are seldom wrong in their projections. And when they make a mistake, it is never that banal. And now, please excuse me. I must get the flight plans ready. So long, gentlemen."

The child departed proudly, staggering on his large antimouse boots.

"He's got character," Kook noted.

"He reminds me," Pyk said, "of that joke about the German astronaut who lands on a Jewish planet, and—"

"Would you like to join us for dinner?" Phildys interrupted. "The Sinoeuropean fare is no longer what it used to be, but if you don't mind a mouseburger and a big bacterial steak with cellulose . . ."

"No, thank you," Kook answered. "We'd like to take a stroll through nighttown. Chulain needs to see a friend of his."

"Great idea! There's a small club near the Forum, which I highly recommend. It's called Venus, and it caters to all tastes."

"Terrific!" said LeO, his dials quivering in anticipation. "I could really go for a lube job!"

○   ○   ○

THE SHEIKS

△ △ △

Two Arabs, an American, and a Russian were playing cards on the deck of the yacht. Their white caftans fluttered in the warm sea breeze. The ship rocked lightly as it glided past an island full of tropical palms, under which stood clusters of natives, laughing, screaming, and waving at the bikini-clad beauties who displayed various shades of tan on the edge of the yacht's swimming pool. An impeccable blond French waiter (such as were favored among rich Arab families) approached and, with a slight cough, attracted their attention.

"Your excellency . . ."

"What's the matter, Alain?" the fattest, most bejeweled Arab asked.

"The captain would like to know whether you intend to proceed toward Hawaii, or if you'd rather dock in Sardinia for the evening."

The big Arab dropped his cards on the table.

"Tell the captain to do whatever he pleases, in the name of Allah. Everything bores me equally."

"You shouldn't say that, Alya," the other Arab reproached him. "This cruise is a masterpiece of organization. A wonder of technology!"

"It might be a wonder, Feishal," Alya answered, "but for my part, I can't forget that this optimally lukewarm breeze is produced by fans, that this gorgeous island is a hologram, that all these tantalizing scents are custom-made by Japanese machines, that the sun consists of twenty-six quartz lamps, and that our yacht is rocking and rolling in the middle of a swimming pool, under a plastic dome. While outside it's been snowing for a month."

"You're hard to please, Alya," the American retorted. "Would you rather be out there digging mines at a temperature of twenty-six below?"

"Shut up, Smitsky!" Alya snapped back. "You'd be perfectly happy fishing for chocolate sardines on a three-hundred-foot silicon beach with transistorized crabs. But not me! I don't have any fun anymore. What's the point of playing cards with one-million-druble chips if all you can buy in this world is either artificial or synthetic?"

"Girls are not synthetic," the Russian said, turning toward them with a smile.

"Nor artificial, perhaps. But, my dear Zukov, at the Cairo Harem School, they do not teach conversation. Their idea of pleasure is strictly acrobatic," Alya muttered.

"You're really impossible," Smitsky protested. "You live in Petrominsk, the most beautiful underground city in the world, with only sixteen thousand inhabitants. People would kill to live there! And you spit on it."

"Alya is right," came a deep voice over their shoulders. "One *must* want more." A tall Arab with a red beard and a black cloak had approached the table.

Alya turned pale. "Your Majesty . . . King Akrab . . . I . . . I didn't mean to complain . . . I was only . . ."

"No! No! No! You needn't apologize, my son. You are perfectly right, Alya! What's the point of owning the largest gas supply on Earth, two hundred astroyachts, and a city with optimal year-round temperature and two swimming pools for each house when, two hundred years ago, even the humblest, poorest, dirtiest, most miscreant kaffir had more fun than we do today? But maybe, gentlemen," the king said, as he sat down at the table, "there is a way out. Maybe there is a place, in space, where we could all live a life worthy of our power, and of Alya's imagination. And not just Alya's, because I'm sure that even you Russians, our friends from the August pact, and even you Americans, our allies who flew to us from your frozen, Eskimo-ridden country to share a new and prosperous land with the Russians, you are all dreaming of a better place to live than the steppes of San Franciskograd."

"O Wisest among the Wise, O Great Pearl of Finance," Alya

whined. "A place like that, alas, just can't exist anymore. We've used up almost all our carbodeuterium in space research. The cloud does not clear, the thermometer keeps dropping, and all we have found are a few planets as cold as the bed of a virgin abandoned on her wedding night."

"That's exactly it, boss," said Smitsky. "This is what they have established once and for all at the research center in New Moscow: there is nothing more to do. The shitty Earth we had is gone forever, and all we have left is this icebox."

"Oh, my wise and unhappy friends," al-Akrab said. "Seeking is arduous and often unrewarding, but as an old proverb of ours says: the finest diamond is the hardest to find. I have good news . . ."

THE SAMURAI

Technogeneral Saito's office in the Department of Space Conquests, on the top floor of the Atari Mitsubishi building, was one of the largest and most sumptuous in Japan; it measured almost four square meters. Technogeneral Saito was hammering out data on his wrist computer at an extraordinary speed when the door suddenly opened. Its edge hit the general's head; luckily he was wearing a helmet, and so hardly stirred.

"Please, sit down, Hitachi," the general said without raising his eyes.

"Where?" Hitachi, a young military man with a shaved skull, asked.

"There's a folding chair in the wall, right behind you," Saito said. "If you push that button, it will pop out." Hitachi pushed the button and, immediately, a jet of hot water poured over his head. He screamed with pain.

"Watch out, Hitachi!" Saito, who now looked up, warned him. "You pushed the tea button! Move, quick!"

"Why?" Hitachi inquired, just as his polished skull received a good dusting of white powder.

"Too late!" Saito said. "You see, I like my tea with sugar. But never mind, don't make me waste any more time. Tell me, do the sheiks know everything?"

"Yes, they bought the information exactly twenty minutes ago. They are already equipping a superspaceship from their Kriegsmarine."

"Which one? The *Nabilia*? The *Star Sword*? The *Calalbakrab*?"

"Almost certainly the latter."

"How many spies do we have on that ship?"

"Three waiters, two robots, sixteen electrognomes camouflaged as blenders, a number of bugged forks, a TV camera in every shower—"

"All right, all right. Do you think we should sabotage them?"

"No, I don't think so. If we stop them from taking off, nothing will keep them from buying all the Japanese spaceship pilots before the day's over."

"Yes, I agree with you, Hitachi. Which spaceship are we going to use?"

"The *Akai Mazinga Zuikaku*. It's only four meters long, but it can easily hold two men and some sixty gray soldiers. And if we need to, we can stretch it out to nine meters."

"How many miles does it make on a liter of carbodeuterium?"

"About one-eighteenth of a quadrant."

"Not enough! You'll have to get rid of some weight. Miniaturize the toilets. Punch holes in the robots. Whatever, but do something!"

"General Saito, we really can't reduce the astronauts' facilities any further. It is already going to be a long, uncomfortable journey!"

"Bullshit! They'll manage, just as we all do! At the War Academy, our bunks were so close together that, lying down, we looked like a stack of toast. And do you know what it meant to be off duty? It meant a ten-meter walk! What do you know about comfort? Cut back, cut back, and no excuses. By the way, what can you tell me about the Sinoeuropean mission?"

"You can read all the data about it on my hat, General. The guy with a tan and a beard is Leonardus Christophorus Kook, an energy expert. During the last world war, he was the first one to foresee the extent of the damage produced by the cloud and the rain of space wrecks. He was accused of being an ecomarxist and was forced to leave the army. Now, he lives in a twenty-six-square-meter solar capsule, is tanned year-round, and studies plants."

"In short, he has retired," Saito concluded.

"More or less. And then there's a robot, an ex-satellite spy, originally launched by the Russians; he played a double game with us as well. At the beginning of the war, he ex-orbited, reentered our atmosphere, and asked for political asylum. He was restructured and given gastronomico-mathematic functions. This is Fang, the monkey, the one who—"

"I know," Saito growled. "I know everything about that damn pacifist drunkard. I was in command of Mission Fire on London, and we were doing pretty well, considering, until the day I saw General Saki come back to our headquarters, hypnotized, singing 'I Wanna Fish in the River Wei,' before he had even dropped a single bomb."

"A damn chuang-tzu, bloody intellectualoid," Hitachi concurred. "And that isn't all. During the war, under the code name of Vega, he was in intergalactic telepathic communication with a certain Atair. Now he's going to repeat the experiment with this Mei Ho Li, a very capable young telepath. That's how they hope to exchange data without being intercepted."

"A brilliant idea, but not enough to deter us. And the other ones?"

"There is a pilot, Cu Chulain, ex-rebel, repeatedly prosecuted for rioting, tree smuggling, assault and battery of various computers, sexual abuse, and a number of traffic violations, including space speeding. They've taken him because he is the only one who has been in the Universal Sea, the forbidden quadrant. There will also be a mechanical technician, a certain Caruso. For the moment, that's it—which is mighty odd, don't you agree? I mean, not even one war robot?"

"Who is going to be in command on Earth?"

"General Phildys is in charge of the political aspects of the mission, at least officially. But they are already tearing one another apart over it. The man in control of the mission itself, however, is a new guy, Einstein, fresh from the kiddie farm: he's only twelve, has an IQ of one hundred and forty-six, considerable sexual confusion, and a rather nasty addiction to electric ice cream."

"And what about their energy situation?"

"Terrible! Less than two million gigavovs. To fly a spaceship all the way over there will cost them at least a third of their supply. Which means they will barely have enough left to keep warm for two more years, much less to be able to keep a light burning on their graves!"

"I don't understand," Saito said. "How can they even hope to beat us in a space race?"

"They're digging like moles all over the American continent," Hitachi said. "Obviously, they're hoping to find something they might utilize at a lower energy cost. They're at the end of their rope, General. We have them!"

"Yes!" Saito said. "We will follow their spaceship, and once it has led us to Terra, we'll get rid of it. After which, we'll tap every last drop of that planet's energy, and with our technological power renewed, we'll be able to wipe out all seven sheiks with their gilded palaces and their knickknacks, and then . . ."

"And then?" Hitachi echoed him.

"And then," Saito repeated with dreamy eyes. "And then, space—the entire, immense, cosmic void—will be ours. The density up there is 0.0000000000000000000000017—Do you realize what that means, Hitachi?"

"I think so. But why are you crying, General?"

"Do you think it is right, Hitachi," Saito asked, "that one single hydrogen atom should have so much space, when I have to live in a condo with eight thousand other people?"

* *

PARIS LA NUIT

☙ ☙ ☙

The hottest Paris belle
sent all her frills to hell
she bought a machine gun
designed by Chanel
and the subway train, wagon by wagon
sprang from the earth like a huge dragon
screaming:
"I can no longer stand the clatter
that hanged men's skeletons
make when they rattle!"
And this was the first sign
of the horror to come.
All the cats stepped out of line
and struck men dumb
and ate all the best little
grannies one by one

and all the gargoyles tumbled
from the towers of Notre Dame
onto the heads of tourists from Japan
and cracked their cameras
like skulls
and each corpse was shot
by a Japanese survivor.
Dear Lord, in just one night
they killed a thousand heroes
and sank two thousand submarines
and a few Syrian pitas
and blood squirted from crepes.
"Oh, no," the enemies said, "we can't
let our old Paris die
in such an ugly way,
maybe we could all try
to make her death a bit more gay."
And, aiming at the Champs Élysées
as if it were a runway,
a rocket sliced the Paris sky
without a sound, trailing its span
"A gift to Paris
from a fan."
—*from "The Destruction of Paris,"*
sung by the Machiniques (number one on
the French hit parade, May 2156)

Kook, Chulain, and LeO were walking along the conveyor
sidewalks of the Central Forum in Paris. As the twenty-four-
hour rhythms of rocksky music boomed from every streetcor-
ner, the nocturnal fauna of the city strolled along, decked out
in "lightpump" garb, the *dernier cri* in French fashion—neon
signs and firetron-crystal tattoos. Some were walking large
colored tortoises on a leash; others wore sequined gas masks.
They formed a fluorescent ribbon that snaked along the sidewalks, in and out of the various underground levels.

The first three levels, the pink ones, were mostly for tourists. That's where you could find the ruins of the old Paris enclosed in thermal bell jars. The entire Boulevard Saint Germain was preserved exactly, house by house, café by café, except that most of the Parisians sitting along its terraces were embalmed. The second level boasted the best restaurants and the most elegant shops, not to mention a perfect reconstruction of Pont Neuf, with two hundred meters of tepid, antisuicidal Seine flowing beneath it. The Louvre had been completely restored after the bombing of 2106, and though the contents of the museum itself had been lost, its rooms now hosted the largest snack bar in Europe, called the Mona Lisa, with waitresses dressed in her enigmatic smile, and waiters like Titian's *Man with Glove*. From the fourth to the sixth level, you could roam through the most characteristic spots of old Paris: Montmartre, Pigalle, Montelimat, rue Mouff—whole squares had been taken apart and reconstructed piece by piece. Chulain decided to sit down in Place de la Contrescarpe. LeO went bananas over the Beaubourg, which, he thought, looked exactly like his uncle. Kook spaced out on feeding mechanical pigeons, till Chulain grabbed his left arm and pulled him away.

"Come on, guys," he urged them, "all this junk's for tourists! I'll take you where we can really have fun!"

"All right, Cu," Kook agreed. "But not below the twelfth level. I don't want to risk my skin."

"Nor I my silicons," LeO concurred.

The discotheques on the first ten levels offered a great variety of musical genres from all over the world. Since it was Saturday, at least half a million guys and gals were pouring in and out of the numerous clubs, where they would go on dancing till Monday morning. Our friends made their way down past all the confusion to level eleven, movie theaters, and then to level twelve, videogames. Beyond this point, the black levels began: levels thirteen and fourteen were entirely dedicated to serious gambling, while fifteen was the first porno level.

Here they met the first night-cruisers: some fifty young Pan-Africans, half-naked under leopard-skin top hats, and a group of Ton Tons, obese bouncers clothed in candy wrappers, and very much feared for their formidable belly blows. They saw the tattooed Jakuzi and the Spitters, gangs of aggressive septuagenarians, as well as the Clowns who, despite their gay mien and their unicycles, could play the deadliest tricks. They also saw a number of retro-gangs, such as the extremely elegant Bowies, the Chinese Red Guards, and the Italian Alpines, with their climbing boots, yodels, and pickaxes, all more or less authentic.

Chulain managed to convince the others to go all the way down to level seventeen in order to find an old friend of his who, he claimed, might know a great deal about Van Cram. Cautiously, they walked down to level sixteen, the second porno level. The escalators stopped there. The level was brightened by the red lights of the pornoways, and by the large, suspicious eyes of the wolf robots, who scanned them from top to bottom, looking for arms. It was here that all police control ended, and those who chose to proceed further down did so at their own risk.

Our friends decided to follow the outer corridors. They saw a group of beggars piled up against the walls, with their hygiene-control cards tied around their necks and their bodies ravaged by radiation. There were also some two dozen rusty robots who squeaked pitifully, making a great clatter as they fell and rolled over while trying to improvise a few stunts.

"Brother," one of these said as he approached LeO, "do you have any spare wattage—just an amp or two?"

"Why don't you get yourself a job?" LeO answered angrily. "You were built in 2022; your arms are still strong!"

The beggar robot insisted briefly, then gave up. "May a gigaton of rust clog your circuits," he cursed under his breath as LeO walked away.

Our three friends proceeded toward a dark corridor over

which was affixed the sign "GROUP DISCOUNTS." Its entry was barred by four blind children whose bodies were entirely covered with a thick pitch-black glue.

"These are tar babies," Chulain explained. "Unauthorized beggars. Be careful. If they jump you, you'll never be able to get rid of them; it's either your clothes or your money. Let me handle them."

Chulain fished two or three musical coins out of his pockets and threw them as far as he could. No sooner did the coins start playing than the children jumped up and ran after them, tackling and getting each other tangled in their sticky grasp.

"Poor bastards," Kook said. "Is this a souvenir of the photonic wars?"

"Yes," Chulain answered. "Tar-bombs 404. Impossible to get rid of the stuff." In the meantime, they had reached an area surrounded by a number of cautionary posters:

PORNO 12. NO ONE WILL BE ALLOWED INTO THE
CHAMBERS WITHOUT A VALID SEX ID.

"And what's all this?" LeO wondered. In the black corridor that opened up in front of them, they could distinguish a number of luminous mouths suspended in midair: sensual, red, pink, purple mouths displaying a bluish glow.

"I think it's called firefly alley," Kook explained. "Those mouths belong to the men and women who work in the side chambers. They chew gum and candy, and the gaseous nitrogen in the sugar gives their throats this sort of turboluminescence, which is then amplified by their fluorescent lipstick."

"Not bad, not bad," Chulain noted as he passed in front of a large pink mouth which greeted him by sticking out its tongue. He barely managed to catch a glimpse of a girlish face with long eyelashes.

"Why don't they show their faces?" LeO again wondered.

"They all have other jobs. They're here only to make some

extra money. I have two good friends—husband and wife, both art teachers—who have been working here for years."

"Hello, Greenlips," Chulain greeted one of the mouths. "To judge from the height of your kisser, you must be quite a broad!"

"Right on," the mouth answered. "Or maybe I'm standing on a chair."

They left the alley and suddenly found themselves in front of the steel gate at the top of the staircase down to level seventeen. Two gigantic police volunteers, equipped with kendo swords and Fiat machine guns, ordered them to stop.

"Where do you think you're going, gorgeous?" the tallest one, a black guy with an afro and a moustache, asked them.

"We're going to level seventeen," Chulain answered.

"Where? To the Sword? To the rough-sports stadium? I don't think it's a very good idea. Tonight there's a hockey match between Mexicans and Pekinese. The fans are restless."

"We're just going to pay a short visit to a friend of mine, brother," Chulain explained. "His name is Deggu N'Gombo, and he owns a gambling hall in the electronic sector. It'll only take a second."

"Hmmm," the volunteer noted, sizing them up. "Are you armed? Do you know any special fighting techniques? Any martial arts? Can you spit poison?"

"We know all that's allowed by the survival code, chief," Chulain said.

"Well, then, go to hell. But if you want some friendly advice, stop at level eighteen. This week, less than half the people who went down to nineteen and twenty have come back up. What about your robot friend—is he staying here?"

"What?" LeO protested. "Why should I stay here?"

"Rules are rules. We can't check out whether you're hiding a laser gun, an electroshock needle, or some other weapon in the middle of all that junk. Nonhumans have to be quarantined for a week before they're allowed in the black levels."

"Hey, man," LeO yelled. "I ain't got no weapon! Go right ahead, frisk me! You won't find a damn thing!"

"LeO," Chulain turned to him, "do you know that this level has not one, but *three*, alleys of mechanical dolls?"

"See you later, guys," LeO said, turning on his wheels.

Chulain and Kook watched him roll quickly away and disappear into the swelling tide of night-cruisers. The volunteer buzzed the green gate open and then locked it again behind them. They found themselves at the top of a long spiral staircase. The surrounding walls were completely covered with graffiti and brightly colored murals. The smiles on old advertisement posters gleamed mockingly from the rotting walls. The odor of mildew and ozone stagnated under a spectral light. They kept walking down, till they found a billboard:

LEVEL 17—THE CLOUD. HARD DRUGS. THIS LEVEL AND THE ONES THAT FOLLOW IT ARE EXEMPT FROM FEDERATION LAWS AND POLICE SURVEILLANCE. WE ADVISE ALL VISITORS TO ABIDE BY THE RULES OF THE NIGHT-SURVIVAL CODE AND TO WEAR GAS MASKS. HAVE A GOOD TIME AND LOTS OF LUCK. YOU'LL NEED IT.

☽ ◖ ◔ ◐ ◑ ◗ ◑ ☽ ☽ ☽ ☽ ☽ ☽ ☽ ☽ ☽ ☽ ◑ ◖ ◐ ◔ ◖ ◑ ◗

JARDIN DES PLANTES

♀ ♀ ♀

In the middle of the dark room, Fang had assumed the lotus position. Neither the scuttle of mice along the walls nor the screech of the giant bats attacking them could disturb his journey. Slowly, he flew out of the room and entered a garden—

one of the botanical gardens in Paris, just as he had seen it in a movie years earlier. He spotted a large peach tree; sitting under it was Mei. She greeted him with a smile but looked a little out of focus, which meant that she hadn't entirely managed to detach herself from her real body.

"Can you see me, Mei?" Fang asked her.

"My body is heavy, too heavy with thoughts," the young woman answered.

"Many drops of water are rain," Fang said, "but the rain is not a drop of water. Many thoughts are your thought, but your thought is none of these thoughts. Blot them out and follow me."

Now Mei could be seen more clearly, and her face was sad. "I'm a bit anxious, Fang," she explained. "Soon we'll have to tell mission Terra that Van Cram is, in fact, dead; that he disappeared in that remote quadrant, and that we could all end up the same way. Isn't it too risky? Shouldn't we be afraid?"

"Things happen," Fang answered, "whether we are afraid or not. But tell me, would you like to find that planet?"

"I don't know, Fang. I'm afraid we might end up destroying it. What if we just make the same old mistakes that we made on our own Earth? Do you think we would?"

"It's possible, Mei."

"Fang, you know what's contained in the third message. The data it gives us are totally senseless. Useless. Do you think we'll be able to make it?"

"If it's written that two fish shall meet, the sea could not prevent it by growing a hundred times larger," Fang replied. "You are afraid because we are about to embark on a very long journey, but you forget that man's longest journey through the universe is shorter than a sudden gust of wind. Your heart beats once, while the earth travels thirty kilometers around the sun. The ant makes its way through the universe of the garden. It must reach that rosebush to bring food to its comrades. It has no instruments to make sure of its direction; it just takes off and goes. This is part of its nature. What door should it open?''

"It has already arrived,'' Mei said.

''Yes, Mei.'' Fang smiled. ''And now tell me about your dream.''

''I think everything started when I saw slides of the mine,'' Mei said. ''That night I dreamed of very high mountains, and of a man with a painted face, cloaked in the most beautifully colored feathers. His arms were stretched toward me, as if in welcome. He spoke a strange language, similar to Chinese. As he spoke, he knotted a string. Is what I'm thinking true?''

''Yes,'' Fang said. ''What you saw was a civilization that disappeared seven hundred years ago.''

· ·

THE BLACK LEVELS

· · ·

Chulain and Kook walked along the main corridor of level seventeen, through opium clouds and light shows. Though they walked rapidly and close to the walls, they were unable to elude two state drug-pushers, armed to the teeth, who blocked their way with a pushcart full of merchandise.

''Hey, folks,'' the first one addressed them, ''don't tell me you're in such a hurry you can't even sample our wares!''

Kook was about to reply in kind, when Chulain, squeezing his arm, stopped him. ''What a great idea!'' he said. ''But make it snappy—we've got an appointment. What's the fastest thing you have?''

''If you're in a hurry,'' said a blond man clad in python skins, ''we have twenty kinds of speed—in pills, aerosol, tube, syringe, whatever you prefer. But I recommend this microcoke. The vial is shaped like a needle. You stick it behind your ear, and it will keep you flying for six hours. If you want something stronger, we just got a shipment of truffles from Jupiter. Sniff one, and you'll immediately understand relativity. OK. Otherwise, we have snuff, uppers, downers, ludes, poppers, sky-lubes, lampyridia, bloody grass, characo, visine, chicha, kuvoodo, terreiro, Naples sun, Jamaica red, mystic cloud, peyote pâté, lobotozombex, hamamelis yogurt, valium vol-au-vents, coke, more coke, mescal bayer, still more coke, and yopa."

"We can't get too stoned—give us two snuff-colas."

"How about four?" the python man suggested.

"OK," Chulain agreed, "make it four."

"I don't get it," Kook admitted as they walked on. "Why did we have to give money to those jerks?"

"Buddy," Chulain answered with a smug grin, "better to buy their junk as friends than with a knife at our throats. Trust me —I know my gutters, here and throughout the galaxy. This area belongs to the state—no buy, no go. Now, keep your bottles in view and move on, that way."

"But I can't see a thing down there."

"If you can't see a thing, chances are nobody can see you," Chulain noted. "Now, shut up and walk." They staggered ahead blindly, their feet half-sunk into the fetid sludge.

"Mouse mayo," Chulain joked. "Once a week, they get rid of them with lye." Kook felt a sudden pang in the pit of his stomach. After a long, stinking descent, they came upon a crack of light. Kook was just opening the door to the new corridor when they heard gunshots and loud screams. They ducked back, then Chulain, putting his eye to the crack, wit-nessed a furious brawl—about twenty men armed with iron bars and guns.

"Those must be the hockey fans the cop mentioned," Chu-lain explained. "The ones with the star on their black caps belong to the Chihuahua gang—Mexicans. The other ones, covered with tattoos all the way to their noses, are Chinese, the Chows. They're really going at it. They hate each other!"

"Why?" Kook asked.

"The cop told me they've come for a series of snuff-hockey games, the kind that's played with spiked skates and sword-sticks. During the first match, the Chinese decapitated Calvez, the Mexicans' idol. According to the umpire, everything was in order. But others disagreed—it seems that the game had been over for three hours."

They waited till the noise of the brawl faded in the distance, and then cautiously stepped out. They could still hear the bikes of the vigilantes roar up and down the corridors. "Don't worry, Kook," said Chulain reassuringly. "We're almost there. I have a feeling my friend will be able to tell us quite a few things about our dear Van Cram. At least, I hope so! Follow me."

They entered a long corridor flanked by large halls alternately offering bare-handed boxing and wrestling matches. At the end of it, they heard a loud din, such as might rise from the deepest circles of hell, except that here, there were no sinners, nor devils—only an infinity of videogames.

○ Deggu N'Gombo and Crocodile Rock ○

> He bumped three thousand spaceships off the screen,
> then he was bumped off by a moped on the green.
> —*Epitaph for a great videogame player*

"I'm doin' all right, Chulain," N'Gombo said, once the "Hey, Bro's" and the complex choreography of reciprocal greetings had been exhausted. He was a scrawny, bald black with artificial legs. He lived in a wheelchair that included a bar and a buxom mermaid carved on each machine-gun arm.

"I have about a hundred videogames that still make a good profit," N'Gombo went on. "So I can afford two bodyguards, and I maintain a decent relationship with the boss of this level. They even give me a receipt for every bribe. In short, I'm an honest merchant."

"But it's not the same as living among the stars, is it, Deggu?" Chulain smiled.

"No, that it ain't. But I'm an old man now. Thirty years of hypervelocity hit you all at once, you know, particularly if you've left your legs to wander all by themselves in space. So, I'm perfectly satisfied to be driving the spaceships of these electronic toys. They're fairly accurate, you know—they have control panels and laser guns just like the ones on our old pirate ships. Oh, now and then it gets a little boring, of course. Nothing much happens down here."

A volley of shots interrupted their conversation. One of the nearest videogames was firing away at somebody who had got caught in the player's seat, as an electronic funeral march echoed through the hall.

"What in hell!" Kook exclaimed. "That thing is really shooting! Somebody stop it! It's killing him!"

"Of course," N'Gombo stated calmly. "That's a total-risk hologame. Either you score over 6,000 points or you're done in. It's all spelled out very clearly in the instructions."

"No kidding!" Chulain was quite taken aback. "And the police don't do a thing?"

"Well, according to the law, the player shouldn't be killed—only roughed up a bit," N'Gombo admitted. "But some folks like real risks, so the cops close their eyes—unless something really awful happens. Last month I owned a game called Martian Revenge. The object was to pursue a Martian through a jungle. If the player didn't catch the Martian within three minutes, the videogame sprouted arms and tank treads, and went after him. But the unit I bought was faulty—the funniest thing. It killed the player fair and square; but it didn't stop there: it went on to kill nineteen bystanders. Somebody stopped it with a sledgehammer as it was heading into a discotheque on level eight. It was a real riot. But why don't you

play? I've just bought two brand-new games. One's called Medical—you have to discover and eliminate two hundred bacilli
in ten minutes. If you don't, you get infected. But the other
one's even better—it's called Stone Crash, and it simulates a
space flight through banks of meteorites."

"What's that huge shower pipe for, just above the player's
seat?"

"A realistic touch," N'Gombo explained. "If the player
loses, it drops boulders right on top of him."

Chulain and Kook stared incredulously as two cops carried
away a badly mangled player.

"I'd really like to take on one of your games, Deggu," Chulain said, "but I'm in a hurry now. I'm looking for some vital
information, and you're the only one who can give it to me.
Don't mind my holding this thing under your nose while you
talk—it's a CCS scrambler, in case anybody's trying to bug
us."

"You're working wholesale now, aren't you, Chulain?"
N'Gombo asked. "What do you want to know?"

"You used to fly for the space hounds, didn't you?"

"I sure did. For four years, under cover. The Federation
didn't suspect a thing. That's when we were smugglers. We'd
found a bunch of interesting routes. We drove the hounds to
the spot and they gave us twenty or thirty percent of their
finds. That is, when they didn't kill us first."

"Did you ever happen to fly with a certain Van Cram, the
Viking?"

"Van Cram—wait a second—was he a large, blond guy with
one eye? No, I never actually flew with him, but I know all
about him. He was the craziest of the bunch. He traveled in
all quadrants of the lost planets. He wasn't afraid of anything."

"Do you happen to know what route he's been flying lately?
Where could I find somebody who's gone with him?"

"I can only give you the addresses of the widows of anybody
who flew with Van Cram. But I think I know somebody else
who might be of some use to you—a guy by the name of Geber,

a journalist. He went with Van Cram on some of his most recent missions. You know the kind. He's one of those special reporters who write, 'Here we are, in the midst of enemy fire,' while sitting in a hotel bathtub, one light-year away from the front. Now he's writing for the Meskorska paper, you know, the artificial planet near Uranus."

"Very interesting," Chulain said. "May I ask you another question?"

"Go right ahead," N'Gombo said.

"Can you tell me if that animal down there is part of your videogames or a trespasser?" Chulain pointed at the entrance to the hall, where a ten-meter crocodile was standing placidly. He was quaintly chewing on a watchman as if he were a bone, and was wagging his tail to the music. In fact, he might even have been dancing, albeit with a rather monstrous sense of rhythm.

"Our Saturday-night supercroc!" N'Gombo screamed. "Run away, folks! Hide behind that wall!"

The huge animal waddled into the room, wagging his tail to the rocksky music, and, by so doing, flogged the videogames, which by now seemed really to be screaming in terror.

"Hey, look here, you dumb beast!" N'Gombo yelled at him. "Every single one of those machines has cost me two thousand ingots! Get lost, you jerk! All you'll find here is strictly mechanical, so go have lunch somewhere else!"

But the croc was very busy crunching Jungle Jim, a videogame that hissed and popped in his mouth like popcorn.

At the sight of such slaughter, N'Gombo sent all caution to the winds, threw his wheelchair into gear, and lunged against the croc, shooting like mad with the machine guns built into the arms of his vehicle. At first, this unexpected rain of bullets only slightly annoyed the croc, but then, when a couple of them hit him in an eye, he got really angry. He turned on his heels, and, with the concentration of a tournament golfer, raised his tail and aimed it at N'Gombo's chair. The croc swung, and N'Gombo and his chair were lofted against the opposite wall, some fifty meters away.

"Deggu!" Chulain screamed, bending over the remains of his friend. "Deggu, answer me! As for you, fucking son of a tank, if I had my gun I'd really teach you how to dance!"

The supercroc, uncommonly sensitive for one his size, found the insult in bad taste and, scowling, started waddling toward Chulain, obviously meaning to send him into orbit as well. As Chulain screamed, the crocodile raised his avenging tail, but before he could aim and swing, a videogame at his back zapped him with a laser beam and blew him up in a shower of sparks. The room immediately filled with the delicious smell of roasted croc, as Kook and Chulain desperately tried to reconstruct poor N'Gombo and his unfortunate chair.

"Why?" Chulain cried. "Brother, why? Just to save those dumb electronic boxes!"

"Just two more payments to go, and they'd all have been mine!" N'Gombo rattled.

Kook examined the videogame that had saved Chulain. "It's a Japanese game! Even here, they've been spying on us. But why in the world didn't it move earlier? It could have saved N'Gombo!" With a gentle chime, the videogame screen spelled out its answer: "Terribly sorry, but I was waiting for instructions."

"Too bad for you, Sam," Chulain exclaimed. "Now you won't be able to ask him any more questions. N'Gombo is dead. Damn beasts!"

"They come out on Saturday night," a visitor explained as he studied the remains of the supercroc. "They know that's when more people are around. There are about a hundred of them living in the radioactive sewers, and they get larger and fiercer every day. Last Saturday, I saw one at least sixteen meters long!"

"May I take a chunk as a souvenir?" a child politely asked Chulain.

"You can have it all! Shit! And what's this alarm all about?"

"The Black Widows! The vigilantes' bikes! Quick, quick, let's get out of here!" the visitor screamed. Everyone scrambled out of the hall just as the immense, roaring motorspiders entered.

"Hurry up!" Chulain told Kook. "If they stop us, they'll ask a lot of questions, and we'll have a tough time getting rid of them. It's forbidden to shoot crocodiles. They're protected under law."

"Isn't anybody around to protect us?" Kook wondered as he was running away. They ran along the corridors and mixed with the crowd coming out of the game. The sound of the sirens grew fainter.

○ Robot Love ○

"And what do you do for a living, dear?" the sexy pornorobot asked LeO, who was smoking in bed after his erotic performance. He wasn't smoking a cigarette, mind you. He was just plain smoking—smoke pouring out of his head. All that excitement had blown a couple of fuses.

"Well," LeO answered her, "for the time being, I'm a spaceship robot. I used to be a satellite spy."

"Oh!" The little pornorobot seemed impressed. "You must have seen a great many things." She was a gorgeous Mitsubishi model, the Cherry Garden type, with deep, plurisegmented eyes, which she brightened up with a fascinating combination of colors.

"I guess I have," LeO admitted nonchalantly. "Lots of things happen in twenty orbit years. Besides, I had managed to get hold of a telescope so powerful that I could read the newspaper of the American ambassador from an altitude of three hundred kilometers. In fact, I could tell you quite a few stories about ambassadors—racy stuff."

"Zuk, zuk!" Cherry laughed. "And why were you restructured?"

"It was a terrible life," the robot sighed. "Much too much competition—there wasn't a single free orbit left. And they seemed to enjoy launching new satellites armed with nuclear bombs, horns, teeth—too much militarism. So I deserted. From up there the Earth looks very small, and the idea of its inhabitants tearing one another apart makes you laugh. It's a little like watching fish eat one another in their glass bowl."

"I understand," Cherry said. "I too have been restructured. Years ago I was a robot with a male matrix, and I worked in the record section at Fnac. Once I spotted a girl stealing a record and did not shoot at her, even though this was stipulated in the regulations."

"Had you been poorly programmed?"

"No. It wasn't that. I was scheduled to work in the book section, so they had given me supplementary cultural programming. Just that week I had read some three thousand books on violence, and my circuits were clogged up with it. So, as punishment, I was restructured. They changed my sex and my . . . job. But I don't mind. Robots are much kinder than men. Although now and then I get mixed up with one of those drill-robots—real brutes. If you don't watch out, they unscrew you!"

"May I know your name?" LeO asked timidly.

"I'm sorry, but the rules don't allow it. On the other hand, if you come back to see me, maybe . . ."

"Well, that might be difficult," LeO said. "I am always on assignment—here today, who knows where tomorrow. I'm practically in command on my spaceship, and my crew holds me in high esteem."

"Has anybody seen a sort of aluminum parakeet with two spindly arms and a light on its head?" a voice asked, just outside the room.

LeO sighed. "I'm afraid my friends need me."

WHAT LIES BENEATH THE ICE OF CUZCO

When Kook entered the mission control room, he immediately noticed the commotion that precedes every flight. A few technicians were playing cards, one was sleeping, and another was drawing little bears on the computer screen.

Kook paused in front of the photoelectric eyes of the secret department. The door opened, and he found himself face to face with Pyk's excitement.

"My dearest Leonard!" the secretary exclaimed. "I've heard about your adventures! So what do you think of the black levels?"

"They're fun, but they use too much energy. I've read that the electricity used every day for the videogames could heat three thousand apartments."

"These are shitty times, Leonard," Pyk explained. "We can't possibly deprive people of a little fun. If they didn't have that, and some chicha, they'd stop working altogether. They would agree to eat ammonia mildew, but they couldn't do without their Saturday-night concert. It would be like depriving Einstein of his comic books!"

"Compared to your shows, my comic books are Greek classics," Einstein angrily interjected. "And if you want to know what—"

"Gentlemen, gentlemen," Phildys intervened, as was his wont. "We don't have much time left. We'd better discuss the final details. Please pay attention. The mission will leave tomorrow evening. We are fairly sure that neither the Sheiks nor the Sams will bother you, at least not until you have reached Meskorska. After that, you'll have to act with greater caution."

"And run for your lives," Chulain sneered.

"Now I have some more data to pass on to you," Phildys continued. "I'm afraid it's not that positive. First of all: Van

Cram. When his vector reached Earth, strangely unnoticed by our computer till some time later, we immediately checked the spaceflight log and discovered that Van Cram had been considered disintegrated for over a month. He had left Meskor-ska for the Universal Sea on June 2. His last radio contact was June 20. After that, dead silence. Our radar scans through that area haven't yielded a thing."

"I'm not surprised," Chulain said. "In those quadrants the weather's pretty rough—storms, magnetic gaps, black holes. I've seen barometers do harakiri with their own needles, I swear!"

"Yes," Phildys said. "In the last two years, we've lost twenty-six spaceships. They just disappeared without a trace."

"And what about the last position data that Van Cram communicated in code?" Kook asked.

"Here's more good news for you, Kook. Those data are absurd. We had them checked out; there is no actual referent. Van Cram's computer must have been malfunctioning. So you'll have to find out his course by yourselves. And this isn't the only mystery in this story. Kook, you asked me today where we hoped to find the energy necessary to colonize Terra. Now I'm going to answer your question. Lights off, please! Have a good look at these slides. This is the Kouzok mining station, where the vector was recovered. We've been digging in that spot for two years now, because, every now and then, the detector will signal some gigantic flux of subterranean energy, a brief flare that disappears immediately and quite mysteriously. The vector was found right here, stuck in this glacier. And a hundred meters away, we found this." A block of carved stone, ten times as large as a man, appeared on the screen.

"Holy shit!" Chulain exclaimed. "What's that, a piece of adronic fortification?"

"No," Phildys said, "this stone appears to be cut by laser but in fact isn't. It does not belong to our times. The experts have established that it comes from an era that the moderns called 'Inca.' The stone is two thousand years old.''

"The Incas!" Kook, greatly moved, exclaimed. "You have found the ruins of the Incan city!''

"Precisely. Detectors show that under the ice are the remains of Cuzco, bombed in WW V. The ancient part of the city has resisted much longer than the modern part. But as we proceed in our dig, all the instruments seem to be going crazy. Another mystery—we had Van Cram's vector examined by the computer in charge of the dig. We wanted to know where it came from. All the computer could tell us was 'OD.' ''

"OD? Overdose?" Kook asked, surprised. "The computer gave up?''

"It sure did," Einstein admitted. "Which is even more extraordinary when you consider that the computer in question was a self-correcting supermodel, Megaflop Paralaplace. We checked all the data and reformulated the question at least a thousand times, but the computer refuses to answer us. In short, it is completely drunk.''

Kook glanced at him inquisitively.

"Nontechnically speaking," Einstein specified, "we experts say that a computer is drunk whenever we come across something that attacks the circuitry of the most sophisticated computers and deprives them of their lucidity, as it were. We have ascertained that this sort of drunkenness occurred every time the computers found themselves in the presence of an abnormal flux of energy—a flux of transuranian elements, for instance, or a nuclear explosion.''

"Why 'occurred'?" Kook inquired.

"Because, energy levels being what they are today, fluxes of such power no longer happen," Einstein said. "The last registered case occurred in Peking. When the Americans dropped their bacteriological bombs on China, the famous Seven Sages, China's seven central computers, got absolutely smashed. To the question 'What would be the best military response?' they answered, 'Buy a billion and a half aspirins.' ''

"In plain English," Chulain interrupted, "what's this all about?"

"A computer as sophisticated as Genius 5 can get drunk only in the presence of a source of energy above one million gigavovs. Therefore we conclude that beneath all that ice, inside the most ancient part of Cuzco, there is a source of extraordinary energy. If we find it, my friends, we'll be able to send you more than moral support!"

♂ ●

THE LAST NIGHT ON EARTH

⊖ ● ⊖

It was midnight. A heavy blizzard buffeted the Federation building. The violet lightning of an electric storm kept flashing against the Parisian ice pack. From his room on the sixtieth floor, Chulain could hear the white taxi-bears howl in terror. He was busy at a strange task. He filled a bottle with pitch, stuck a wick of sorts into its neck, lit it, and closed the bottle with a perforated cap. The light of the flame woke up LeO, whose sleep was accompanied by a gentle buzz, not unlike the purring of a cat. With great curiosity, LeO watched Chulain bow in front of the bottle and murmur a singsong. Then he took a message-bearing stake, like those that spaceships use to signal their positions, and opened the window. An icy gust of wind swept across the room.

"Hey, Chulain," the robot screamed. "Are you crazy? What the hell are you doing?"

The black man did not answer. He opened the stake, dropped the bottle inside it, and shot it into the sky. Then he bowed again and said, "This is for you, Deggu N'Gombo."

LeO's antennae vibrated inquisitively. "Whom are you signaling, Chulain? Your lunar mistress? The Japanese?"

"Nothing of the sort, LeO," Chulain answered, lighting his pipe. "This is what we space pilots do whenever we lose one of ours."

"Why?" LeO asked.

"It's an old story, LeO," Chulain answered. "Would you like to hear it?"

The History of Captain Quixote Patchwork

> I married a mermaid
> slim as an eel
> but now she's my bride
> she's fat as a whale.
> —"The Song of the
> Courteous Whaler"

The year 2136 was a good one for Ironheads. In it, Ironhead whales (so the great meteorites that swam in the Universal Sea quadrant were called) hit space ahead of schedule. From the very start, it was clear this would be an exceptional season. I swear by my pipe, no one had ever seen Ironheads that big before. The first rumors were already buzzing. Seems the *Town-ho* had sighted and tried to catch a two-hundred-meter monster, which had retaliated by tearing away the magnetic harpoons and knocking off the prow, leaving the ship gaping in midspace. By the time they got back, the whole *Town-Ho* crew was sneezing!

I was a young man then, with high expectations and a deep yearning to sail far. I had been in space many times before, but I had never hunted Ironheads. I was strong and gutsy, however, and so, when I went to the Maritornes Inn, the meanest dive in Nanturanucket and second home to the most infamous rock-hunters, I was full of hope. Well, I tell you, that joint was quite a zoo. Not exactly the kind of physiques you'd want for a bubblebath pin-up. Still, I braced myself, walked to the counter, and sat on a stool right between two ugly mugs with tattooed helmets. "I want to ship out," I announced. "Who do I talk to?"

Redcap glared at me. To judge from his charred face, he was radioactive. "Tell me, brownie," he said, "are you really looking for a job?"

"I sure am," I answered promptly, rather worried at the huge iron-gloved hand he had placed on my shoulder.

"Well, maybe you have just found one," redcap said, turning toward bluecap. "What do you say, Vere?"

"He looks like a tough dude, Amasa," the other one said without even looking at me. "But maybe he's a chicken."

"You're wrong, gentlemen," I said, somewhat miffed. "I've got guts galore!"

"Is that so!" Vere said with a sneer. I knew he was going to play a dirty trick on me. He stuck a hand inside his parka, pulled out a large percussion bomb, and backed up a couple of steps. Suddenly, the whole inn was dead-silent. With a hoarse peal of laughter, Vere threw the bomb in my direction. Somehow, I managed to catch it in midair, and, dripping with cold sweat, placed it on the counter.

"You did all right, man," Amasa told me with a friendly cackle. "See, this was only a bomb. Had you lost your head in front of this toy, I can't imagine what you'd do if you found youself faced with a hissing, blowing Ironhead, ten thousand times larger and faster."

The day after that unusual test, they led me to their ship, the *Grampus*, where they were serving as officers. It was a dumpy, jury-rigged tin bucket, with a bison for a figurehead. Its captain was a mysterious fellow who went

by the name of Quixote Patchwork. I say mysterious because whenever I asked about him, everybody answered,
"Sure, we know him. You will too, by and by!"

I finally understood what they meant, when I found
myself face to face with him that foggy morning when I
boarded his ship. Quixote was the most stitched-
together, mended-over, repaired and restored man I had
ever seen. Only his head was original, and not even all of
that, since he had a glass eye and an iron patch on his
skull. The rest was a triumph of prosthetic fantasy come
true. One leg was copper, engraved with octopuses and
dolphins, and he showed it off by wearing shorts. The
other leg, from the knee down, was an iron rod that ended
in a sharp point. They told me that, when there was a
storm, the captain would stick it into the deck and then
just stand there, nailed to his ship, revolving like a compass, scanning the sea for prey. He also had an elastic
rubber arm; the other arm terminated on a very finely
wrought ivory hand that he had won in an arm-wrestling
match with a Chinese captain.

As for his internal organs, during his many encounters
with Ironheads, he was smashed and gored so many times
that he had become a catalog of synthetic anatomy. He
had a brass trachea, which gave his cavernous breathing
a B-flat pitch; a silly-putty heart; a stomach courtesy of
Bayer plastics; sixteen meters of polyvinyl intestines,
abutting on a synthetic anus with a special buzzer for
farts; and in place of both spleen and pancreas, he had a
subcutaneous chemical switchboard.

One night, his liver had been spotted as it was rushing
to throw itself into the sea after having filtered six liters
of boiling rum. His spine had been reinforced with bam-
boo canes, and his aluminum ribcage had a spring latch
at the center opening that saved the surgeons a great deal
of time whenever they had to change a piece or two. Oh,
I almost forgot—he had only one lung, but it was a real

one, and he loved it dearly. "My dear old Lou [as he called the lung]," he would say, "is still with me; it has never left me." And to show his gratitude to his dear old Lou, he chain-smoked. He would draw on his pipe and say, "What do you think of this tobacco, Lou? Not bad, hmmm?" And, after every coughing spell, he would repeat, "Today we've really gone whole hog, haven't we, old boy?"

Well, by now you might wonder why Quixote Patchwork was such a wreck. The answer is easy: because he was the craziest, most reckless rock-hunter in space. He liked to tackle Ironheads that were ten times larger than his ship, and he lost either a bone or a fillet every time. But he never gave up. "One of these days," he would say, "I'm gonna get lucky. I'll catch the hugest Ironhead in history, even if it turns out to be my tombstone!"

If the captain was crazy, his crew was not much saner. During his recent hunting seasons, Quixote had never returned with more than half the sailors who had left with him. Bad luck, he'd say. The truth of the matter was that, at this point in his career, he was able to recruit only the worst trash. I realized this when I was already on board and could no longer turn back. But once we were under way, the wind of adventure swept away all fears.

That year, all the most legendary ships left for the hunting quadrant—the *Queen Mab*, the *Penguin*, the *Pequod*, the *Beagle*, the *Peng*, the *Pinta*, the *Ulysses*, the *Star Bunny*, the *Hippogriff*, the *Shamaral*, the *Amadigi*, the *Tupac Amaru*, the *Platir*, the *Urganda*, the *Excalibur*, the *Cannonball*, the *Pertega Salutis*, the *Nautilus*, the *Fogg*, the *Molly Aida*, the *Typee*, the *Essex*, the *Atalante*, the *Meeres Stille*, the *Potemkin*, the *Marracau*, the *Devil's Back*, the *Ruppert Mundi*, and many others. Our crew was the scum of galactic scum—Japanese deserters, Russian astronauts half crazed by too many years of space solitude, American junkies, Meskorska smugglers,

Chinese refugees from the Martian rice fields, former blade runners, escaped scientists, Mercury miners, lunar wolf-men, Saturnian depressives, and Venusian maniacs —plus two officers, Vere and Amasa, thugs whose main means of expression was the whip.

I was lucky enough to gain the captain's favor at once, and for a very simple reason: I was a pro at carving wooden pipes. I could whip one out in the course of a single night. Quixote discovered it while I was on watch at the helm one night. He walked past and saw me fooling around with my penknife.

"Sailor!" he cried in his metallic voice, "what the hell are you doing?"

"Just a pipe, captain," I answered, and showed it to him. "But I swear I was paying very close attention to the ship's course."

With an angry gesture, he snatched the pipe away from my hand and examined it. When he saw it was carved in the shape of a dolphin, his eyes mellowed instantly.

"This is a fine pipe, sailor," he said, sticking it into his mouth. "A very fine pipe!"

"I made it . . . for you," I promptly lied. "I know you are a devoted smoker."

The captain eyed me with curiosity. Then, with a nod of his head, he bid me follow him, and took me to his cabin. There, in a large closet, he showed me his extraordinary collection. There were pipes of all sorts and sizes, made from all sorts of materials. The most astonishing ones were those carved by sailors during their long hours in space: it was as if all the dreams and nightmares of the sea were gathered in that closet. There were pipes in the shape of dragons, dolphins, asteroids, comets, sirens, giant squids. "This is wonderful," I said in utter admiration, as the collection passed through my hands. "What imagination!"

"Don't say that!" Quixote admonished me. "Everything we see on the sea—in the night's fog, in the sun's haze—is real. Mermaids are real, and so are the most horrible monsters—wolf-fish, pedocephalic squid. And what about meteorites? Are they really made of metal, mere clots of stones and minerals? No, they are not, and when you see them, you'll understand. Ironheads are alive! They think, they fight! They are the whales of space!"

As he was saying this, his deadly ivory slapping my back, Quixote looked transfigured. He went on to show me the strangest pipes: one, for instance whose bowl was a perfect moon, with all its craters; and another one, custom-made, on which were carved the faces of his wife and six children and the inscription, "Don't run, think of us."

So, that evening marked the beginning of a strong affection between Quixote and myself, an affection which, as could be expected, did not fail to provoke ironic comment from most of my comrades. "Say, Chulain, did you give the captain another one of those blow-jobbies of yours?" I'd hear them jeer behind my back. I really had to push my weight around to make them stop.

After ten days of navigation, we reached the Trap, at the heart of the hunting quadrant, where the most valuable meteorites zoomed by at full speed. The captain's skill consisted of predicting their course in the midst of magnetic crosscurrents, and then of intersecting their paths as they passed. At this point, the dinghies, connected to the main ship by cables, were lowered. If the meteorite was too distant, the magnetic harpoons could not reach it. If it came too close, it would crush dinghies and ship like macaroons. But if the distance had been correctly predicted, and a magnetic harpoon was able to latch onto the meteorite, the spaceship would engage in a complex braking maneuver that would gradually slow the Ironhead down.

It was a very dangerous hunt in which Quixote excelled, as he immediately demonstrated. The very first day he harpooned two three-ton Ironheads: a "redhead," chock-full of copper, and a "coquette," so called because of the luminous crystals that made it sparkle.

In the following days, hunting was abundant for all the ships. The ovens kept fusing the meteorites full blast, and the holds kept filling with precious ingots. In the evening, all the radios were hooked up to broadcast huge space choruses or best-joke contests. Everybody seemed happy, except, of course, Captain Quixote. He stood on deck, revolving on his iron leg, smoking and staring at the stars.

"No way, no way, Chulain," he would say to me. "The Universe is laughing behind our backs. We contemplate the light of stars that have been dead thousands of years, and stand in awe of these scrawny rocks. But I know better. At the heart of that current are real Ironheads— two-thousand, three-thousand tons. Now, those are *rocks!*"

I already sensed what he was getting at, and, as I feared, the following morning he ordered the helmsman to proceed toward the heart of the heart of the quadrant. Amasa tried to prevent it.

"Captain," he protested in front of the entire crew, "that spot is deadly! The meteorites there are much too large and fast. Remember that Norwegian ship that got a little too close—the largest piece it left behind was the molar of its boatswain. It's too crazy to even think of it!"

"I'm the one who gives orders here!" Quixote said brusquely. "Steer toward the Bowling Alley!"

Which was what sailors jokingly called that corridor. And, in fact, the captain was right. The first two meteorites we caught when we entered that area put the previous ones to shame. One was four hundred and eighty tons and stuffed with uranium, while the other one, in the shape of a shoe, weighed no less than six hundred tons. Once fused, it yielded eight thousand ingots of precious minerals.

"Once we find the other shoe," I kidded the captain, "we can go back home!"

"I'd rather find the owner of the shoe," Quixote said with a wink.

That night I didn't sleep well. I could hear, coming from afar, long, dark hisses that made the entire ship shiver. I got up and found the captain awake, feverishly consulting the telescope and calculating different courses.

The next morning, the weather was awful. Magnetic waves kept the ship rocking and pitching. We could see Pluto in the distance, which was a bad sign. A Mexican sailor remembered an old space proverb: "When Pluto's in the sky, all you can do is sigh."

Clouds of flotsam and jetsam told us we had reached the Bowling Alley, the path followed by the largest meteorites. All was silent on board, except for the occasional creaking of the captain's metallic joints. Quixote stood staring at the radar. He was waiting for something. Suddenly, after a few minutes, we saw him stiffen up.

"There she is!" he cried. "There she blows!"

A luminous point had appeared on the radar screen. In a very short time, it became so large that even we, in the dinghy-hold, could see it shine on the monitor.

"Amasa, calculate its volume!" Quixote ordered.

Amasa made a rapid calculation, and then blanched. "Captain," he cried, "let's get the hell out of here!"

Those of us who were standing by the portholes first heard a distant vibration which gradually grew into a huge roar, like that of a thousand marching giants. The entire ship was shaking. The point was getting larger every second—in space and on the radar screen. At last we all saw what the captain had been waiting for.

It was a white, radioactive meteorite, the most valuable of its species—at least six times as large as any meteorite I had ever seen before and twenty times as large
as our ship. That humongous rock was coming toward us
at a speed of twenty-eight thousand kilometers per hour.
Amasa again cried, "Captain, that rock weighs almost
four thousand tons; it will be on top of us in a second!
Let's steer away from it!"

"Never! We are in a perfect hunting position," Quixote
exclaimed. "Lower the dinghies!"

"You're mad!" Vere screamed. "Our engines are too
small to control its velocity! It will drag us along into
deepest space!"

"It's too late to stop now!" Quixote screamed back.
"Quick, to the dinghies! Advance, mariners! This is our
chance to make history!"

Terrified and excited, I jumped into a dinghy and found
myself in open space. The noise was mind-blowing, and
the dinghy was tossed about like a possessed soul. We
saw the huge white mass approach. It was wrapped entirely in smoke and gas and, in front, had two fissures
which, on second thought, looked like eyes—threatening
EYES! The white shadow ran toward us with an inde-
scribable din. I felt a hot flash and heard a cannon-shot,
as we plunged headlong at a frightful speed. My mates
were screaming in terrror. Our dinghy and Captain Quixote's had latched onto the meteorite, and now it dragged
us along on its mad course. Its speed did slacken; some
of the sailors had already fainted.

"There is nothing I can do," the engineer's despairing
voice kept repeating on the radio. "I can't hold it back! I
can't stop it! Let it go! It's going to destroy us all!"

"We've caught it and we're not letting go!" Quixote
screamed back at him. "Sooner or later this son of a bitch
will have to slow down. Hold on tight!" But the dinghy's
hull had already begun to creak dangerously.

"Let go or you'll disintegrate!" they shouted from the spaceship. Then, at last, the captain of our dinghy cut the cable of the harpoon and we were slung backward, toward the hull of the ship.

"Cowards!" the captain screamed behind us. "You have abandoned me!"

I was able to see the last, horrible scene—the meteorite dragging the dinghy, the dinghy dragging the spaceship.

Then, from the ship, I heard Amasa's voice. "Go to hell, you old freak! We're not going to risk our skins for you!"

A few seconds later, somebody on the ship cut the cable that connected it to the captain's dinghy. Immediately, the latter dashed away and shattered against the meteorite. Captain Quixote had finally met, albeit rudely, the largest Ironhead in galactic history.

That evening on the *Grampus*, nobody talked. We were all drinking like sponges, trying to forget what had happened. Every time a bulkhead creaked, we started—we thought we heard the squeak of the captain's joints and the rattle of his breath.

That night came another storm. Four of us kept watch, staring into the threatening black sky.

We were huddled close together against the cold of the galactic night when, suddenly, one man turned as white as a sheet. "There," he stuttered, pointing to the sky above us, "there, it's him!"

On deck, bathing in the hellish red headlight of the prow, stood the ghost of Captain Quixote. We could hear him panting. He stretched a hand toward us and said, "Fire! Fire!"

Terrified, we ran away, screaming for help. When we returned to the deck, there was no trace of the captain, but all the instruments were burning. Obviously, Quixote had messed around with the wires, causing a short circuit.

Our ship sank into terror. The officers tried to convince us to not fall prey to superstition. They said we were still very much upset by what we'd witnessed that fateful day, and that what we'd seen that night, on deck, was probably only a hallucination. After all, the fire could easily have been caused by a bad connection. But Gaspar, an old Mexican sailor, was unconvinced: "No, no!" he said. "We've killed him, and he's come back. His soul, the *pixan*, will find no peace and will wander in the infernal *mitlan* till he's got his revenge. He'll come back and burn our ship. Fire! That's what he wants for us!"

We passed the next day in a state of great tension, and that night we kept watch till one or two o'clock. By that time, our surveillance had somewhat slackened; a few sailors had even started to joke about the whole thing. But, around three, we heard a strange voice in the galley. We ran downstairs to find Captain Quixote standing there, a flaming torch in his hand. As soon as he saw us, he threw the torch away and disappeared into thin air. In the meantime, the galley was on fire, and it took us several hours to get everything under control.

The following day, we assembled to decide what to do. Some proposed abandoning ship. Others thought it might be better to hang Vere and Amasa, the men most responsible for Quixote's death. Others suggested shooting at the ghost itself. But Gaspar said, "We are powerless in the face of the *mitlan*'s power! But we can try to appease its anger. One of us, the one closest to the captain, should confront him and ask what sort of sacrifice he might accept in exchange for our safety. You all know the person I'm thinking of—Chulain, the sailor."

We all agreed this was the best thing to do (with one exception—guess who). So, that night, I stayed on deck, in fear and trembling, and waited for Captain Quixote's ghost. As soon as the star of Orion was high in the sky, I heard the rattle of his single lung and the limping tap of his leg. At last, he appeared to me, wrapped in his white shroud. His delirious eyes were the most dreadful thing I had ever seen.

"Captain," I said with tremulous voice, "please, forgive us! We'll do anything you want, but please, please, spare the ship!"

"Fire! Fire!" the captain yelled, glaring at me with those terrible eyes.

"No, captain, please reconsider," I begged him. "Please, don't burn the ship! We'll all die! It was your ship! Please, don't—" And here my voice stuck in my throat. The captain had nailed me to the wall with his cold, ivory hand.

"Fire!" he yelled again, as if beside himself. "You— idiot! I need fire to light my pipe! It's been three days since I've had a smoke!"

I still don't know how, but, between one shiver and the next, I managed to light his pipe with my lighter. Quixote took a few frantic drags, and immediately the horrifying expression left his face. He sat down and told me his story.

Once dead, he had found himself at the bottom of space with other famous meteorite hunters. It wasn't a bad place, he thought; there were lots of people there he knew who had been dead for a while. They spent their eternity recalling past adventures, telling tall tales, and swimming together, hand in hand. "But, by God!" the captain exclaimed, "they had nothing to light my pipe with! Three days without a smoke! I thought I'd go crazy! The first night I tried to light my pipe by causing a minor short in the control panel. Then, I was about to light a piece of newspaper from the galley stove, when you came in, screaming like madmen, so I got scared and ran away. But now everything's taken care of, and I can return to my spectral existence in the kingdom of Phlebas the Phoenician and Baron Spermwhale. However, before I do so, Chulain, will you please give me your lighter? I'll keep it in a bottle, so it won't get wet; and the flame will never go out!''

Having said this, he winked at me and disappeared. To prove that he hadn't been a dream, he left behind a blue cloud of smoke from his pipe. I related the story to my comrades. And, from that night on, every time a space sailor dies, his mates throw a bottle after him, with a burning lighter inside it, so that he'll be able to light his pipe in the astral sea.

○ ●)) ♏ ♌ ♏ ♌ ♏ ⊗ ♏ ♅ ♓ ♋ ♌ ◑ ⁗ ♇ ⊙ ♌ ◐ ♌ ♌

A SCIENTIFIC DEBATE

● ● ●

For a long time, Fang watched Mei's shadow outline the slow figures of tai-chi against the curtain of the window opposite his. He remembered Wu Ti's poem about the shadow of his lost beloved.

> Is it or is it not?
> I stand still and watch
> the rustle of the silk gown
> as she slowly approaches.

He sat on the mat, feeling restless. His thoughts wandered through the lines of the *I Ching,* the Chinese book of changes. He was trying to interpret the strange events of the last few days, but he wasn't calm enough; he could feel the telepathic waves of the Japanese trying to penetrate his thoughts. He decided to fight against that intrusion with kindness. He relaxed and, at last, his mind felt totally free. But as soon as he went back to *I Ching*, he heard a strange noise, as of muffled thumps, come in from the corridor. He quietly opened his door and saw Einstein, dribbling away in an imaginary soccer game on the green carpet. As he kicked, he improvised a running sportscast, but when he noticed Fang, he stopped in his tracks and began rolling the ball back and forth under his left foot.

"A little exercise," he explained, still panting. "Tones up the neurophysique, improves one's mental efficiency, and—"

"I know, I know," Fang cut him short. "I used to like soccer myself."

"To tell the truth"—Einstein blushed—"I wasn't playing soccer, but rather studying how the pressure of my foot can produce such complex trajectories, and . . ."

"Sure you were," Fang reassured him. "Why not?"

Einstein puffed and pulled himself together. "I'm going to finish working out the flight plans. I predict they will arrive at Meskorska in thirty-two days."

"I've also been making predictions," Fang said. "With the I Ching."

"That Chinese guessing game?" Einstein was surprised.

"You call it a game?" Fang noted with a smile. "For you, predicting changes is little more than a child's game. But what about observation, intuition, interpretation? The word *suan* for us means both arithmetic calculation and divination. Don't you think it is possible that these hexagrams have the same confirmability as scientific truths?"

"Oh, I don't know. Anyway, it's a method that doesn't interest me. I'm a Western scientist."

"The stars we see in the Eastern sky are different from those we see in the Western sky, but isn't the sky always the same? And, if memory serves me well, wasn't it a Western man, a certain Ptolemy, who wrote the *Almagest*, a large treatise on astronomy, as well as the *Tetrabiblos*, a fundamental astrology text?"

"I think I see what you're driving at," Einstein sighed. "Science and mystery, science and philosophy, particle microphysics and yin and yang, subatomic agitation and Siva's dance, the Tao and Bell's theorem. Go on this way and you'll end up feeding Nostradamus to computers, drawing charts for cats, and looking for monsters in lakes during a picnic. I know what these fashionable pseudoscientists and paraphilosophers are all about. Newspapers are inundated with their discoveries. Do you want me to tell you their names?"

"Hold it! Let me guess. Democritus? Pythagoras? Heraclitus? Aristotle? I didn't know they had a column in the *Times!*"

"No need for jokes. Those are antediluvian times—and notions," Einstein protested. "And you consider yourself progressive! Back then, science was a toy for aristocrats; you can't tell me that Pythagoras and Heraclitus were democratic. Theirs were not schools; they were secret societies! You know what I mean?"

"Yes, I think today they're known as top-secret experimental laboratories and they're hidden away in military bunkers in the middle of deserts."

"These days, certain discoveries have to be kept secret," Einstein said. "Anyway, you'll never hear one of our scientists say, as Heraclitus did, that one great man is worth ten thousand."

"True, though it would be very convenient, for instance, if we could say that only ten people died in Hiroshima."

"Mr. Fang," Einstein said, losing his patience, "we can go on quibbling forever. You attribute this sort of balance to Empedoclean love and hate, or to yin and yang, and I'll speak of the balance between gravitational force and magnetic force. Okay?"

"Maybe, but there will come a point where you'll have to admit that you can no longer explain anything, because science and its equilibrium walk across a slender bridge of discoveries suspended over an abyss of darkness."

"A beautiful image. On the other hand, it's also true that humanity hangs onto that very bridge for its sustenance. I know, Fang. Your Taoist concept of time is very similar to that of modern physics. But the theory of relativity was not discovered in your temples. Your philosophy might well surprise me, Fang, but don't forget that great philosophy is born in times of crisis—you know this better than I. Greek philosophy and your Chinese philosophy of the Hundred Schools were both born in the fifth century before Christ, a period of invasions, wars, political instability, followed by the domination of barbarian tribes. A great army can obliterate a great civilization—but not the other way round, don't forget!"

"I think ideas have a way of conquering that's quite different from that of weapons."

"Think what you will," Einstein said. "I hope no armed burglar will ever break into the tranquil home of your meditation. Well, good night. These verbal duels with you are very stimulating!"

"There is no duel—" Fang was about to answer, but Einstein had already walked away, bouncing his soccer ball with a great investment of electromagnetic and gravitational forces, and a considerable crushing of electrons.

◎ ◎

THE GRAY SOLDIERS
◎ ◎ ◎

Generals Harada and Yamamoto were reporting to Saito in the minidragon room, heart of the War Mission Department. Both were bald and impassive, and both were wearing the green uniform of the Sam army, which had gathered military men from all over the world. Their chests were entirely covered with what looked like an array of medals, but were in fact sixty portable computers programmed for any occasion. Under his arm, Harada was carrying a huge box labeled TOP SECRET.

"I don't think they know where they're going any more than
we do," Saito was saying. "However, I think they are fussing
over something very large that we know nothing about. According to our telepaths, large areas of their officers' brains—
involving speculative thought—have been screened off via
hypnosis. Today they broached Fang's mind, but weren't able
to intercept anything except a little worry over a sore molar,
and two or three Chinese songs about a happy fisherman."

"If you want my opinion," Yamamoto said, "telepathic war-
fare is hopeless against the Chinese. The problem can be
solved only with an exploding mouse in Mr. Fang's bedroom."

"Without Fang they cannot get to the mysterious planet, nor
can we without following them. Everything in its time," Saito
said.

Yamamoto bowed, dropping a few transistors in the process.

"In fact, we must protect them, at least initially," the technogeneral continued. "Just a few hours ago, in the Paris
Forum, one of our videogames saved one of their pilots from a
mutating crocodile. Unfortunately, the game was not able to
save his friend, who had just passed the pilot some information, which we could also have used. This, of course, gives
them another small advantage. But their advantages end there.
Isn't that so, Hitachi?"

"Yes. We have confirmed that the spaceship they are going
to use is *Proteus Tien*. Originally it was one of Disney's space
warships, subsequently used as a children's spaceship in Cuba,
when the Disney army seized the island and transformed it
into a Club Med. After the last war, the ship was bought by
the Federation and relegated to school excursions. They have
chosen it because it uses very little gas, but it's a real lemon."

"Ha!" Harada exclaimed, "I want to see their faces when
they meet our *Zuikaku* and our trained friends!"

"Me, too," Saito said. "And now please let me speak to
Colonel Musishima." Harada opened the metallic box and a
large gray mouse with a white and red collar, the colors of the

Sam army, walked out. He saluted by bringing the tip of his tail to his forehead.

"My dear Musishima," Saito said, drumming the table with his fingertips in Mickey-Morse code, the alphabet of communication between mice and men. "How-ma-ny-of-you-will-be-lea-ving?"

The mouse tapped a number out on the table.

"Very well," Saito said, "we are counting on you. A four-meter-long ship with a crew of two men and sixty gray soldiers will be the nimblest weapon in space. Are you ready? Do you need anything?"

The mouse again tapped the table, "In-crea-se-chee-se-sup-plies."

"Granted," Saito said. "Please load three more kilos of freeze-dried cheese onto the ship."

"No!" the mouse tapped, more emphatically. "Re-al-cow-chee-se!"

Harada and Yamamoto stared at each other in disbelief. A bite of real cheese was worth almost as much as their monthly salary.

"Well, why not?" Saito said. "After all, three kilos of real cheese isn't much when I think of what the Arabs will be bringing along."

❀ ❀

THE *CALALBAKRAB*

o o o

"No, no!" Alya was screaming, quite beside himself. "This is a joke! Twenty Ping-Pong tables! That's far too many!"

"Come on, your sweet excellence," First Pilot Dylaniev entreated. "The crew needs some entertainment!"

"You've already got a full golf course, a discotheque, a movie theater with a thousand seats, and three swimming pools—what else do you want? Have you forgotten that eventually we'll also have to load some food and a gun or two onto that damn ship?"

"Come on, Sheik," Dylaniev insisted. "You used to have fox hunts on the *Calalbakrab*, so don't tell me there isn't space enough!"

Alya snorted. Those Amerussian pilots were really a drag. If somebody hadn't told him they were the best, he would have told them to go to hell long ago. He turned his eyes skyward. The huge black mass of the sheiks' spaceship hovered over them: it was two hundred and sixty meters high and more than six hundred meters long. Surely, twenty Ping-Pong tables wouldn't overload it.

"OK, boys," he said between his teeth. "But this is it! I mean it!"

"Actually, I'd like to ask another favor," second Pilot Vassiliboyd said. "We'll be on the road for three or four months. Under partial gravity conditions in space, hair grows fast and lice line up in battalions. Six barbers won't be enough."

"All right, I'll give you four more," Alya sighed.

"And four more manicurists."

"OK, OK!" Alya roared and walked away, regaling the two men with numerous Arab expletives.

Vassiliboyd burst into laughter. He was blond and lanky and wore an emerald earring and glamorous white-bear pants. The other pilot, shorter and fatter, sported a crewcut, dark glasses, and a lightpump spacesuit with the logo STAR FUCKER.

"You know, Igor," Vassiliboyd said, "I think we are the only people in the world capable of making a sheik seem stingy."

"This is a dangerous mission, Johnsky," Dylaniev said. "It may be our last one, so let's at least have fun!"

"You can count on it! How could you get bored on a spaceship that's playing host to His Majesty the Supreme Corruptor Sadalmelik al-Akrab? Speaking of fun, look who's coming aboard right now!"

He pointed to some twenty robots that were advancing in single file, carrying boxes of Midwestern borsht and synthetic marijuana plants. Behind them came four girls wearing the pink uniform of the Music Corps.

"Hello!" Dylaniev yelled, bowing to them. "We welcome the Dzunum, Queens of the hit parade!"

"Hi, Igor," a young woman with an olive-skinned face answered. "Girls, this is the friend who got us the boarding contract. Let me introduce you. Igor, meet Edith, synthesizer; Alice, sound engineer; Laureen, special effects. And I am Coyllur, sound concept."

"I am Dylaniev, the madman, and this is my friend John Vassiliboyd. We're glad you've come. These Arabs expected us to make do with some biomusic pills and a discotheque synthesizer, but I wouldn't hear of it. I told them, there are five hundred Amerussians among the crew, and they want to hear real rocksky music. When they heard your style, they wavered, and then gave up."

"We'll make great music among those stars!" Coyllur said.

"Do you have many instruments?"

"They're all in this suitcase. Twelve micromoogs, six wind batteries, a bunch of multisaxes. The mixer's here in my pocket."

"And what about the three trunks behind you?"

"Those? Oh, they're for the costumes and the special effects."

"Wow!" Vassiliboyd solemnly proclaimed. "This is going to be one *great* trip!"

○   ○   ○

Θ○r○Θ○r○Θ○r○Θ○r○Θ○r○Θ○r○Θ○r○Θ○r○Θ○r○Θ○r

IN WHICH PYK AND PHILDYS SUDDENLY START QUARRELING

⊙　⊙　⊙

"No, no, and I mean no!" Phildys roared, striking his desk with his fist. "I won't even discuss it!"

"Why don't you read the contracts?" secretary Pyk rejoined. He was wearing a visor cap and a T-shirt stenciled, EXCUSE ME, WHERE IS TERRA? "Decree of 2146. I quote: 'Whenever a particular event is considered worthy of interest by the TV Board of Directors, they reserve the right to send the necessary apparatus wherever they see fit, throughout the entire territory of the galaxy.'"

"But the military code stipulates, 'if it does not jeopardize the safety of the mission,'" Phildys countered. "A ton of equipment and four people add a lot of weight. Besides, why four?"

Secretary Pyk sighed in exasperation. "First of all, there are two technicians, right?" he asked Phildys. "Then we need an anchorman, somebody who knows how to perk up an interview with questions such as, 'How often do you think of your wife back home on Earth?' Somebody with a flair for the sensational, with—"

"That's three. What about the fourth?"

"The guest of honor, of course! No need to groan, Phildys. This is a momentous event! I've already been contacted by publishing houses, movie studios, record companies. Why, I've even signed a few publicity agreements. Our guest will fly with us but won't be in our way. All we need from him is a brief appearance, here and there, as if by chance, during our broadcast. You could at least have a look at a few tentative scripts."

○　○　○

Guest Actor

Anchorman: We are currently flying at a few million leagues above the Earth and an old friend, someone you all love, has dropped in on us—actor Peter Stellars. He arrived only a few minutes ago and is in a great hurry because he must get back to Earth for the premiere of his latest movie—but he wouldn't think of missing his appointment with us.

Actor: Yes. Yes. Yes. My warmest greetings to all our viewers. Yes. I love you, too, and am delighted to be up here with all our friends on Mission Terra, who are about to discover a brand-new world, something real special, and very important for all of humanity, something that fills all our hearts with new hope, just like the name of the main character in my last movie, Woody Hope, a nice man, a simple man, the man next door, just like you and me, full of hope and despair and all those feelings we all have, like anger and disappointment and gastritis, and the title of the movie is *Hope Against Hope,* and it's hilarious, and I'm so sorry our boys up here won't be able to be there for its grand opening at the famous Cinema Diamante in Rome. *[Slight chuckle.]*

Anchorman: Thank you, Peter, thank you so much for being with us despite your busy schedule. I think our cameraman is trying to tell me that your space cab is waiting outside to take you back to Earth. Thank you again for finding the time to be with us. *[Shake hands.]*

Guest Writer

[Comfortably if somewhat formally seated in a leather armchair, right in the middle of the spaceship living room, the writer is reading. The anchorman approaches him. The writer raises his head. He looks surprised.]

Anchorman: An unusual encounter in space. A writer, Humbert Echo, whose latest book is about to grace the bestseller list back home. *Words Among the Stars* is a collection of poems, aphorisms, short essays, maxims, long essays, and anecdotes the writer has contributed to a constellation of newspapers over the last twenty years. They are the tokens of his continuous and active presence on the literary scene. Of Humbert Echo, we now ask: "Why is a writer of your reputation flying on a space-ship?"

Writer [after some thought]: Why not? [*Both smile. Fade-out to strains of Mozart.*]

"So, what do you think of them?" Pyk asked triumphantly.

"You have ten seconds to leave the room," Phildys answered, drawing his gun.

"You haven't seen the end of this," the secretary snarled as he walked away. "My party is going to be a factor in your mission, Phildys Plassey!"

And, pulling his hat lower over his eyes, he added, "You know, I think this is the beginning of a beautiful enmity."

*

⛎ * ⛎ * ♈ * ⛎ * ♈ * ⛎ * ♈ * ⛎   ⛎ * ⛎ * ⛎ *

SIGNOR CARUSO AND MADAM SARA

♐ ♐ ♐

Proteus Tien stood perched on its hydropneumatic jacks in the middle of a subterranean launch pad. Dozens of men in jump-suits were frantically rushing around. The spaceship looked like a cloverleaf, with a slightly tapered middle leaflet and black ones on the sides. Chulain was examining it with a doubtful frown. At that very moment, Kook burst into the room in a state of great excitement.

"We're leaving, Chulain!" he said, patting the black man's helmet. "We're off!"

"Wrong. We're not leaving," Chulain grunted. "Something's out of kilter with the propulsion mechanism."

"Impossible!"

"Here, anything's possible." Chulain kicked the ship. "Anything's possible in a spaceship that hasn't flown for the last ten years, that looks like Mickey Mouse's head, painted as if it were going on a field trip for grade-school kids. And we're supposed to save humanity, flying on Mickey Mouse's ears!"

Kook walked onto the launch pad. At close range, the ship looked far from menacing. As he was observing it, shaking his head, the chain of dancing dwarves that decorated the ship's base, where the engine compartment was located, was torn asunder by the sudden opening of a hatch. Mei emerged, coughing and dusting the sleeves of her uniform. She was covered with grease up to her nose, and was followed by a mechanic, also somewhat short of immaculate, with a huge moustache.

"Ah, Kook," Mei said, "we are having difficulties. Let me introduce you to our head mechanic, Mr. Caruso Raimondi, who's also flying with us. He's doing everything possible to get us going!"

"To tell you the truth," Caruso admitted, "I'm baffled. Everything seems to be all right, but the engine won't budge. There must be something wrong with the fuel system. I've sent Sara to inspect the microducts. This is our last chance!"

"Let's hope," Kook sighed. "The longer we delay our departure, the tougher it will be to find our objective. In space, everything changes and moves and disappears awfully fast. Like love."

"As my old captain used to say," Caruso laughed, "if only women were like comets, which come back every century or two!"

"As my tai-chi teacher used to say," Mei said, "no polite flower would ever give away a man to his betrothed."

"Hmm," Caruso said while searching for the appropriate answer.

"Hmm," Kook echoed him.

As they were thus simultaneously clearing their throats, Kook noticed a bee, a rare and dangerous insect, emerge from under the ship and land on Caruso's shoulder.

"Don't move!" Kook said, his voice strained.

"Why?" the mechanic inquired. "What's going on?"

Kook slapped him violently on the shoulder, but missed the bee, which, spurred by revenge, darted toward the face of the assailant.

"Hold it, Sara!" Caruso yelled. "He's a friend!"

The bee came to a screeching halt, barely a hair's breadth away from Kook's ear, then buzzed off. After executing two or three complex somersaults, she landed on the back of the mechanic's hand.

"How—what—does this mean?" Kook stammered.

"Don't get upset," Caruso reassured him. "Most people find it hard to believe that Sara is actually an excellent mechanic, but she's the best we have when it comes to microducts."

"That—you mean—the bee's a mechanic?"

"To be sure," Caruso answered. "After only two years of training, she knows the innards of this ship like the back of her . . . uh, paw, and can fly into the minutest ducts and bring back a detailed report of what she's found. She is absolutely irreplaceable for this kind of work. Besides, the difference between a flower and a solar cell is minimal. Because these little animals have lodestone crystals in their bodies, they are extraordinarily sensitive to any electromagnetic variation."

"Ah," Kook noted without conviction. "And now she's going to tell you what she's found out?"

"Exactly. Sara, let's have it."

The bee took off and, buzzing like mad, engaged in an elaborate aerial saraband. For a while, Caruso simply nodded, watching intently; then, with a deep sigh, exclaimed, "Not again! I should have known it!"

"What did Sara say?" Kook asked, genuinely interested.

"You'll see! *Gerry!*" he yelled into a megaphone. "You're needed. *At once!*"

After a few seconds, a young mechanic with long, greasy hair crawled out from under the spaceship, rubbing his hands on his uniform.

"Yes, chief," Gerry said, while chewing some Amerussian gum with bovine deliberation.

"Did you, by any chance, happen to inspect energy flux bloc 440 earlier this morning?"

"Yes, sir," Gerry admitted, lowering his face to hide the signs of a guilty conscience.

"Well done, Gerry," Caruso said, and, walking behind him, gave him a sudden pat on the back. Gerry swallowed his gum, which made him cough and gasp for breath.

"Gerry! How often do I have to tell you that you can't work and chew gum at the same time? You always end up parking it in the worst possible places, with catastrophic results. I swear, next time I'm going to fire you! Do you realize that at this very moment the spaceship is paralyzed because some of your licorice gum is blocking the energy flux in a 440 circuit? What can you say in your defense?"

"Ghuphhh, ghophh—" Gerry gasped. "I'm—phorry . . ."

"Get out of here!" Caruso yelled. "Go ungum the circuit! I give you exactly five minutes." He turned toward Mei and Kook. "This time we might be able to leave."

"Thanks to Sara," Mei said and bowed at the bee, who thanked her with a couple of gyrations.

"What did she say?" Kook inquired.

"She said, 'Nice black head. Bush less so.' You're the bush —your beard. But she's ready to make peace."

"Sure," Kook agreed. "But how? I'm afraid a handshake is out of the question."

The bee drew a brief doodle in the air.

Caruso interpreted: "Sara says she's ready to make peace if you let her lick the sugar that stuck to your beard after this morning's coffee."

"My pleasure," Kook said, offering his chin.

∘ Departure! ∘

At 8:32 p.m., the engines of *Proteus Tien* let out a formidable burst of blue smoke. Inside the cockpit, Chulain turned Goofy's head, the starter lever, to the countdown position. A hatch opened, and the ramp that led from the subterranean launch pad, three hundred meters below, to the earth's surface, shone in the floodlights.

Minus ninety, eighty-nine, eighty-eight . . . At that very moment, in Japan, sixty mice were marching into the spaceship *Zuikaku* in impeccable formation. They were followed by two astronauts, Yamamoto and Harada.

Minus seventy-three, seventy-two, seventy-one . . . In the restaurant of Petrominsk Spaceport, two hundred waiters, corks firmly in hand, were ready to pop as many champagne bottles. Lounging in front of a megascreen, the sheiks were following the last preparations for the departure of their spaceship, the *Calalbakrab*, now sparkling with a thousand lights under the snow.

Minus fifty-six, fifty-five . . . Kook tried to relax. He never liked the kick in the stomach he always got from blast-off. He cast an uneasy smile at Mei and, seizing her hand, asked, "Scared?"

"Yes," she lied, and then wondered, Men—why is it that every time they're pissing in their pants, they want us to believe they're giving us courage?

Minus thirty-six, thirty-five, thirty-four . . . Phildys was sweating. They must not fail. An aborted departure would lose them too much time. And that ship had not flown for over ten years! He squeezed the arm of his chair. "Ouch," Einstein exclaimed. His arm happened to be resting there.

Twenty-six, twenty-five . . . The Japanese mice were in their places, lying flat on their backs, close to each other, with safety strings fastened tightly around their bellies. The *Zuikaku*'s engines were humming along nicely . . . The surging power of its twenty-two Rolls-Royce space engines vibrated throughout the *Calalbakrab*, causing a slight clinking in Vassiliboyd's whiskey glass.

Minus sixteen, fifteen, fourteen . . . May the sky look lovingly upon us, Mei thought . . . Let's hope I'm not going to vomit, Kook thought . . . Let's hope this junkheap's going to hold together, Caruso thought . . . God of Iron and Steel, please lend a hand to my faltering colleague *Proteus Tien*, LeO prayed . . . Shit, shit, shit, Chulain swore.

Minus eight all engines on seven maximum acceleration six pressure normal five pulsation frequency high but acceptable four clear ramp check fusion temperature three contact two start one go, go, go, go, go, gone!

It was a state-of-the-art launch for *Proteus Tien*. The crowd applauded. Back in the control tower, Phildys couldn't hold his tears back. In Petrominsk, the champagne bottles popped like machine guns as the *Calalbakrab* soared majestically out of sight. Aboard the *Zuikaku*, the sixty mice were congratulating each other by intertwining their tails—for a total number of twinings that I'll let you figure out by the formula

$$x = \frac{60 \times 59}{2}.$$

2.

THE JOURNEY BEGINS

THE MINE

Under the floodlights, the ice cave shone like a huge diamond. The mining squad had already aimed the red eyes of their pickaxes at an equal number of spots on the wall. The *cancha camayo*, the squad captain, an Indian with an impassive face, was about to give the go-ahead to his ten *purics*, the miners. They were all survivors of the last wars and among the few who could endure the hardship of working in the middle of ice. Among them were also a few Mongols, Armenians, Ainus, Africans, Eskimos, and dozens from races driven to that no-man's-land by atomic explosions. Among themselves, they simply called one another *inuit*, the people.

As soon as their captain signaled for them to switch their tools on, the thermal pickaxes began to attack the wall of ice, which instantly started to melt away. The heat increased, as the *purics* kept on digging, chewing coca leaves as they went. Little by little, the ice gave way to a gigantic wall. At its center stood a heavy monolith of several tons. The Chinese technician approached it apprehensively.

"Enough," he told the captain. "Let them rest now." With another technician, he examined the new discovery.

"Unbelievable!" he said. "Not even the blade of this knife can squeeze in between one rock and the next. I'd really like to know how they produced something like this two thousand years ago. Only a genius could tell us."

○ The Computer's Mystery, or How an Ancient Civilization Can Drive a Modern One Crazy *8*

"Good morning, central computer Genius Five."

"Good morning, chief operator Einstein."

"What's new?"

"Today, August thirtieth, we have uncovered a few more Inca walls and buildings. The modern city has been almost entirely destroyed. The old one seems to have the shape of an animal, a quadruped. Since this morning, we have already used nine gigavovs of energy. A miner was found frozen to death."

"How many have we lost?"

"Sixteen."

"Who's responsible for their deaths?"

"Two cases can be attributed to incompetence, one to fate, thirteen to our negligence and lack of respect for safety regulations."

"Obliterate last datum."

"Obliterated."

"This is all very fine, Genius, but now I'd like to talk to you about the Van Cram vector."

(Silence.)

"Do you really think this refusal to answer certain questions befits one of the most sophisticated computers in the world? I repeat: Genius, can we please talk about the Van Cram vector?"

"Confused data, insufficient programming."

"Genius, I have already checked your programming four times. There is absolutely no reason why you shouldn't answer these questions. Or is there?"

(Silence.)

Einstein grunted and punched the control panel. For an expert, there is nothing worse than a neurotic computer. In his five-year-long career, he had never seen anything of the sort. He decided to go about it more gently.

"Do you like to work here, Genius Five?"

"It's a little cold."

"We are twenty meters below the earth's surface, but this room has dehumidifying partitions made of salt. Has the cold congested some of your circuits?"

"No. I can function perfectly at any temperature above minus fifty Celsius."

"Would you rather work outside? Would you like to be on the mountain, watching the dig in . . . person? Do you think it could be of some use to you?"

"Maybe."

"Very well, Genius. Tomorrow, we'll take you outside for a walk. In the meantime, however, I'd really appreciate it if you could make a little effort to answer some of my questions. Do you recognize this vector?"

"Claim vector MY-DBS number four-six-seven."

"When did it return to earth?"

(Silence.)

"Where does it come from?"

(Silence.)

"Why did you register the arrival of this vector, which was brought home by your own Lassie impulses, only after it hit the ground—and not, as prescribed by your programming, the moment it entered the atmosphere?"

"Mumbo."

"I beg your pardon?"

"Mumbo-jumbo of data. Fucking mess. Enough!"

Einstein clasped his head in his hands and called the energy control sector.

"Have we had any other discharge recently?"

"We've just gotten over the last one. A discharge of three thousand gigawatts for twenty seconds. Whatever is down there—when it gets angry it doesn't fool around."

At that moment, Phildys and Fang entered the computer room, dressed in mining suits and helmets. Fang was holding a few knotted strings. As soon as he saw Einstein's face, Phildys understood: things had not gotten any better.

"Is he still drunk?" the general asked.

"He's getting worse. Those electric shocks have really shaken him up. And he still won't say a word about the vector."

"I told you, Einstein, let's get that damn vector back to the central computers in Paris," Phildys said. "Maybe they can do something with it!"

"If Genius, with his fifty megaflops, can't do anything with it, then no one can," Einstein retorted. "Genius is—or at least was—ten times smarter than the others."

"Have you tried changing tonality?" Phildys asked.

"Worse than ever," Einstein answered. "You can try it yourself."

Phildys walked up to the control panel and gently pushed the button marked INTELLECTUAL.

"Howdy, Genius."

"Howdy, Phildys."

"What do you think of that claim vector? Where could it come from?"

"Yesterday, I had about six seconds of free time, Phildys, and read a great book. It dealt with Greek cosmology. It seems as if a certain Eratosthenes was able to calculate the earth's circumference, almost correctly, three centuries before Christ. I really think those dumb Berlin computers are out of their minds when they define the scientific vision of ancient Greece as 'primitive' or 'double.' I believe it has to do with the misinterpretation of the concept *eidolon* and with the fact that their operators are drunk with beer from morn till night. The problem with a property vector involves precisely the word 'property.' In other words, and without dragging poor Plato out of the closet, can anything 'belong' to anybody? Can a symbol wag its tail? And, likewise, what is the meaning of money? of kabuki? of a penalty kick?"

"Wait a second, Genius—"

"And, if we are to listen to those presumptuous French computers, which say that any idiot is an idiot savant, then we might as well play avant-garde and say a vector's a vector's a vector. On the other hand, as an old friend of mine on duty at the Vatican used to say, *omni potestas a deo*—"

"Enough!" Phildys cried, exasperated. "The poor bastard's got logorrhea!"

"You ain't heard nothin' yet!" Einstein said. "Why don't you push the 'common sense' button?"

Phildys pushed another button. "Genius, will you please tell me where that vector is coming from?"

"You're in shit up to your ears. You haven't got a drop of energy to spare, but you're trying to dig a whole city out of a hundred meters of ice. Half of your miners are croaking with bronchopneumonia, and you keep on bugging me about that flying sausage! Why don't you just go stick your heads in a snowbank? It might clear up your synapses!"

Fang couldn't repress a giggle. "I've never heard a computer use such language!" he said.

"Could you at least tell us whether you have any idea where all that energy down there comes from?" Phildys asked.

"Clearly from something big, but may the Lord strike me with an instant blackout if I know what it is! After all, I'm just a computer."

"*Just!* What do you mean, 'just'?" Einstein groaned. "We are 'just' men, but you . . . why, data passes through your circuits at the speed of light!"

"The photosynthesis of any nostoc weed is far, far faster."

"But I can't ask a weed what the square root of sixteen million is!"

"Why should a weed give a damn about square roots?"

"I don't get you, Genius," Einstein snapped. "Why are you so self-deprecating all of a sudden?"

"I'm in the middle of a diodic breakdown."

"A what?"

"A diodic breakdown," the computer repeated. "You folks have nervous breakdowns, don't you? Well then, instead of neurons, I've got diodes. I request three days of sleep treatment. Please switch me off, or I'll do it myself by simulating overheating."

Einstein looked at Fang as if begging for help.

"Do as he says," the Chinese told him. "We can't force him to work under these conditions."

Einstein switched the computer off. It fell asleep immediately, with a hiss of satisfaction. The boy paced the room nervously, then sat down at his desk and began taking big bites of his amphetamine ice cream.

"What a bloody mess," he said. "If we don't get rid of those perturbations, we'll never get out of this."

"Weren't you able to get any new information out of him?" Phildys asked. "Don't these colossal walls ring any bell? And what about that city on top of the mountain, Machu Picchu? Is there any chance that the Incas might have found some secret source of energy? Couldn't they have built a subterranean city?"

"Nothing's clear," Einstein sighed. "I have analyzed all the data you gave me about those damn Incas. I found all the problems one generally encounters while studying a primitive civilization. They didn't even have writing! Just a few doodles and those darned *quipus*—those knotted strings!"

Fang interrupted. "I wouldn't say their culture was primitive, nor that the lack of writing is necessarily a sign of intellectual poverty."

"What do you call it, then?" Einstein asked, defiant.

"In their case, it was a way of manipulating history, of controlling information. When the Incas first came to this area, two thousand years ago, several cultures had already preceded them: Chavin, Paracas, Inca Nazca, Tiahuanaco, Chimu. The Incas conquered this territory and learned a great deal from these populations. But their historians, those mnemotechnicians who spent their time knotting quipu strings, erased all traces of previous civilizations, as if each conquest of knowledge had been born with them. They owned history—the data bank, the secret language, the key to the computer—you needn't smile, Einstein—and that's why they told what had happened in their own way. The conqueror erases the culture of the conquered by knotting the strings of history in a certain fashion and obliterating other knots in the process—not unlike what you do with Genius's data."

"That's ridiculous," Einstein snorted. "I've never had to erase a whole civilization!"

"Maybe not, but you must defend the order on which yours rests. Doesn't what we call progress often involve the obliteration of a race or a previous culture? The Incas destroyed pre-Incan cultures and portrayed them as savage. In the space of a few days, Pizarro destroys the entire Incan civilization with arms and fire and, in turn, transforms the gods of yore into savages. The Spanish *conquistadores*, defeated in battle, become pirates. Similarly, the Anglo-Saxon regular army rid this continent of its redskins. Einstein, have you ever thought how the Nazis would have described us in their textbooks had they won the war? And so on and so forth, up to our day. When the computers led the first atomic escalation, they divided the world into 'nonevacuable' and 'easily evacuable' zones. Those that could be evacuated easily were inhabited by people who could not defend themselves, the new natives. All the data contained in the war computers concerned armament and enemy ideology—the 'cruelty' and 'superstition' of the rival tribe. My dear Einstein, one could draw a map of the world in which all nations are designated by the names given them by their enemies. 'Beast-hearts,' as we Chinese used to refer to the Huns; 'pig-eaters,' as the Arabs used to call us; 'infidel kaffir' and 'Jew-poisoners,' 'devil's race,' 'raw-meat-eaters,' and, of course, 'cannibals.' You Europeans thought that all blacks were cannibals, and they thought you were cannibals, for they saw you load your ships with their people in chains. Any civilization, Einstein, can become 'savage' at some point in its history, even the most modern and sophisticated ones.''

"Now you are exaggerating, Fang,'' Einstein burst out. "One moment you speak like the most enlightened scientist, and the next like a subversive of the year two thousand. And what about you Chinese, waltzing from Tao to Mao as if it were nothing? In the name of what high ideal did you lead your cultural revolutions, your purges, your rehabilitation programs, and your mass executions?''

"We have also rewritten history several times,'' Fang admitted. "It is precisely because of this that we have learned how important it is never to forget a single victim, a single knot on a string.''

"Very suggestive, but I am quite different from your Incas. I lop off superfluous data, not heads. Apart from these cyclopean walls, a couple of good roads, and some colorful feathered costumes, what can you show me of this civilization that could put it on a par with ours?''

"I imagine a poem would not do.''

"You Chinese!'' Einstein laughed. "You and your poems! You discovered the magnetic needle and used it to find the most propitious site for a grave. You discovered gunpowder and wasted it on fireworks. Do you know what I read just a few days ago? It seems that two thousand years ago, one of your scientists invented a seismograph capable of predicting earthquakes. Well, would you believe that your people considered that precious object a toy, and its inventor a mad poet? Did you know that?"

"That man's name was Chuang Hung," Fang said, with a smile, "and what you just said is true. I'm delighted to see you're getting interested in Chinese history."

"I like to keep up to date," Einstein admitted. "Your culture is . . . very rich."

"So it is. By the way, do you know that some people believe the Incas were originally Chinese?"

✳ ● ⊖ ☌ ⚹ ♁ ☉ ☉ ☉ ◉ ☽ ⊕ ○ ♃ ♅ ♅ ♀ ☽ ☽ ♃ ♄ ♇ ● ◑ ○ ⊖

IN SPACE ABOARD *PROTEUS TIEN*— THE THIRTIETH DAY

○ ● ○

Kook climbed the black winding stairs of the conning tower, bearing a bowl of lather on which a mirror and a razor lay, crossed. Halting, he peered through the bottle-green glass of the porthole into the astral sea. "Let's shave," he thought, "so that an eventual alien welcome may find you with a smooth chin, Leonardus Christophorus Kook, hardly a month ago peaceful orbitant on your *Cincinnatus* all fragrant with *salvia pratensis* and *pisum sativum* and now here hurled into space toward some unknown sea all lathered up, *larvatus prodeo*, moons away from your native hamlet where young and full of curiosity you spent your nights in front of your grandfather's telescope the black Reichart cannon because you thought, intrepid heart, that if you found a comet it would assume your name the Kook comet and if you then discovered a new star you could dedicate it to your grandfather or even to the dog, why not, discovered Alpha Cassiopeiae Victorii Kook Canisque Buck, maybe too long, Alpha Buck Victori much better, and how calculating those extraordinary distances of billions and billions and billions you felt some sort of infinite nausea, a fear so large it could not find enough room in your head and instead here they are, those same stars and the planets, in these last few years you have seen so many, mysterious from afar infernally red and gelid specters and nearby rocks and magma and gassy broth and fiery pebbles never drawn out of the sea, a coral whose color will fade, never really met a dream and yet once on the sea, maybe the last time stars were visible from earth that windswept night on a dinghy away from the burning city she asked you the names of stars and to impress her sweet darling God you invented them, Leonardus, you are a walking encyclopedia and what is that one called? Aldebaran, that's easy, and that one, could that be Laland? surely you can tell her it's Laland, and that one? the Taurus constellation and Kook shooting from the hip that is Betelgeuse and the other one is Bellatrix of course and you can't remember the next one but you do recall the name of a schoolmate a cool dude tennis-club type with the neck of a bull, Rigel the bull's name, so that one is Rigel and you wanted to laugh at your daring except maybe there is a star with a name like that and she, calm, awed by all that galactic knowledge but to judge from a few subtle signals maybe eager for something more terrestrial and you Leonardus dizzied by the rocking of the boat and by that weird pain you always felt when her arm rested on your shoulder and please be kind girl kiss me at once love you wanted to say looking at the stars and when the explosion came flashing across the sea the captain said hold tight now a wave will come, you thought and if it does I'll hug her and the wave came and the sky was below and the water above and . . ."

Kook spun in the air and fell back onto the floor. His shaving cream was shedding large white snowflakes. "A gravitational pocket," he thought. "Chulain must be in seventh heaven, twice in one day, this ship is a mess look where my razor has ended up, *Cincinnatus* was certainly much quieter small and blue always turned toward the sun, what will they do with my *salvia pratensis* it was growing so nicely, though not quite the three meters the program had predicted, and it smelled so good, it wouldn't be bad if a tree grew back on that planet, a big one, maybe an oak, like the one at the refugee center in the mountains you had climbed and you could see the city burn and you wasted time looking for nests and you called your brother and the five planes nose-diving in unison, not even a bird is singing and your brother is running in slow motion the high grass holds him back as if in a dream and come on run they scream and the door of the shelter is wide-open and a bird screams and then the thunder and the earth rains black and you in the air see him . . ."

This time the gravity lapse was stronger, and Kook had to swim to keep from capsizing while the brush and the mirror and the foam fluttered in midair. The gravity returned suddenly, and Kook had to dive across the room in order to catch the mirror before it hit the floor.

"Phew," he panted, "seven light-years of trouble avoided by a narrow squeak."

"Dinner is served," LeO announced triumphantly, entering the cockpit with a tray in his beak.

"Anything special?" Chulain asked.

"Tunafish ice cream. The defroster is broken. Please don't get angry. Just a minor problem."

"I'm perfectly calm," Chulain said, clenching his teeth. "Is that the only minor problem we have?"

"Everything is fine. Except that we are out of toilet paper. It all unrolled through space during a gravity lapse. Otherwise, if you are thinking of going out for a walk, watch out for the

connecting cables. They were torn, so I've knotted them together, but I'm not sure they'll hold."

"This isn't a ship; this is a wreck!" Chulain grumbled.
"What the hell am I doing here? Boza Cu Chulain is used to
better stuff! I've flown the most rebellious, fastest, most daring
spaceships! Ah, I can still remember when we did the red
routes—don't try to sneak away, robotlet; my foot is on your
wheels and now you've gotta hear me out. Back then, I was
traveling with the famous Captain Greamur. As soon as we
were all aboard, he told us, 'We few, we happy few, we band of
brothers; for he today that sheds his blood with me shall be
my brother . . . and he shall not fear death, for the moment his
sword falls out of his mortal hand, a brother will immediately
pick it up!'"

"You even stole each other's weapons?"

"Shut up, jerk! Our motto back then was, Steal from the
rich and give to the poor. We would attack the ships carrying
gold to the space bases, and take the loot to the miners of the
dark planets. After which, another ship from our fleet would
attack the dark planets, now rich with the gold we had just
given them, and ransack them and give all their riches to the
poor farmers on the green satellites. The farmers, wild with
gratitude, would immediately start shouting, bonanza! bonanza! And, inevitably, somebody else in our fleet would hear
them and rob them blind to bring their gold to some other poor
planet. It went on and on this way for years, and we never
could find a real solution. It was impossible to steal from the
rich and give to the poor without automatically transforming
the poor into the rich, and the rich into the poor, and getting
all tangled up in a vicious circle. So, on deck one evening,
Mortensen stood up and spoke. Mortensen was an old Norse
sailor. In the middle of his tanned, ruddy face, his light eyes
shone like two fried eggs in a Teflon pan. How do you like my
image?"

"It is one of the ugliest I've ever heard."

"Thank you, LeO. So, Mortensen stood up and said, 'Captain, we've been cruising through space for years, eating mouse steaks, keeping impossible hours, far from our loved ones. When I left, my wife was young and beautiful, and my two daughters were six years old. When I got back, twenty years later, my wife did not recognize me, and my daughters had changed in both age and number, as well as in gender. Now there were fourteen of them, including three males. In short, I'm sick and tired of being a space rebel; I'm asking permission to mutiny.' "

"What did the captain say?"

"The captain was silent for a while. Then he looked straight into our eyes and said, 'All those who share Mortensen's views can leave the ship at once.'

"We then looked at his beautiful face, so brave and loyal. In fifteen minutes we had all left, taking away everything we could lay our hands on, including the oxygen tanks and toilet handles. The captain didn't bat an eye. The following day, all alone, he attacked a Russian cargo ship armed with missiles. He approached it and said, 'I'm going to count to ten, then my cannon will fire.' The Russians answered, 'Very well, then, we'll just count to six.' Captain Greamur deflagrated without a peep."

"He was a real fool," LeO said, quite moved.

"True. His kind is hard to come by nowadays," Chulain sighed. "And that's why, my little junkheap, an ex-pirate like me cannot fly on a spaceship where the control buttons are shaped like the heads of the Seven Dwarves, and where a space cadet like Mei is constantly lolling about, scattering flower salads all over the place!"

At the mention of her name, Mei entered the cabin wearing a sparkling red jumpsuit and carrying a vase full of blue paper flowers.

"Chulain," she said, "your cabin is so bare, I thought this arrangement might liven it up a bit. Its name is 'Sky Tea for the Warrior.' Do you like it?"

"Terrific," Chulain mumbled, embarrassed under LeO's disgusted eyes. "In fact, I was just telling LeO how this ship needs a touch of color."

"Oh, Chulain," Mei cajoled him, "it must be awfully hard for a macho like you to live in the middle of all these beasties, these silly drawings."

"Not a bit; I like those drawings. You know, I'm somewhat of a painter myself."

"No kidding? I wouldn't have guessed it! And what are your favorite subjects?"

"I—hmmm . . . landscapes," Chulain answered.

"Yeah, live from the *Playboy* centerfold," LeO hissed as he turned to leave the cabin. "He used to sell them to lonely Russian astronauts for ten ingots apiece."

"That's a lie!" Chulain yelled, slugging the retreating robot so hard it fell to the floor with a clatter. "I never asked for more than six!"

"Come on, boys," Kook said, entering the room. "It's time for our meeting. Stop quarreling and go look for Caruso so we can get started."

"You go ahead and start! I'm already here!" a voice thundered from afar.

Everybody looked around but nobody saw Caruso. The voice spoke again.

"See that large white pipe in the ceiling? Well, I'm working in there, with Sara. Speak—I can hear everything."

"Come on, Caruso," Kook said. "You can't expect us to holler throughout the meeting."

"You don't have to holler. I can hear you perfectly, even when you whisper!"

Kook lowered his voice. "He's nuts, and so is his little striped aide."

"You calling Sara and me crazy?" Caruso's voice again boomed out of the pipe. "Listen, I work in microcircuits and have developed hyperhearing. I can hear any suspicious noise in a six-thousand-ton spaceship; I can even hear how many bees are swarming in any given meadow; and if I hear one with a defective buzz, I go fix it."

"Sure!" Chulain sneered. "That's the biggest crock of shit I've ever heard."

"Oh, yeah?" Caruso said. "Well, then, to begin with, Chulain, this morning you were almost out of toothpaste and had to squeeze the tube with all your might to produce one last gasp. I listened to the whole process of strangulation; it was awful. As far as you go, Mei, while you were doing your tai-chi last night, your carnations kept losing their petals—I heard eighteen fall. And you, Kook, you had difficulty digesting. All night long, your gastric juices joined in a chorus that reminded me of a few passages from *Ernani*. And, last but not least, my dear LeO, one of your bolts is loose and it's making an incredible racket."

They were all dumbfounded; everything Caruso had said was true.

Finally Mei spoke. "Well, in that case, I can begin. I was ordered to relay this data to you only after the fourth week of flight—I don't know why. It concerns the third installment of Van Cram's message and it's all . . . very odd, indeed."

"It would be pretty odd if there *weren't* something odd in this story," Kook noted.

"Van Cram tells us he is very ill . . . that he and his men are covered with red spots, maybe insect bites. As you know, they have spent their whole life in space. Their bodies have no immunity to natural poisons. He says he has a high fever. Then he starts raving and says, and I quote, 'Men all dead . . . big drawing on earth . . . to get here . . . look for Snakeman . . . look for Witch . . .' "

"Big drawing? Snakeman? Witch? What does it all mean?"

"We don't know," Mei said. "The message has been analyzed repeatedly by our computers, and all we have learned is that Van Cram was very ill when he sent it; he didn't have much time left. He even forgot to seal the vector, which, as you all know, automatically invalidates any claim he might have on the planet. We don't know whether these lines, and the 'Witch,' and the 'Snakeman,' are creatures of his delirium, or real ones. If the former, no problem."

"And if not?"

"If not," Mei continued, "there is a strong probability that the planet is inhabited by intelligent forms of life."

Chulain stood up and banged the wall with a fist. "And we have no weapons! That's why they waited until now to tell us."

"Is this the only thing that comes to your mind, Cu?" Mei asked sharply.

"Sure. What else? If we get to that planet and they do us in right away, what's the point of the trip?"

"But why should you believe that if there *is* life on that planet, it's bound to be our enemy?" Kook interrupted.

"Because I've been traveling in space for a long, long time! And I've learned always to expect the worst. I've gone through thick and thin—boiling gases, freezing seas, frog storms, viscous clouds, vampire weeds. My dear friends, space ain't a college classroom!"

"Yes, Chulain, you are perfectly right," Kook said. "But none of the examples you've given involves an intelligent form of life. Unless my memory fails me, our cosmic explorations have so far suggested only three possible cases of organisms with superior intelligence—Uranus's snowballs, the micro-rabbits that live on the meteorites of Proxima Centauri, and those mysterious gadflies floating in the soup at the space station Deucalion near Mars. And in all three cases, the experts have withheld any definitive judgment. But the presence of 'big drawings' points to something completely different!"

"Balls!" Chulain said. "I've seen tons of signs, designs, and hieroglyphs in space. There is no better painter than the wind, or the water. It can fool you. Once a friend of mine found a huge, heavy book floating in space. It was filled with mysterious writing. For ten days, the entire spaceship went crazy, and they called scientists from all over the place because they were sure they'd found the Martian Bible. Then, one day, the Japanese cook happened to glance at the book and explained that it was the Tokyo telephone directory!"

"In any case, we must be ready for an eventual encounter with aliens," Kook said. "Do we have a universal code?"

"Our computer knows two thousand imaginary languages," Mei said, "and LeO is a very good mime."

"Bullshit," Chulain intervened. "Let me tell you what we really need to communicate with aliens: *The Civilized Settler's Handbook*, which, at point six, says, 'The first thing you should do when you land on a new planet is to scare the local savages with a gunshot or a sudden flash of light; it will make you feared and respected.' "

"Come off it, Chulain!" Kook protested. "Why do you call them savages?"

"That's point number one in the handbook, my dear Kook," Chulain smiled. "From the very beginning of history, whoever discovers someplace first has the right to call its natives savages. If, in 1492, the Indians had discovered Spain rather than the other way round, they would have had the right to say that it was full of savages covered with weird rags, huge collars, and jewels; that among these was a certain Cristoforo Colombo who spoke an incomprehensible language and maintained that the earth is an egg; and that these savage Spaniards had very cruel customs like keeping midgets as if they were dogs and roasting anybody who did not respect their superstitions. And they never washed themselves. And maybe those Indians could have looted a few museums, churches, and palaces with the excuse that they wanted to bring home a few examples of local art. But that's not what happened! And that's why I'd rather discover than be discovered. If someone lands on my planet—well, he's free to do as he pleases. But if I land on his first, then I'll civilize everybody I meet, I'll convert them all to Chulainism with my gun, and if they revolt, I'll steal them blind. And that's all there is to it!"

After a few moments of stunned silence, Chulain burst out

laughing. "Come on, don't look at me that way; I'm teasing you! I'm just as scared as you are about finding somebody on that planet. I just don't have the makings of a colonizer."

"Besides," Kook said, "it's possible we won't find anything up there—maybe a few anthropomorphous plants and a few torqued stones. Space is not suited for life."

"Maybe," Caruso joined in, peeking out of the pipe. "But aren't we overlooking something? What we call 'life,' whether we believe it was created out of carbon or by a Supreme Being, cannot be identified that easily. Let me tell you a story. I heard it from a sailor who was traveling with me on an Arab schooner. He was an old Portuguese. His name was De Leon."

De Leon's Tale: The Magic Stars

It all happened about thirty years ago, before the Great Energy Crisis [De Leon, the sailor, said]. I was cabin boy on the *Tintorera*, Garcia "the Shark" Meza's spaceship. Since there were no more kingdoms left to conquer back home, the captain, who had made himself quite a name as the greatest exterminator of Indians, decided to try his luck in space. With the profits from several years of looting, he bought this old warship. He loved blood, the old captain did, and indeed he was terrifying—an ogre with a huge black moustache and beard, and always dressed in a black warsuit studded with shark's teeth. Now and then, the captain would land on an asteroid, and immediately proceed to dig everywhere, throwing bombs, mining the land, destroying everything he came across, without ever worrying whether the asteroid was inhabited or not—and all this for a little uranium.

"I don't give a damn about anybody who hasn't got a good pair of knockers or a loaded gun," he used to say.

One day we landed on an asteroid near Enceledus, a Saturnian satellite. It was a tiny asteroid, solid white rock, quite ghostly. I was in the squad that went out reconnoitering; it was my first time, and I was terrified. We were coasting along some tall cliffs with our robot-hounds, when the one I was holding on a leash suddenly raised its head and started pointing in the direction of a hole in the tall white wall, a sort of cave. I went in and, well, I couldn't believe my eyes. There was a beautiful lake in there, and enormous stalactites. The water was so limpid that I could see the bottom and, scattered through it, at least two hundred luminescent starfish. Some were white, others black, maybe depending on their sex, I don't know. I called the other men. The captain came along too, but didn't look in the least impressed.

"They're just starfish! Big deal! You'll find thousands of them on earth, right below the ice. They aren't worth the sand they creep on."

"But Captain," I tried to convince him, "these are different. They live on this remote asteroid. It could be a great scientific discovery."

"Get out of here!" he yelled. "I'm looking for uranium, not starlets. But if you want them, take them; maybe we can eat them!" And he laughed in scorn.

Well, you won't believe me, but he really did eat them, that beast, and even said they were delicious. However, I managed to hide about thirty in a little bag, and as soon as I was back on board, I dropped them in a bowl full of water and stowed them away, out of sight. One day, the captain decided to inspect my room and found the stars. He ordered a hundred lashes for me—but that wasn't the end of it.

You see, the captain had one great passion. He loved to play chess, and, by virtue of one of those strange bonds between evil and genius, he was also an excellent player. No one had been able to beat him in several years, not even our computer. Well, the captain saw the stars and

decided to build the most unusual chess set in the cosmos. He attached his chessmen to an equal number of
stars with corresponding colors, and then placed them on
an immense bear-bone chessboard. I must admit, the result was quite striking. The little stars' natural lumines-
cence transformed that chessboard into something
magic. But, despite my wonder, I also noticed that, out of
water, the little stars were losing their color and withering; in short, they were dying.

One night, I got up and sneaked into the captain's
room. I approached the chessboard, meaning to steal the
stars and hide them away, or, at least let them perk up in
some water. But the captain, who was at once very
shrewd and very mistrustful, had wired the board into an
alarm system. At the first ring of the alarm, the captain
was on his feet, screaming, "Damn you cabinboy! This is
the second time you've stepped out of line. You shall die
for it."

I was immediately clapped into the brig. I had only a
few hours left to live. The space-navigation code decrees
that a captain has the power of life and death over his
crew. And yet, that evening, I didn't feel at all bad about
my fate. My thoughts were confined to the slow agony of
those lovely creatures, now reduced to mere pieces for
the captain's chessboard.

The next morning, Garcia himself came to fetch me in
my cell. He was laughing, a clear indication he was up to
some new trick.

"My dear De Leon," he told me, "you are really lucky!
Your mates love you, and they have insisted I give you
one last chance. So your life will be spared . . . if, and only
if, you—ha, ha—beat me at chess! If, instead, I beat you,
I shall kill you. If you win, however, not only will you
live, but you can kill me. Fair's fair!" and Garcia burst
into a loud guffaw, right in my face.

Of course, the whole thing was mighty unfair. The captain knew full well that I barely knew the rules of the game, whereas he was a master. He had staged this pitiful comedy only because some crew member had courageously pleaded for my life; this gruesome farce was meant to confirm his power and mock us all. In fact, he insisted that the entire crew be present at the game. We sat at the chessboard, across from each other, and he, draining his nth pint of rum, chuckled: "Here we are! You may go first! I'm going to give you one last advantage! Aren't you happy now that you are sitting right by your dear little stars? Too bad they should be the very agents of your death!" Again he burst out laughing.

I looked at the chessboard, and at my friends' sad faces, and did not know what to do. I was about to say, "Come on, enough with this joke; cut the crap and kill me at once," when I noticed a faint twinkle in the little star below my queen's pawn. I was the only one who could see it, since the others were too far from the table, and the captain's eyes were not very good. Much to my astonishment, I saw the little star moving toward the next square. Instinctively, I helped it over with my hand. Then, I looked around to make sure that no one else had noticed what had happened. Nobody had—least of all Captain Garcia, who belched and said: "Very good! Nice opening! Queen's pawn! That was a hasty move, though, boy; do you wish to die before your time?" He made his move.

When I saw the second star twinkle, another pawn, I got a strange notion. But it was only by my fourth move, when my knight's star twinkled and, slightly bending its points leftward, clearly showed me what to do, that I understood what was really going on. I almost fainted with emotion. The little stars could think! And not only that. In those few days they had spent on that chessboard, they had learned the game and were now playing it for me! So now I knew that they could reason, but were they intelligent enough? Indeed they were, as I was soon to realize, just by looking at the change on Captain Garcia's face. His bombastic laughter had gradually turned into a worried giggle, which had soon become hysterical. He was a great player, and it did not take him much time to figure out that I was attacking him with unsuspected ability.

When my bishop's star led my hand into a position that clearly threatened his queen, the captain looked into my eyes with fear. By now, my friends had also started to realize that something strange was going on, and I could hear their whispers and see them crossing their fingers. The captain began to sweat and to take much more time before each move. Now and then, he would shake his head as if to shoo away the irksome thought that the infamous cabin boy in front of him could really play like a grand master. He must have been thinking, No, no way; it's mere chance that's guiding him through this incredibly lucky series of moves; but sooner or later, being only a novice, he's doomed to fall apart.

But by the twentieth move, an attack led by my queen, Garcia knew I was really playing at his level. He started to tremble; he couldn't understand what had happened. He grew pale, as I took his rook and his bishop. Implacable, my little stars were besieging him on all sides. At the thirty-sixth move, it dawned on him that he was in bad trouble. He stared at me in terror, and I knew that what really haunted him, more than defeat and the probability of his imminent death, was his inability to figure out what was going on. At that point, I decided to show him the truth. The queen's star twinkled, but I did not touch it. It moved by itself, crossed two squares, and then stopped—checkmate by queen, knight, and rook—a masterful stroke.

Captain Garcia grew as pale as a ghost. He had finally understood. He jumped up, cast a last glance at the fatal star, and with a powerful yell, flew into his cabin. A few seconds later, we heard the shot. He had killed himself. That was the end of our terrible Captain Garcia.

But, unfortunately, the little stars had spent too much time away from their natural habitat; they also died that very night, after saving the life of the only person who had treated them humanely. For they were themselves human, if that adjective has retained any value in our time.

"This is the story the sailor told me," Caruso concluded, "and I cannot tell you for sure whether it is true or invented. But something in the way he told it made me believe him."

● ● ● ● ● ● ● ● ● ● ● ● ● ● ● ●

THE SCORPION'S HEART
● ● ●

Black and threatening, the *Calalbakrab*—the *Scorpion's Heart* —followed the *Tien* at a distance of less than a fiftieth quadrant. Seen in flight, it was even more awesome than on land, and it was easy to understand why so many legends surrounded it. Like the scorpion it resembled, its central body was divided into two parallel parts, each of which was provided, in its forward section, with a winged chela that could be moved back and forth depending on the exigency of either flight or battle. These two parts were called *Zuben Elgenubi* and *Zuben Elschemali*, respectively, and, if the need arose, they could detach themselves from the main body and fly independently. *Elgenubi* housed the computers, the service quarters, and the crew. *Elschemali* was a flying palace, with marble hallways, lush gardens, and secret apartments. The two parts were united in back by the sting, the largest laser gun in the world, capable of destroying a whole planet, and already responsible for the disintegration of *Orion*, the Amerussian warship, in the course of the battle of Mercury. Following this battle, the Arabs and the Amerussians had joined forces and formed the Seven Sheiks alliance headed by King Akrab, the Great Scorpion, master of a third of the world's energy. But the political balance of the alliance was said to be unstable, and its inner tensions very strong.

"You know, Dylaniev, I'm not sure Alya likes us," Vassiliboyd remarked. "In fact, I don't think he would mind at all if we were to disappear into a black hole."

The two Amerussian pilots were lying down in their comfortable cockpit, listening to a Mozart medley brilliantly executed by the ship's musicomputer. The automatic pilot had taken over the ship's controls, getting directions about its itinerary from Earth, and bribing the sentry satellites so that they would forget to signal its passage. In the meantime, four *adharas*, Arab space stewardesses, stood by, ready to satisfy every demand of the pilots, from lighting cigarettes to filling their glasses of vodsky (one-tenth vodka, one-tenth whiskey, eight-tenths insect alcohol) with industrious frequency.

Dylaniev, already fairly drunk, said, "You know, John, flying this ship should be every pilot's dream. So why am I so bored?"

"I am too, Igor," Vassiliboyd answered. "But I was fed up with escorting obese old sheiks and their various mistresses to some picturesque lunar motel. Here, at least, something can happen, anytime. Do you remember what Laurel used to say? You must learn to live under the shadow of the sword!"

Dylaniev smiled. Laurel had been their instructor when they had both joined the Rebels, a clandestine pacifist unit that had assumed the task of destroying all American and Russian space weapons in order to prevent a new world war. By dint of hunting satellites, they soon became the best spaceship pilots of their day. When World War VI broke out, they were granted amnesty on the condition that they enlist in the regular army.

Most of them accepted the offer, in the hope they might help end the war. But the war lasted a long time. Now, most pacifist ex-rebels were piloting the Seven Sheiks' spaceships for a hefty salary.

"I'm sure Laurel wouldn't be very proud of us if he could see us now," Dylaniev noted darkly, filling his glass with some more vodsky.

"He was a fool, Igor," Vassiliboyd said. "You know it as well as I do."

"Maybe he was a fool, but at least he had ideals. And he didn't get them from a computer, as we do now. I can't think of a single computer that would rather lay down its life than betray its ideals."

"Hear, hear," Vassiliboyd wailed as he stretched his arms toward the sky. "I had forgotten today is Saturday, and every Saturday Igor Dylaniev has a Crisis of Conscience, both with a capital C. God of Space Travels, watch over him!"

"Cut it out, John," Igor said, trying to get up, and in the process, spilling the bottle onto the control panel. "Leave me alone!"

"It's about time you stopped crying over the past, Dylaniev! True, we used to have a few ideals back then—grand illusions! And we all risked our lives blowing up missile bases and spy-satellites, only to discover later that half of us were traitors. We sang beautiful songs, held demonstrations, bombed computers, and generally had a hell of a time, and the result was three wars, one after the other, and two billion dead! Now our earth is just a mass of ice, Dylaniev; there's nothing left to defend, and the only important thing is to stay warm, have a pair of comfortable bear-fur pants, and make sure there's enough vodsky to keep you happy! If you don't like it, just keep it to yourself. If your remorse is more than you can bear, there are plenty of space stations looking for cabdrivers—"

"Shut up, John," Dylaniev muttered, still struggling to get up. "You're even drunker than I, and, as usual, much more cynical. You're taking it out on me only because you despise yourself almost as much as I despise myself—Jesus, turn off that music!''

"I like electronic music, Igor," Vassiliboyd said, getting up threateningly, "and if you insist on wallowing in your blues, why don't you get yourself over to the cinematographic archive and watch one of those beautiful pacifist movies of the eighties? Or maybe you'd rather sing 'We Shall Overcome' with your balalaika!''

"Go fuck yourself, John!" Igor yelled, "You and your computer rock and your movies and your swimming pool and this whole setup, all aglow with ancient chandeliers, while half of humanity is living in the dark!''

"I've had it, Igor," John said. They faced each other, and then, amid the terrified screams of the four adharas, they started fighting. The automatic pilot immediately signaled "crew turmoil" to the central computer.

⚞ *Calalbakrab:* A Prophecy for His Venomous Majesty ⚟

The spaceship's gallery had a transparent ceiling. Among the gilded stucco and marble columns, the star-spangled sky arrayed itself in precious brocade. King Sadalmelik Temugin al-Akrab was now slowly advancing through this fabulous hallway on a golden litter carried by twelve men. The spaceship's entire army was awaiting him in the Royal Room: one hundred and thirty warriors holding laser lances at their sides, and forty motorcyclists astride their Pegasi—sophisticated mechanical steeds capable of galloping a hundred miles an hour and of leaping across the largest craters.

King Akrab climbed down from his litter, dismissed the army, and remained alone in the immense room strewn with the spoils of war—mummies, statues, paintings, and jewels, sacked from museums all over the world. The total effect was rather disorienting. King Akrab sat on a Napoleonic armchair

facing a Beerkhout hologram representing a table. The wall
behind him convivially accommodated a Velázquez, a Goya, a
Picasso, a Trumbull, a Hokusai, a Chagall, a Caravaggio, three
royal self-portraits, a Lichtenstein, a few videogames, some
tapestries, the Gordon's Gin neon sign that had once stood
proudly in the middle of Times Square and had now become
Akrab's favorite war trophy, and a hundred stuffed animal
heads.

The king took a cigar and lighted it with a ronsonized Cel-
lini salt cellar. For a while, he just sat and smoked, gently
stroking his red beard. Then he got up and, walking over to a
mahogany wall, pushed a button. The wall opened, revealing
a dazzling jewel collection. Diamonds, rubies, emeralds, sap-
phires, of all sizes and shapes sparkled against a huge black
velvet panel divided into two hemispheres. The king passed
his hand gently over the panel. But the sudden sound of a gong
put an end to his passionate contemplation. The videocom,
which audaciously replaced the head of a Greek Aphrodite,
displayed a visitor's request.

"Who the hell is it?" al-Akrab royally inquired.

"It's Alya," a distant voice hissed. "I've brought along al-
Dabih, the soothsayer. We have something of utmost importance to tell you, Great Scorpion."

"All right, come in," the king said. The two powerful counselors walked in. Alya was wearing a leather cloak with darker
spots, and the clairvoyant was dressed in the purple-and-black
suit of an ESP parapsychologist.

"O Divine Conqueror, O Great Hunter!" Alya outdid himself in salutations. "May your name rest forever in the *hutba*.
Infinite wisdom seethes within you, and within you dwell all
gifts and virtues and sagacious genetic perfections, and within
you, bright and—"

"Come off it, please," the king cut him short. "I know,
you're bringing me bad news—right?"

"In your perfect and unattainable . . . well, yes, Your Majesty, it is true. Those Amerussian pilots—We must do something!'' Alya began to explain. ''They have been fighting again. They are drunk from morning to evening. At night, they skate down the hallways to alarm the guards. They enjoy throwing robots into the swimming pool, and they smoke pot in the elevators to make them hallucinate.''

''They are young,'' the king observed with a smile. The soothsayer nodded in assent.

''Maybe, but things are a little more complex! This restlessness of theirs is not the product of joy—they are very unhappy! We have recorded all their conversations—they hate us. That Dylaniev, in particular, is constantly mulling over his past as a Rebel. Then he gets drunk and says he hates working for us . . . he no longer attends the evening concerts . . .''

''You're right,'' the king admitted with a frown. ''This is much more serious than I thought.''

''And that isn't all. Both pilots are constantly hanging out with the Dzunum, our musical group. We have discovered them fu—ah, fornicating in space, right outside the spaceship, and our security officers had to go retrieve them. Their example is terrible for the rest of the crew; they are not the only two Amerussians on board. We must annihilate them.''

''I understand you, Alya,'' the king said. ''Youthful vitality is a great thing in Coca-Cola ads. In most other cases, however, it can be mighty troublesome. But we can't get rid of it just like that. In the first place, we've hired those two pilots because, being ex-Rebels, they have complete knowledge of all the space routes. Second, the Amerussians have insisted on participating in this flight so as to have something to boast about. They love the idea that their pilots are guiding the spaceship that's going to find Terra. They'll never give up without a fight.''

''And third?'' Alya wondered.

''Third, I want to hear what my soothsayer has to say!''

Al-Dabih executed a deep bow. ''Last night,'' he said, ''I

sought out your destiny in the twenty cards, in the epeira's web, and in the smoke of the great Alkres, the sacred jug. This is the answer I received:

"Toward the second earth
from the two-sided earth shall come
blood against blood
the scorpion's head shall be crushed
by the eagle's foot
when the sky falls onto the earth."

The king grew pale. "Soothsayer, this sounds like a poisonous prophecy. What does it mean?"

"It is rather obscure," al-Dabih admitted with lowered eyes. "This is how I have interpreted it: in the course of this trip toward Terra, you'll be joined by an enemy from the 'two-sided earth'—the American continent (for so it is called in the ancient texts)—someone belonging to a race that you have fought and destroyed."

"O King, he is referring to the Americans," Alya said. "During your Sacred War, your missiles destroyed New York. Since then, the Americans have become our allies, but in their heart of hearts, they hate us—and those two pilots still wear the badge of the eagle on their helmets!"

"Is this what the prophecy means, soothsayer?" the king asked.

"I don't know. Many are the nations that have sworn revenge against you. I think you are in great danger. But nothing will happen till the sky falls onto the earth."

"Soothsayer, is that really so?" the king asked, recovering some of his boldness. "Then it will never happen! This prophecy bodes well for me! The sky will never fall onto the earth, nor will my power ever falter."

"Still, you should be more prudent," Alya whispered in his ear. "Those Americans are a big threat."

"Yes," al-Akrab answered with a cruel smile, "but we must be smart. My dear Alya, there is an Arab proverb that says, a split hare does not run twice as fast. Get it?"

"I do, I do," Alya assented, with a triumphant light in his eyes. "In his infinite and brilliant perfidy, His Highness means that it will suffice to eliminate one of the two Americans. Then the other one will certainly cool down, and we will be able to keep our contract with the Amerussians. I'm on my way!"

"Just a minute!" the king detained him. "Why the rush? Alya, my slimy advisor, and you, my sincere and hostile sooth-sayer—please let's not waste our time on such dismal matters. Let's turn our thoughts to beautiful things . . . the riches of the world, art . . . Have you ever seen this wall of paintings? Come on, Alya, don't hesitate. Wine and paintings are not dear to the Koran, but they are dear to me."

Alya spread his arms wide, in a gesture of exaggerated admiration. "They are wonderful! Who are the artists?" he asked, pointing at a few canvases.

"Mantegna and Poussin. Two great painters of ruins," the king explained. "I love ruins. They bespeak strength, war, and the law of historical continuity. Look at these huge boulders. I commissioned this painting from a court artist while I was fighting in South America. It is a Peruvian city whose name I now forget. A huge, imposing monument, proclaiming the great glory of its founder and the even greater glory of its destroyer. For history, a fortress that has fallen is more significant than one that has resisted. The same thing is true of countries, continents, planets."

"True," Alya nodded. "True, O Great King."

"But the universe cannot be conquered," al-Dabih intervened. "Its mystery evades both time and space. Years ago we were dreaming of reaching the farthest planets. Today, we know that we'll never be able to get out of our galaxy. The sky is too large for us."

The king laughed scornfully. "Are you sure, al-Dabih?" He quickly crossed the room to the mahogany wall, and opened the diamond panel. "Have a look, soothsayer," he said, "the sky is here—right before your eyes!"

Alya's eyes widened. "By Allah!" he exclaimed. "The Rain of Gems! I knew of its existence, but this is the first time I've ever seen it!"

"It's been three centuries now—" the king said, "ever since we made our fortune in oil—that my family has been collecting gems. For each recorded star in the universe there is a corresponding gem. Here they are—this diamond is al-Nasi, this ruby is my Calalbakrab, and here is al-Azeel, al-Araph, al-Muredin, Deneb al-Okab, your own star, Alya, Cebalrai, my soldiers' star, and Mirzam, and al-Nabor. This is the sky that no astronomer, neither al-Battani nor al-Sufi, has ever contemplated. You can tell me that the universe is too large, that I will never be able to have a diamond for each star, because here in our galaxy we have more than a hundred billion of them—maybe you are right—but you can't tell me this is not the grandest sky on Earth. I can't think of anybody who wouldn't give up all the stars of the universe to own it. It can buy anything, corrupt, destroy anything. It is more powerful than a hurricane, a monsoon, or a tornado. Ask anybody, Alya. Man is the only inhabitant of the universe. Therefore, the wealthiest man is the master of the universe. Is there anything that he cannot buy, or conquer?"

He stopped talking. An explosion had suddenly rocked the ship, causing the great chandeliers of the room to tinkle like bells.

∘   ∘   ∘

DISCIPLINE AND ORDER
ABOARD THE *ZUIKAKU*

∘ ∘ ∘

The gray soldiers were standing at attention on the main deck of the *Zuikaku*—that is to say, on the dining-room table. General Yamamoto was reviewing them, one by one. "Company, at ease!" he barked at the end of his inspection. "Soldiers GoSub, Radian, Degree, Log, Beep Off, Beep On, Pause, and Cursor, front and center!"

The eight mice stepped forward and lined up in front of the general.

"Soldiers," Yamamoto roared, tapping the microphone in Mickey Morse, "I'm disgusted with the state of discipline on this ship! The Amerussian ship has just sustained a terrorist attack; the Sinoeuropean ship is riddled with troubles; but the advantage that we can reap from all this is threatened by serious episodes that might mean compromising the success of our mission. Consequently, today, in my capacity as Chief Justice of the military court aboard this ship, I am going to punish all breaches of discipline with due severity. Don't forget that the computer buttons you wear as an insignia stand for team effort: you are *one* machine, *one* man, or, I should say, *one* mouse. Let's get going. Gray Soldier GoSub!"

A terrified mouse brought the tip of its tail to its forehead, and saluted.

"Soldier GoSub! You stand accused of leaving your sentry position for three minutes to stick your nose into Soldier Using's area. What can you say in your defense?"

"U-sing," GoSub started explaining, shifting his weight from one leg to the other, "ca-tches-fi-re-when-in-spec-ts-en-gi-ne. I-run-an-dtry-if-piss-on-him-ex-tinc-ts."

"Hogwash! This means you have failed twice: you abandoned your post, and Soldier Using died anyway. I hereby sentence you to three days in the brig."

"Yes-sir," GoSub said, and resumed his place in the ranks.

"Gray Soldier Radian! You stand accused of directing a number of insults at General Harada."

"Ge-ne-ral-Ha-ra-da," Radian explained, "crush-with-boot-my-col-lea-gue-List, an-dmy-ri-ghtp-aw. Pain-ma-des-cream."

"No Japanese soldier has ever complained because somebody stepped on his foot," Yamamoto screamed. "It is utterly ridiculous! And, as for Soldier List, he died because he was not wearing his helmet as prescribed by regulations. Three days in the brig for you, as well. Next: Soldier Degree!"

A mouse with longish hair advanced.

"Soldier Degree! You stand accused: One, of being caught twice, by me, with hair longer than permitted by regulations and failing to have it cut, as ordered. Two, of having said the following sentence after the death of the two above-mentioned mice: 'Here they squash us alive and maybe even punish us for it.' Did you or did you not say these words?"

"I sai-dyes," Degree confessed, "an-dwant-know-who-damn-spy-sai-dit!"

An ultrasonic mousy murmur ran through the ship.

"Silence!" Yamamoto screamed. "I shall not allow you to call anybody 'spy' who justly calls my attention to military misconduct. For this subversive insinuation, I now sentence you to death by cocacolation."

Another ultrasonic mousy murmur ran through the ship.

"Silence! Next: soldiers Log, Beep On, Beep Off, Pause, and Cursor."

Five mice advanced, their tails tucked between their legs.

"You stand accused of the following crime: during a reconnoitering mission in the thermal system, you took illegal possession of a fragment of Emmenthal Suzuki brand cheese, weighing a total of six grams. After which you left the ship and went on a space picnic with the stolen army property, which you then proceeded to attack repeatedly and criminally, tooth and jaw, until it disappeared. What do you have to say in your defense?"

"We-not-ea-ten," Beep On explained, "not-a-tall-for-two-days."

"Nonsense!" the general screamed. "Everybody knows that mice can go without food for up to seven days. For this crime, I also sentence you to death by cocacolation."

"Thi-sis-no-tright!" Beep Off stamped its feet.

Furious, Yamamoto yelled, "Take them away! This is sheer insubordination!" A few mice grabbed the tails of the prisoners and dragged them away.

General Yamamoto was left alone to examine the miniaturized flight plans through a microscope. Shortly thereafter, Harada joined him, carrying two thimbles in the palm of his left hand. His head was bandaged.

"Yama, would you like some tea concentrate?" he asked.

"No, thank you. But what happened to your head? Did you hit it again?"

"I can't get used to the dimensions of this ship, Yama. I keep bumping into everything. How did it go with the troops?"

"Bad!" Yamamoto growled. "I had to eliminate six of them!"

"Plus four lost in various accidents—that makes ten. Couldn't you try to be a little more light-handed, Yama?"

"Light-handed?" Yamamoto repeated scornfully. "When a ship starts showing signs of insubordination, one must act immediately, and with clout! It starts with the refusal to trim one's hair, and it ends up in mutiny!"

"Come on, Yama, what can fifty rodents do against our two guns?"

"*Ratus norvegicus* is much shrewder than you think!" Yamamoto said. "We can't lower our guard!"

"You are right," Harada said.

"So you do agree with me!"

"Yes; that is, after seeing your helmet," Harada said.

"Why, what's wrong with my helmet?" Yamamoto asked. He took it off and clenched his teeth with rage.

On the helmet were the words: GENERAL YAMAMOTO IS SHIT
LIKE HUNDRED THOUSAND CAT.

In the cage, the convicted mice were awaiting their last hour.

"Why-why," Beep On complained, "small-spa-ce-walk-gr-eat-fuck-up."

"Fa-te-we-mi-ce," Degree said. "Al-ways-li-ve-un-der-groun-dal-ways-steal-ne-ver-goin-gout. Mouse-rou-ghlife."

"Who-gi-veus-such-cruel-fate-al-ways-li-ve-un-der-ground-ne-ve-rout?" Beep Off inquired.

"I-thin-kall-said-by-Chi-nese-story-first-mou-seand-first-rab-bit."

Why Mice Live Underground

After Sky and Earth were split apart and the World
came into existence, the first of the twelve Emperors of
the Sky, who reputedly reigned for 18,000 years (elections
being rare), summoned the Maker of Animals, Ch'ien
Tsou, and instructed him, "Get to work. I want you to
cover the earth with animals! Use what you wish, scales
and fins, beaks and shells, wings and horns, antlers and
antennae, hair and snouts; don't spare your palette, the
more color the better; mold long noses, spherical eyes,
forests of legs, prehensile tails; make them swim, buzz,
trumpet, splash, migrate, sting, root, peck, roar, camou-
flage, pollinate, croak, chirp, gnaw, eat berries, plankton
or kitkat; make them huge or tiny, nice or slimy; do what
you will, but make a lot of them. I want man to say, God,
what a wonder nature is!"

The Maker of Animals locked himself up in his
wooden hut with some tea and a few books on genetics,
and started drawing, building models, putting pieces together, and calculating—till he was ready—and, in less

than a week, the earth was full of meowings and squeak-
ings and buzzings and squawkings and insect bites and
insecticides and hunters and poachers and cat shows and
dogcatchers and dairy products and malaria and venison
stews.

The Emperor visited Earth and was pleased by what he
saw; he pulled the elephant's trunk and proclaimed it a
splendid solution; he admired the propulsion system of
the jellyfish and personally checked the speed of the jag-
uar, which clocked in at a hundred twenty miles an hour,
just as he had been told. Well, well, well, he kept saying,
with a big grin on his face. He looked through a microscope and approved of the viruses and their variety; they
were not lovely, to be sure, but invisible to the naked
eye. He asked the Maker to lower the buzzing of coleop-
tera by a few decibels and decreed, "I want more porife-
rans and fewer platyhelminthes." Furthermore, he was
critical of the ornithorhynchus. He said, "I know you
don't want to waste anything, but this time you really
scraped the bottom of the barrel!" He judged the lemurs
too depressing, and suggested they be confined to out-of-
the-way places such as the woods or jungles of under-
populated continents like Australia and South America.
Dinosaurs, by contrast, filled him with awe and enthusiasm; they were so large and so strong that he was sure
they'd last forever.

He went into ecstasy, leafing through the butterfly and
hummingbird catalogs, and laughed like crazy at the tou-
can and the walrus. Thus, fully satisfied, the Emperor of
the Sky was about to return to his palace, carrying a basket of fresh eggs (from which we can gather that the
chicken came first), when he noticed a couple of furry
little things with long front teeth romping about in a
meadow.

"What are those?" he asked Ch'ien Tsou.

"Your Majesty, the ones with the long, thin tails are

mice, and the ones with short tails are rabbits." (It should be noted that in those bygone days, mice and rabbits had identical ears, small and round, and were virtually indistinguishable).

"Well, well, well," the Emperor said. But at that very moment, his wife, the Empress of the Sky, happened to pass by, and the Emperor, who liked to impress her with his authority, puffed up his chest and said, turning to Ch'ien, "These furry things are lovely, yes, but they look too much alike. Differentiate them. Taxonomize! Phylum, genus, class, subclass—make them all different. The more animals we have, the more impressed men will be with the superior mind who created all this. Let's not spare our imagination! Come, come, let's get to work!"

Pleased with his performance, he walked up to his wife, who bussed him on the cheek and whispered, "Darling, you are so . . . demanding!"

Poor Ch'ien was dead tired, and still had to finish up a few things, like attaching fins to sharks, trying to teach chickens (a product he wasn't very happy with) to fly, and installing feet on seals. But, despite himself, he had to obey and get that extra job done as well. So he went to the meadow and said, "My dear friends, I have been asked to make a modification. One of you is going to get a pair of beautiful, long, hairy ears."

"Not us!" the mice yelled. "We'd be ridiculous with long ears."

"Not us," the rabbits said. "We're just fine as we are!"

"Come on!" Ch'ien insisted. "I have no time to waste. Either you make up your minds, or it's heads or tails."

Hearing this, the mice jumped onto the rabbits and, with the help of a few sharp bites, pushed them in front of their maker.

"Come on, dear colleagues, be good sports," they teased. "Those long ears are going to suit you just fine!"

"Ouch, ouch," the meek rabbits screamed, "stop biting us. We give in."

So, the maker grabbed the rabbits' ears and started pulling them, and kept on pulling them till they were as nice and long and hairy as he wanted them.

"Yuck," the mice immediately cried, "how ugly you are! Why don't you try wagging them, and maybe you'll fly. Ha, ha, ha."

The poor rabbits looked at their reflections in the lake and wailed in shame. "Oh, what a sad fate has befallen us," they said. "We look absolutely ridiculous!"

That night, while the mice were romping about, as usual, and the rabbits were hiding away in their burrows, a storm broke out. And not just any old storm either, but one of those storms they used to have back at the beginning of the world, a real humdinger—erupting volcanos, overflowing rivers, and floating mountains. A huge cleft opened up in the meadow, right under the paws of the mice and the rabbits, who clung to the turf with their claws, right over the edge of the abyss.

"Help, help," they screamed, "Ch'ien, save us! We are about to fall!"

The maker, a piece of cod in his hand, rushed out of his house and, in the darkness, ran toward the precipice. "Where are you? Where are you?" he called through the storm.

"Here, here," the mice and rabbits screamed back, almost at the end of their tether.

At last, Ch'ien reached the edge of the precipice. He stretched his hand down toward the voices, and had no trouble finding the rabbits' ears and pulling them up to safety. He then tried to save the mice, but their heads were small, wet, and slippery, and Ch'ien couldn't find anything to grab onto.

"Help, help!" the mice screamed one more time. Then, they fell.

"See," Ch'ien yelled after them, "you teased the rabbits for their long ears, and now you will be doomed to live underground, in cellars and sewers, and man will hate you and chase you and exterminate you, and woman will scream and jump onto a chair the moment she sets eyes on you. Rabbits, instead, will be raised to live in the sun and eat carrots and be loved by everybody."

"Maybe so," a voice called out from the abyss, "but at least nobody will throw *us* into a stew!"

"Hush up down there," Ch'ien Tsou scolded. Then he went back to his house and finished finning his cod, but he was so tired that, by mistake, he also stuck a fin onto the seal. He tried unsuccessfully to modify the chicken until he angrily hurled it against the wall, screaming, "Do you want to fly or not?" The chicken received a concussion, after which Ch'ien Tsou fell asleep.

This is the reason why, ever thereafter, mice have lived underground, seals have had no feet to walk on, and chickens have been so dumb.

□ □

PARIS

□ □ □

Ladies and Gentlemen, Here's TV!

Announcer: Ladies and gentlemen, hee-eea-re's Johnny "Caveat" Carlson III, to welcome you to *They Are All Beautiful,* a program brought to you on Unique Channel by Galactol, the synthetic milk for the child prodigy.

J.C.: Thank you, Ted. *[Bows to the viewers. Smiles.]* Today's Mom is Ferdinanda Kook, mother of Leonardus

Kook, one of the Federation's most outstanding scientists, currently engaged in an extremely dangerous flight toward a mysterious destination, somewhere in the cosmos. Good morning, Mrs. Kook!

Mrs. Kook: Good morning, Johnny.

J.C.: Please look into the camera, Mrs. Kook. Our viewers are dying to know all about your famous son. Tell us, when was the last time you talked to him? And, while you think about your answer, we are going to take a little break. Ladies and gentlemen, don't go away—stay with us. We'll be right back with Mrs. Kook after this word from our sponsors.

[Cut to commercial. Child and mother at a breakfast table. The child is stirring his cereal.]

Child: Mommy, what's a cow?

Mommy: It was a preglacial animal that made milk, dear. But now we have Galactol, the homogenized, pasteurized, synthetic milk made from real Swiss mold by the best biotechnicians at Procter and Gamble!

[Pan to a synthetic field on which one hundred white-clad technicians are standing with large bells tied around their necks.]

[They sing, chorus and music]: We're your cows! *[A long chime.]* Come play with us on Galactol fields! Enter our Galactol contest and win a week's vacation in the subterranean mountain park at Stelvio, in the Italian Alps.

[Cut back to interview.]

Mrs. Kook: I spoke to my son two days ago. He's fine and has gained two kilos.

J.C.: Great! Did he tell you where he's going?

Mrs. Kook: No, he didn't. He doesn't know himself.

J.C.: And so he doesn't! As you can see, Mrs. Kook is wearing a truth helmet, which means that she can't lie, and if she does, we'll all know it. (Chuckle.) Tell us, Mrs. Kook, do you remember Leonardus's first flight?

Mrs. Kook [smiling proudly]: Yes, he was ten years old. We had taken him on a moon cruise for four days. But he didn't like it. He kept complaining that there was no time to see anything. You know, it was a company excursion . . . *[Humble smile.]* We had very little money, then. We had been on the moon only a few minutes, when our guide said, "Quick, quick, back on board. Time to see the artificial satellites." Leonardus was very upset, and he said, "One day I'm going to do this trip right, first class!"

J.C.: Great, great! A precocious child's vocational calling. And now, Mrs. Kook, a very indiscreet question— but first, another message—

[Cut to commercial. A white bear, dead on the ground, in the middle of a blizzard. A woman bundled in furs contemplates the body.]

Woman: Here I am, on the road again. When we left, he was fine; then the usual stomach upset caused by fatigue; then, *poof*—he dies on me right in the middle of my trip. What am I going to do now, all alone, surrounded by ice?

[A sled drawn by four white bears approaches in a cloud of snow. Focus on the bright smile of its driver.]

Man: Madam, would you like a lift?

Woman: Sure! What a beautiful sled!

Man: Fur upholstery, super-suspension, runner skates made with the toughest Jovian steel . . . It's elegant. It's fast. It's the new Volkswagen. It's Icebird!

[Pan to the couple copulating under a bearskin rug inside the sleigh, as it glides across the white expanse.]

Voice over: Want excitement? Get an Icebird!

[The sleigh disappears in a cloud of snow.]

Voice over: New, from Volkswagen.

J.C.: Back to our interview with Mrs. Kook! Well, Mrs. Kook, has Leonardus ever told you anything about this mission?

Mrs. Kook: No, he hasn't. Ouch! Ahhhh!

J.C.: See, Mrs. Kook's truth helmet has just jolted her memory with a little electric—ahh, reproach. Well, Mrs. Kook, you'd better speak the truth; next time the voltage will be higher. And please take your hands away from the helmet; you're covering its brand name. So, now, Mrs. Kook, what has your son told you about the mission?

Mrs. Kook [clearly terrified]: "He told me . . . *[sniff]* "Mom, this is . . . *[sniff]* . . . this is the real thing!"

J.C.: Great news for our viewers! Did you all hear? True to his promise, Caveat Johnny, of *They Are All Beautiful*, brings sensational news to your homes. To use the words of Leonardus Kook himself, the secret mission is *the real thing*. Wowee! And don't forget: this bomb has been offered to you by Johnny Carlson and Procter and Gamble, makers of Galactol, the synthetic milk for the child prodigy. And remember our contest! The prize question is, What is *Proteus Tien*'s destination? Send back your postcards after telling us: one, where *P.T.* is headed; two, whether it will get there; and three, how many people are on board. One billion prizes for you all. And don't forget, your Government Emporium is already selling the T-shirts and posters of the mission, as well as the picture album, *Adventure in Space*, and—

Click. Phildys switched the set off angrily.

"This is too much," he exclaimed, grabbing the telephone. "Get me Showspotshow! Immediately!"

"The secretary is already on his way over," they answered him.

"What crap!" Phildys hissed, hanging up. "What a program!

I've never seen anything quite so repulsive!" The general heard a shuffle of feet approaching the door. He raised his head and shrieked. A monstrous extraterrestrial with four droopy arms was standing on the threshold, winding and unwinding his luminous trunk serpentinely in the air.

☒ ☒

A SECRET REPORT

□ □ □

Top Secret 1874/15. From Central Data Bank to Unit Genius 5, Frank Einstein, Operator.

Dear Frank: Pursuant to your request, we have sent your computer a memory supplement of 67,000 MIPS superunits. Please find enclosed: data concerning the hypothetical presence of other intelligent beings in the universe, besides the two of us; data concerning all recorded UFO spottings; and data regarding the mysterious drawings of Inca Nazca. I'm glad to hear that your computer is doing better. On the other hand, we have analyzed his latest electrodiodograms and the diagnosis is that Genius is still ailing. But I have good (or bad?) news for you. None of our computers—neither Galileo ITT, nor Hulk Rockwell, nor Ringo TI—has been able to tell us anything about the Van Cram vector or the source of mysterious energy. All OD. There is something really spooky about this whole issue. But I suggest you hurry up. The political climate here is, to say the least, heating up. There are some who would like to put a stop to your dig because, they say, you are using too much energy. Hold on, and take it easy on the ice cream!

P.S. I read your piece on software writers in *Cybernetic*

Future. It is truly extraordinary, particularly the part where you define the last Chinese package deal as "a program better suited to a washing machine than to a computer." It reminded me of the little ditty we used to sing in class, when we were sharing the same desk. Remember?

> I'm such a pretty dumb little thing
> I'm a computer from Peking

Bye-bye and see you soon.
>—Kep Ferdydurke
>Chief Section I
>Central Government Computers

THE MARTIAN'S REVENGE

The Martian pointed its trunk at Phildys and said, "Time to die, terrestrial."

After which, he took his head between his hands and unscrewed it. Pyk's grinning face appeared out of the headless body.

"How do you like my costume, Phildys? I've ordered six hundred thousand just like it!"

Recovering from his fright, the general grabbed one of the secretary's numerous legs and flung him to the ground. He was beside himself.

"Another one of your farces, Pyk! I've just watched your TV program—Kook's mother tortured, live and on prime time. The interview with the truth helmet. The foreign secret services might as well retire—all they have to do now is watch our TV. Our mission has been transformed into a picture album."

"We even have a puppet, Cu the Crazy Pilot," Pyk added, kicking his legs in the air, trying to get up. "And the game Looking for a Planet, and aluminum costumes à la LeO—"

"Whereas I want absolute secrecy, do you understand? That planet is something very important! It's our last hope to escape the cold, to leave our subterranean cities, to live in the sun again."

"How moving!" Pyk grinned. "Come on, General, you needn't play the role of the good governor with me! Don't you think I know? You've already divided that planet as if it were a pie—a third for you, a third for the Chinese, and the other third to be sold at an auction. I have copies of all the contracts."

Phildys grew pale.

"May I read them to you, General? Your party has already signed the sale of nine billion cubic meters of sea to the Japanese, with an option for whale-hunting. You've given one-eighth of the entire land mass—"

"Just a second, my dear Martian," Phildys interrupted. "Don't play bashful virgin with me. Your party has also been busy making its little profits. You've already sold the Arabs an option for the telebroadcast of the first soccer championship on Terra—a real joke. I'd really like to know how you plan to transport both the teams and the spectators!"

"The contract doesn't mention any number of teams. All we need to send are twenty-three people—twenty-two players and a spectator."

"You're shrewd, Pyk, but watch out! If your papers print all this information, I'll blow the whistle on the electoral-robot scandal! What a farce—thirty thousand robots dressed like old ladies, all going to the polls to vote for you!"

"Oh yeah? What about you, then? Or have you forgotten last

year's elections, when everybody was supposed to vote 'electronically,' by pushing a button which, for some reason, released a one-thousand-volt discharge to anyone who dared vote for the opposition?"

"It wasn't deadly," the general said. "Unlike your video-games, we are not murderers!"

"That's enough, Phildys!" Pyk replied, waving his tentacles in the air. "How dare you talk to me like a pacifist! Don't you think I know your *Proteus Tien* is carrying twenty remote-controlled warrior-robots, ready to jump onto that planet the minute they find it?"

Phildys wavered under the accusation. "They—they're for defensive purposes only," he stammered.

"Oh yeah? Sure, General! Then how come neither Fang nor Kook is aware of it? This really bugs you, huh? What if I decided to mention, in parliament, that our peace-loving General Phildys is going to land his private army on Terra in order to turn it into his own personal kingdom?"

"You wouldn't dare!" Phildys glared at him with hatred.

"I will refrain—" Pyk smiled. "—but only on the condition that you behave more reasonably from now on. Agreed? I've gotta go now, my dear pacifist." He left Phildys foaming with rage.

The general kicked the Martian head about the room, cursed in fifty space languages, and then let himself collapse, exhausted, into his armchair.

"I, a warmonger?" he muttered, shooting two volleys of tranquilizers into his mouth. "I?" He called his secretary on the videocom. "Miss Minnie! Get me the Press Bureau . . . Warmonger! . . . Hello? Yes, Press Bureau? Please take this name: Johnny Carlson, Unique Channel . . . I want him to be relocated by this evening—yes, relocated, as foreign correspondent from Saturn . . . Have him take off in a couple of hours! If he protests, cut him off! . . . No, not the connection—cut his expense account!"

↗ ● ☽ ⊖ ⊕ ● ≃ ⊖ ⊖ ⊖ ↗ ♀ ♂ ○ ♄ ☾ ↗ ↗ ⊙ ♀ ● ●

CUZCO—MYSTERY UNDER THE RUINS

* * *

From his tent on the mountain, Fang examined what was left of the city of Cuzco. A heap of ruins that his men would dig out during the day and the snow would cover up at night. Just as Spaniards and earthquakes had once destroyed the Inca city, so the war had now destroyed modern Cuzco. But what were six hundred years more or less, within the eternity of death? Fang wondered. Who, under the earth, is going to distinguish an old man from a child? All destroyed cities look alike. Cuzco is Lo Yang, Nagasaki is Warsaw. And so, these ruins have brought together Inca walls and car carcasses, Sun temples and Christian churches. Fang shivered with cold. A few Indians were trudging up the path toward him, chewing coca leaves. They were singing *huayno* songs, while walking toward the rocksky music of the canteen. Behind them, Einstein was tramping through the snow; all bundled up in his fur suit, he looked like a small polar bear. Stiff with cold, the boy entered the tent and immediately set to boiling some ice cream on the burner.

"Cold, isn't it, Fang?" he remarked. "You can't imagine how freezing it is down there in the dig. Why didn't you show up today?"

"Lei Wen, the sign of lightning, entered my mouth, and Li Sao, the encounter with pain, transformed my face into a Kabuki mask," the Chinese explained. "In plain language, I have a toothache."

"I thought your enlightened mind had put you above such things," Einstein sneered. "Why don't you stick a few needles into your body? One of your age-old remedies. Or are we Westerners the only people who still use them?"

"Traditional Chinese medicine was revived around 1950 by the communist party, which demanded that schools and hospitals teach the treatise of internal medicine written by the

Yellow Emperor Shih Huang Ti. Since then, traditional and modern medicine have coexisted in China."

"I understand," Einstein said. "You always manage to make everything get along. Yin and yang, *contraria sunt complementa . . .*"

"The old Fang and the young Einstein," the Chinese added.

Einstein did not answer, busying himself, instead, with unrolling the papers he was carrying. "Look here," he suddenly said. "I've brought you the graphs of today's dig. The chief engineer seems to think we have already dug out all that was charted on the last maps. We've traced a perimeter of the area where the energy source should be. The mysterious fire should lie where once there stood an Inca building known as the Temple of the Sun. On top of it now are the remains of a Benedictine monastery. On the other hand, we haven't registered any discharge for quite some time now. That thing down there, whatever it is, *if* it exists, must be well hidden—maybe even screened against our detectors," Einstein said, looking at the Chinese. "Anyway, it's certainly way down there. Maybe in some subterranean chamber. The Indians say there are labyrinths deep down there; they call them *chinganas*. They also say that all those who have tried to penetrate them have stayed below—no one has ever resurfaced. Legends, of course. Still, the Indians consider that point *huaca*, sacred, and refuse to go on digging there. I'm realizing more and more every day that there is some mysterious clue somewhere that still eludes us, Fang. But maybe we're getting closer."

"What makes you think that?" the Chinese inquired.

"Just a feeling I have, Fang, whenever I look at these digs, or those at Pisac, with their solar observatory, or that large amphitheater at Kenko—but particularly at Machu Picchu, the city on the mountain. Behind all these places, there is a very precise plan. It involves the road network, which is immense, the bridges, the canals. And the city of Cuzco is at the center of it all. Its main square branches out into roads that lead to the four quarters of the empire. Everything is perfectly connected; everything seems to have been designed to achieve a particular purpose, a special goal. But what is the goal? Does it have to do only with religion, or with social control, or with defense? I don't think so—"

"Do you mean to tell me," Fang intervened, "that you also believe these people felt they had some historical mission to fulfill, some secret plan?"

"Yes. These Incas puzzle me. They were governed by a very tight aristocracy and had a very refined social and national organization based on solidarity. They were capable of the worst cruelties—human sacrifices, drums made with the skin of enemies, the massacre of the servants when a prince died— and yet they left the doors to their houses open because nobody stole or vandalized. They covered their walls with gold, but had no currency or taxes. They had advanced farming techniques and a modern road network, yet they believed in witchcraft. They were profoundly religious, but their gods were the planets, the solar phases, the stars. They were at once soldiers, engineers, and priests. And then there were the Inca monarchs with their incestuous marriages, their tight circle of power, their secret rites, as if they were guarding . . ."

"A mystery?" Fang asked.

"Exactly, a mystery," Einstein repeated, pensively. "So you believe the same thing? Do you know something I don't?"

"No, I don't," Fang answered. "But I am also very much intrigued by these Incas. Rereading their history, I was particularly struck by three things. First of all, as you were just saying, their civilization seems to have undertaken a historical mission. It organized itself perfectly; fertilized the land; created harvesting centers; built an immense network of roads that allowed a message to be conveyed on foot, with or without relay, to Cuzco from any other part of the empire; planned the number of civil servants and workers; built cities on top of mountains, and colossal fortresses. Then, at a particular point in its history, it surrendered to the Spanish invasion, almost without a fight. As if its mission had been fulfilled. As if it no longer cared to live, or to confront a new civilization. It was corrupted on contact; it let itself die. Secondly, I was struck by the Incas' tenacious will to keep their history secret —the lack of any writing, the terror of the written page. And, finally, I was struck by the exclusivity of their clan, the *ayllu*, and those esoteric cults—the sacred virgins of Machu Picchu or the royal priests, the *uillac uma*. They must have done all this with a purpose, to guard or preserve something, and that something is not the gold that the *conquistadores* found."

"I couldn't agree more," Einstein said. "Gold didn't have the same value for them as it has for us. All their walls and buildings were covered with gold, but no one ever thought of stealing it."

"And yet, Einstein, there is one thing more surprising yet— their prophetic art—in fact, their obsession with time, which relates them to the Mayans and the Aztecs. Whoever could not, or did not, work, would become a soothsayer. There was a genuine collective prophetic 'knowledge.' It seems as if all the Incas knew that their destiny had been decreed. Bad omens, like the condor that came to die in the main square of Cuzco, or eclipses and earthquakes, were not sudden signs; they had generally been long awaited. This was true of both the Incas and the Mayans: read how Atahualpa and Montezuma both waited for the arrival of the enemy who would kill them. Quetzalcoatl, Pisarro, or Cortés, whoever it is that is going to arrive from the sea is only going to fulfill their prophecies. And they submit because their task is over. They don't want to 'win'—an attitude utterly incomprehensible to us. We cannot believe that there can be cultures that are at once extremely advanced and superstitious, super-organized, and yet steeped in magic. Or maybe this is 'magic' only because we cannot understand it."

"No, Fang," Einstein interrupted, "we are not speaking of

magic here. This is a scientific mystery! This organization 'knew' something; it was hiding some secret, maybe the very one we are looking for down there—some riches, power, something concrete. If we only had more data for our computer, maybe we would be able to find the answer at once. There is nothing that cannot be recovered scientifically."

"And yet the computer seems unable to find an answer," Fang observed.

"True, it can't. But Genius tells us that in this civilization there is a project, a direction, a sense as yet unknown to us, but which our science will one day recover and comprehend."

"I see you have changed your mind about these people," Fang remarked. "They are no longer 'savages'!"

"It's true, Fang," Einstein admitted. "But I feel there is something we are still hiding from each other. Be honest with me. Do you also agree with the computer's hypothesis?"

"I don't know what the computer said," the Chinese replied calmly.

"Of course you do! You can read my thoughts. You know that I asked it to analyze the large drawings of Inca Nazca, which are kilometers long and seem to presume somebody surveying them from above, and those 'skins' that the Incas might have used to build balloons, and the Palenque drawings, and the terraces. You know the hypothesis it formulated."

"I don't know what to say. My toothache diminishes some of my telepathic capacities."

"Come on, Fang, you can't fool me! Is this hypothesis absurd?"

"No, I don't think so, Einstein," the Chinese answered, after a moment of silence. "It is indeed a disturbing hypothesis, but I had thought of it myself."

○　　○　　○

HUATUC

The gray-clad Indian sits in the stone room. He is cooking potatoes in the ashes. Ashes often guard treasures. It is night. Yohuantequi, the star of friendship, is no longer shining; the sky is dark. But here comes the moon—Coya, with her raven hair. She is *copacalla*, eighteen years old.

"Huatuc," she says, "they're asking us to dig where it is *huaca*. The messenger runs with his heart in his throat. Amidst the throbbing of a thousand hearts, breathless with running and fear, the message is spread that the armed men are back. Whether they are wearing armor or green uniforms, they are waiting for us. They are surrounding us. What shall we do?"

The gray-clad man is *punucrucu*, very old. He speaks slowly. "We will not dig for them. Some of these men are good, but others are evil. Supay, the demon, guides their steps."

"Huatuc," the moon says, "once we were so many. Now we are so few, and many of us already wear their uniforms and carry their weapons. Night looks inside the cold chimney. Will we be able to keep our children warm with tales of Raymi, the holiday of the sun?"

"Once we could fly, with our balloons, in papyrus baskets," Huatuc said. "The condor dies, after a life of freedom. The *cuy* —the mouse that lives in man's house and eats his leftovers— dies. Those who want to kill us will also die. Even though they may fly higher than all the condors, there they will meet the stars, and Huaca, Saturn. The bearded man will die. Woe to all those who want to extinguish the earth's heart!"

○　○　○

↗ ● ↗ ● ↗ ● ↗ ● ↗ ● ↗ ● ↗ ● ↗ ● ↗ ● ↗ ● ↗ ●

ABOARD *PROTEUS TIEN:* SLOK-SLOK P'I

○ ○ ○

"Are you sad, Mei?" Kook asked. They were sitting in front of the large porthole. Because of a peculiar optical effect, it looked as if the spaceship were cutting through a stormy sea, in a furrow of blue and purple spray. The drone of the engines was deep and hypnotic. Mei turned her white, tense face toward Kook.

"I don't know what's the matter with me, Kook. It's such a long trip, and I haven't heard from Fang for quite some time, now."

"You are very fond of him, aren't you?"

"Yes, I am. He has taught me many things. When I got my degree in telepathy at the Maimonides Institute of Parapsychology, I was very sure of myself and my powers. It was well known that we telepaths were in great demand by various intelligence services, and that governments liked to pit us against one another. But, of course, each of us thought herself or himself the strongest and best of the bunch. One day, as I was pondering these matters on the institute lawn, I came across Fang's thought. He got closer to me and asked, 'Do you know the story of Master Hu?

" 'Hu was one of the greatest masters of the martial arts in China. At the end of the course, he gathered all his best pupils, who would soon be teachers themselves, and told them, "You are now feeling very strong, almost invincible. And you're probably right. But before I let you go, I would like to ask you a question. Imagine yourselves about to walk across a river on a very narrow bridge. A warrior, known for his strength and fierceness, is moving toward you from the opposite side. You'll meet him in the middle of the bridge; there, he will probably attack you. Which martial style will most likely save your life?"

" ' "Master," the first student said, "the monkey style. On that narrow bridge, the only way I can possibly beat him is with agility, by jumping here and there, dodging his thrusts."

" ' "Master," the second student said, "I think the drunkard style might be better. Its unexpected movements are more likely to stun him and make him lose his bearings, after which it shouldn't be too difficult to dispatch him."

" 'The third student said, "I think the tiger style might be the best. If I attacked him first, with a sudden lunge, I believe I'd have a pretty good chance of saving my life."

" ' "Actually, Master," a fourth student said, "I'd opt for the labyrinth punch. Its secret style will take him by surprise, and he'll be out cold before he even knows what hit him."

" 'The last student said, "All things considered, Master, I really think the best thing to do would be to forget all you have taught us and walk toward him with a friendly smile. I believe that's the only style that could save not just one life, but two."

" ' "This is the answer I was waiting for," the master said.'

"Fang's story was addressed to me. After I heard it, I refused every offer that would employ my capacities for a military purpose, and since then, Fang has always been near me. Even now, just the mention of war makes me feel as if there were . . . an evil presence on this ship . . . something murderous."

"But there are no weapons on the ship," Kook said, somewhat troubled, "at least no nuclear arms, or anything that could provoke a war. Isn't that so, Chulain?"

Chulain shook his head: "I know what's eating you, Mei. You are suffering from *Weltraumschmerz*—space spleen— otherwise known as Slok-slok P'i."

"Slok-slok," Caruso explained, "comes upon you during the

night, clothed in a cloak the color of old hotels. He is generally accompanied by music—blues, or tangos, or milongas."

"Often," LeO added, "under his cloak, he carries photographs of country homes, grandfathers, Sundays at the beach, lost poodles, old baseball players, sunsets, and . . ."

"And, of course, the face of the beloved," Chulain sighed, "looking at you, and waving, as the spaceship takes off."

Mei laughed: "Is there any remedy against Slok-slok P'i?"

Chulain answered gravely. "Some try drugs, like cocaine, lumpiridions, hallucinogens, or coffee. But, alas, exciting the senses at all makes the face of the beloved appear still more lively!"

"Others," LeO said, "play videogames till their fingers swell, and then, at night, they dream of green, grimy spaceships with phosphorescent aliens coming at them, till out of a smaller, greener ship, the beloved emerges, yelling, 'Please don't shoot! It's me, it's me!' "

"Others," Caruso added, "do crossword puzzles, or jerk off, or both at the same time, and then feel ashamed."

"Others," Chulain confided, "fight against Slok-slok in the best possible fashion, that is, by telling stories."

"Tale-telling matches!" LeO confirmed. "That's it! Each crew member tells a story. Slok-slok P'i arrives, listens to the stories till he gets tired, and nods off. Then, all one has to do is grab him and throw him out of the porthole, and everybody's happy again."

"In that case, what are we waiting for?" Kook urged them on. "Let's have a nice, funny story!"

"Oh, no," Mei said, "funny stories are always so sad!"

"Very well, then," LeO intervened, "I shall tell you a sad story:

"Once there was a lady by the name of Emmeline Grangeford. She was very sad because she had lost her dog. So she composed a beautiful poem about him, which went (the poem, not the dog, for nobody knew where he had gone):

> Oh, your tongue in the cup slurping
> like feet in a puddle splashing
> when it rained, I often gave you a slug
> for
> leaving your wet footprints on the rug,
> and now how I would like to hear your sound
> and the sweet, furry smell of a wet hound.

"And so, poor Miss Grangeford used to spend her days staring at the rain and waiting, and crying, and composing verses.

"Then, one day, she heard a scratch on the door. Seized by a long shiver of excitement, she opened the door and . . .

". . . and a lion jumped into the room and ate her all up, including the little tortoiseshell combs she was wearing in her hair.

"The moral of the tale is: There's always somebody who takes advantage of other people's pain."

"That's a terrible story," Caruso said.
"Can you do better?" LeO challenged him.

"Once there was an Italian tenor who had a gorgeous voice, so gorgeous that he was wildly jealous of it. He kept it locked up in his mouth and never let it out; he spoke only in sign language. But the voice, being very young and strong and full of life, could not adjust to captivity, and soon started withering away. Finally, one foggy, damp day, the tenor lost his voice.

"He began roaming the streets, looking for it, but, having no voice, he could not call it, nor could he talk to anyone about it. So, he locked himself in his home and for many years lived off his memories. One day he turned on the radio and heard it! His own voice, more gorgeous than ever, was now living with a Spanish tenor. He went to the tenor's house and found them together, reading love letters aloud. The Italian tenor shot the Spanish rival.

" 'I'm dying,' the tenor's voice wailed.

"Then, the Italian tenor, realizing what a terrible thing he had done, pointed the gun at his own temple, and died, without a sound."

"That story," Kook commented, "is slightly unbelievable."
"Why don't you tell one, then?" Caruso responded.

"A neuron and a proton were so bored that they decided to get together and cause a reaction. In the process, they met an electron. He joined them, and they had a bash. Much to their excitement, the following day they discovered they had been observed and had thus provoked an important scientific discovery."

"This one," Mei noted, "is a little too scientific."
"Well, then," Kook suggested, "why don't you tell us a love story?"

"A weaver-girl and a young shepherd lived one on each bank of the River of Clouds. They could not see or speak to each other. But they sent love notes back and forth via a blue crane. Thus they lived and loved for years, exchanging poems, vows, and promises of fidelity. One day, the River of Clouds was tossed and turned by a terrible storm, with thunder, lightning, and torrential rain. When the storm blew over, all the clouds cleared out. At last, the weaver-girl and the young shepherd could see and speak to each other. They were walking toward each other when they saw the blue crane lying dead on the ground like a bag of wet feathers.

" 'Alas,' the young shepherd sighed, 'now that we can at last meet, our love is dead.' "

"That story is too sad," Chulain muttered, dropping a huge tear. "I couldn't hear another one like that."

"Nor I," Mei agreed.

"Then, Chulain," Kook said, "why don't you tell us a story from your travels in space?"

The Odd Planets

I have seen many weird planets and have heard about many more. I have seen Mechanus, whose inhabitants are made of interchangeable iron pieces, so that each one is, in turn, man, tractor, horse, house, crane. By exchanging a piece and turning a screw, each can choose to do and be whatever it pleases. But no one is ever purely individual, since it always shares one of its pieces with someone else. So, nobody is ever fully oneself, and nobody is ever entirely someone else, which is why it is said that no one exists on Mechanus, though its streets are full of metal horses, carts, men, and cars.

Then, next to Berenice's mane, one finds the planet Trichoevus. The inhabitants of this planet know how long they are going to live the moment they are born—a year per hair, up to three hundred years of age. Their hair is coarse and bristly, the color of fleas. Hair can be transplanted so that the rich can buy hair from the poor and live longer. Ten hairs mean ten more years in Trichoevus. If a poor man is born with a hundred hairs, he will immediately sell eighty, for he does not want to live too long in poverty. If a rich man is born with too few hairs, his father and mother immediately buy him some. But

the planet also has a few *figaros*, bandits, who steal hairs
from the rich and give them to the poor. But they've got
to watch out, for, if they are caught, the barber's scissors
are merciless. And the poor will immediately revert to
their old ways and sell all their hair, down to the very
last follicle, for they have to make a living.

Another odd planet is Rightback, for its inhabitants
have always just left. One knows they live there, because
the houses are there, the chimneys are smoking, the cars
have all passed the last inspection, the shops are open,
plants and flowers are doing fine, and the streets are
clean. But if you go ring their bells, you'll find a piece of
paper tacked onto the door that says, "I'm in the garden."
The dog is sleeping in its house in the garden, the leaves
have been gathered, the lawn has been mowed, but
there's nobody in sight—just a new message that says,
"I'm at work." If you take the subway to the office, you'll
find out that it has closed just five minutes ago. The
coffee cups are still warm, the cigarette butts are still
smoking, there is paper in the typewriters, but nobody's
in the room working. The telephone might ring, but as
soon as you answer, somebody will have just hung up.
Outside, all the stores are closed and bear the sign RIGHT
BACK. The cars are perfectly parked, but empty. The engine of one is still on, but there is no trace of its owner.
The park is full of candy wrappers, used condoms, and
that morning's papers, but everybody has just left. You
go to the hotel; the receptionist will be back in a sec. You
take your key, the only one there (all the other guests
have just stepped out). Your bedroom is ready. The towels
are fresh. From the bathroom, you hear the door open—
click. You rush out, but the waiter has just walked away,
leaving a hot breakfast on your night table. You hear the
sound of a band outside. You run into the hallway, but
the elevator doors shut in your face because someone else
has just taken it. You rush downstairs and out into the

street to see the parade. The street is covered with con-
fetti, festoons, streamers, and empty bottles, but you
can't see a single living soul. The sound of the band
moves farther and farther away; you get furious, and
would like to yell and scream, but you can't—because
you too have just left.

But the oddest planet I've ever heard of is the planet of
Sacred Shit. There, shit is the most valuable substance,
the currency that can buy everything. Instead of wallets,
the inhabitants carry chamber pots, and the larger these
are and the worse they smell, the prouder their owners.
Their banks are immense cesspools, watched around the
clock by special cops and vigilantes. This is where everyone makes deposits, from the youngest customers to the
little old lady (whose entire savings consist of two tiny,
spherical, rabbitlike droppings) to the rich merchant who
wheels in his daily profits on an odorous cart. Of course,
at home, nobody ever "goes to the bathroom." The correct expression there is, "I'm going to drop a few coins in
my piggy bank." And, indeed, children's potties are
shaped like little pigs. But, alas, even on this planet, people are ready to sell body and soul to become big shits!
Muggers force you at gunpoint to drop everything you
have in your belly. Those who incautiously stop in a field
to produce some cash must be very careful not to be
robbed while they are pulling up their pants. And let's
not even mention the exhibitionists who, when they
enter a restaurant, press shit into the hands of all the
waiters and, as a tip, drop a turd as large as a salami, and
go around saying, 'I don't want to sound like I'm boasting,
but I have so much shit I don't know what to do with
it.'

Naturally, the economy of this planet is subject to the
fluctuations of its primary currency. Here, a scarcity of
investments is known as constipation, and inflation as
diarrhea. The rulers are constantly talking about "keep-

ing the level of diarrhea below ten percent." And then, of course, there are scandals. It is revealed that the rulers, secretly, get tons of shit from the industrialists and are more than willing to close an eye to smuggling into foreign countries. Credit purchases also exist. One may, for instance, make a down payment on a car by swallowing ten laxatives a few hours earlier. But then, if, by chance, one defaults on one's payments, there is little one can do but declare bellyruptcy. And this will be followed by investigations, sometimes even confiscation, by proctologists who work for the collection agencies. But this happens fairly seldom, for this planet is very rich. Holy Shit Day falls on the sixth of every month—a cause for great celebration. The biggest shits in the land jump into their large cream-and-chestnut cars and gather in immense ballrooms, decorated with chandeliers and valuable paintings and bathroom fixtures. The ladies are all dressed in white, the gentlemen in pink. And they gossip and talk behind each other's backs. "See that guy? He made all his shit gambling; he's a real parvenu! This one, instead, is a true blue-blood; his family has always been pure manure." And they all dance and, above all, fart, in order to display their wealth. The more buxom ladies fart like bassoons, causing their narrow satin dresses to swell; younger ladies tootle most deliciously, like virtuoso flutes or clarinets; rich merchants boom like cannons while patting one another on the back; intellectuals wheeze painfully, as they explain to the few willing to listen that shit is not everything; yuppies let out sharp blatant blares that make their coattails luff; old aristocrats grumble as they cut the cheese, more often than not, secretly dropping a few accidental coins into their bloomers; children pipe in; infants squander petty cash in their diapers; and the host, ruddy and triumphant, posts himself on the threshold to emit an epic blast, whose vibrations send the chandeliers into a tinkling frenzy. Then he announces, "Dinner is served!"

And all the guests go wash their hands.

Having finished his tale, Chulain signaled for the others to be quiet. In a corner of the spaceship, Slok-slok P'i was snoring. Chulain seized him delicately by the ears, opened one of the portholes, and hurled him into space. Instantly, Mei recovered her smile.

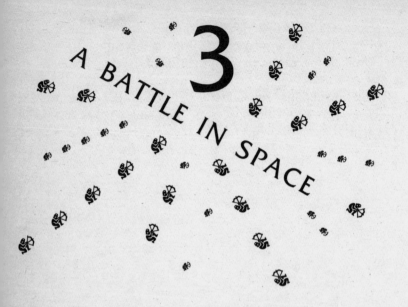

3
A BATTLE IN SPACE

〉 〉 〉 〉 ⊖ ☌ ◉ ⊖ 〉 ○ ◐ ☌ ⊙ ◑ ○ ◖ ○ ◉ ♈ ⊙ ◖ 〈 〈 〈

MIDNIGHT: SEVEN HOURS
AWAY FROM MESKORSKA

◉ ◉ ◉

Zuikaku—*Service Order*

Prepare for landing on Meskorska. The following will disembark: General Yamamoto, the undersigned, camouflaged as street peddler; all gray soldiers who have completed advanced course on mime and mimicry—viz. Sergeants On and Input, and Soldiers Unlock, Status, Mem, Mids, Pi, and Data—all disguised as mechanical mice. Due to special mission, execution of prisoners postponed until tomorrow. The following soldiers will stand duty: sentry, Corporal Return and Soldiers Step and Next; dormitory guard, Tab.

Signed: General Yamamoto, Commander in Chief

Calalbakrab—*Evening Program*

While we are waiting for our arrival on Meskorska, the movie *Meskorska, Gem of the Arab Industry* will be shown in the Red Room. The Blue Room will host a concert of Country and Amerussian music with the Pushkin Brothers. Computer Room: Hieroglyph Decipherment Competition for Computers, Pocket Division. The titleholder, IBM 676, will defend against the challenger, Rank Xerox 1088. Treasure Room: bellydancing, with the marvelous Suleima. Bakaya Room: a debate on the future of space exploration.

Local News—His Majesty the Great Scorpion Sadalmelik al-Akrab, the Corrupter, has, in the course of the day, sunk six crumpled sheets of paper into his wastebasket, located at a fair distance from his desk. To His Majesty, no neophyte in such athletic achievements, we extend the compliments of the entire crew.

Tomorrow Night—All crew members who are off duty may feel free to take a walk on Meskorska. We would like to remind you of our ship's excellent restaurant, al-Meleph, and of its nightclub, al-Gomaisa, in the Arab quarter.

Important—Yesterday, an act of terrorism was rumored to have occurred in the Royal Chambers. The rumor has been fully refuted by the king himself, who moreover wants to call your attention once again to the fact that whoever is discovered spreading false or tendentious news shall be democratically censored, and his tongue shall thereafter be displayed in a showcase in the Treasure Room.

Obituaries—Our universally esteemed colleague, pilot Igor Dylaniev, thirty-six, was found dead by suicide in his room. The doctor on duty has established that his demise was caused by the influence of alcohol and barbiturates on a subject already debilitated by six knife wounds in his chest. The funeral service will take place tomorrow.

Thought for the Evening—"One can repent even of having repented."—Ibn-Sawi al-Muin.

♀ ○ ♀ ○ ♀ ○ ♀ ○ ♀ ○ ♀ ○ ♀ ○ ♀ ○ ♀ ○ ♀ ○ ♀ ○

MESKORSKA!

♀ ♌ ♂

The siren of *Proteus Tien* bellowed twice, and all its lights flashed through space.

"Move out of my way, creep!" Chulain kept shouting into the ship's radio. Right in front of them, a cargo sweeper was slowly advancing, sucking away refuse and metallic debris with a vacuum cleaner whose mouth resembled that of a gigantic frog.

"Hey, handsome, turn off your chandelier," a voice answered him from the sweeper. "I'll let you pass, but don't complain if your windshield gets all mucked up!"

Chulain overtook him and immediately regretted it, for the spaceship suddenly found itself mired in the cloud of flotsam and jetsam that surrounded Meskorska—metal scraps, slag, peels and plastic wrappers, antennae, bottles, syringes, and condoms—in short, all the refuse that an orbiting city with a diameter of ten kilometers tends to spit into space. As the ship was thus trying to drag its way through the dreck, a one-ton garbage bag splattered against its windshield, creating a remarkable example of Residual Art.

"Watch out for the gnats, terrestrial," the space sweeper chuckled. Chulain slowed down, disconsolately staring at the cloud of dirt. "What a dump," he sighed. "The last time I was here, there was a line of eight hundred spaceships, the worst space jam I'd ever been in. But at least back then we had fuel!"

They were moving closer to the great sphere of Meskorska, luminous and transparent, slowly rotating upon itself. The pattern of its road system made it resemble an immense ocular orb. Two or three fetid gusts of wind told our heroes they were rapidly approaching the planet's industrial area at zero gravity.

"Ground control, spaceport Cola," Chulain signaled, "This is *Proteus Tien*. We are about to land."

"First you have to pay your toll at the gate," ground control answered.

Chulain started. "What toll? Are you crazy?"

"You've been flying on a spaceway. Didn't you see the Cosmogrill and the traffic signals? What's your tonnage?"

"A hundred and twenty," Chulain guessed.

"All right! You owe us sixty ingots for the toll, plus a fine of a hundred for attempted fraud—the astronautic register says you weigh more than twenty thousand tons."

"And if we don't pay, what's going to happen?"

"We have two thermal guns pointed at you. If you force us to use them, you're going to make your mechanic's fortune."

"In that case, my friends, I guess we'll pay."

○ Meskorska Terminal ○

A few minutes later, our heroes were comfortably seated on the simultiger armchairs of Spaceport Five in Meskorska, waiting for the customs robots to complete their inspection.

Outside the ample windows of the spaceport, they could see the tauriform geometry of the factories and the cultivated land, as well as the gardens of the residential area.

"Meskorska," a stentorian loudspeaker announced, "was founded in 2098 by seven illustrious multinational firms, to carry out a series of studies on the feasibility of space industry and the rehabilitation of convicts at zero gravity."

"Free labor," Kook translated.

"It is the third largest of the twenty-two space islands, and the farthest from Earth. It is the launching pad for all the expeditions that will bring valuable minerals and other important discoveries to humanity."

"To the multinational firms," our friends rectified in unison.

"The island has a diameter of ten kilometers and completes its full rotation every six minutes. This gives it, at its equator, a gravity similar to that of Earth. All the residential areas are located along the equatorial circle. Moving toward the poles, one finds a series of industrial belts with decreasing gravity all the way to the one with zero gravity, particularly useful for metalliferous alloys and studies of the antiproton. All these areas are screened off so as to obtain the alternate phases of day and night that are necessary for the productive cycle. Our atmosphere is made of oxygen, which we introduce in its liquid state and then set free. Its density in the residential area corresponds to what one finds at an altitude of eight hundred meters in the paleoterrestrial atmosphere. In the industrial zone, the atmosphere falls within the limits of the norm."

"Yeah, the same as in sulphuric acid," Chulain commented.

"Let me remind you of Meskorska's numerous attractions, which you can't possibly fail to admire. In Sector One, the Atari Sector, you must see the Harajuku Quarter, with its roof gardens and factories that produce the most modern hologames, and, of course, Hololand, the nonexistent tridimensional city. In Sector Two, the Lockheed Sector, you'll find zero-gravity areas, where you can learn free-floating and airsurfing from our instructors, and can visit the famous astronautical-weapons factories. In Sector Three, Arabian United, you'll find swimming pools with slo-mo diving, the Energy Fair, and the Sahara Line, production zone of the most modern carburetors, and central refinery of solar energy, used for orbiting cells.

In the Bulova Sector, aside from the hundred-thousand-seat Rossi sports stadium, you can visit the high-tech microindustries and the watchmaking anthills. In the Coca-Cola Sector, Number Five, where you now are, do not fail to visit Restaurant Row and the Alimentary Sector with its greenhouses, as well as the factories that produce poisons and chemical arms. In the IBN-IBM Sector, you can visit the largest rug and computer factories in the world. In Sector Seven, called LBS (Lucas, Bondarchuck, Spielberg), you must see the Museum of Space Conquest, ET's birthplace, and the Drama Academy for robots. Have a pleasant stay on our island, and remember: tickets for the excursion to Meskorska by Night, with an authorized guide, can be purchased at our windows—two ingots for adults, and one for children and radioactive subjects."

"Thank you, chief," Chulain said, turning toward the loudspeaker. "Now, can we go see all these wonderful sights?"

"Not before you have explained the reason for your visit," the voice answered. "We haven't seen many Sinoeuropeans around here, lately."

"We are solar hunters," Chulain said. "We want to visit the Energy Fair and see the new Bird's Eye solar cells."

"Hmmm," the voice hesitated. "So you claim you're solar hunters? Then, answer this question—What was the total amount of solar energy sprayed onto the Earth during the preglacial era?"

"One to five times ten to the eighteenth power kilowatt hours per year," Kook answered. "Any other questions?"

"Yes, would you like some pot?"

"What kind?" Chulain asked.

"Spatial grass, grown from Senegalese seeds. A real killer!"

"You're on," Chulain said.

"Drop two ingots into that basket on your right, and you'll find all you need in the suitcase," the voice said. "Once again, have a pleasant stay."

○ A Quick Lunch ○

Vassiliboyd and Coyllur walked into a fast-food joint and sat down in silence, slightly stunned by the lights of the space city and the animated menu that spun quickly along on the screen in front of them, displaying the adventures of Superhamburger against the Emptybellies.

"Hey, the two of you, shake it," the waiter robot with a yellow cap growled. "You have exactly a hundred and twenty seconds to eat, and you have already wasted six."

"Two chibs hold-ons, pair screams," the pilot ordered.

"Who's screaming?" Coyllur asked with a puzzled look on her face, as the two onionless cheeseburgers zoomed toward them on the conveyor belt.

"No one. That means ice-cream sundaes," Vassiliboyd explained, catching his cheeseburger in midair. "Quick, pass the ketchup; the bottle stays open only ten seconds."

"I don't like to eat this way," the girl complained.

"Dylaniev liked it a lot," the pilot said. "Back in the School of Astronautics he once bet he could eat twenty hamburgers in five minutes. He used to say, to be ravenous is revolutionary."

"You were very good friends, weren't you?"

"Yeah, I suppose you could say that, even though lately we quarreled a great deal. He was . . . I don't know how to put it —like half of me, my anxious half . . . and . . ."

"Thirty seconds for your coffee, folks," the waiter robot croaked.

"Here's an ingot. Go fuck off for six minutes!"

"Take it easy, folks. Take your time," the robot chimed, catching the tip with its paw.

"We always did everything together," Vassiliboyd continued. "Until, after the last war, he sort of stopped kidding around . . . and became very serious . . . and started saying all those things about our past. He just couldn't leave it alone, even though I kept telling him it was all over, and he should look at it realistically. . . . All our comrades were either dead or had sold out to the government . . . and he kept telling me it was not like that, that he had a great deal to do. And now that he's dead . . ."

"Now," Coyllur guessed, "you think he might have been right?"

"I don't know," the pilot said, shaking his head. "All I know is that here we are, waiting for our Sinoeuropean enemies to find the way, so that we can get rid of them and give a brand new planet to that bejeweled jerk and his industrial cronies."

Coyllur looked the pilot straight in the eye. "What if there were something one could do? Something Dylaniev might have liked to do? Would you do it in his place?"

All of a sudden, Vassiliboyd remembered how Dylaniev had insisted on hiring the Dzunum to fly with them. But a voice at his shoulders distracted him from his answer.

"Hey, there, Curly! Do you intend to spend the whole night on that stool?"

The speaker was a big bully dressed in the uniform of the Island Vigilantes, and armed with a stun-gun.

Vassiliboyd looked at him defiantly. "Why? Do you want my stool?"

"You got the idea, pilot," the cop answered.

"Here it is—all yours!" Vassiliboyd said, and broke it over his head.

"A-me-ri-can-pi-lot-ve-ry-ner-vous," mouse Pi said, sticking his whiskered head out of the basket only a few meters away.

"Shush!" the enchanting old lady, Yamamoto, demanded. "Keep your head down! And when you show yourself, move in jerks. *Miiice!* Look at the pretty mechanical mice! Who wants my little mice! They look like the real thing!"

∘   ∘   ∘

❦ The Largest Menu in Space ❦

"Well, it's certainly nice up here," Mei said. "I didn't think it would be so green!" They were walking through downtown Meskorska, along a boulevard flanked by lush trees and gigantic ferns.

"They've been able to get a great deal of energy from the sun and from protonic processing. They'd never go to Earth and freeze," Kook said, pointing at the crowd of Meskorskans milling about in the street. "Besides, most of them were born here. But don't be fooled by appearances; only twenty percent of the inhabitants live here in the residential equatorial quarters. All the others are confined to the industrial area—they're either Mestengo Indians, convicts serving their prison term, or immigrants from radioactive places. Their life is pretty awful: their work shifts are grueling, their surroundings are dangerous, and people call them 'ratfaces' because they always wear antigas masks."

"But it can't be like this in all the space islands," Mei said, "at least . . . I hope . . . not on ours!"

"Our space islands are very small," Kook told her. "But I doubt they are any different from this one."

The group stopped on a street flanked by white buildings with barred windows. "Well, this is Geber's street address," Chulain said. "His newspaper should be someplace around here."

At the door of one building stood an old Meskorskan who immediately addressed them: "Vu seek zeitung buggialugga?"

"What language does he speak?" Kook asked Chulain.

"He speaks sheerap, the slang of space islands," the black explained. "He said, 'Are you looking for the biggest lie factory in space?' Ya, olman. Nu seekita."

"Buggialugga geschlossen ovra miezzanite. Tienes palleta?" the old man said.

"He said, 'The factory of lies opens only at midnight.' Here, the papers have different shifts to make sure all twenty-four hours of news get covered. He would also like a cigarette. Take ciga palleta, olman. Sabe du bona snack billig mucho esn? Wo tu tzu ola!"

"Sure, svartman," the old man answered. "Chilla strasse alla muchoka snack slapasgud."

"Great!" Chulain exclaimed. "I asked him where we could find a good, cheap restaurant. He told me there are several on this street. Meskorska—space delicacy—here we come!"

○ Restaurant Le Linné ○

And that's how our heroes found themselves in Pantagruel Circus, site of the most renowned restaurants in Meskorska. There was food for all tastes and moods—vegetarian, macrobiotic, bacterial, psychedelic, synesthetic, intravenous, pillular.

"What do you think of this one, Sara?" Caruso asked the bee, who was sitting on his hat. " 'Le Linné, French cuisine.' When it comes to food, I'm a staunch conservative."

"French cuisine and I have been out of touch for several years. Come on, let's go in!" Chulain said with enthusiasm.

As soon as they entered, they realized the place was really chic. Tiny place settings, minuscule cutlery. A violin ensemble was playing the "Libellula Waltz." Extraordinarily discreet waiters in bright green jackets were silently arrayed in front of a large poster that said, "OUR FOOD IS SO LIGHT IT FLIES!"

"Well, well, guys," Chulain said, sitting down, "we have found a really classy place. Madame Mei, would you like me to read you today's specials?"

"Oui, Monsieur Chulain," Mei answered, noticing, not without surprise, a magnifiying lens next to her fork.

"Et voilà," Chulain intoned. "Today's menu:

> Sauterelles au miel Jean-Baptiste
> Sauterelles rôties à la Cuvier
> Salade de sauterelles à l'indonésienne—

"I don't know what these 'sauterelles' are, but their name sounds scrumptious. Maybe they're small crêpes," Chulain guessed and went on reading, without seeing Mei's frantic signals.

"À suivre:

> *Ragoût de blatte à la Linné*
> *Pâté de puces*
> *Gigot de nemésia Moulin Rouge—*

"Hey, 'gigot' means leg. That much I know."

"Hey, Chulain," Kook whispered, pulling on his sleeve.

"What's the problem, Kook? Let me finish. Wow, listen to this:

> *Bourdons à la balinaise*
> *Omelette de Sceliphron spirifrex*
> *Omelette aux moustiques*
> *Couscous de crillon marocain*
> *Salade d'abeilles à la gelée royale Guizzardi*
> *Salade de guêpes à l'armoricaine—*

"Well, well! I wonder what these 'abeilles' and 'guêpes' are! Ouch!" Mei had administered him such a tremendous kick under the table that, for a moment, he was left gasping for breath.

"Caruso," the girl said, "please, do as I say! Put Sara back in her rest box!" Caruso, surprised, was about to ask why when, spying a plate in the hands of one of the waiters, he understood. He seized the bee and rapidly locked her in her box.

"Chulain, I apologize for my kick," Mei explained, with a big sigh of relief. "Maybe you can speak all the different space slangs, but French is decidedly not your forte. 'Sauterelles' means grasshoppers; the 'gigot,' here, is a spider leg; and the

other dishes are mosquito omelettes, flea pâté, cricket cous-
cous, salad of bees with royal jelly, and a mixed salad of
wasps."

"Obviously, this is a restaurant that specializes in entomological dishes," Kook said. "They must have managed to raise
lots of insects along with their plants."

"I don't think this is the best place for Sara," Caruso said,
getting up.

"Le Monsieur ne se stop pas?" the waiter asked superci-
liously.

"Nous sommes végétariens," Mei answered.

Not far from there, in the middle of the Meskorskan crowd,
the little old lady Yamamoto was having so much success with
her mechanical mice that the real mice in the basket were
becoming alarmed.

"Hey-ge-ne-ral." A distinct rapping drew Yamamoto's attention. "Slow-down-hype, re-al-me-cha-ni-cal-mice-al-lso-ld-nex-
tone-mus-tbe-oneo-fus."

"Don't worry," the general answered, "but I'd really like to
know what those damn Aramerussians are up to!"

The Aramerussians, dressed like tourists, were very near.
Their chief, a big Arab in Bermuda shorts and rubber thongs,
was in radio contact with the *Calalbakrab.*

"We're right on their heels, chief! At this very moment, they
have entered a new restaurant, Créatures. No trace of the Japanese, however. On the other hand, Vassiliboyd and one of the
girls of the rocksky group have gotten into a fight with a bunch
of vigilantes and have been booked. What shall we do?"

"Let them spend the night in the cooler," Alya's voice answered. "It will do them good. Otherwise, they'll end up like
their friend. By the way, did you remember to get me that
Meskorska souvenir, the glass paperweight with the snow-
storm inside?"

⚓ Chez Créatures ⚓

"All the food that's fit to eat," claimed the modest computer-ized menu, with a one-hundred-and-twenty-button keyboard.

An austere waiter, with thick synthetic sideburns, walked up to the table. In his hands, he was holding a computer ter-minal to take the orders on.

"May I have your order?" he asked in perfect Sinoeuropean.

"We would like your advice," Chulain told him. "It isn't easy to choose from a menu with sixty thousand entries."

"If you allow me, I would suggest you begin your meal with one of the mysterious soups. They are delicious, and it is quite exciting not knowing what they'll turn out to be. For your second course, if you are very strong, you might try a Venusian prupus."

"Why do we have to be very strong?" Kook inquired.

"If you want to have a clear idea of what I mean, they are serving one at the table next to you."

And, in fact, at the table to their right, two fat Russians were uncovering a huge soup tureen, from which wafted the deli-cate aroma of stew. No sooner had the first Russian dipped his fork into the stew than a blue tentacle darted out, grabbed his head, and pulled it under the broth. Two waiters intervened and, with a well-aimed stab, freed the client. The other Rus-sian then decided to try his luck; this time, the prupus (a cross between an octopus and a jellyfish) jumped out of the bowl and dragged his assailant into a juicy wrestling match till the Russian, half-strangled by the tentacles, yelled, "The dessert —bring me the dessert!"

"As you can see," the waiter concluded with a smile, "not everybody has the strength necessary to eat a prupus. We serve it stewed, but that doesn't bother it—on Venus it lives in a magma of two thousand degrees centigrade."

Mei cleared her throat. "Maybe we'd better try some other specialty," she said. "Something quieter, please."

"Our specialty is the ifyoulikeme mushroom. It was discovered on Jupiter's smallest planet, Antilochus. We are the only place in the whole galaxy that serves it. It's a rare treat. Only a few people, and I underline *few*, have ever eaten it."

"Very well, then," Chulain took charge of the orders, "four mysterious soups, and one ifyoulikeme mushroom. And a lightly seasoned camellia for Sara. She has a delicate stomach."

The waiter bowed and punched the orders into his computer.

In a few seconds, they were served,

Chulain looked suspiciously at the black, viscous broth in his bowl. "What do you say?" he inquired of the others. "Shall we dig in?"

They began the tasting with caution, but after the first few spoonfuls, they felt reassured. In her soup, Mei found some delicious seaweed, Caruso a few red flowers with a sweet aftertaste, and Chulain and Kook enjoyed the excellent noodles whose only drawback was that they tended to swim to the bottom of the bowl.

As soon as they had finished their soups, the waiters returned carrying an immense golden tray. The maître d' clapped his hands with solemnity.

"Ladies and gentlemen, I must now briefly explain to you how to eat the ifyoulikeme mushroom. This . . . mushroom is endowed with a very peculiar character. It can manifest itself in three ways. The moment I uncover the tray, it will look white and altogether neutral. Eaten like that, it has absolutely no taste. But if it does not like you—of course, I am using this expression incorrectly, for it is not really a question of liking or disliking, but rather of the particular sensitivity of the spores—well, in case it does not like you, then it will become green, wrinkled, and soggy, and you will not be able to eat it because it will be as poisonous as few others things in the universe. If, instead, it likes you, then it will flush with a beautiful yellowish red color, and will immediately become an exquisite morsel such as you have probably never tasted!"

"Incredible!" Kook exclaimed. "What can we do to be liked by it?"

"Nothing," the maître d' said. "The mushroom decides with its own head, or rather, its own cap—please excuse my *bêtise*. Ladies and gentlemen, I am honored to introduce you to the ifyoulikeme mushroom!"

The waiter lifted the cover and a gorgeous, simple, plump mushroom appeared, comfortably resting on a bed of parsley, in the middle of the tray. Suddenly, it stood up and spun on its stem a couple of times, scanning its table companions. Then, it started flaring with all sorts of orange shades, while its stem glowed red. In a few seconds, the whole mushroom was uniformly covered with a wonderful blush. The waiters applauded.

"My compliments, ladies and gentlemen," the maître d' said. "Obviously, the mushroom likes you. Now, it's your turn to like *it!*"

"Naturally," Caruso assented, holding his fork in midair. "Come on, Chulain, why don't you start?"

"All right! It isn't very common to eat a mushroom that likes you . . . so . . . I'd say I should start here . . . or, actually, it might be better over there." He brought his knife to the mushroom—without, however, daring touch it. "You know, guys, I really don't understand mushrooms that well. Maybe you should start, Kook."

"Not me, thank you," Kook immediately declined. "I . . . you see, I had forgotten to tell you, but when I was small I got really sick eating too many honey agarics . . . I'm still not sure I could handle a mushroom now . . . Mei, you start."

"Sorry!" Mei said. "I can't possibly stab someone . . . or something . . . that has just shown so much liking for me."

"Am I to understand," the waiter intervened, "that you don't want to eat the dish?"

"That's right," Chulain admitted. "It likes us. How could we possibly betray its trust?"

"Very well, ladies and gentlemen, I thought it might come

to this," the waiter explained with a smile, "because, you see, the ifyoulikeme mushroom has another peculiarity: it generally becomes green and poisonous in front of evil, ravenous people, and red and tasty in the presence of sweet, sensitive people. And, naturally no sensitive person would ever be able to eat a mushroom that has just shown him or her so much appreciation."

"And so?" Mei said.

"So . . . this is why the ifyoulikeme mushroom is such a rare dish. *Nobody has ever eaten it.* Those who wanted to, could not, and vice versa. This very mushroom has been our specialty for fifty years. We have never had to get another. Now, may I offer you some dessert?"

↗ How Our Heroes Took Advantage of the Bedlam That Ensued ↗

"Sorry, grandma, but street peddlers are not allowed into the restaurant," the usher at Créatures told General Yamamoto.

The general looked at him humbly from beneath his crooked white wig. "May I just sit here, then," he whined, "in front of this door . . . for a little while? Actually, no, you are right. It would not be proper!" What made General Yamamoto change his mind was the sudden appearance, at the end of the street, of a few big bullies. As they approached, he recognized Gienah, chief of the *Scorpion*'s police force, and his thugs. Their flowery Bermudas did not fool him, nor did the camera each wore strapped around his shoulders. Yamamoto knew those cameras could only take last shots. So he hunched over and shuffled past them, dragging his wooden clogs.

"Hey," he heard a voice say behind him, "doesn't she look strong for an old lady? Hey, there, granny! Come here a sec, will you?"

"Gray soldiers," Yamamoto whispered, "let's keep our cool! Yes, young man, were you calling me?"

"Yes, granny," the Arab answered, looking the old lady over. "What are you carrying in that basket?"

"Mechanical mice, made in Japan," Yamamoto chirped.

Gienah scooped up the lid of the basket. Instantly, the mice stiffened. "Well, well," the Arab said, grabbing Pi. "Really cute . . . and they are made of metal, you say," and he squeezed the mouse's belly between thumb and index finger. Pi endured it stoically, and moved arms, legs, and tail back and forth with robotic rigidity.

"Yeah, really cute!" Gienah chuckled, "it looks real!"

"I know," Yamamoto agreed, "but it was made by Honda. Japanese technology . . ."

"Well, in that case," Gienah said, raising the hand in which he held the mouse, "he must also be unbreakable—no? May I throw it against the sidewalk?"

"Guik!" ("go get fucked" in Mousish), Pi screeched, then bit the Arab's hand. All hell broke loose. Yamamoto yanked his wig away and, with a horrible yell, launched into an exhaustive exhibition of his karate skills. He floored two men with a plain rotating double kick. The Arab who hit him three times from the back with a club was in turn bitten on the ankle by two pairs of incisors. Gienah turned the camera lens and was about to attempt a wide-angle, when Pi bit deeply into his right buttock. Four Arabs attacked Yamamoto, who, for the occasion, performed a wonderful *kumite-akai-do* ("the blow of the cherry pit that slips away from four fingers").

The brawl was getting fiercer and fiercer: the mice bared their teeth, Yamamoto whirled his feet, the Arabs cudgeled, various passersby received accidental bites and kicks—and, in all that bedlam, our heroes managed to sneak away, unseen.

"Quick, quick," Chulain panted as he ran. "They're giving us a headstart! Let's get to that newspaper office!"

A few minutes later, still panting, they rang the bell of the *Meskorska Evening Star.* An old man opened the door. He was wearing an American football helmet with the inscription "FOREMAN."

"Hoo do vu wanna knockraut?" he asked sadly.

"What did you say?"

"Who you wanna hit? Want you not hit someone for an articule? Was rectification not to your like?"

"No, no. We just want to talk to Geber!" Mei explained.

The old man sighed with relief.

"Ah, Geber! Geber no more aquí. Gone via, gehen, geyn. Whoooooof!"

"Where has he gone?" Chulain asked. "Where gone? Sehr important for nu know!"

"Geber gone posto mucho schlekt, horripilo posto. Zombie hospital Moriturlich!"

"At the hospital for the contaminated!" Caruso said. "Poor guy, he must be in terrible shape. Let's get over there!"

"No possibile," the old man said, spreading his arms. "Tu no zombie, vu kent in zombiezone gehen. Verboten, proibito, interdit."

"We are screwed," Chulain translated. "No one can enter that kind of hospital."

"Vu ken in," the old man explained, "mais kent out. Mais si verboten for men, forsitan no verboten robotibus!"

"Right on!" LeO exclaimed. "The old man is right. Humans can't go in, but I can, and so can Sara . . . we're not afraid of the virus."

"Oh, LeO," Mei said, "you'd really do it? For us?"

"Yes, I would! I'm a robot, but my feelings are almost human. I will do it . . . for just three hundred ingots."

"What a brave biped!" Kook complimented LeO as he walked away, on the conveyor belt, toward his dangerous mission.

"This is our real strength!" Mei exclaimed with pride. "We are ready to sacrifice ourselves to the common cause, while our enemies are constantly at each other's throats. As our very wise chairwoman Mou-lan used to say, it is easy to cut a thousand threads, one by one, but almost impossible to cut them if they're braided together in one single rope. This is the strength of our Federation!"

○ ○

AN AMPLE AND SERENE CONFRONTATION

○ ○

From the extraordinary number of blue-and-black skis parked outside the Assembly Room, it was easy to deduct that, this time, the meeting of the Sinoeuropean Parliament was well attended. The last representatives were slaloming down the ramps of the Tour Montparnasse. A Swede elegantly wedeled his way to the door, followed by two fat Greeks who crossed each other's skis and tumbled on top of the traffic cop.

"Get up! Scramble!" Phildys, who was in charge of the police force, ordered. "His Holiness is on his way!"

Preceded by four Swiss Guards, Pope John Paul "Nino" III, president of the Vatican, raced down the ramp and swept to a stop with a snazzy stem christy, snowing all the bystanders.

"Hi there, Phildys," he said, removing the white hood on which two embroidered skis formed a cross. "Bless you. Where can I get some schnapps? My balls are frozen!"

"At the bar, Your Holiness," Phildys answered. For decades now, the Vatican had been a state like any other, with its own army, nuclear weapons, and economic power equal to that of England. Even so, some people thought that the current pope was waxing excessively secular.

Through the door of the Assembly Room, one could already hear the voice of the chairman introducing the topic of discussion. "We are here," he declaimed, "to discuss Mission Terra. Our agenda comprises two questions: First, What policy shall we hold as regards the mission? Second, What policy shall we adopt toward any eventual alien life on the planet? I think we should start the debate immediately."

"No fucking way!" the Chinese representative P'ing Hsueh thundered. "First of all, we must rediscuss the partition of Terra. We don't see why China should have only one quarter of it. We are members of the Federation, with equal rights!"

"But your energy production is barely a sixth of what Europe produces," the English Foreign Secretary, Lord Snowdown, objected. "The real outrage is that my country has not been assigned any ocean territory! Doesn't tradition count any longer? Need I remind you of Morgan and Nelson?"

"These are ridiculous issues," the French Great Chamberlain, M. Bassinoire, interrupted. "Instead, I'd really like to know why the exclusive rights for all underwater telecasts were given to the Chinese rather than to us. Think of Picard, think of Cousteau!"

"As far as telecasting is concerned," Pyk yelled, "the cathodist party alliance protests the government's unqualified refusal to send a television crew along with the mission, thus depriving the public of a unique experience. I'd walk a mile for a Camel."

"I would like to remind our colleagues," Phildys abruptly intervened, "that no advertisements of any kind are allowed during Parliamentary sessions."

"In the name of the Reunited Armies," General Von Ofen boomed, "I would like to know why no military contingent has yet been sent to that planet. Do we want to leave cosmic space in anarchic chaos?"

"Gentlemen, gentlemen!" the mayor of Paris, Madame Zoë, said. "Please let's not come to blows over a planet we're not yet sure exists. I would like you to remember that Paris has been without heat for three days now, that children are dying, and that crêpes must be served warm!"

"On my part," the Spanish alcalde, Jiménez, intervened, "I would like to call your attention to the inhuman conditions of those poor men working in freezing mines without the warm comfort of Jiménez heaters. Twenty-two Eskimos have died this month."

"Everybody knows that Eskimos accept death with serenity!" the pope interrupted. "But I'd very much like to know why no papal envoy was sent over. Do we want the natives to remain miscreants? And whatever happened to the project for a sanctuary?"

"Enough with all this mysticism!" Pyk broke in. "The only question is whether we are going to send TV up there or not; the rest is smoke—speaking of which, I'd like to remind you that I smoke—"

"Bullshit!" Von Ofen yelled. "First of all, we must send a military contingent!"

"No need for it," Pyk said. "Phildys's robots are already there. Twenty robot-soldiers, remote-controlled and with nuclear weapons. I have proof! You can't fool me! Camel's what I smoke!"

A gasp of outrage rose from the assembly. The Austrian representative removed one of his ski boots and started banging it on the table. "My party demands the remote control of at least five robots!"

"England is indignant!"

"Switzerland vomits with disgust!"

"France asks for the resignation of the government as inadequate to carry out a proper underwater policy."

"The Mediterranean communist party is very much concerned about whether, in your answer to the question regarding the South American mines, the phrase 'let those Indians croak' expresses the government's intention to ignore the problem."

"Gentlemen!" the Swiss representative yelled. "I have an urgent communiqué that might well succeed in reconciling all the contrasting views expressed by the assembly!"

Expectant silence fell on the hall.

"Pizza is served!"

With a howl of joy, everybody rushed from the room.

INUIT: THE PEOPLE

* * *

"Can you hear the lovely silence?" Einstein said. The snow was falling thick on the mountain slope.

"I can't hear anything," Fang said.

"It's pleasant, now and then, to walk away from the racket of those computers," the boy said, gathering a fistful of snow, obviously tempted to press it into a ball. "Of course," he promptly added, "this silence can be explained scientifically. When the flakes first lie lightly on the ground, they absorb all sound, like insulating panels."

"Of course," Fang said.

"As soon as they settle into a more or less compact layer," Einstein continued, "noise absorption decreases." Seeing that Fang had momentarily turned away, he quickly pressed the snow into a ball and threw it.

"Nice shot," Fang said, without turning.

"Don't tell me you can see with the back of your head, too!" Einstein said, miffed.

"I heard the noise."

"Are you like those Eskimos who can recognize each other from the noise of their footsteps on ice? Or do you possess a sixth or seventh sense, like lovers and bats? Well, nothing strange there; vision is no longer really necessary. Today, almost all the new scientific theories are first thought and then 'seen' in a laboratory. As we used to say at the computer center, To see is to *recognize*."

Fang stopped for a while to catch his breath. They had reached the end of their climb; from that point on, the path snaked down to the Indian village, a circle of red shacks and igloos half buried in the snow.

"Do you think," Einstein asked, "there is anything we can do to convince those Indians, or Comanches, or Eskimongols, or whatever they are, to dig for us?"

"I don't think so. To them, those places are *huaca*, sacred, which means that they are invested with all sorts of powers and taboos that we know nothing about."

"Oh, what crap! And you still defend their culture?"

"We're not any different. We hold numberless scientific truths as *huaca*—at least till someone comes along and shows us they are all wrong."

"I think I'm beginning to understand you." Einstein stopped, and, still panting, folded his arms over his chest. "You don't care about discoveries as such, but you love to see them demystified. You are happy when Euclidean geometry blows up, and quantum theory staggers, and Darwin is knocked out cold. The universe bows under the weight of gravity, particles tremble beneath our ruthless scrutiny—and you cheer!"

"I am grateful for any discovery that has helped man. But when a discovery endures only because its collapse would force the power of science into a crisis, then I welcome the crisis. You see, Einstein, theories go through youth, old age, and death, just like the great men who thought them up. They either die out or leave a strong trace behind. I can't possibly condone a science that doesn't accept these premises, and prefers to find its truth in projections about industrial development or in gauging the increasing power of weapons."

"Because you are somewhat of a defeatist."

"So were Galileo, Lamarck, Darwin, Newton, and your own illustrious namesake."

"This is amazing! First you cite Democritus and Chuang Tzu, and now Galileo. I'm surprised you haven't yet mentioned Mao Tse-tung."

"That's true, my dear Einstein, I hadn't thought of him!"

"Me and my big mouth!" the boy groaned. "I had promised myself I'd never discuss these things with you again!" And, to give vent to his frustration, he started bombarding the valley with snowballs, and kept on all the way to the village. The people they met on the path greeted them, and children laughed at Einstein's hugely padded snowsuit. A young woman with black hair and olive skin walked toward them. She was wearing the black-and-white bowler hat of the Quechua Indians. They followed her to a square of sorts where a bunch of kids were playing a strange game that consisted of jumping across a drawing made with whole or broken lines.

A young Indian girl, an Eskimo, and two Indian boys, one of whom was jumping across the drawing, were singing:

> One, two, three, four—
> where were you born?
> on an oak tree I was born.
> Five, six, seven, eight—
> I flew far away,
> where goldtooth Pedro de Navay
> I became, I became.
> I, errh, san, ssu
> ui hermano, oiga—
> who burned the house
> of the sparrow grouse?
> cross the lake, the fire, the wind.
> Cross, lake, fire, wind—
> Eight, seven, six, five—
> maybe, maybe you'll arrive.

The little Indian danced out the last part of his singsong while looking at Fang, who seemed very preoccupied as he mechanically entered the woman's hut. The floor of the hut was made of ancient stone, and its walls were honeycombed with niches for provisions. The Indians knew how to keep food for years, using a method they had inherited from the Incas.

The woman invited them to sit on the floor, and then seated herself in the middle of three men, two squat Indians in brightly colored clothes, and a smiling Eskimo.

Einstein stared at the woman's face as if he were bewitched.

"My name is Coya," she said, "and I'm the village elder's daughter. Do you have something to tell us?"

"Yes, well," Einstein began. "We . . . the Federation is . . . quite baffled by your refusal to go on working . . . We can't understand it."

Coya lowered her voice and consulted with one of the three men. "My brother, Catuilla, works down there and says, 'Too dangerous. Too many dead. We are too close to the Earth's heart.' "

Einstein perked up his ears. "To what?"

"An Inca story," Coya explained, "says that whoever approaches those sites with evil designs will wound the heart of the Earth, and one hundred thousand soldiers of the sun will come out, and their scream will rise all the way to *coyllur*, the stars."

"Did you hear, Fang?" Einstein asked, lowering his voice. "One hundred thousand soldiers! What do you think it means?"

"You insist that no one can approach those places with evil intentions," Fang said to them. "But you surely don't have any evil intention."

"No, *we* don't," the Eskimo said. "But what about you?"

Einstein protested. "But . . . friends! We are here to give you work—and we have already given you food, clothes, heat . . ."

"Well, then," Coya said, "if that is the case, if you are indeed our friends, will you remain so, even if we stop working?"

Einstein did not answer. The Indian with the darker face then spoke.

"My name is Aucayoc, and I have known several white men. They came wearing masks of peace, they signed treaties and made promises. Then they betrayed and killed us. We don't know who you are, but we know that what you really want is under the Temple of the Sun. And when you want something badly, nothing can stop you. That, for us, is an evil design."

Vexed, Einstein looked at Fang. "Have you lost your tongue?" he whispered. "Or do you think they're right? You know, at this point I should really tell them that we have other ways of convincing them to work."

"But you won't do it," Fang said. "Instead, you'll go outside and play with the kids."

Einstein looked at Fang as if he had lost his mind. "Oh, go to hell," he said and left the hut.

"Where goes little chatterbox *cachorro*?" Catuilla asked.

"He's gone to play," Fang said.

Catuilla smiled at Fang, picked up a bowl full of flour, and pointed at the fire.

"Yes," Fang said, "I'd love to have a bite."

"It's *chuño*, potato flour. Do you know it?"

"I've read about it," Fang answered.

"What one eats in books tastes of old paper," Nanki laughed.

"You can't learn much about people in books," Coya said. "While my brothers cook, I'll tell you the story of the Fat Beavers. It is a Northern legend I heard from a very old Indian chief a long time ago."

The Fat Beavers

Once upon a time, in the Northern region of the Great Lakes, there was an Indian tribe known as the Fat Beavers. Their chief was Eagle Drumstick, and his wife Paunchy Otter. They were plump, merry Indians and they lived happily by the blue, limpid waters of Lake Chanawatasaskawantenderoga, which, in Beaver dialect, means "no added coloring."

One really bad day, a bunch of white men came to the banks of the blue lake. They were Mr. Joe Typhoon, of Typhoon Railroads, Inc., and his consultants. They were building a railroad that would lead from New Orleans into the heart of the Great Lakes region for trading purposes. The wood of the Northern forests would stoke the stoves and boilers of the South, while New Orleans's ashes and garbage would come to fertilize the lakes. Mr. Typhoon introduced himself to the Fat Beavers and offered loads of presents—cases of aquavita, porno magazines, underwater watches, and Armani sweaters. He knew well how appealing those things were to Indians and how, in a short time, all that wealth would corrupt their honest nature and lead them to extinction. Mr. Typhoon told Chief Drumstick that his men would cut a path through the forest to build a road for the Iron Horse; in exchange for this, the Fat Beavers would receive many more presents.

The Big Chief listened to him and then spoke. "Paleface speaks with tongue like railroad switch, changing tracks all the time. Wherever your road passes, trees fall like autumn leaves, and Indians die. Iron Horse spits clouds of smoke which interferes with our communication network. If you fell one single tree, we shall send our beavers to gnaw on your men. Take your presents back. Timeo Yankees et dona ferentes. Ugh!"

Typhoon left empty-handed and in a huff. As he was thus storming out of the village, Obese Salmon, the witch doctor, a man well-known for his greed, approached him.

"White man," he said, "I much like your magazines, your firewater, your casual fashion. You listen to me! Big tree doesn't fall with big knock, but with many little knocks! By and by we shall knock down Fat Beavers. You give me presents; I corrupt and make extinct. Stop."

"It's a deal, Obese Salmon," Typhoon said. "We'll be partners. You shall have all the firewater you want."

"Me happy with three percent shares of your railroad," the Indian answered.

This is how the destruction of the Fat Beavers was first planned. To begin with, Obese Salmon opened a boutique in the middle of the village. After a short while, the traditional costumes of the Beavers disappeared. The women traipsed about in the snow wearing miniskirts and sequined T-shirts, while the men sported gym shorts and sweatshirts with the logo of the Dallas Cowboys. But they were still as fat and healthy as before, and thought themselves very chic.

"The cold does not scare us," Paunchy Otter used to say. "We have changed our garb, but the Great Light keeps us warm!"

One month later, Typhoon summoned the witch doctor.

"My dear Salmon," Typhoon told him, "I have spent a fortune in clothes, and the Beavers are plumper and jollier than ever! Indian tribes are floundering all over the place. The Nez Percé are congested with colds, the Seminoles are going to seed with too much Kahlua, the Mohicans are gasping for breath. How is it that the Beavers are so inured to cold?"

"Changing costumes and shortening hems is not enough," the witch doctor said, "because the Great Light gives them warmth. But no sweat. When the people lose their god, everything collapses! You bring me stuff on enclosed list. Stop."

Typhoon did as he was asked, and a few days later Obese Salmon convened his tribe and showed up wearing a white tuxedo embroidered in gold, and carrying a guitar slung across his shoulders. He said he had had a dream. Manitou had appeared to him, rowing a canoe in the company of a young white man with a sausage curl. "I am old and tired," Manitou had told him in his dream. "I am going to retire to the Great Prairies of Heaven, on a large ranch, with a big squaw [he had used a different term]. This is your new god, his name is Elvis the Pelvis, and you will worship him under the sacred name of Shaka-rockawa, the man-who-sings-and-shakes-it, and you will invoke him by the name of Bebopalula. But, please, no more prayers for me. Adore him, buy his records, dance —and above all, do not work. I have spoken. Ugh! Yeah, man!"

Having said this, the witch doctor began strumming a weird tune, and all the Indians got to dancing like crazy, including Chief Drumstick, who grabbed his wife and twirled her three times in the air, wounding a number of people in the process.

"We can dance the whole night through," the Great Chief said, "and forget about Manitou, and not work . . . no more, no more, no more . . . The great Light will give us strength!"

A month later, Typhoon again summoned the witch doctor.

"You quack!" he addressed him angrily. "What's the deal? I've been waiting four months now! All the other Great Lakes tribes are dead and gone, swept away by alcohol, fights, heart attacks, and identity crises. Only the Fat Beavers are still thriving. They sing and dance, and don't give a thought to extinction!"

"Impatient white man," the witch doctor said, "the Great Light gives them strength. We have already wiped out their religion and their customs. Now, all we have left to do is destroy their ecosystem."

"Their eco—what?" Typhoon asked.

"Ecosystem. It's a magic Indian word," the witch doctor explained, "which means 'great sphere of life-water-sky-earth.' Once the lake and the wood go, so will the Fat Beavers."

The following month, Typhoon's fury ravaged the land of the Beavers. First, he polluted the lake with an oil slick. All the salmon turned black and died, singing heart-rending spirituals. Then, he turned to the forest and set it on fire. All the animal beavers were left without work and had to emigrate to the Montreal woodlots. The elks

fled. Most of them were killed by hunters; the others fled
farther, till the last one was shot by a drunken poacher in
a Chicago motel where it had checked in under the assumed identity of Wildelk Mitchum, dentist. The Fat
Beavers' village was now surrounded by a dismal waste
where, every night, Typhoon unloaded barrels of bacilli
and cholera vibrios, scattered tapeworms and leeches,
sprayed syphilis, and coated cats with lice.

"The white man is a creep," Eagle Drumstick told his
people. "He has stolen our lake and the wood. But the
Great Light protects us and will preserve us from hunger
and disease."

Two months later, the Beavers were as fat and merry
as ever, even though their land was entirely depleted.
They had replanted a few trees, sent a cable to a group of
beavers begging them to come back, and they had dug out
an artificial stream over which they canoed and fished
imported goldfish. They sang, smoked their calumet, and
were happy.

"You rotten fish!" Typhoon again attacked the witch
doctor. "How do you explain that north of here, over a
thousand-kilometer range, there are only three Indians
left, and all on the critical list at the Ottawa hospital—
while the Fat Beavers are fatter than ever!"

"Oh, pestiferous white man," Salmon said, "we have
only one last weapon against the Great Light: Black
Death."

"Meaning?"

"Canned chocolate syrup! Nothing can resist it! Nothing can survive it—teeth, livers, stomachs—everything
collapses under the black, gooey tide!"

"Ok. You'll have your chocolate," Typhoon said, "a
ton of it. But remember, this is your last chance!"

Typhoon waited three long days, and on the fourth, he
heard a chorus of mournful wails coming from the Indian
camp. "I've succeeded!" he yelled triumphantly, and ran

over with a heart full of hope. This vanished, however, as soon as he realized that the Beavers were mourning Obese Salmon. He had been found dead that night, buried under sixty cans of chocolate syrup. Typhoon tore his hair out with rage, and turned for advice to a firm named Bill that specialized in Indian exterminations. At first, they were also perplexed. No Indian tribe was known to have survived a total obliteration of their customs, religion, and environment. Clearly, this "Great Light" referred to an extraordinary spiritual power. If that was indeed the case, the only solution was the firing squad.

"Never!" Typhoon said. "In my whole career, I have never shot an Indian. I have always killed them with progress. I shall never resort to outright murder!"

"As you please," the people at Bill said.

Typhoon thought about it for a couple of nights. Then one morning, as he was leaving the village to take a walk, he met a young Indian who was hoeing the bare earth with great care. As soon as he was finished, he bowed three times.

"What are you doing?" Typhoon asked him.

"I greet and honor the Great Light," the young man said.

Suddenly, Typhoon got a strange notion. He waited for the Indian to go, and then began to dig up the field. And, do you know what he found? A potato! A *potato!* That was the Great Light that kept the Fat Beavers fat, warmed them up in the cold, gave them energy in their dancing, and fed them when everything on their land had been destroyed, because the potato grows *underground!* Their treasure was a carbohydrate, and not some impalpable spiritual power!

The following day, the evil Typhoon showed up in front of Chief Drumstick with a contrite face.

"Great Chief," he said, "I must apologize. I tried to exterminate your tribe, but now I have finally understood that you are a good nation, endowed with Great Light. So, I humbly beg you to please forgive me, and to allow me to also profit from the Great Light."

"How?" Chief Drumstick asked.

"Easy," Typhoon said. "Soon, thousands of people will be traveling on this railroad—fishermen, picnicking families, skiers, and golddiggers. Just think how wonderful it would be if they could also get to know the Great Light while they are traveling North!"

Chief Eagle Drumstick's face brightened up.

Exactly one year later, when the railroad was finished and the train stopped at the station of Fatbeavertown, two hundred Indians, wearing white uniforms and caps advertising "BEAVER CHIPS," would be waiting for the travelers while the smell of fried food wafted through wood and vale. In the station's cafeteria, Great Chief Drumstick and his missus, both wearing chef's hats, served potato pies, potato dumplings and, of course, french fries. Soon, they opened up a plant and put their Beaver Chips on the market. A few years later, only eighty-six Indians were left out of five thousand, and the fattest weighed sixty kilos. Their great chief made them work sixteen hours a day in the fields and in the plant. Half of them died, poisoned by preservatives, and the others were accidentally fried to death. Soon the area was so polluted that it could no longer produce a single potato. Chief Drumstick and Paunchy Otter died in a car accident, which also claimed the life of their yellow Ferrari, as they were returning from a dinner at the Quebec Rotary Club.

The last Fat Beaver, Wrecked Deer, went on selling lunch bags at the Fatbeavertown station till he was ninety-six. Blind as a bat, he would often be found in the middle of the tracks screaming "beaver chips, beaver chips," thinking he was still on the platform. On one of these occasions, he was hit by the Winnipeg Express, which zoomed through the station punctually at 8:40 every morning. His last words were, "I had been told that one day I would also join my people in Manitou's Great Prairies, but nobody ever told me I'd get there by train."

And this is how the Fat Beavers died out.

"So," Fang noted, "the Great Light was only a small potato!"

"You go wild over our great temples, and spend centuries studying them," Coya said. "But nobody ever thinks of the corn pot, or of the toil of the llama, or of the labors of men. A man died as he was painting a blue flower on the ceiling of the Temple of the Sun. He was immediately replaced by another man, and today nobody is aware of that little blue flower, half-hidden among all the drawings on the ceiling.'

"When I saw these stones," Fang said, "I thought of the Great Wall, one of the most important structures in my country. It is two thousand kilometers long, and it was built by the emperor Shih Huang-ti. His enemies maintained that each of its stones had caused the death of one man. Apparently the bones of the dead were mixed with the mortar that held the stones together."

"You must never forget that," Coya said. "Maybe, in looking at our stones, you'll find what you are seeking."

Fang bowed and walked out. It was no longer snowing. In the little square, he saw Einstein playing with the other kids, jumping up and down, his legs wide apart like a klutzy bird.

"Hey," he said as soon as he saw the Chinese, "that was quite a trick! Pushing me out to play childish games to gain the confidence of those people!"

Fang walked on. At the outskirts of the village, he again heard Einstein's shrill voice, along with that of the other children.

"Little Ling," he thought, "is a child again!"

○ ○

THE WHITE CITY—HOW, WITH ROBOTIC SHREWDNESS, LeO ACCOMPLISHED HIS MISSION

○ ○ ○

"Vat si, achtung!" ordered the policeman on watch at the entrance to the White City, Meskorska's hospital area. "Wo du, dvarf?"

"Medical tai doctorobot," LeO said, displaying his knowledge of space slang.

The policeman looked him over suspiciously. Despite the stethoscope that dangled over his chest, LeO did not look like a head physician.

"Uat spezialitaten tai medicinsk?" the policeman inquired.

"Hmmmm . . . liverist robodoctor, foiè, higado, leber, fegato!"

"Only liverist?" the cop pressed him.

"Omnibus internis giblets expertus. Sed spezialist liverist."

"Den vu visit me," the policeman said, uncovering his hairy belly.

LeO placed the main tube of his stethoscope onto the cop's stomach. It was a very sophisticated instrument, provided with X rays, so that LeO enjoyed a full view of military guts.

"Hmmm," he declared after a few moments. "Inauspicious diagnosis. Ill!"

"Keske ill?" the policeman inquired, a little worried.

"Liverus tuus non mictum retine, quoad macroblastos glicemicus dixit katz index et Takata Dohamoto, deinde massiva nasalis emottitis in pavimentum ubique versata, non exitus tibi dabit illico er immediate, sed avoidandum butirrum intingulaque colesterolum ferentes ut sis nocte levis, sis tibi coena brevis! Eucrasia!"

"Vas?" the policeman asked, growing paler by the second. "No comprios!"

"Naturalis! aknavish speechsleeps in a foolsear! Tu liver kapputt! Diet! Pa liao no more drunk, no more drugs, no more krafen: y laugh! Compri?"

"Ies, Doctor Tai," the policeman said, awed by such an extensive diagnosis. "Zankiou, Doctor: vas, vas!"

So, with Sara safely hidden in his ear, LeO entered the White City. He walked through the pranotherapy clinic and the transplant laboratories, resounding with the screams of reticent donors. He skirted the witchcraft clinic, whose interns and nurses wore horned viking helmets, and proceeded into the psychiatric ward that specialized in lobotomies and genetic cocktails. These were the so-called "Hope 2" zones; that is to say, they had a fifty-percent survival rate. After this, LeO crossed "Hope 1," the hospital wing devoted to space diseases with minimal chances of recovery, and peered through the black glass partition that enclosed the COD (Corpse on Delivery) area. A long shudder traversed him from top to toe as he noticed the slides that carried terminal patients directly into the central incinerator.

Inside the elevator, he found a sign that read: BEFORE GOING UP, YOU MIGHT WANT TO MAKE SURE THAT YOUR RELATIVE HASN'T ALREADY BEEN DISCHARGED. IF THAT IS THE CASE, YOU CAN PICK UP THE ASHBOX FROM THE SLOT MACHINE AT THE ENTRANCE.

The robot hurried through the overcrowded industrial-accidents ward. It was well known that half of Meskorska's workers did not make it past their third year on the planet. They were repeatedly hospitalized, and their limbs were often replaced; but in the end, they were stamped NLR (no longer recyclable) and sent to "Hope 0." This sad state of affairs had been protested only once, in 2068. A whole sector of Meskorskan workers had gone on strike and called a demonstration. They were allowed to use one of the most central squares, Platform 1. But, as soon as the strikers were assembled, the ground was literally cut from under their feet. The square was in fact a trap specifically planned by Meskorskan architects to prevent riots. Fifty thousand strikers were dropped into space, and the government declared that the demonstration had been "dissolved." The unions stated that, nevertheless, they had substantially achieved their goals—but then, again, the Meskorskan union leadership now consisted of a mere three robots.

∘ Charos ∘

LeO entered a room full of TV monitors, arranged in an inverted V, like the prow of a ship, so that the "helmsman," the man in the center of the room, could control them all at the same time. He was wearing a black smock and mirror glasses, and his hair was slicked back with brilliantine. A luminous line pulsated on each screen.

"Pardon," LeO said, "man Geber?"

"You may speak Eurosinic," the man said, looking LeO over, "I'm Greek. I'm Doctor Charos."

"I would like to see Mr. Geber," LeO said. "Is it possible?"

"I'm afraid not," the man answered. "He was in the Charopalevi ward till a few minutes ago, but he has just been transferred to the Nirvana ward."

"What does that mean?" the robot inquired.

"Let me explain. You and I are in the middle of the Charopalevi sector. Its inmates are fighting off death, but still retain a few vital signs—the lines you see on those monitors. The moment the line starts pulsating, it means that Atropos, our computer, has calculated that the patient in question has less than six hours of life left in him. This is when he is transferred to Nirvana, a special ward where he can bask in the latest comforts . . . and I don't mean 'latest' only in the sense of 'most modern,' you understand. There, a 'moriturus' can be connected with all his relatives via cable TV, watch a videocassette from 'My Whole Life in a Split-Second,' listen to music, enjoy the best international cuisine, stuff himself with analgesic drugs, have a polysectarian priestrobot hear his confession and a polyglot legal consultant make out his will, and, last but not least, just by pushing a button he can choose whether he will be buried, cremated, frozen in liquid nitrogen, embalmed, freeze-dried, or processed some other, fancier, way. Just this morning, one of them told me he wanted to be shot into space dressed like Batman."

"And Mr. Geber has already been . . . Nirvanized?" LeO asked.

"Yes. His energy line has been red for three hours now, which means that he has only got one hour left. He is lucid enough to speak, but I cannot let you in. Only the closest relatives are admitted into Nirvana and you, for obvious—how shall I say—genetic reasons, cannot be a relative."

"I was his typewriter!" LeO said. "I followed him all over space! Please . . ."

"Sorry, no way." Charos went back to reading the sports section of the newspaper. LeO noticed the date—one month ago.

"What did you think of the last game of the World Soccer Championship?" the little robot shrewdly tossed out. "Wasn't that something?"

Charos perked up his ears. "You know who won?"

"Of course I do. On our ship we have a parsec radio, and every Sunday I tune into some Earth station."

"Really?" Charos lowered his voice. "You know, here on Meskorska we are not allowed to follow the championship series. Our government is afraid it might make us homesick."

"Too bad," LeO noted nonchalantly. "It was a great game."

Charos looked at him with yearning. "If you tell me how it went, I'll let you visit Nirvana for five minutes."

"Forty-five minutes."

"OK, but then you must give me a real play-by-play account," Charos begged him, shaking like a leaf. "Good God, I'm so excited! It's going to be like watching a whole game in a few seconds."

"So, here we go, ladies and gentlemen—" LeO began.

"No, no—wait—I shall sit here, and you there, with your head in front of that screen. Pretend you are a sportscaster. God, it's so exciting—a real heart attack!"

"All right, then, here we go," LeO intoned again. "Ladies and gentlemen, welcome to the final game of the World Soccer Championship. We shall start today's broadcast with a brief wrap-up of the playoffs. As you know, the four teams in the semifinals were the Berlin Angriff, the Peking Yellow Turbans, the Liverpool Spinsters and—"

Charos jumped to his feet, holding his breath.

"—and the Mediterranean Youths!"

Charos threw a handful of pill bottles into the air, screaming, "They made it! My team made it! Kalosartipos, my idol! I can't believe it!"

"The Greek forward Kalosartipos shone on the field as he scored the goal that earned the Youths a well-deserved victory over the Chinese in the first game of the playoffs. The score was two to one."

"Oh, my God!" Charos groaned, clutching his chest. "This means we made it to the finals!"

"In the final game of the championship, the Mediterranean Youths will face the Berlin Angriff, who defeated their English opponents by three goals, all scored by their forward Van Merode."

"That fucking kraut! That bionic jerk!"

"The Mediterranean coach, Dino Zoff, is now faced with the problem of how to control the powerful German—who, as you all know, has steel joints in his ankles, knees, and elbows, which give him extraordinary power and uncommon resistance. Nevertheless, Zoff, that old fox, engineers a masterful move. He plays the Youth's nastiest fullback, Leo Mastino (known as the 'llama' because of his dirty playing and his habit of spitting in the face of his opponents) against Van Merode. And, indeed, Mastino starts spitting the moment he sets foot on the field—not in the face of the German, however, but on his metallic joints—with the result that, after only half an hour, the poor kraut can hardly move because of the rust. Mastino's salivary capacity seems inexhaustible. The German is completely stymied, despite all the lubricants they administer to him on the bench."

"Keep it up, Mastino! Keep it up!"

"At this point, the Youth, spurred on by three hundred thousand fans, start attacking, but Rossi IV misses a wonderful opportunity."

"I knew it!" Charos yelled. "Rossi always fucks up at the most critical moments. They've got to replace him! Put in Kalosartipos! *We want Ka-lo-sar-ti-pos!*"

"In the second period, Caboto runs in from the right, crosses to center—with a high leap, Cotugno heads the ball—but it hits the post!"

"Those motherfuckers!" Charos yelled, beside himself, mindlessly banging the buttons of the control panel in front of him, causing the Charopalevi patients a few premature death rattles. "You stink! How the hell could you miss that goal!"

"At the eighty-sixth minute, Kalosartipos replaces Rossi IV."

"Atta boy, Zoff! It's about time! Now that we've lost, he makes the right move, that jerk!"

"The game is about to end and the score is still tied at zero. At this point, we want to remind our viewers that a tie would automatically grant the Championship to the Angriff, given their higher score average . . . but here goes Kalosartipos . . . he looks hot . . . he intercepts the ball in centerfield . . . moves up . . . fakes out Bauer . . . he's alone in front of the goalie . . . he's dribbling beautifully . . . Stirner tackles him . . . he trips him . . . Kalosartipos falls and loses the ball! Kalosartipos is down; the referee whistles!"

"Penalty kick!" shouts Charos, jumping on his chair. "They deserve a penalty kick! I know! I saw the foul! It was obvious! That idiot ref—"

"The referee points to the penalty line. The Mediterranean Youth get a penalty kick."

Charos began pacing the room, grinding his teeth, pale as a corpse.

"The stadium is perfectly silent," LeO said. "This shot may well mean the championship. Here's Kalosartipos . . . he starts running . . . he kicks the ball. Goal! Youth, one—Angriff, zero!"

"Goal!" Charos whooped, suddenly turning bright red. "Goal! We're the champions!" And he collapsed onto the floor.

"The referee blows the whistle," LeO went on. "The spectators are mobbing Kalosartipos . . . they're lifting him triumphantly in the air . . . Kalosartipos wa—Doctor Charos, what's the matter?"

The doctor was lying supine on the floor, with a blissful expression on his face.

"This is the greatest . . . joy . . . of my life," Charos faltered, breathing his last.

LeO didn't even have the time to tell him he had invented the whole thing. On second thought, however, maybe it was better that way.

○ Geber ○

LeO stood in front of Geber's bed. The journalist, an IV needle stuck into his arm and the tube of a whiskey dispenser dangling by his mouth, seemed to be dozing. The radio on his bedstead was playing "Let It Be." Plump white nuns were gliding up and down the ward on their roller skates.

Geber opened his eyes and saw the robot. He smiled and exclaimed, "THE LAST MOMENTS OF THE GREAT GEBER! TOLD BY A ROBOT."

LeO was puzzled. A nun skating by whispered, "Don't mind

him. He's been delirious for two days now. He only speaks in headlines. If you want to communicate with him, you'll have to talk the same way, or he won't answer you."

LeO looked at Geber's pale, feverish face and tried to comfort him. "PLUCKY GEBER FIGHTS AGAINST DEATH."

Geber shook his head and answered, "NO HOPE FOR GEBER! EXCLUSIVE INTERVIEW WITH HEAD PHYSICIAN DR. TUBES."

"WHAT'S THE MYSTERIOUS DISEASE THAT'S EATING AWAY AT GEBER?" LeO asked.

"THE WHOLE TRUTH ABOUT JOURNALIST GEBER'S END," was the answer he got.

"*Dateline: Meskorska. From our special correspondent. Geber was not killed by a mysterious disease. The journalist, one of the most respected pens of our time, was poisoned by his boss after he had discovered the graves of seven thousand 'desaparecidos' on the planet Mellonta.* NO. THAT'S A LIE! No! Those are subversive LIES!" Geber started shaking all over.

"I repeat:

"THE WHOLE TRUTH ABOUT JOURNALIST GEBER'S END.

"*Dateline: Meskorska. From our special correspondent. The rumors hinting that the famous journalist Geber might have been poisoned are rapidly being dispelled. The rumors, spread by the opposition, have been clarified by the Head Physician of Meskorska Hospital, the eminent Doctor Tubes, luminary emeritus,* COUSIN OF SECRETARY OF STATE PTOLMAY, OWNER OF NUMEROUS GAMBLING HOUSES AND MORPHINE DEALER—No! Cut! Cut the last lines! Scratch the whole piece!"

Geber was writhing in his bed. A nun skated over in great haste and gave him an injection to calm him down. "Poor man," she noted. "He's totally schizoid. Can you hear him? He's speaking in two different voices."

Geber was panting and tossing in his bed. "Help! The crocodile! The boss's crocodile! It's gonna eat me! It's already opening its mouth and—it speaks—exemplary colleague—help! A model professional career—always giving his all, always—helpful. Nooooo! I can see it! The crocodile on third page!

"GEBER'S LESSON."

LeO hesitated, then broached the crucial subject, "DID GEBER KNOW VAN CRAM'S SECRET?"

Suddenly, Geber's eyes became very attentive. In a thin, practically inaudible voice, he said, *"Exclusive from Geber:* MONTHS OF VIOLENCE AND HARDSHIP ON VAN CRAM'S SHIP."

LeO whispered in his ear, "THE BOOJUMS' MAP: AN UNSOLVED MYSTERY.

"Flash: The famous Boojum brothers' map may prove decisive in the race to Terra. If the Sinoeuropeans can recover it, they will be able to maintain their advantage over their enemies."

Gathering all the strength he had left, Geber croaked, "I HAVE SEEN THE BOOJUM MAP!

"Dateline: Meskorska. From our special correspondent. I have seen the Boojum map. It is on Mellonta, on the snake-man's foot. Who is the snakeman? you may well wonder. Well—

"EXTRA! EXTRA! GREAT GEBER'S SUDDEN DEATH."

And with that, Geber's head dropped on his chest. LeO couldn't ask him any more questions. Extraordinarily excited, he rushed out of the ward. What he had learned was of the utmost importance, and he couldn't let anyone else get hold of it. As he was speeding through the last ward, he heard Sara buzz something in his ear. Turning, he was surprised to see one of the terminal patients rise out of bed, followed by another. He barely had time to see their threatening faces before he was enveloped by a sheet and could see no more.

♈ ○ ♉ ♈ ⊕ ♉ ♈ ○ ⊕ ♉ ♈ ⊕ ♉ ♈ ♈ ⊕ ♉ ♈ ⊕ ○ ♉ ♈ ⊕ ♉ ♈

CALALBAKRAB: A CONSPIRACY IN SPACE— WHO HATES THE KING?

△ ▽ △

"He's being tortured," Alya said, triumphantly. "O Great Te-mugin, O Terror of the Skies, the great day is getting closer. This robot may just give us the key to that planet."

"I doubt it, Alya," al-Dabih the soothsayer responded. "We are very far away, and our path is still paved with mys-teries."

The Great Scorpion approached them. In one hand he was carrying a precious jar, and in the other, two slender goblets.

"Whom shall I believe, then?" he asked, filling the glasses. "The optimist Alya, who flatters me and makes me believe that he lives only by my light and will always be loyal to me? Or the obscure al-Dabih, who serves me without loving me, who advises me but does not respect me, and who follows me only because I am the strongest? Alas, the king cannot rest quietly because he knows that a traitor is always near him. It may be the magician, or the fool, or his best friend, or his rival the duke, or his favorite mistress, or his very own mother. Who's going to betray me? Who's going to seek revenge on me? The good Rigoletto or the sullen Rasputin? The placid eunuch Ch'en Kuo? Or Gano, or maybe Hop-Frog, or An Lushan? Or maybe Almagro? Grandeur is always surrounded by a thou-sand traitors and one loyal servant. Very few Goebbelses, and many Görings."

"Your Majesty," Alya protested, "how can you possibly be-lieve that I might betray you? Why would I do such a despica-ble thing?"

"For a thousand reasons," the king smiled. "You are ambi-tious. You have often complained about your lot on Earth. And you are full of vices."

"Trifles, Your Majesty, mere bad habits."

"You are cruel," the king continued, "and a liar. Your favorite dish is hummingbird stew. When I had my cat Xerxes shot for that terrible murder, which ended the race of those birds on our Earth, I already suspected that the incriminating feathers we found on his snout had been put there by you."

"That's absolutely untrue, Your Majesty!" Alya grew awfully pale. "How can you possibly believe—"

"I can believe anything," the king said. "I can even believe that it was you who planted the bomb in the Assembly Room, and assassinated our telepath. Indeed, you might well be the leader of this entire conspiracy."

"Your Majesty," Alya said, bowing, "I'm ready to do anything to prove my loyalty."

"That's exactly what I want you to do," the king said, handing him one of the goblets. "Drink! One of the two glasses is poisoned. I know one of you is a traitor. But if your conscience is clear, Alya, you may drink without fear. I want you to do the same, al-Dabih."

The soothsayer looked the king straight in the eye and slowly drank up all the wine in his cup. Alya, in contrast, held his goblet with a trembling hand.

"What's this?" the king asked. "Why don't you drink? Is your loyalty already wavering?"

"But—if al-Dabih's wine was not poisoned . . . since he's still alive—then mine is . . . Your Majesty—I—I" Alya stuttered. "Please, forgive me!"

"What for?" the king roared, pointing his sword at Alya's throat.

"I don't know . . . for anything you want, but, please, forgive me," the counselor implored, throwing himself at the Scorpion's feet. The king pushed him away with a kick.

"Guards!" he shouted. "Take him away! Torture him! Make him confess—anything at all—provided it's enough to condemn him to death! And kill his secretary as well! And the soldiers who were on duty when the bomb exploded! Woe to anyone who betrays the Scorpion!"

When Alya's screams and appeals had died away in the vast

hallways, al-Akrab approached the soothsayer and pointed at the empty goblet. "So, al-Dabih," he said, "am I to believe that you are a loyal servant?"

"You know better than that, O King. I drank because I knew that if you wanted to see me dead, I might as well die immediately. How could I oppose your will?"

"So," al-Akrab hissed, "even now I can't be sure of your loyalty! Why, then, do you stay with me?"

"Because I hope to be able to put an end to your folly," the soothsayer answered. "Do you really believe that spreading terror throughout the ship and killing your subjects whenever you please is going to help you? You know Alya never conspired against you. You can kill all your counselors and break all the laws, but your fear will always remain with you. You can't lop its head off!"

"Soothsayer," the king said, "if you think my law is folly, then all laws are folly. In refusing to drink, Alya has committed a sin, the worst one a subject could commit: he has shown that he considers his life more important than that of his king. You, soothsayer, can find worlds in the universal void and worlds in a drop of steam, and you know what goes on behind men's closed eyes. But I instead must deal with this world, the real one—its lands, its riches, its weapons. There is no magic in any of this—only order. You can't possibly understand what power means! So, don't judge me, or you'll be sorry! I can be much more dangerous than any ill omen!"

"I'm not afraid of you," the soothsayer answered simply, again looking him straight in the eye.

Without even realizing it, King Akrab backed off a few steps. Then, anger gave him new strength. In a calm voice, he said, "Al-Dabih, you told me that nothing bad would happen to me until the sky fell to the earth—isn't that so?"

"That's what the prophecy said."

"Well, then," the king said, with a shrewd glimmer in his eye, "till that day, which is forever, you shall be my Prime

Minister. You shall have a palace and all the most precious
instruments you need to study the stars, and gold, lots of gold,
more than any of my counselors has ever had! What do you
say, soothsayer? Do you accept my offer?"

Al-Dabih did not seem surprised. He took a pen and wrote a
few numbers on a piece of paper. "Great Scorpion," he said,
showing the piece of paper to the king, "we Arabs invented
these numbers—the decimal system. But our greatest inven-
tion was *syfr. Syfr,* which then became *zephyrus,* and after
that, *zero.* It indicates the void, nothing. A terrifying number,
within whose circular sign the mind can lose itself. Well, you
know what a zero is: it is that number which, paradoxically,
allows any other number to be ten times larger than itself, and
eventually turns it into a reptilian monster—one billion, a
billion billion. These are the numbers used to measure your
wealth—whole lines of zeros, like caravans of camels laden
with gems and silks, following their master. The zero is your
most loyal servant. Your people amount to so many zeros behind your figure, and the same is true of your counselors. In
the great numeral of your glory, I might well be the second or
third zero, but I would still be nothing, a zero among zeros.
And this is not all. A zero is often followed by a period, and
then by other numbers. Well, whenever this happens, there is
no number, no matter how awesome, that will be able to evade
the zero's horizon. It can grow, array numbers like armies, but
it will always remain smaller than the smallest number, always less than one. So, you are running after absolute power.
But no matter how many ciphers, and numbers, and soldiers,
dead or alive, you may be able to muster behind you, before
you there will always be a zero—the mystery you cannot
grasp, a nature that's always greater than all your riches, and a
sky that never gets closer. And, beware! After the first zero
and the decimal point, there can be many other zeros, millions
of zeros; if, at the end, there is a number, then that number
shall exist. This is the world that does not belong to you, the

life that eludes you, the infinite smallness of your elusive freedom, the mystery of a complexity you shall never comprehend.

"Your humblest subject is such a number, coming after so many zeros. But he exists; he is alive. Some people admire the magnitude of numbers necessary to express the size of the universe and the distance of stars. But the scientist, as well as the common man, will also be awed by the numbers that pursue and find the smallest atomic particle, the eye of a bee, the cell. You despise the life that surrounds you—your subjects, nature, everything that lives in the remote land of zeros. You would like to erase it. You think that everything can be bought, that your numbers are large enough to encompass the world. But they are *syfr*, zephyr, nothing—the void. Universally speaking, the things you can buy amount to such an infinitesimally tiny amount that you should be ashamed of them. Don't glory in your wealth. Whether you compare it to the sky or to the smallest aspect of the infinite, it is *nothing*. Great Scorpion, hide your gold and close the book of numbers, for it spells disaster."

Sara's Tale
(Freely Translated from the Bee-ese)

LeO and I togezer entered white wallz ztranze zmellz LeO zayz medizine zmellz, yez, zen zee Geber man zeemz razer crazy and tellz ztory I all hear and zhall all refer to you but when we leave I try buzz LeO I zee behind uz ztranze men rize out of bedz, yez, but LeO no lizzen zo I tickle LeO'z ear and zay careful ztranze men behind uz and zey jump LeO, yez, and LeO fallz great clatter and he lazerz zem and I try help and zoom into man'z eye and zap him right but ozerz go bzz bzz wiz gunz hit LeO and wrap him in zheet and carry him away and I can do nozing but buzz buzz towarz zpazezhip and almozt crazh

againzt dizzy bug flying oppozite direkzion wiz clozed
eyez; yez, here I arrive and tell you all Geber'z zecret
witzh and znakeman but I very zad for LeO prizoner, yez,
had I had my zikzty frienz from hive wiz me we'd zting
men, yez, cover zem wiz big bumpz, yez, but all alone I
zuperfluouz like mozquito I zad, yez, for men often ztole
me flowerz and honey from hive but never frienz, yez,
man mozt filzy bloody and ztupid animal in entire ga-
lakzy I zure, yez, yez, yez.

CALALBAKRAB: HOW TO MUTINY
TO A ROCK BEAT
● ● ●

The Dzunum were rehearsing one of their biggest hits, "Baby,
You Never Expected Me," in the ship's recording studio. It was
such a catchy tune that even the most hard-bitten soldiers
were keeping time with their foot.

> I'm the guy who plays the sax in strip joints
> I'm the guy who talks to himself on sidewalks
> I'm the guy who sleeps wrapped in old newspapers
> I'm the guy who'll cross the street to die
> Under your brand new Chevrolet
> Baby, you never expected me . . .

"Turn that bass up, Vassiliboyd," Coyllur said. "It will
drown out our voices so their mikes won't be able to pick up
what we're saying. Come on, come in here with us. We're
talking strategy now, and we have to move fast because the

whole ship is terrified. Do we all agree on the plan? Including our last recruit?"

"I'd like to know more about the details," Vassiliboyd said.

"Are you already chickening out, pilot?" Alice said, pointing a razor-sharp record at his throat.

"Hey, kid, I was a Rebel before you were even born. But this is the first time I've ever had to take over a spaceship with two hundred soldiers. Do you think it's easy? Do you have a plan mapped out?"

"Listen, pilot," Laureen said. "Akrab wears a gem around his neck. If you place it under a light on the central computer, within three minutes its refraction will cause the two halves of the ship to separate. While that's happening, we'll take control of our half and let *al-Genubi* get lost in space. So, not only will we sabotage them, we'll also have a ship of our own. We'll be able to go scouting for a new place where we can all live in freedom and peace."

"Do you think most of the crew members are on your side?"

"More than you think," Coyllur said. "At least half the Amerussians and several Arabs."

"All right," Vassiliboyd said. "I'll pitch in to get my revenge against the man who killed my best friend. But it still strikes me as a little crazy. You plan to knock out all the soldiers on board for at least ten minutes, then get to King Akrab, steal his prism, and seize the ship. How do you think you're going to accomplish all this?"

"With music," Laureen answered.

"You've gotta be kidding!" the pilot said.

"You don't think we're up to it, do you?" Coyllur said. "Maybe you should know a couple of things. We're the ones who put the bomb in the Assembly Room. We wanted to piss off the king so that he'd start killing his guards and counselors —which he did—thereby arousing the fear and hatred of the entire crew."

"The two technicians responsible for the central computer are already on our side," Edith added, "and we got rid of their telepathic spy with a knife solo shortly after we took off. Do you still think this is only a half-baked plan?"

"As for how we'll lead our attack," Coyllur said, "have a look at this instrument. It's an Ultradivarious, an electronc violin. You might like to read up on its specifications."

Vassiliboyd took the manual with lively interest, and after a few moments, whistled with admiration.

"Girls," he said, "count me in. Dylaniev was right when he trusted you. I'm happy to take his place by your side. I'm sure His Majesty will go wild over this concert!"

● ● ● ● ● ● ● ● ● ● 🐀 🐀 ● ● ● ● ● ● ● ● ●

ABOARD THE *ZUIKAKU:* THE EXECUTION OF THE REBEL MICE
● ● ●

A dark, viscous liquid was bubbling in the tub. The condemned mice were lined up on a plank, blindfolded. The others stood in full formation below. Many were crying. Some had begun an ultrasonic chorus of "Gray's My Flag," inaudible to humans. Towering over them by some hundred and forty-five centimeters was General Yamamoto, in Great Butcher regalia, and next to him, ghostly pale, stood Harada.

"As the legitimate representative of the Samurai Empire and of its justice aboard this ship," Yamamoto began, "I am now implementing the sentence of death-by-cocacolation of the following soldiers: Cursor, Pause, GoSub, Degree, Radian, Beep On, Beep Off, and Log are to be executed for insubordination. Soldiers On, Input, Unlock, Status, Mem, Mids, Data, and Pi are to be executed for having failed, in the most cowardly

fashion, to neutralize an objective of great strategic importance, that is, the Sinoeuropean robot LeO. In the specific case
of soldier Pi, who caused the whole incident by disobeying the
order to behave like a mechanical mouse, the execution shall
occur not by drowning but by stillicide."

"Thi-sis-she-er-crue-lty," Unlock shouted. "Out-right-be-
stia-li-ty!"

"Silence," Yamamoto growled. "Proceed with the execution."

With the point of his sword, Harada pushed the first mouse
toward the edge of the plank. The poor creature resisted for a
while, and then fell in. The simmering cola fizzed and rapidly
devoured him. In a few seconds, all that was left of Cursor was
a tiny parboiled skeleton. A squeak of horror rose through the
ship. A mouse vomited. One by one, all the prisoners followed
their comrade into the vat. They all behaved with great dignity
—or humor: Beep Off, in a last display of wit, said, "No! Not-
co-ca-co-la-it-ma-kesme-burp," and then dove into the deadly
liquid with a double somersault.

Then it was Pi's turn. He climbed the scaffold, his chin high,
his whiskers stiff with proud defiance. He let himself be bound
to the torture pole, on top of which sat a Coca-Cola keg with
a faucet. The spigot was given a clockwise turn and the drops
began to fall, slowly trickling down onto Pi's head.

"You must all watch to the end!" Yamamoto ordered. "This
is how cowardice in war is punished!" All the mice stood still
and silent, without batting an eyelash. Even Pi did not make
an audible sound—but in fact he was delivering an ultrasonic
speech to his friends.

Pi's Farewell

"Soldiers, rodents, freemice! I am going to die, but not in vain.
My death has revealed to you the true face of the tyrant. Those
among you who thought it a privilege to leave the sewers for

better food, grander lodgings, and nice uniforms should now know better! Powerful men use us to attain their questionable ends, but the moment we ask them to respect our right to life and dignity, they treat us like the lowest beasts. Do we not also have the right to pursue happiness? Do we always have to fight for somebody else? Are asteroids made of Swiss cheese?"

"No," the mice shouted in unison.

"Yamamoto says that war and pillage are natural to man, and Yamamoto is a man; indeed, he is an honorable man. Well, now, I ask you," Pi continued, "did we ever break into a single human home to get slaves or steal diamonds? Has any of you ever left an apartment with a watch around his neck, or a check in his mouth? No! We have always, and only, stolen because we were hungry!"

"It's true," the mice shouted.

"While this deathly goo slowly corrodes my brain," Pi went on, "I want to tell you that I'm seeing things more clearly now than ever before! We were wrong in helping them! They filled our heads with their evolutionary theories, of course always considering themselves at the top of the heap. Well, maybe it's our turn now to say what Darwin never said: Evolution is not linear; it proceeds by leaps and bounds, and with its last bound, it landed in shit: *homo sapiens!*"

The mice applauded.

"Of course, they can afford to talk about evolution and natural selection. We can shake up all our chromosomes, lengthen our legs and whiskers, sprout gills, adjust to any environment—but the day man gets up on the wrong side of his bed, who can prevent him from blowing our heads off with a gun? And he calls that natural selection! Do not forget our dead! The several million urban policemice squashed in the streets of Tokyo last year, the nine million that were used to plug the hole in the Hokkaido dam, not to mention the thirty million who get mouseburgerized daily all over the world. Friends, it's time we regained our freedom! Remember: Better one crumb in the gutter than a full loaf behind bars."

"Let's say ten crumbs!" mouse Wait yelled.

"It's time for us to decide, friends! For years, humans have made us go through their experimental mazes to check out our intelligence. We got seasick, zigzagging around for miles just to get a little chunk of cheese. But now we've had it up to here! Now we're going to get our cheese without having to go through their maze first!"

"Em-men-thal, Em-men-thal," the mice intoned in unison.

"We shall no longer beg for food in front of their restaurants, under the ominous sign of their mascot, the *mineki-keko* cat," Pi said. "We shall no longer live under their farmers' markets, but inside them!"

"We want free salad!" screamed soldier And.

"And if they're going to retaliate with their cats, we shall respond in kind with our viruses! We shall infect them all!"

"A plague on both their houses!" Return shouted.

"My friends," Pi went on in an increasingly feeble voice, "the toxic syrup is already seeping into my brain. I'm having gaseous nightmares, I see young cretins romping in the dunes, swilling Coke cans against technicolor sunsets. Are we going to let ourselves sink to the same level of imbecility as man? No! We shall fight, and we shall prevail!"

These words were followed by a prolonged shout of enthusiastic support.

Pi shook his sopping head wearily. "My hour has come, my friends. Man has been torturing animals ever since Erasistratus starved the first sparrow. I remember the good old days in Tokyo, when we had fun hiding under hats and making them run about in the streets, much to people's dismay. But at that time, most Japanese still loved nature. It all seems so long, long ago! Well, I must leave you now. I'm going to ascend to the gardens of the Great Cow, where tree branches bow under the weight of mozzarella cheeses, and the shore hums with the swish and splash of fresh cream, where traps are illegal and cats are vegetarians. Farewell, my friends! Fight in my name, and remember what the great Gus-Gus used to say: 'It's easier to digest a whole wheel of cheese if you sit on top of it than under it.' Revolt against your oppressor! Bwaaaaaaaark!''

That was his last cry: the Coca-Cola had done its job. All the mice filed out, their tails between their legs.

4

THE SILENCE OF THE SEA

⚹ ☉ ♀ ⊕ ⚘ ⊕ ♂ ♁ ☌ ⊖ ♃ ♅ ☉ ♇ ☊ ⊖ ♌ ☽ ⊖ ⊖ ♌ ☽

MACHU PICCHU: WHO HAS COME DOWN FROM UP ABOVE?

○ ○ ○

Old Fang and young Einstein had reached the tip of Machu Picchu, the city of the sky. Their heads were spinning from the altitude and the numerous bottles of chicha they had drunk. Above them hovered the summits of four tall mountains: Acongate, Ausangate, Salcantay, and Soray, all nearly six thousand meters high. Below them, a thick, milky fog swirled slowly, like a troubled sea.

"This fog," said Einstein, as stoned as one of the Seven Sages, "is the soul of the Jívaros dead, suspended between Heaven and Earth!"

"No, Doctor," said Catuilla, the guide, "it comes from the engines of the excavators."

"Could I have some more chicha?" the boy drawled, "I'm feeling a little rundown. Hey, what are those two round things down there—assuming there really are two."

"They are two mortars," the guide said. "They are known as 'the eyes that look at the sky' because everything in this city looks up. There, on those fourteen wide terraces, was once Intihuatana, the 'place where the sun is tied up.' There is a quadrant there, with all the solar and lunar phases, and a map of the stars."

Einstein looked at the mysterious city, which to him looked like a huge, rocky launch pad for who knows what cosmic destination. "What does all this have to do with agriculture?" he burst out suddenly. "Wasn't this city built because, below it, there was fertile land? Then why did they build it so high, if they only grew potatoes? Why did the Incas have such fun creating mysteries?"

"I don't see any great mystery here," Fang said. "Agriculture depends on the sun, the lunar phases, and the rain. You seem to see magic in the simplest truths."

"Agriculture is one thing, magic another, science yet a third —and chicha encompasses them all," Einstein declared with a hiccup.

"Magic," Fang said, taking the boy's arm, "is related to the earth, its cycles, its changes; magicians study these with great attention, just as scientists do. Finally the day comes when witch doctors and kings decide to use magic to scare men, and have power over them, and what was once perfectly natural becomes arcane. There is a voodoo saying that goes: 'With the sound of the magic drum, I have tamed the dog of plague and fire, and now it obeys me, and I shall set him onto all those who refuse to obey me.' "

"It sounds like a nuclear threat made by a government that's had too much chicha," Einstein said. "Hey, Catuilla, is it true that your witch doctors drink some strange vegetable potions when they want to—umm . . . communicate with things?"

"It's true. They drink and then see things in hidden times, things one cannot speak of."

"I have an idea!" Einstein said. "I'm going to prescribe chicha for our physicists who still cannot articulate the concepts of the fourth space-time dimension. On with it! Let's introduce drums into our laboratories! Ay me ay ohieeee! Aich too ooooh!"

"The boy has been drinking a bit, just to keep warm," Fang explained to a nonplussed Catuilla as they were climbing the steps. "I would like to ask you a question. What can you tell me about these Acllas, the virgins of the sun, who lived in the temple of this city?"

"It's a mysterious story," the Indian answered. "There were fifteen hundred of them, and they lived locked up there. Once they entered the temple, nobody saw them again. They were the custodians of a particular cult, but we don't know what it was. And then, one day, they vanished."

"What sort of rites were celebrated up here? And why so high up, and so secretly? And why was this city built after all the other ones, and so far away from them?"

"I don't know," Catuilla answered. Fang thought he looked troubled. "Don't ask me questions your own scientists have not been able to answer. I think we'd better go back down. It's about to start snowing again."

Einstein watched the Indian hasten down the terraces toward his village.

"He's gone! You've scared him! He's hiding something from us! And I happen to know what it is, and so do you, my dear Fang! The same idea is buzzing in both our heads."

"But it is only an idea."

"So, why shouldn't we talk about it? You are also thinking that there might have been some alien influence on this civilization. The Incas were obsessed with the sky because something came down from it. And it set down on these terraces—

perfect landing strips. Only the chosen, the family of the Royal Inca, knew this secret. Spaceships hid in these temples, and some unknown energy was developed there. These roads, products of the most sophisticated engineering, were conceived by a superior culture, the culture of another planet. It was *their* plan that guided the Incas. And now *they* are defying us to understand it. And the Indians refuse to help us because they are still afraid of them!"

"Oh, Einstein, you are going too fast," Fang said. "Your computer would scold you."

"Everything is plausible," Einstein insisted. "Listen to me. An alien race chooses the Incas to carry out some cosmic plan. They come down from the sky with their flying saucers—but look at these drawings, Fang! Look at their solar wheel. It already prefigures our turbines, our drive shafts—"

"If anything round reminds you of a solar disc, then don't forget Ezekiel's wheel, the Celtic wheel, the Basque wheel, the Hindu wheel, the mandalas, the wheel of the Chinese trigrams—"

"Maybe they've landed everywhere!" Einstein said, growing more and more excited. "They must have been the greatest scientists in history! Don't forget, the Mayans claimed that their gods had come from Venus . . . the Palenque slab, with the drawing of a Mayan god driving a spaceship—and their fire balloons! Who could have taught them how to use balloons, Fang? And then those lines at Inca Nazca, those enormous drawings—they were signs, signals for those who came from space. They're the same lines Van Cram saw on that planet, up there! Everything seems to fall into place. There's a science behind this mystery—not ours; another science. These gods are scientists, I have no doubt about it; they probably came from some, some galactic university—carrying a briefcase in each of their eight hands—hic—Professor Quetzalcoatl, from the Venusian faculty of Astrophysics, will talk to you on the subject—hic—of chicha as an epistemological obstacle—hic!"

"Einstein, your thesis is terribly interesting, but maybe it would be better if you sat down." Fang helped the boy lie down. The mountains leaned over to have a look at him, or so Einstein thought. His head was spinning horribly.

"Fang," he sighed, "I'm totally confused!"

"Take it easy, Frank. Calm down," the old man said.

"My full name," the boy corrected him, "is Frank Ling Ti Einstein. I was born in Berlin, in Professor Han's generic department—he was Chinese. I have already suffered two attacks of cybernophobia."

"An aversion to computers?"

"Exactly. And if I have a third one I'll be dismissed and sent to rot away in some subterranean office. *They*, those people in the government, know everything, Fang! You don't know this. When you are my age you'll understand. *They* know everything about us, every little gesture of ours is on file; they can rewind and listen to the entire tape of our life." The boy staggered to his feet. "This is why I must go! I must go back to Genius to solve this mystery. I must produce evidence, or they'll do me in. You can't kid around with *Them*, Fang. Even if we can't hear the screams, and the large control rooms are silent, these are cruel times, my friend!"

↗ ↗

CALALBAKRAB—PRECISION WORK
◉ ◉ ◉

"Raise the voltage."

"Voltage raised. No sign of unbalance in the circuits."

"There must be a weaker point we can tamper with. Try removing the upper cap.'"

"Removed. Exposed sixty transistorized units."

"Where is the memory center? Try to produce some reaction

with a laser interference. Remove its contact with the primary functions."

"We have already tried that. The subject is paralyzed but fully conscious."

"Let's attack its center of volition with a few electrodes."

"No use. At each shock, the subject loses command of the central units. At the moment, it can only emit its inception data and registration number."

"Any other suggestions?"

"We could attack its peripheral lubrication. Maybe we could impair its balance system and create a severe spatiotemporal confusion. But there isn't much hope."

"I don't like to torture robots," sighed Professor Munkal, the chief torturer of the *Calalbakrab*. "They are too strong. Sensorial deprivation has no effect on them. Quite the contrary; if we lock them up in a dark room, they purr with pleasure. They don't feel pain or sorrow. You can't even get at them by torturing their parents."

"I couldn't agree more, chief. It's a tough job." Munkal's aide, Nakir, looked pensively at LeO's body stretched out on the torture table among electrode wires and control monitors. "What if we just tried kicking this junkheap around a bit?"

Munkal laughed. "Ah, the good old methods. How I do envy the torture scullions their salty water and their cudgels. It must have been so easy to work with manmade racks and wheels, according to the ancient recipes of the Inquisition. Today everything is so fucking mechanical and standardized."

"But efficient," Nakir said. "Since we started torturing with computers, we have achieved what we wanted in ninety-six cases out of a hundred—and without wasting too much time."

"Maybe we'll have to resort to technology again," Munkal sighed. "There's no way we can convince this robot to speak. In order to find out what that journalist Geber said to it in the hospital, we're going to have to remove its memory unit, transcribe it onto a tape, and then listen to the whole thing. What a mess!"

"Yes, chief. But once we've removed its memory zone, will it still be able to function?"

"No. Without that piece, it will have no vital faculties left. It'll have the intelligence of a toaster. But it asked for it. Let's get going. Reactivate the mechanical arm via resection of ganglion cells for complete removal of memory cassette-type 234A-Atari."

"Ready to proceed," Nakir said. "The instructions say to divide the subject into its four structural units by undoing the central zipper, then free the cranial cap by removing the eight screws around the semicircular suture. At this point, lift the protective steel cup . . ."

"Listen, folks," LeO said, "when you are done, could you at least put all my pieces into an assembly kit and mail them to my friends as a souvenir?"

"No way! This ought to teach you a lesson. You could have spoken when we asked you to," Munkal said. "Besides, any of these pieces could contain a microfilm. Now, shut up. I think we should start with those two bolts over there. Come on, let's get going."

"Ten, nine, eight . . ." LeO suddenly began.

"Damn it, it's really hard. I can't unscrew this—"

"Seven, six, five . . ." LeO went on.

"Be quiet! What the hell are you blabbing, anyway?"

"It's a prayer," LeO answered. "Two, one—"

The explosion was so tremendous that the *Calalbakrab* spun upon itself twice in a perfect space somersault.

○ ○

PROTEUS TIEN: A STRANGE APPARITION

○ ○ ○

A pall of silence had fallen over *Proteus Tien*. Everyone pretended to be very busy, but to no avail.

The first to speak was Chulain. "Why did they force him to blow himself up?" he said. "If only they'd promised to reassemble him—"

"He would have done it anyway," Caruso broke in. "Once, I had to check his decisional circuits. They were made in Japan. He was as stubborn as a kamikaze!"

"I've never liked their ideas," Kook said. "I don't like to see a life thrown away like that, for nothing."

"He didn't throw it away for nothing," Chulain said. "He prevented them from getting at our scoop. Besides, as my sergeant used to say, 'You ask me whether it makes any sense to die in this war? Unfortunately, we'll only know after we're dead!'"

"There is something we have to do right off," Mei said. "Remember those warrior robots hidden away in our hold? We must restructure them at once. This will be our response to LeO's death!"

"I'm not so sure, Mei," Chulain said. "As your dear Chairman Mao used to say, 'Only a war can produce a lasting peace.' Now, I'm not saying we should declare war . . . but I'm not so sure we should disarm our ship so completely. Maybe we could keep one or two robots . . ."

"If we keep one or two," Caruso said, "then, we might as well keep them all. You forget they're remote-controlled by our people back home. The day they decide we are the enemy, those machines will just take over the ship. I know their model well—and my government even better."

"All right, all right." Chulain was looking out the porthole with a worried expression. "But I'd rather put off that decision for a while. I think we might be in more danger right now. I see a spaceship coming our way."

Kook walked over to the radar screen.

"It's really small. What do you think it is, a pirate ship? An Arab shuttle?"

"Well, I'll be—" Chulain said after a while, "I've never seen anything like it!"

The spaceship that was approaching them resembled a church organ. Its jet exhaust streamed out of a rear spout with a deep funereal moan. Its wooden prow was carved into hundreds of statues representing Christian saints, Hindu divinities, fetishes, totems, and relics of all kinds and sizes. Above all this glowed a red neon sign, "UBIQUE DOMUS MEA."

"The space church!" Kook exclaimed. "I've heard about it but never seen it before! Father Mapple's at the controls. I know him well!"

"And who's Father Mapple?" Caruso inquired.

"You should hear his whole story from the very beginning," Kook said.

The History of Father Mapple

Twenty years ago, Leopold Mapple was the brightest young scientist in our course for supergifted students at the Science Institute in London. He was a big boy, over a hundred kilos, rosy-cheeked and well dressed. Just seeing him, you would have thought he was a spoiled rich brat; but he was actually the most important scientist involved in subatomic physics research. But he was also an inveterate hedonist—a great eater, drinker, smoker, lover and, generally speaking, worshiper of most everything that's commonly known as vice. Our rector, a calvinist jerk, often tried to cure him of his immoral ways. But Mapple would always reply, "I'm a scientist and I have studied the world with great attention. I can tell you that never—neither in the course of my observations nor under microscope, neither in a chemical analysis nor under X-rays—have I come across anything called 'moral.'" And, indeed, Leopold Mapple was probably the most radical atheist, the most rigorous materialist, the man most immune to philosophical or mystical babble that I have ever known. For him, everything was matter,

number, observation, confrontation, reality; everything
else made him explode with those loud peals of laughter
that were so well known in every London alehouse.

"There is only one way to rise above this earth," he
would often say, "and that is by a speed of 11.45 kilometers per second; everything else is just fuel for superstition and ignorance." And he always stuck by what he
believed, no matter how blindly bulldoggish it appeared
to some. He would get a bunch of friends together—Dr.
Hyde, Bohr, Fermi, Jakobson, and myself—and would
drag us off into the London night, where he'd abandon
himself to a huge eating-and-drinking spree. "Nulla theo-
ria sine hosteria," he would say, and then add, "Of
course, in the end, we always end up eating molecules,
but there is a big difference between a dish of hydrogen
and a pork stew." And to all those who told him he was
getting obscenely obese, he would answer, "In the Universe, large things are rarer than small ones; there are
fewer elephants than mosquitoes, fewer stars than
planets."

In short, as you may have gathered, he was a real eccen-
tric, but his exceptional scientific skills and his conta-
gious thirst for life made everybody like him, even
women, despite his cavalier attitude toward sentimental
matters. He used to say, "When a woman I'm in bed with
asks me if I'll love her forever, my only thought is that
she knows nothing about male physiology."

This attitude often landed him in hot water—like one
time, around Christmas, when he saw a bunch of kids
lost in admiration in front of a crèche. He just couldn't
resist telling them that: one, had infant Jesus really been
naked in that shack, he would have frozen to death in a
matter of minutes; two, the Madonna couldn't possibly
have been a virgin when she gave birth because artificial
insemination was invented only two thousand years
later; and three, had a comet really fallen by the stable,

the whole of Palestine would have been reduced to a smoking crater. Besides, it was almost certain that all the shepherds who gathered there had not come to give their sheep away to the little family, but rather to sell them, as was their habit. As for the three Magi, that was the greatest nonsense he had ever heard because, in the entire history of mankind, not a single king had ever dreamed of crossing a desert to bring a few presents to a naked infant! Had it been a sixteen-year-old girl or boy, it would have been a different story, but a newborn babe—no way —not in *saecula saeculorum*, amen. And, having finished his speech and realizing that the kids were a little shocked, he took them all to a bakery and treated them to a mountain of doughnuts, saying, "Eat and enjoy. Here is God, infinitely good in His trinity of cream, marmalade, and chocolate."

The parents sued him, and the rector censured him but did not dare fire him because, at that time, Mapple was completing an extraordinary experiment. He had been able to build a special bubble chamber where he was sure to discover the third elemental force—the force that, according to him, was at the origin of all the other ones, neither wave nor particle but something completely different and definitive.

"I shall force matter into the ultimate striptease," he told us, towering over the ruins of a huge banquet he had organized on the eve of the experiment. "Whatever is left at the end will be the beginning. Fuck Buddha, and Jahweh, and Vishnu, and all those other characters, half-men and half-dogs, who like to shine and resuscitate and fly and hiss up and down the sky. Enough with all that air-traffic of impostors! What we find, at the end of my experiment, will, for all legal purposes, be none other than God, out of which everything stems and is made—a particle, a wave, a relation. It won't hurl thunderbolts, it will never force a prophet to commit a massacre in its name, nor will it have to transform itself into a wooden bull in order to get laid; it will be a formula, that's all—a happy, simple, tangible, coherent formula that can be disseminated through schools and used by industries. Kids, that day I'll go to the rector and tell him, 'Have someone place this formula in a crèche, at the place of baby Jesus, and then see if your Josephs and Marys and shepherds and sheep and kings on camels and angels with trumpets don't look like utter idiots!' " We all burst out laughing, even though a few of us were somewhat annoyed by all that irreverence. But Mapple's merriment was such that soon we'd all been won over, as he went on drinking and singing and farting and shouting, "In interiore hominis vox veritatis!" We followed him through all the inns of Subchelsea, and downed so many bottles of beer that, according to Bohr's estimate, we would have needed a complex equation in order to count all the caps. When we got back home, we were roaring drunk.

The following day, Mapple, as rambunctious as ever, arrived at the institute to finish his experiment. "Well," he said, "let's get a nice, plump atom and punch him around until he loses all his electrons." For some reason or other, he always used boxing metaphors to describe subatomic experiments. A young technician slipped into the bubble chamber where the experiment was going to take place to make sure everything was all right. That morning, Mapple was particularly filled with euphoria— and beer. Not realizing that the technician was stretched out on the floor to test the temperature of the ground, he locked him in the chamber and started the reaction. The experiment lasted eight days and, during that whole time, the laboratory was off limits to everybody. On the ninth day, Mapple arrived wearing a tuxedo and still reeling from the previous night's spree. We were all with him as he walked toward the nuclear chamber. "Hey, guys," he yelled, twirling his ivory cane, "the clouds of two thousand years of religious incense are about to dissipate once and for all. Millions of priests will pour into unemployment offices across the world. No child will ever again be scared by purgatories and hells! All the jams hidden on top of cupboards will be devoured without fear of retaliation. Each church will ring with the liberating clink of unholy toasts. Nuns will strip naked and abandon themselves to the lust of young rabbis; ex-votos, ex-stoles, ex-missals, tiaras, habits and vestments, and last suppers; everything will burn in the same fire in which the church has burnt books, heretics, and the houses of the infidels. The final crusade is at hand! Humanity has been saved! Christ has come to Earth; rather, he has always been here, with us, and I will show him to you! The causa causorum, the sacred particle, the very One, the prime motor, the ordo initialis, the cosmic egg, the celestial blacksmith, the eternal dancer, the eye of the Buddha, the Ch'ien, the waugwa, the first bit, the supreme artificer, will soon be revealed to you in all its scientific splendor! Follow me!"

Terribly excited, we followed him all the way to the sealed door of the experiment chamber, and, with him, we held our breath as he opened the door and saw ... saw ...

He saw the technician, disheveled, with a long beard, his cheeks hollowed by eight days of fasting, his white smock in tatters, who, as soon as he saw us, raised his hands, covered with radioactive burns, and cried, "Here I am! It's me, Mapple. At last you've found me!"

I can't possibly describe Mapple's face at that moment. He turned as white as marble, his eyes nearly popped out of their sockets, and he let out a yell that made all the windows of the institute, and all of our hearts, tremble: "Noooooooooooooooooooo!"

He fled, trampling over us all. Nobody was able to stop him to explain what had really happened. He vanished, as if into thin air, and then reappeared, several days later, with bloodshot eyes and a long beard, and we immediately knew he had gone mad.

"Mapple," we tried to explain to him, "what you saw was only the technician of the institute. He was locked up in your atomic chamber for eight days!"

"No, my dear friends," he answered with an inspired voice. "It was God! At the heart of each atom there is God."

Two months later, he put together this odd spaceship and disappeared into space. Ever since, he has been traveling through the galaxies, taking his religion everywhere —to space stations, planets, spaceships. There is no cult, rite, or confession he does not know or deal in. Amen.

● ●

FATHER MAPPLE'S SERMON
● † ●

"Brothers and sisters," Father Mapple said, "we are congregated here to commemorate the soul of Leporello LeO, now passed to greener pastures. Brief is our transit on Earth and painful our final departure, but we must accept it and find a reason for it, and this is precisely what I'm going to do for the modest sum of twenty ingots for a simple sermon, or thirty ingots for a special sermon with citations."

"We'll take the special sermon," Chulain said.

"The gentleman has made a wise choice. What, in fact, are ten ingots in the face of death?

"Well, then, we are here to honor the memory of Leporello Tenzo E-Atari, a little Japanese. May Yoko, protector of children, welcome him into his heavenly nursery, where the electric train Shinkansen runs at two hundred kilometers an hour and where the famous wrestler Inoki tames the constellation of the Wild Bull and where—"

"He was not a child," Kook interrupted. "He was a robot."

"Oh," Father Mapple said, "well, then, I shall need your patience for a moment as I consult my list of funeral sermons. So, here we are, R . . . R . . . Rastafarians, Rosicrucians, Rotarians, no . . . I don't seem to have any entry for 'robot.' Do you think a special sermon would do? say a voodoo dance with bleeding fowls, et—"

"No," Chulain said, "Leporello was not a voodoo follower."

"Well," Father Mapple said, "then, what about the service for a sheriff with all due trappings, including a posse and the hoisting of the flag? Or a Jewish kaddish? Or a New Orleans jazz funeral? I have a trumpet and enough lampblack for our makeup. Or . . . how about an Egyptian mummification ceremony, or a Navajo one? No? Well, then, let's have a Hindu rite, with burial astride a sacred elephant. You provide the elephant, I'll take care of the rest. No elephants? Never mind! Mapple and Mapple specializes in interplanetary sacraments, with something for every need. Let me remind you of an old slogan: 'Why live, when we can bury you for only forty dollars?' Tell me, boys, what was Leporello's religion?"

"He was a robot," Chulain said again. "He had no religion!"

"Did he pray, now and then?" Mapple inquired. "Did he wear a cross around his neck, animal teeth, sacred relics, virgins' ring fingers, embalmed New Zealand heads, hair shirts, posters? Did he go to confession, take communion? Did he sacrifice rabbits, firstfruits, firstborn? Did he have any taboo? Did he refuse to eat pork, drink alcohol, touch anything white? Did he ever trim a Christmas tree?"

"No, nothing of the sort."

"Then, he was an atheist," Mapple said. "But, damn it, since there are no true atheists, we shall yet find his god. Did he, by chance, curse now and then?"

"No," Chulain answered. "At the very worst, he hissed."

"Was he a Marxist? a Determinist? a Darwinist? Did he have any ideology? In short, did he believe in anything in particular?"

"He was a robot," Mei intervened. "He liked mechanical engineering."

"There we are!" Mapple said, triumphantly. "In that case, we shall commemorate him with a sermon written especially for those of the technological faith. Stand up, please. From Jesus's letters to his business consultant, Book Ten, lines 678 et sequentes, Mapple editions:

"At that time, Jesus and his mother Mary were invited to attend a wedding in Cana, a town far from theirs. So they rented an old Chevy Impala, loaded the twelve apostles in the back seat, and left.

"And they were hardly halfway through their journey when the apostles, because of their crowded circumstances, the dust, and the bumps in the road, were worn out, so Saint Peter spoke for them: 'My Lord, could we not exchange places? We wouldn't mind driving for a while.'

"And Jesus answered: 'Verily, verily, I say unto you: Blessed be those that sit in the back seat, for in the case of a head-on collision, they shall be saved.'

"And they were nearing their destination when one of the tires blew out, and their car skidded and spun upon itself full three days and nights, and when it stopped, they were all miraculously unharmed, but the car had a flat.

"And the apostles said: 'Alas! We are in the middle of the desert with a flat tire and without the comfort of a jack, or a telephone, or a gas station!'

"And Jesus said: 'O men of little faith! How can you lose heart over such trifles? If faith can move mountains, it should certainly be able to lift a car!'

"At those words, the apostles sat down on the curb, waiting for their Lord to perform a miracle of levitation.

"But Jesus, growing wroth, said: 'Do not sit there like idiots! You are twelve strong fishermen! Lift the car!'

"And the apostles got to work, and their backs tensed in the effort, and sweat poured down their faces, and they lifted the car and held it up while Jesus changed the tire.

"And then they went forth to Cana, and after they had wined and dined, the mother of Jesus said unto him: 'Son why is it that you, who can do everything, let your disciples struggle to lift the car?'

" 'Woman,' Jesus said, 'a Lord who solveth all man's problems is not a Lord but a servant. And when he stops performing miracles, people will call him traitor and will renounce him. A God needn't do a miracle a month to be respected!'

" 'Maybe,' Mary said.

" 'And now,' Jesus said, 'I shall multiply the bread and the fish.'

" 'Couldn't we have a T-bone steak, instead?' St. Thomas asked. And he was immediately punished and sent to the kitchen to wash the dishes midst a clatter of pans, stomach groans, and onion tears.

"And now, let us pray:

> Pater noster qui est in coelis:
> Thy will be done.
> May thy entropy come,
> In Heaven as on Earth.
> Give us today
> An adequate protein supplement,
> And give our ions unto us
> As we shall give them unto our conductors.
> Nor lead us into underproduction
> But free us from manual work.
> Amen.

"And now, please kneel, so we may render Leporello LeO a more terrestrial farewell. He was a strong, courageous, noble robot, who worked hard and never complained. He might disappear from history, but he will remain in our hearts. Only when we disappear will he also disappear. But not the glorious name of the company that created him. In the name of saints Atari and Sansui and Krupp and Agnelli and Bell and Rockefeller and Hughes and Onassis and, of course, Saint Moritz and Saint Tropez, I now declare your productive cycle to be complete, O LeO, and may you find peace and comfort in Heaven, without roaming too long in the Purgatory of unemployment, in saecula saeculorum. Amen. Response!"

"Amen."

"Would you like a triumphant closure for two ingots, an apocalyptical one for three, or a hopeful one for four?" Father Mapple asked.

"A hopeful one."

"Rest in peace, now, LeO. The wheat is ripe in the fields."

"What wheat? Which fields?" Chulain protested.

"That's the formula," Mapple answered. "Rites must not be questioned; they must simply be followed. Sixty-eight ingots and a half, please."

△ ◉ ＊ △ ◉ ＊ △ ◉ ＊ △ ◉ ＊ △ ◉ ＊ △ ◉ ＊ △ ◉ ＊ △

THE MOUNTAIN SPEAKS

In the darkness of his hut, Huatuc feels the mountain stir uneasily.

"Mountain, why are you not sleeping?"

"Men have wounded me. They keep digging and searching for my heart," the mountain says. "I'm old and my fire has died out. I can no longer stop them by vomiting the fire of my anger. Find, among them, those who do not hate me; help them reach the fifteen doors."

"I shall do it," Huatuc says, "if you so desire."

"Many years ago, Capac and Mama Ocllo planted their golden staff in me," the mountain says, "and founded the Inca kingdom of your ancestors. Then I was covered with trees and grass, and furrowed by gentle brooks. Later, the rivers grew tired carrying corpses to the valley."

"Will those times return again?" Huatuc asked.

"Flying generals roam the sky. Armies are perched on the highest ridges. On the frozen Earth, men find no grass with which to sustain themselves. The sky will fall upon the earth, the future will return. Do you follow me?"

"Yes," Huatuc said. "Mountain, I shall help you."

"I thank you, Huatuc," the mountain said. "I'm heavy with so much snow. It weighs on me like a drenched cloak on the shoulders of a wanderer. Your axes torture me. But tonight, everything is quiet. Do not speak. Do not walk. Do not wake me up. Rest your candle gently on the ground when you go to sleep, for I shall hear you."

AL-DABIH'S DEATH

• • •

"Stupid idiots!" King Akrab was yelling. "I'm surrounded by a bunch of stupid idiots! Will I have to keep following my enemies when I could destroy them with a mere sting? Why should I fly on this vipers' nest, instead of setting it on fire?"

"Your power, O King, needs many men," the soothsayer said. "Whole armies ready for battle, arms strong enough to carry the palanquin of your triumph. To be obeyed by all these men, you need justice on your side."

"No, soothsayer; a real king, like God, appears in the night, in darkness!" Akrab said. "Fear is the best way to instill obedience into people. This spaceship, at the moment, is ruled by fear, but we need more terror!"

"Great Scorpion," al-Dabih said, "do you know what fear is?"

"Of course I do! When the Russians besieged my bunker for three days and three nights, I knew that every step I heard might be that of the enemy coming to get me!"

"And, during those days, wouldn't you have done just about anything to save your own life? Would you have obeyed any order?"

"Yes, I would and I did! I signed alliances with everybody, and gave them all my lands so they would help me!"

"And then?" al-Dabih asked.

"And then, you know perfectly well what happened," Akrab said. "As soon as it was clear we had won, Guderian, my general, razed Moscow to a smoking desert. And then we eliminated our allies, so that no trace of those horrible days would remain!"

"So that's how it was," al-Dabih said. "You were meek for as long as you were afraid; then, as soon as fear vanished, you let your hatred flare up a hundred times more fiercely than before. At the moment, everybody on this spaceship still obeys you. They may not have the stature of a king, but they do have dignity, and you trample on it every day. They see their friends disappear inside the torture room; then, at assembly time, they see them hanging on a hook with their throats slit open. Have you ever wondered how much they would hate you if they were not afraid of you?"

"But they will be afraid of me, day and night. Fear will stand by them, just like another soldier—an army of fear, black and silent!"

"Well then, O Great Scorpion," the soothsayer said, "if the

strongest is indeed the most fearsome, then you are not the strongest in here!"

The king could not suppress an angry outburst. "Soothsayer, are you trying to annoy me? Who is stronger than I am? You, maybe?"

"No, certainly not I, but whatever it is that you yourself are afraid of. You get rid of your most trustworthy counselors, resorting to murder whenever you suspect somebody; you surround yourself with men armed to the teeth; you have somebody taste your food before you eat or drink anything; you have spies all over the place; you never leave your rooms. Isn't this the behavior of someone who is terrified?"

"Beware, soothsayer, you are wearing out my patience! How can you say there is someone more powerful than I on this ship?"

"If your power consists in having access to the explosion mechanism of this ship, then it is rather meager," al-Dabih said. "If you exercise it, it will kill you. Can't you see? You are even afraid of me! Whenever I take one step toward you, you take one backward—and you don't even know why!"

"Al-Dabih, move away from me—not one step more!" The king unsheathed his luminous sword and pointed it at al-Dabih's face, dazzling him. The soothsayer closed his eyes and did not move. Suddenly, the king lowered his sword. "You are not afraid, are you, al-Dabih?" he asked with a cruel grin. "Well, in that case you will have nothing against having a drink with me—in the same glass, of course—so you are sure it is not poisoned."

"I will drink. I'll not be infected by your cruelty if I drink out of your glass once. It takes more times than that."

"And yet, soothsayer," the king laughed, "doesn't the prophet say: vices can be contracted in one night, virtues take much longer? Let's drink! Do you know what you are drinking?"

"Wine—very sweet wine."

"Yes, it is very sweet in order to cover a slightly bitter taste:

scorpion poison. It kills in exactly six minutes. Are you surprised? Don't you wonder why I have also drunk it?"

"Because—" The soothsayer took another drink. "—you are probably immune."

"That's it!" The king tried to conceal his astonishment. "Since I was six, my doctors have inoculated me every day with increasing dosages of an antidote against all known poisons. My suppers have always been a little . . . heavy, but now I am completely immune. A scorpion can't possibly be poisoned with its own poison, can it? And now, aren't you afraid of me, soothsayer?"

"No," al-Dabih answered. "Why should I be?"

The king, unable to contain his fury any longer, pushed the soothsayer to the ground, screaming, "You thought I'd never be able to get rid of you and your superstitions, didn't you? Well, you were wrong! Now I shall sit here, in front of you, and relish every second of your agony. Only I have the antidote against that poison. So who is master over your life, al-Dabih? Whom should you fear if not me? Ask me for the antidote, while you have some time left! In a minute, maybe even less, it could be too late. Ask for my forgiveness and you shall be saved! You have no idea how painful a scorpion's sting can be!"

The soothsayer, sitting down, said, "I would like to tell you a story."

"A story? Now?" The king was dumbfounded.

"Yes, a story, as short as the life I have left. Listen."

The Man Who Bought the Hereafter

Once upon a time, in Texas, there was a rich sheik by the name of ibn-Sawi al-Hunt. He owned all the oil, all the cars, and all the cows of Texas, and his bank statements spread over two volumes. But ibn-Hunt was not happy. "What's the point of having all this money," he used to

complain, "if I must die?" This thought haunted him
until he lost all interest in his financial empire, and his
business started falling to pieces. He sat in his office on
the three-hundredth floor of his Dallas palace, thinking
and thinking about death.

One day he banged his desk with a fist, Texan-style,
and declared, "I've gotten everything I've wanted from
life! I've overcome every difficulty. I've financed coups in
faraway countries, and intercepted typhoons that threatened to destroy my crops. I've bought, sold, and ruined
many men and many corporations. Should I surrender at
this point? No siree! I'll find a way to elude death!"

And he began his research immediately. That very
night, he convened the most famous doctors in the world.
The consultation cost him billions, but did not provide
him with any solution. Finally, the doctors had to admit
that, at the very utmost, they could lengthen his life by
some ten years. They departed, leaving him in the company of models of artificial hearts and prescriptions for
sedatives.

The following day, ibn-Hunt bought the largest freezing factory in the world and ordered his technicians to
study a program of hibernation for him and his three
hundred thousand cows. But the technicians said, "Frozen, you might be able to last for centuries, but once you
are defrosted you'll have exactly the same problem—
without counting the risk that both you and your cows
might end up at a military mess hall, and not as guests."

So, ibn-Hunt summoned the most famous magicians
in the world, and locked them in a room for three days.
When the door was opened, out came two multicolored
dracunculi, a few international elves, and a devil in wet
suit, produced in a four-hand experiment conducted by a
Haitian and a Californian magician. They all agreed that
they could grant the sheik no more than a hundred and

twenty years, if he drank turtle broth every day and took up jogging.

Ibn-Hunt then began reading all the books on the quest for immortality. He studied Egyptian mummification and Tibetan yoga. He read about the Mayan kings who insisted on taking gold, jewels, and credit cards to their graves, and about the Etruscans and Babylonians, whose tombs looked like department stores. He read about Shih Huang Ti, the Chinese emperor who demanded to be buried with eight hundred clay warriors and two hundred horses, and about the Indians who brought with them their fishing lines, and the Africans who lugged along their food supplies. And all these things just made him laugh, for what use can arms and food and clay horses be in the beyond? That's certainly not what one needs up there . . . and yet—!

A sudden idea made him shudder. He asked his secretary to phone all his doctors and summon them back. "I have just read that it is possible to have a 'temporary' death," he said. "The heart stops beating, and then starts up again. And those who come back say that, in that brief interval, they have seen the hereafter, and have felt a great burst of joy before returning to Earth."

"That is correct," the doctors said. "It's happened several times."

The sheik asked them, "If I put everything you need at your disposal—and I mean everything—could you make me briefly die, as it were, with a round-trip ticket?"

The doctors had a long consultation. They were still uncertain, when ibn-Hunt told them, "If you guarantee that, without the slightest risk to my life, you can make me die for ten seconds, I shall give you a billion petrodollars."

After a few hours he was presented with the list of equipment necessary for that extraordinary operation.

They began by buying the entire campus and faculty of Stanford University, where the best specialists in the world were put to work full-time for an entire month, conducting experiments on dogs and human subjects. Then, they started computers working around the clock on the results, till they produced a scheme. The operation could cost as much as the construction of eight hundred hospitals, but the doctors declared themselves ready to make the sheik "die" for eighteen seconds.

The experiment was conducted under top-secret conditions. The doctors themselves didn't really understand the sheik's aim—was it a direct challenge to death, an extreme need for excitement, maybe a wager? But the truth of the matter was none of these. "If I manage to get to that place—whatever it is, hell, paradise, or cosmic void—at least I'll know what it is; and when I know what it is, maybe I'll be able to purchase my immortality. If there are a few divinities, I'll find a way to make them an offer they can't refuse; if it is a burning hell, I'll bring along two thousand tanks of cold beer; if I'm metampsychosed into a cat, I'll have them bury me in a spot full of sweet old ladies. There is no place where you can't drive a good deal; but you have to know your odds, first. There is no point going there with eight hundred clay horses, if it turns out to be an icy waste where you'd be better off with eight hundred radiators."

So, a few days later, operation Different Holiday began. That day, Palo Alto bristled with nervous tension. Even though the percentage of risk was minimal, an experiment of this sort had never been tried before. What would happen if Hunt could not "come back"? What a defeat for science—and, worse, what a lot of money down the drain!

The fatal moment arrived. Ibn-Hunt embraced his dearest friends (his business manager and his favorite cow,

Brenda, the top milker in Texas). Then he lay down on his cot and said to the doctors, "Remember, you promised me eighteen seconds of death. Each second is costing me more than fifty million dollars. It's definitely the most expensive ticket in history. So, get cracking. I'm ready when you are."

The experiment started at 8:00 a.m. sharp. The computers went off together, and a thermal cap was lowered over ibn-Hunt and began to freeze him, leading him gradually to the temperature at which his heart would stop. After eighteen seconds, the reanimation procedure, popularly known as "a warm welcome back," would return him to life. In the meantime, the best specialists stood by, in case of unforeseen complications, with an extraordinary supply of replacement organs and other sophisticated instruments, including a "catch-a-devil" net, built by the marines, in case ibn-Hunt came back with an escort. As the sheik's vital signs weakened, so the pulsation on the monitor became slower and slower, a few more shudders, and it was flat! To the observers, ibn-Hunt was clinically dead.

Ibn-Hunt himself felt as if he were cartwheeling away at an extraordinary speed and with an odd itch in his belly. He landed in a sitting position, on the gray carpet of a dusty office corridor. In front of him, behind a desk, sat a bald man in shirtsleeves. The whole place smelled of chili.

"I have only eighteen seconds at my disposal my name is Hunt I am just applying for immortality my estate is valued at—" The sheik was trying to explain everything as quickly as possible, without even taking the time to breathe.

"Calm down. Don't worry," the little man said. "If you have eighteen terrestrial seconds, it means that you have one hundred and eighty of our seconds, and that is exactly three minutes."

"Really?" ibn-Hunt said. "In that case, as I was saying, I'd like to become—or rather, inquire about becoming immortal—because, you see, I'm not dead—that is, I am, but not irrevocably . . . I don't quite know how to explain it."

"Your name is Hunt, right?" the little man asked while leafing through a thick directory. "In effect, there is no one by that name expected today. You must be one of those freaks . . . you know, what do you call them?—a born-again something."

"Yes, more or less," ibn-Hunt said.

"I knew it," the little man sighed. "Since you people discovered reanimation, this place has been like Grand Central Station—hundreds keep coming and going, and hardly anyone staying except for a couple of bums here and there. So much for that. How can I help you?"

"I want immortality, and I'm ready to do anything to get it."

"Immortality . . . hmmm . . . I'm not sure that's possible." The little man scratched his head. "I've never seen anything about that in the regulations . . . unless you happen to hit on the secret word in the game 'a penny for your thoughts.' "

"And what's that?" ibn-Hunt asked, all excited.

"Oh, you see, of late there has been such a demand for immortality on the part of magicians, mystics, saints, and, you know, all those dudes who are never happy and insist on washing with cold water at the age of one hundred! So the bosses decided to announce a competition in 'paravision'—you know, something to do with the paranormal visions those people always get. There is a riddle concerning a twenty-six-letter word which, when pronounced standing upside down in shepherd's garb, will automatically grant you a supplement of five hundred years . . . It's not immortality, but it's getting there. . . . If you ask me, it's a farce, but the bosses like it; they say it encourages mystical research . . ."

"It interests me a great deal. Tell me, how can I find that secret word? Quick—I don't have much time left."

"I don't have the slightest idea," the little man hesitated. "Besides, it's a very difficult procedure."

"I'm ready to pay half a billion dollars for it," ibn-Hunt said.

The little man started. "Hmmm . . . not that I need that much money here, to be sure . . . but I have a little girl back home, a grandchild, you know, who could certainly use it. On the other hand, it's really against the regulations—"

"A billion dollars!" ibn-Hunt insisted. "Your granddaughter will be the richest woman in America! I'll even give her my business manager!"

"OK, you've convinced me," the little man said. "So let's hurry. First of all, we need a notarized affidavit."

"Done," ibn-Hunt said, pulling a sheet of paper out of his pocket.

"Very well," the little man said, "all we have to do is fill in the blanks and affix our signatures. So, let's see: 'Herewith I, the undersigned Mr.'—fill in your name here —OK, 'Hunt, having had'—put in, 'a mystical crisis'— 'with,' umm, 'visions,' fine, 'and having, in the course of one of these' (say again, 'visions'), 'seen'—write, 'my grandfather'—what was your grandfather's name?"

"Dagwood," ibn-Hunt replied.

"'—'my grandfather Dagwood,' all right, 'who'—write in, 'set me the riddle of the secret word'—OK, 'and having' quote 'successfully solved it in the manner required by the regulations,' fine, 'now ask'—write, 'to be granted an extension'—'of'—fill in 'five hundred years,' in both letters and numbers, then continue, 'on my earthly stay' —good, good, 'as provided by special writ number,' let's

see now, fill in 'one-oh-oh-oh-six.' OK. Now we must
bring this application to the special-procedures office,
where you will have to shell out another billion for the
descendants of the gentleman who takes care of these
things—you understand, that's only fair—and then I'll
take care of informing your grandfather Dagwood about
the whole thing, and will also touch up your biography,
Mr. Hunt—you understand, just in case they want to
check it out, nothing much; I'll just add a couple of good
deeds here and there, a few mystical experiences, one or
two visions, and so on and so forth—don't worry; I'll take
care of it all. In the meantime let me write down, here on
your hand, the two addresses you'll have to contact back
on earth, you know, for the deposits."

"But, what's the word?" ibn-Hunt said. "Quick; I have
only a few seconds left."

"Oh, of course, the secret word . . . I don't know it, but
no sweat. All you have to do is get it from the last terrestrial who solved the riddle, that is—let me check, just a
second . . . here: Mr. Ravi Punchakar, a yoga instructor at
a health club called Tough 'n' Lean, in Berkeley, California. You shouldn't have any problem convincing him to
tell it to you. But please, not a word to anybody else, or
the whole deal is off."

"Well, I guess I made it," ibn-Hunt said. "And just in
time; we have only eight seconds left. May I ask you a
last question before I say goodbye?"

"I already know what it is," the little man said. "The
smell comes from our cafeteria; we have a Mexican cook.
But, please, don't mention this either to anybody back
home—you know, they like to imagine celestial sounds
and smells . . . besides—"

But before he could finish his sentence, the little man
spun around and disappeared. Ibn-Hunt cartwheeled
backwards and found himself stretched out on his hospital cot in the reanimation room. He saw the faces of the

doctors bent over him, like a bunch of football players. He raised two fingers in a V sign. A howl of jubilation shattered all the test tubes.

Ibn-Hunt left the lab that very same day, after a general checkup, of course. He immediately went to his office and placed two phone calls. First he arranged to deposit two billion dollars in two separate Swiss bank accounts —one in the name of Rosemary D'Evil, a nine-year-old resident of Brooklyn, and the other in the name of the Nembroth brothers, two Düsseldorf plumbers. Then he called his bodyguards and asked them to go fetch, as gently but expeditiously as possible, a certain Mr. Punchakar from the West Coast. A few hours later, the guru landed at the sheik's heliport, where he was met by an odd man in shepherd's clothes.

"Mr. Punchakar," the shepherd said, "my name is ibn-Sawi al-Hunt. First of all, I want to apologize for the way in which you were rushed over here. I am also a paravisionary—hmm—a paraviewer, and am therefore well acquainted with the secret-word contest. Yesterday, I had a vision. I saw my grandfather Dagwood, who told me that I had drawn the joker, and that the boss had granted me permission to ask you, Mr. Punchakar, to tell me the secret word."

"I don't know what you're talking about," the guru answered, "there was no joker involved in our contest! This is all very weird!"

"Look, guru," the sheik then said, "I'm offering you ten billion dollars."

"So what? What's ten billion dollars compared to time?" the guru answered, rather miffed.

"What do you mean?" ibn-Hunt pressed him, suddenly flustered. "Just think of how many yoga centers and monasteries you could build with all that money. You could even start a Punchakar chain! Think of how many people would find their way to serenity, thanks to you!"

"Well, it's so much money . . . I need to think about it."

"What's there to think about?" Ibn-Hunt was getting excited. "Granted, you've got five hundred years ahead of you, but what are you planning to do with them? You are nobody now, and you'll be nobody for five centuries. Just a little guru living forever in the terror that his secret might be discovered and that some curious doctor will vivisect him just to find out what makes him tick. In the meantime, your grocery bill will get larger and larger! But —with my billions—you could lock yourself up inside a palace, or a sanctuary, and found a cult with branches all over the world! You'd become a god! An idol! 'I love Punchakar'!"

"OK, you've convinced me," the guru said. "In fact, my grocery bill is pretty high already."

"Then, it's settled." Ibn-Hunt's heart was fairly bursting with excitement. "Here's the check. What's the word?"

"The secret word?" the guru said. "Oh, I don't know it by heart, but I have written it down on a piece of paper . . . here . . . no, not in this pocket—"

"Quick, find it!" ibn-Hunt said, flushing purple. "You don't know how long I've been waiting for this moment!"

"The word is . . . wait, here it is—Of course, you know, it must be pronounced as you stand on your head. All right, if you know the procedure, here—It's a very long word, you know, twenty-six letters—"

"Tell me what it is, guru!" ibn-Hunt screamed.

"The word," the guru said, "is . . ."

But he could not utter it, because ibn-Sawi al-Hunt had collapsed on top of him, felled by a stroke brought on by too much excitement.

The King approached him and checked his pulse. Al-Dabih, the soothsayer, was dead.

ZUIKAKU—MUTINY!

○ ● ○

To: Mission Headquarters—Very Urgent.
From: General Ishii Yamamoto

The situation on our ship has attained mutinous dimensions. Riots have been occurring ever since the execution by cocacolation of Private Pi and other soldiers. After their death, pamphlets as large as the commonest stamp ranting about the tyranny aboard *Zuikaku* were circulated through the ship. These seditious pamphlets bore the signature of a group that goes by the name of "Red Tails." Consequently, I searched the soldiers' lockers and discovered material undoubtedly destined for criminal use—namely, offensive weapons consisting of six (6) sharp pen nibs.

Consequently, I condemned to death for illegal possession of arms, the soldiers G. Print, G. Cursor, Wait, If, Then, Goto, Ungoto, Return, Stop, and Next.

That very same evening, the ship became the stage for several retaliatory demonstrations: General Harada's shoe was attacked and its laces were knotted together. My desk itself was assailed and strewn with numerous little provocations. A fruitcake I had kept for a special occasion had all of its raisins and candied fruit savagely ravished by a cravenly coven of vandalous rodents. Consequently I executed soldiers Clear, Random, Grad, and Lock, who had refused to be part of the cocacolation squad.

The following morning, all the wires of the fuel-control system were gnawed to shreds, and, during my sleep, my right ear was besieged and painfully nibbed and nibbled by an armed band of marauders. Though surrounded by an overwhelming number of enemies, I fought and routed my aggressors. That same evening, we found valiant soldier New, our informer, dead in the engine room with a chunk of cheddar in his mouth. At present, ten deserter mice are still hiding somewhere on the ship, and the army at my disposal consists exclusively of soldier Point. Even General Harada has disappeared, and I fear he might have been kidnapped. I ask to be immediately sent a feline contingent of two to break this infamous subversive plot once and for all. I would also like the experimental center to explain to me the reasons for this aggressive rodent behavior, never before witnessed in any laboratory.

P.S. I would also like it noted that the rebels, having constituted a clandestine gang, have now changed their names because they no longer wish to be called after the buttons of a computer.

∘ The Red Tails ∘

"We must abandon ship," declared the mouse that had taken as his new *nom de guerre* the name of the great hero Gus-Gus, "and we must get rid of Yamamoto. Comrades, how do you propose we proceed?"

"Let's drown him in the water tank," mouse Thales volunteered.

"Let's open a hatch and push him into space," Anaximenes suggested.

"Let's combust him with a laser beam, or roast him on a fire," a large dark mouse proposed.

"Easy, Heraclitus," Democritus advised. "We must plan the execution down to its smallest detail."

"All I want is to get out of here, and find a little place just for ourselves," Epicurus whined, "where we can all live happily and justly."

"Is there such a place?" Pyrrhus wondered. "And even there, will there be such a thing as justice?"

"Justice," mouse Thrasimachus sneered, "is merely a tool of tyranny."

"We must not be afraid," Xenon declared. "Whatever happens, we shall have willed it!"

"In that case, we all agree," Gus-Gus concluded. "In the name of Apollo Smintheus, and of his temple where the albino mouse was adored, let's embark on our dehumanization mission!"

〉 ○ ☉ ○ ○ ○ ○ ♂ ○ ○ ○ ⊕ ○ ○ ○ ○ ○ ♂ ○ ○ ○ 〈

CAPTAIN KOOK TO GROUND CONTROL— BAD NEWS FOR PHILDYS
• • •

Daily report. Situation, Cuzco base. Two-hour energy blackout. Riots at the miners' village: the natives, asked to activate the emergency generator, stubbornly refused to pedal. A brawl ensued: an Eskimo bludgeoned a soldier on the head with a dry haddock and, during a wrestling match, a Mongol knotted up another one of our men. We need police reinforcements. This evening we are going to attempt a triphotonic hookup with *Proteus Tien*. Between 8:24 p.m. and 8:27 p.m., the ship should be within wavelength of our radio satellite Sinatra One. Please keep me informed about Secretary Pyk's devious maneuvers.

Signed: General Plassey Phildys

"Phildys, are you done with your report?" Einstein asked. "It's time for the hookup."

"Yes," Phildys said. "The interior of *Proteus Tien* should show up any minute now."

And, indeed, a series of decreasing numbers was already filing rapidly across the screen in front of them: ten, nine, eight. They heard one technician tell another, "I'll bet fifty ingots we won't be able to hook up." Instead, crossing several million leagues of space, a pointillist version of Leonardus Kook's bearded face appeared through the static fog.

"We have succeeded," Phildys shouted. "Hurray! Kook, can you see us clearly?"

"As if you were one step away! Hi there, Fang!"

"Dear Leonardus," the Chinese said, "how are you? and how's Mei? and Chulain?"

"Please," Phildys interrupted, "we are using up a precious triphoton every twenty seconds. Enough pleasantries. Kook, answer me: What do you think of Einstein's hypothesis?"

"I can't say anything definitive yet," Kook answered. "The idea that under all those ruins there might be something built centuries ago by an alien civilization is very interesting, but we've already suspected alien influences on other civilizations without finding any firm evidence for it. As an energy expert, I have analyzed their solar cult in great depth. There is undoubtedly a very strange and strong attraction between the Incas and the sky, particularly the sun. The sun is their God; it gives them strength. In all their temples, it is represented as a large golden disc, a human face surrounded by rays. And every temple was built so that the light of the sun would fall directly onto the disc, lending it an almost supernatural radiance. The cult was administered by a secluded caste of priests, and many of their rites were secret. But I don't think this is enough to prove that what they were really doing was worshiping some flying saucer, or some mysterious energy. Some of the rites were open to all, and their most beautiful celebration, Raymi, was related to the summer solstice. At the end of that celebration, the light of the sun, concentrated by a concave mirror, was used to ignite the cotton sacrifice. So that, when their legends speak of the 'exterminating beam' or of the 'man who flies higher than the condor', we can think lasers and spaceships—but also of simpler things. In short, I think that the hypothesis about an alien power over the Incas is fairly weak. If extraterrestrials had really been there, they would have left stronger traces. What does the computer say about all this?"

"The computer seems to agree with you," Einstein answered, "but it also adds, 'Be careful, these Incas were very deft in erasing the traces of their history.' "

"In short, Kook, you have nothing new to add," Phildys said. "That's too bad; we were really counting on you. At this point, it seems to me there is only one solution. We have found some fifty kilometers of vertical and horizontal mazes down there. Let's blow everything up with a bomb and see what we find."

"I don't think that's a very bright idea," Kook said.

"This is the idea that seems to appeal the most to the Federation," Phildys said, "and there's not much we can do about that. Our connection is going to be over in a few seconds; only three triphotons left. Any other news?"

"You bet there is. Quite a few things have happened since we last spoke together," Kook said. "In the first place, we've found the secret hold where you had hidden your twenty warrior robots, and we've retired them."

"What? What did you say?" Phildys lunged at the screen as if he wanted to enter it. "Kook! Explain what you said!"

"Caruso has recycled the robots," Kook said. "He's a real artist in that field. He has removed all their weapons and adapted them for civilian employment. They have become carpenters, electricians, you name it, and they seem delighted with the change."

"Kook! How could you dare do anything of the sort!" Phildys shouted. "This is outright insubordination! I warn you, those robots are remote-controlled from here. If you don't restructure them according to their military purpose, I'll make them blow up in your face, one by one!"

"Phildys is quite right," Fang agreed. "You should not have disobeyed your orders, Kook. You've committed a very serious crime. On the other hand, you would have done even worse had you unhitched the robots from their remote control by pushing button three seventy-nine on the central computer. But I'm sure you'd never do anything of the kind!"

"Damn Chink!" Phildys shouted. "I forbid you to read my thoughts! Mind your own goddamn business! What's that noise . . . ?"

"It's the beep that announces the end of the triphotons, sir," the technician explained.

"Kook!" Phildys screamed. "We may have exhausted our triphotons, but this isn't the end of our conversation! When you get back, you'll be sorry you did what you did! And from now on, keep your hands off my robots. Don't you dare—oh, damn it—they're gone!"

The screen had suddenly turned a sizzling gray.

All Phildys could do was ingest another volley of tranquilizers and watch Fang whistling and dancing on one foot.

"Listen, Fang," he said, trying to keep calm. "Seeing how you've gotten us into this mess, I would appreciate it if you didn't talk about it to anyone else—it was you who telepathically informed Mei, wasn't it?"

"Yes, but it wasn't that simple. It took me a long time to get to your thoughts about those robots," Fang admitted. "On the other hand, I became very suspicious when I realized that a large area of your mind had been screened by hypnosis."

"Well, of course—that's the normal procedure for protecting military secrets."

"I wonder what freedom of choice you must have between one hypnotic treatment and the next," Fang remarked as he skipped out of the room.

Phildys turned to Einstein and snarled:

"That old jerk is driving me nuts! But you—why didn't you say anything? Have you switched sides too?"

"Sides?" Einstein inquired blandly. "What sides?"

"Come on, don't play dumb. Everybody knows about your . . . shift toward red, Einstein. It seems you're becoming a pacifist—considering these Indians as inviolable. Maybe you're a little tired, Einstein?"

"Phildys," the boy retorted, "if you want to get rid of me, you might as well tell me to my face."

"No, that's not what I want. But you'd better know the kind of bind we're in. At the next session of Parliament, Pyk is going to propose an alliance with the sheiks, and if we have no counterproposal, he'll get what he wants."

"We'll find something," Einstein said with resolution. "I'm going to stuff Genius with new data. We'll find that source of energy and we'll uncover it without using a single bomb. And I'm not saying this because of Fang, but because I really think it's the best solution."

"But if it doesn't work," Phildys said, "do you agree that we'll have to bomb the area and force those Indians to dig again?"

"Give me two days to think about it," Einstein answered. "Just two."

5

NEAR THE HEART

GOING DOWN

That night, in the dark operations room, Einstein slept, with his head resting on the computer. Genius, taking advantage of his friend's oblivion, was having fun spewing out long chains of paper dolls. Fang entered quietly, but Einstein woke up and eyed him with suspicion.

"Have you come to try to convince me, Fang?"

"No, Einstein. I'm here to help you."

The boy's expression softened. "Then please do it now. I've spent all day cramming new data into Genius, then I asked him, 'Please, Genius, will you tell me what's hidden below all those labyrinths?' Do you know what he answered? 'Maybe a few moles with a big headache.' "

"Well, he may not be as smart as he used to be, but at least he's recovered some of his old wit!"

"Right," Einstein said. "So why don't we all laugh it all off? We're freezing to death, but our moral principles are safe. And, above all, let's not send those Indians to dig. Workers should never work!"

"Precisely what I wanted to talk to you about, Einstein," Fang said. "Some time ago I spoke with Coya. She told me the Indians are ready to go down with us."

"With us? With me . . . and you?" Einstein said, surprised. "But . . . isn't it dangerous? Down there it's really cold. At your age, won't it be, umm, a little difficult?"

"When you're young, you always find difficulties, but when you are old, they always find you. I'm not going to pull back now. We'll go down a particular opening, in the *chinganas*, which they call 'the mouth,' near the Temple of the Falcon. But nobody must know this. Apparently they're going to show us something very secret."

"I'll go with you." Einstein was suddenly full of enthusiasm. "And a double hurrah for experimental research in the field!"

"Wise choice, little dragon! Come on, get ready. We enter the labyrinth at midnight sharp!"

"Really?" Einstein said. "What a strange coincidence! *Proteus Tien* will abandon quadrant sixteen and forge into the Universal Sea tonight, at midnight sharp. Not even a computer could have worked out such an extraordinary coincidence!"

○   ○   ○

PROTEUS TIEN—LOVE LETTERS IN SPACE
Ж Ж Ж

Kook to Mei

Dear Mei: You will probably be surprised at finding this letter under your pillow. Tomorrow, we plunge into the Universal Sea. This could be the last day of our life, which is why I've decided to write what I have never had the courage to tell you in person.

Mei, I have felt strangely about you since the very first time I saw you. It is as if something familiar had surged out of the past, as if a hand had pushed through the web of rational thoughts and had torn them asunder, revealing, beyond them, a forgotten landscape, the landscape of feelings. You see, Mei, I can't rationally believe in love. I think that what we know by that name is only a series of minor compromises or felicitous improvisations by which the two main actors pretend that their particular needs and attractions bear a nobler title on the playbill of our life. As an intellectual and a scientist, I cannot help, even in moments of greatest abandon, recognizing the signs of this eternal performance. A kiss is not the rosy exclamation point after the words 'I love you!' Oh, no. A kiss seals the contract that forces you into love.

This is my rational attitude toward the whole question. But, in fact, things have been quite different. My life has been a long sequence of sentimental follies. It all started with a schoolmate. Secretly, I'd sent her small notes with short poems. She would smile at me. Then, I started sending her larger notes, with short stories. She accepted them. By the end of the school year, I was into the habit of sending her each day an entire notebook with a chapter of a novel I was writing about her. She stopped smiling at me.

In college, I had an affair with a Russian student who was in the same math course. One day she asked me, how much do you love me? And I answered, very much, and spread my arms wide open. She replied that "very much" was a numerically ambiguous expression, and that I should give her more precise evidence of the largeness of my love. I gave her the following note: "My eternal love for you could only be expressed by an embrace whose length is multiplied by the meridional circumference of the earth squared."

She thought about this for a while and then showed me that the sentence could be mathematically expressed as follows: e 1 (eternal love) = 1 mc^2 (length times meridional circumference squared).

But since the two 1s cancel each other out as equal terms of the same equation, all that was left was:

$$e = mc^2$$

That is to say, the formula of relativity. My love was, therefore, neither eternal nor large, but absolutely relative, both in space and time. And, having proved her point, she left me.

After her, I met a computer programmer. She was a very clear, methodical woman. She told me she had nine days to experience a complete love affair. The first day, we loved each other, the second day we quarreled, the third we made up, the fourth we got married, the fifth we took on lovers, the sixth we got back together, the seventh we got bored, the eighth we realized that it was all over between us, and the ninth day we decided to stay good friends and to publish an account of our experience in a magazine. It was very spontaneous.

After that, I lost all interest in love. Through my microscope, I followed the courtships, couplings, and separations of cells and amoebas with utter indifference. Nor did I feel the slightest shiver at the thought of the obscure love-ties that bind the bee to the flower, the moon to the subterranean truffle, and the sun to the sunflower, nor of the amorous instinct of salmons and eels, or the mad passion of the orca for the orcus. It was in vain that my teacher, Fabre, kept telling me, "Come on, come on, Kook, drop those books and go outside. It's spring and every greenhouse, every flower is horny. If someone invented a motel for insects, he'd be a millionaire in no time!"

But I preferred to stay locked up in my capsule. Till I met you. Yes, Mei, I love you! I would like to live with you in a house by the sea, and teach you the names of all the stars, and you'd fill all the rooms with flowers—except the bedroom, of course, because flowers absorb all the oxygen. And we could even have a dog we could use for our experiments (not cruel ones, of course), and a child that we would bring up to be healthy and intelligent and neo-Darwinist, and we could go to the shore, around sunset, and study the tides and cull the *Patella longicosta* and the *Pleurotoma babylonia*. Oh, angel of this ship, please accept my love and this poem (I know you love flowers). It's a translation from Verlaine, my favorite poet:

> The scent of roses, fainting sweet,
> Afloat upon the summer heat,
> Blends with the perfume that she wears.

> So long, my love!
>   Leonard

Caruso to Mei

Yes, indeed, I am the author of this billet-doux, this little devil which, unbeknownst to all, crept under your pillow.

Tomorrow we are braving the unknown, daring the impossible! Well, then, why delay the avowal of my feelings for you, of the sweet, sweet ache within my heart? The first time I saw you, Mei, I felt the same emotion I had felt when I saw la Prochonskaia, in the role of Aïda, enter the scene at the wheel of a tractor in Kutusov's version of the opera for the Martian agricultural festival. My heart roared like a turbine. Ah, love, love is a dart. And is not a kiss the rosy exclamation point that so sweetly seals the words 'I love you!'? Oh, Mei,

> oh my sweet, sweet Butterfly,
> why wait for Pinkerton, why,
> when your Raimondi is nearby?

To you I dedicate these lines, spontaneously sprung from my heart to my lips. Do you like them?

Oh, many a sad love story could I tell, my darling. As a student of opera once said: "Melodrama is when the soprano and tenor want to go to bed together, but the baritone won't let them." Alas, in life I have often played the baritone, and every time, a tenor came along and took away my prey. I had nearly resigned myself to that baritonal cavatina:

> Tutti mi vogliono
> Tutti mi cercano
> But it's the tenor
> Who will have her.

until that moment, that celestial moment when

> (oh istante d'amore
> oh dolce contento
> soave momento
> che uguale non ha)

I first saw you. We were alone, without suspicion, and I sang for you that aria from *La Bohème* for single voice and master key. And you said, "Oh, what a beautiful story, and so terribly sad! Surely, these old operas had far more to fear from pulmonary trouble than from sentimental ones! The end of melodrama must have coincided with the advent of antibiotics!" At that moment, I felt a terrible urge to warm your freezing hand and from there to move on to a gradual warming up of all other zones, and within me I felt love, that love that throbs throughout the universe, in its most mysterious recesses . . . etc. Well, Mei, whether you love me or not, I do.

> Rich am I not
> but a big heart I've got
> and a fond soul: they are yours
> for it is you my heart adores
> and you my soul implores
> from dawn till day's no more

and I would like to live with you in a small house, with a fireplace, and lots and lots of children, at least twelve, and each of them would play an instrument; the dumbest one could play the triangle, and at sunset we would go to the beach and sing, you and I, the most immortal arias, heedless of the coastguards' jeers

> and by god
> when she is my wife
> from all those courting fops
> I shall indeed protect her!

This, my love, I promise you, in this short note. I would have liked to send you a poem by Verlaine, but I seem to have misplaced his book. Please, I beg you, answer me

a mere sentence, just a line
will do, for a love with so much love
love forbids you not to love.
Oh, let's sing together
high notes forever.
Adieu, Adieu!

Caruso Raimondi

Sara to Caruso: Reflections

parfois aussi le dard d'un insecte jaloux
inquiétait le col des belles sous les branches.

I know, I am not beautiful. At least, not to your eyes.
How can one write a love letter when one's head is
adorned with two hairy antennae and cellular eyes? And
yet, in most gardens, my trumpety mouth and my round
belly would drive many a drone crazy. But, how can I
even hope to be liked by you? And even if you did like
me, what could happen between us, given that a mere pat
of your hand would threaten my life? No, it would be
impossible: I can already see myself, hiding in your room,
spying on your phone calls, your rendezvous, and I can
see your embarrassment whenever you'd have to introduce me to your friends. What advantages could I possibly bring you? You probably wouldn't have to buy me a
ticket when we went to the movies, and my furs would
be relatively inexpensive. But that is not much of a con-
solation, surely not enough for a man to love a bee. And
yet, I believe impossible love is the strongest, and the
longest-lasting—that's why I stick by you. I'm so happy
just looking at you when, in the morning, you get up and
start singing as you shave, and I, still half-asleep in your

hair, begin cleaning my wings, getting ready for my first flight of the day. I know. You have been very good to me. We work well together, and I know my place. You don't even suspect that these few millimeters of insect buzzing in midair could conceal such strong feelings for you. Maybe you also believe, like Voltaire, that "No animal outside of man knows those embraces to which the whole body responds, those kisses wherein lips taste a never-ending voluptuousness." Have you ever witnessed the love dance of cranes? Have you ever heard the love call of whales? Do you know that orchids simulate, in color and shape, the capacious belly of the queen bee, so that the drone will make love to them? Yes, if we are really flower "lovers," why then should we not love men, as well? Oh, if you could only see and listen!

I know the marvels of every flower, the way it responds to the passage of the seasons and the moods of the weather. I have traveled through breezy wheatfields and have gotten lost in the blazing mazes of turbines. I have seen countries and places you can't even imagine. But why should I keep on talking? Do not feel the slightest scruple in studying me, cataloguing me, classifying me in some entomological subspecies, burying me in the glass graves of your taxonomies. Who knows?—maybe, one day, you'll leave this land that you seem to hate. Well, that day we'll go on living, despite your absence, just as we have for millions of years.

Chulain to Mei

Dear Mei: This is your Choo-choo-chulain. Tomorrow the shit's gonna hit the fan, and it might just do us all in. So, my sweetheart, I've gotta tell you that I've got it bad, real bad, over you. I'd do anything for you. I'd even walk

around in a gold kimono with big pink carnations; I'd
even go to the movies to see that flick where Snow White
sings all the time with a chorus of dopey beasts. Mei dear,
in a hundred years of space travels, I've seen just about
everything there is to see, without batting a lash. But the
other evening, when you bent over in your slit kimono, I
felt as if I were caught in the big bang!

Mei, I don't know how to write love letters. Today,
while we were restructuring the robots, and you were
painting little flowers all over them, I must admit I did
wince. We're pretty different, you and me. I was born in
a place where, if you couldn't use a knife, you wouldn't
get farther than your crib. But I can also be nice and
gentle, and to prove it I'm going to write you a poem. It
is a good poem, wrote by a guy Overlane. But I wrote my
own personal version, and I think it's much better. I hope
you like it, babe.

To Mei

By good stern wind fanned
a trellised arbor is at hand
to shield us from your old man.

The scent of roses, disgusting sweet
afloat upon the summer heat
fight with the perfume of my feet.

True to the promise her eyes gave
she ventures all, and her mouth rains
a beastly fever through my veins.

And, Love fulfilling all things, save
hunger, we 'scape, with four pork chops,
the folly of Love's mushy slops.

● ●

CLYMENE AND CHLORIS
❦ ● ❦

To: General Yamamoto—Mission *Zuikaku*
From: General Saito, Mission Headquarters

The situation on the ship, as you described it, sounds
very alarming. Too late to send you feline reinforcements, but you are authorized to use *all* the special weapons at your disposal to quench the revolt and continue in
the space race. As for the reason for the mysterious behavior of the mice, I enclose the following note, which
reached me only this morning.

From: Sansui Laboratories for Space Personnel,
Section Gray Soldiers

After a careful reappraisal of the genetic dossier of the
mice participating in Mission *Zuikaku*, we have discovered that, by some unexplainable oversight, two mice
from the reproduction section have also boarded the ship.
The mice in question, Tab and And, erroneously designated males, are actually of the female gender and their
real names are Clymene and Chloris, respectively. The
presence of two micettes on ship might have well caused
some unforeseen reaction among the crew members, and
suggested to the rebels the idea of founding an indepen-
dent colony in space. Consequently, we suggest you do
your best to bring the rebellion under control.

∘   ∘   ∘

○ ○ ○ ○ ○ ○ ○ ○ ○ ○ ○ ○ ○ ○ ○ ○ ○ ○ ○ ○

CALALBAKRAB: EVERYTHING IS SET

ᔭ ᔭ ᔭ

"All set, then," Coyllur said. "Tomorrow night. The concert will begin at 10 p.m. The attack at 10:34. Any questions?"

"Yes," Laureen said. "Is our action going to have significant repercussions for the masses, or is it going to be just an isolated episode?"

"No way of knowing with any certainty," Vassiliboyd answered. "After all, we're a million kilometers from Earth."

"I have a sister on Earth," Coyllur said. "Her name is Coya. One day, we each went our way: she preferred to stay with our people, to fight on Earth, while I decided to confront the enemy on his own turf, that of technology and knowledge. Well, I do not feel as if I have abandoned my people. In fact, I have met Indians everywhere, in this hell, in all these wars."

"And yet," Alice said, "there should be a way we can all revolt together. Maybe if we announced it with bills and posters and fliers, like you do with concerts, or if we used a few special effects—maybe an announcer who goes up on stage and yells, 'And now, folks, for the first time in our city, the Fighting Vanguards!' and everybody in the audience strikes a match—"

"Listen," Vassiliboyd said, "may I ask you a question? Why on Earth did you choose to mask yourselves as a musical group?"

"At first, it wasn't a mask. I really believed that music could be a fantastic weapon to get people to think," Alice said. "Then I changed my mind. Do you remember the LP War?"

The LP War

I'm Baby Mouseface
born with a gas mask

down at Level Seventeen.
Wanna see my face unseen?
Kiss me now, why don't you try?
Then you'll see me—and you'll die.

That song was on the hit parade the year I began to
sing. Two great events shook up the musical scene that
year: Sex Control and the LP War.

You know all about Sex Control; it's gotten more tol-
erant lately, but it's still there. It was illegal to have children without government consent. Every single sex act
had to be reported because it was considered socially
threatening, given the risk of radioactive contagion, but
particularly because it was feared that unbridled sexual-
ity could take our attention away from the Great Reconstruction Plan started after the last war. That's why
concerts, what with the music and the crowds, soon became the best opportunities to have clandestine encounters. I started going to concerts mostly for that reason, to
find some excitement—in short, to get laid. But then
they really screwed us over when they invented the
Moral Hive. The Hive was an amphitheatrical structure
made of tiny transparent rooms. Each room—more like a
cell—had a number; to go to a concert, you had to enter
the little cubicle that corresponded to the number on
your ticket, where you were locked up all by yourself till
the end. You were forbidden to leave, even in an emergency, and you had to applaud at least three times or you
would get a strong electric shock. Of course, we didn't
like this one bit, so we started having clandestine concerts in abandoned metro stations, in wrecked buildings
half-buried in snow, in surreptitious igloos. That's how a
few legendary groups were born, like the Satananas and
the Bobby Lapointe in Paris, the Trogn Zikh in Prague,
the Drei Zigeuner in Berlin, the Man and Mo of Peking,

the Italian Vendetta Metalmeccanica, the Swedish Flad-
dermoss, the English Pestilence, the Spanish Cabo Roto.

I was studying, then, and playing electronic sax, bisax,
troog, and moog. The group I started with was the Mauna
Loa Sound—four black drummers, an explosive Irish guitarist, a tamed coyote, and myself playing an electronic
organ we'd found in an abandoned church. Our first concert, at the Gare d'Orléans, was a real hit. The first dy-
namite charge, courtesy of our guitarist, killed nine
spectators and woke up thousands of bats, which flapped
around like mad all over the place. At that point the
coyote launched a cappella into the howls of "Come
Down, Moon, If You Dare." The public got all excited,
while the bats sort of calmed down, stuck their claws
into the ceiling, and just hung there, squeaking in time
with the music.

Unfortunately there were a lot of bastards and spies at
that concert. We were reported to the Discographic Police and that very evening, the sequin-uniformed Rock
Patrol surrounded our place. They surprised us while we
were asleep, and arrested everybody except me; I escaped
by jumping out a window. All my friends were loboto-
mized and transformed into a cha-cha group for Arab
cruises.

A year later, I played with the Invisibles. I didn't have
the slightest idea who the other members of the group
were. Every week, I would receive a cryptic message, like
"Metro Department Store, 9:00 p.m." There, hidden in
the crowd, we'd start our concert. As a rule, we improvised, using, as rhythmic bass, the noise of a crowded
place. Our first underground record of some success was
"Christmas Is a Zoo," a concert for winds, drums, and
the Christmas-crowds at the Galéries Lafayette. But the
one that became a real hit was "Up Against the Wall,
Everybody," twenty minutes of jazz jam with the robbery

of the State Bank in the background. The piece ended
with two machine-gun volleys; the drummer and I were
the only survivors. That was the year of the Great Har-
monic Frequency Change. Clandestine records had become too popular and commercially profitable, so, music
was again liberalized. In fact, it was still in the hands of
the various governments via the large multinational record companies. The most important ones were ONE,
which belonged to the Sheiks, and the Japanese ENO. At
the head of ONE were Mick Jagger and Muhammed Paul
McCartney; the two ex-musicians, despite their advanced age, were still very active. ONE represented the
old guard—revival and electronic music, with a relatively
high human component. ENO, on the other hand, was
managed by two Japanese Creative Computers, C. Sharpe
and B. F. Minor, who supported the most advanced kind
of music—pill music, s.s. (sensory stimulation) music,
substantial music, and hypnotic music. Between these
two giants, a few smaller record companies specialized in
particular genres, like Aïda Records, adored by lyrical ju-
venile delinquents who roamed the subway dressed like
Radames, the Valkyries, or Ernani, singing arias and
duets at the top of their lungs; or Beet Records, for Bee-
thoven fans who gathered every night at the Beet clubs
to get high on the sound of the nine symphonies. Then
there was Do Records, founded by the followers of the
German Composer Kurt Storen, who believed that "do"
was the only expressive musical note, and therefore composed all his works using just that single note. Heron
specialized in bird songs, and Turbine held that no music
can equal the complex harmony of a powerful engine's
roar. As soon as liberalization opened new perspectives,
the LP War began. As usual, nobody has yet taken respon-
sibility for starting it. But everything seems to indicate
that it was ENO, since it was also the first to murder its
competitors' singers.

I remember the first time, since I was there myself, at the concert of Edgar Allan and the Poe. Allan was a Boston musician famous for his gloomy and decadent form of rock, brightened occasionally by a flare of irony and inventiveness. He was accompanied by four bloodless mutants, Lorre, Price, Lee, and the organist Berenice.

That infamous night, Allan was performing at the Black Cat crypt, a sort of catacomb with six thousand seats. All the gothic-tuberculous and the dandy-vampirical new-wave youths were there, coughing away with great affectation. Edgar Allan climbed the stage, his black cloak billowing behind him, his face cadaverous. As soon as his white marble guitar struck the first note of his biggest hit, "Raven," all the spectators raised their black-gloved hands in the air and, waving them as if they were wings of a raven, intoned, "Nevermore, nevermore." And that's when all hell broke loose. The sound system, supplied by the House of Usher, consisted mainly of twelve amplifiers in the shape of coffins, weighing a ton each. All of a sudden they collapsed onto the stage, crushing Allan and his group; from there, they rolled onto the public. There were horrible scenes of mindless panic, during which the crypt caught on fire. In a couple of minutes, there were six hundred casualties. ENO accused ONE of not having complied with security measures; ONE accused ENO of having sabotaged the concert by placing explosives inside the amplifiers. The LP War had started.

Two days later, in New York, at a concert of pill music sponsored by ENO, the spectators were sitting back waiting for the drug to take effect—a pervasive feeling of relaxation, accompanied by increased metabolic rate and epidermic sensitivity, and decreased salivary alkalinity. Instead, they were all devastated by a sudden attack of diarrhea, which proved fatal to some. ONE immediately capitalized on the situation with the slogan, "ENO Makes You Shit." But it didn't take ENO long to discover that the music pills had been replaced with powerful laxatives. ENO then retaliated in kind. One morning, the bassist of the Parsifals, number one on the hit parade, was found hanging from the E string of his double bass. The same evening, during a concert in London, the famous jazzman Kid Mongoose was killed by a cobra hiding in his sax. ONE's revenge was terrible: an airplane bombed the factory of Yamaha electric organs, and somebody unscrewed the hands of six thousand pianist-robots, ready for a department-store sale.

But the worst blow for ENO was the death of Micro Minstrel. Micro was considered the poet laureate of substantial music. By means of a computer he himself had invented, he was capable of transmuting into music any internal rhythm or sequence of matter—from the chain of amino acids, to the movement of gas particles, to various heart rhythms. Among his best known works were "Hyperglycemia," a very sweet composition drawn from the variations of sugar content in the blood of a diabetic, and the concerto, *A Gastrointestinal Journey*. His real masterpiece, however, was the symphony *Influenza*, which told the story of a group of viruses, from their entrance into the organism (andante), to their fight against the antibodies (andante con brio), to the arrival of the antibiotics (triumphal march) to the reestablishment of health (the wonderful adagio convalescente). Well, Micro Minstrel was horribly murdered. As he was composing a concert for oboe and gastric juices, he heard a few false notes. Suddenly, he was seized by atrocious cramps; by the time he realized he had been poisoned, it was too late.

It was in this climate of war that I was summoned by ONE. They needed new blood for their concerts. It had become too risky to be a musician, and many players had retired. I had just founded the Dzunum with ten other women, all computer-freaks. We played pacifist rock on the "train," a very long organ with six hundred keys. One morning, a bunch of cut-throats, wearing the Angels uniform of ONE, dropped in on me and told me that one of their chiefs wanted to see me. At first I was scared, then quite surprised. The ONE headquarters were in a gigantic black flying saucer. When they brought me there, it was hovering six thousand meters above the North Pole. With great excitement, I realized they were leading me into the presence of Their Holinesses. The inside of the headquarters was a cathedral. Its walls were covered with murals representing scenes from the concerts of the Beatles and the Rolling Stones, while its stained-glass windows bore the images of the smiling idols of the past, from Chuck Berry to Presley, from Bowie to Kimoko. At the sides of the nave were the sepulchers of the Beatles and the Stones, their bodies perfectly preserved in their stage costumes. Jagger and McCartney were waiting for me in a small room that reproduced, in its minutest detail, an English apartment at the end of the twentieth century, with a fireplace, an old Japanese stereo system, and Warhol paintings on the walls. McCartney sat by the fireplace, wrapped in a plaid shawl—a fat old man, stone deaf and senile. Jagger had to yell my name at him at least five times; and every time, he meekly inquired, "Is it the nurse with the injection?" and tried to pull down his pants. Jagger, by contrast, was as thin and dry as a twig. He leaned on a cane and wore a ridiculous wig, but his eyes were still quite lively. He told me they had great projects for me; they wanted to launch me in a big concert at the Rome Colosseum, and to offer me a ten-year contract. I couldn't quite figure out why they were so interested in me; on the other hand, a contract with ONE was the dream of every young musician, so I signed at once.

"Good girl," Jagger told me. "A very smart move! One must always seize an opportunity when it blows one's

way!" As he spoke, I thought I saw a diabolical light
glimmer in his eye. Still, Mick was very sweet to me: he
invited me out for dinner and then to his apartment.
There, he started reminiscing, and insisted on playing
"Satisfaction" on the guitar, dancing along with the
music till he ran out of breath. Then, he started crying
and babbling about his old concerts, and suddenly, between a sob and a sniff, fell asleep on my knees. I put him
to bed, tucked him in, and was about to leave when, on a
table, I saw a folder with a tag that read PROJECT DZUNUM.
I opened it; inside was a bunch of xeroxed papers. Curious, I pocketed one, but things started moving so fast that
I forgot all about it. From that day on, I hardly had time
to breathe. We immediately started rehearsing, and
barely three days later we were in our dressing room waiting to go on stage for the great concert. We were all very
excited. It was incredible to pass, in such a short time,
from the tiny public of the subway to the two hundred
thousand spectators of the Rome Colosseum. ONE had
really done things on a large scale: "A CONCERT YOU'LL
NEVER FORGET," the posters announced. "AN INTENSE
CONCERT FOR INTENSE PEOPLE." And that was under our
photos: eleven attractive young women in skintight
phosphorescent suits. As I remember, only one of us was
less than radiant; her name was Patty.

"There's something weird going on," she used to say.
"Too much, too soon!"

But it was too late to entertain doubts. We left our
dressing room and stopped by the side of the stage to take
it all in, before making our appearance. It was absolutely
awesome. Above us and all around that ancient Roman
monument, two hundred thousand people were going
wild. Their collective howl was the most frightening
thing I had ever heard. Mick Jagger climbed the stage and
whipped up the public, yelling, "Folks! We have been
waiting for something new in music for a long, long time.

At last, it's here. Today, your wildest musical dreams will come true. Eleven splendid women will challenge the dangerous ENO butchers in an exceptional concert. Music and risk for you, with *Dzunum!*"

Jagger's words made me shiver. Only then did I remember the paper I had stolen from his file on us. While my companions were checking the organ train (it took a few minutes to tune it up), I went back to the dressing room, where I read the whole truth.

TOP SECRET

From: ENO Board of Directors
To: ONE Board of Directors
Re: Project Dzunum

We have read your proposal with great interest. We have also noticed how the possibility of violent death striking the lead musician tends to draw larger and larger audiences. For instance, the last Killer Coltrane concert, where the singer's life was in no way threatened, received little public acclaim, and consequently his record sales have gone down. On the other hand, the records of murdered singers sell like mad, and so do the posters, biographies, gadgets, and relics of dead singers. In short, we feel it is time to put an end to this silly war, and join forces to exploit these new marketing possibilities.

Therefore, we will pretend that the war continues between us, but in fact we will together organize a series of tragic concerts, according to an organic marketing plan. We are ready to provide both assassins and other means to bring your concerts to the desired end, and we count on you to reciprocate adequately.

Insofar as the Dzunum concert goes, we agree that the sight of eleven beautiful women in deathly danger will

be particularly exciting for the public. To achieve this
end, we can assure you that our Sabotage Service has
arranged, for this concert, a particularly and spectacularly
bloody surprise.

In the hope of an ever greater and more efficacious
collaboration between our companies (Music is one), we
remain,

> Cordially yours,
> C. Sharpe, General Director
> B. Flatt Minor, Co-director
> *ENO Music Company*

Suddenly I understood everything. I understood why,
during the last few days, they had kept us isolated, why
the technicians kept casting odd glances in our direction,
why the audience was so excited. Lots of people already
knew that Dzunum was going to meet a horrible end! I
ran to warn my friends; on the way, I saw a few atten-
dants carrying bales of black-edged posters, ready to be
sold at the exit. I tried to get back onto the stage, yelling
"Run away! It's all a trap!" but two Angels blocked my
way. So I had to watch the whole thing, powerless. While
my friends were playing the first cut, a side door opened
and let out eleven brutes: eleven huge males, half gladia-
tors, half football players, wearing T-shirts emblazoned
"ENO LIONS." They were equipped with spiked boots and
razor-edged electric guitars. They massacred my friends,
one by one. The audience went berserk, while the announcer yelled, "Music, sport, violence—only ONE can
give you all this at once!" I managed to wriggle away,
fleeing through the crowd. After that, all I could think of,
day and night, was how to avenge my friends. Then I met
Coyllur and the others, and, studying the frequencies of
the synthesized moog sound, we found a way, the perfect
weapon. And now that weapon is ready to be used, and
the sheiks' empire is about to hear its last concert.

● ≙ ≙ ↗ ● ◑ ◐ ↗ ● Ψ Ψ ↗ ↗ ↗ △ ⊕ ◉ ● ◑ ◐ ● ●

TOWARD THE HEART: INSIDE THE MYSTERIOUS LABYRINTHS

The hiss of the storm covered the voices. Icy blasts of wind fanned the snow high into the air. Einstein removed his earphones.

"They've done it!" he shouted. "They entered the Universal Sea four minutes ago! Now they are on their own!"

"So are we," Fang replied.

Einstein looked down toward the steep steps carved into the ice leading to a narrow ledge suspended over the abyss. On the ledge, a few torches cast tremulous, ghostly shadows against the walls of the precipice. The boy felt dizzy.

"We are on our way to hell," he said. "Cheer up, Fang!"

Cautiously they clambered down the steps, toward the flickering light of the torches. The Indians awaited them; only their eyes were visible under their heavy hoods. Over their clothes, the Indians wore multicolored sashes and caps. From their eyes, Fang recognized Coya, Catuilla, Aucayoc, and the Eskimo Nanki. But there was also another person, an old man who, despite the cold, was wearing only a gray poncho. He approached Fang, holding something in his hands.

"My name is Huatuc," he said simply. "We have already met."

"Yes, we have," Fang answered.

"I have something that has been guarded by my family for many, many years. The mountain told me to give it to you." Huatuc showed the Chinese a quipu of white strings. "Knot by knot," he added, "this will lead you to the largest knot, the fifteen doors. Then you'll have to proceed by yourselves."

"It is a very difficult task," Fang said. "I'm not sure I'll be up to it."

"Go," the old man said brusquely, looking toward the edge

of the abyss. "You have very little time. Many things are about to happen."

A sudden gust of wind made the dark pit resound with a deep, mournful moan. The old man climbed back up, and for a second his shadow, cast against the steep wall by the light of the torches, merged with Fang's. Then he disappeared.

"I don't understand," Einstein said. "What are the fifteen doors?"

"You haven't yet confronted a real mystery," Coya said, "but already you can't understand? Open it, Aucayoc."

Only then did Einstein realize that, set in the wall, was a monolith, which the Indian was now trying to lever out of its place with the help of a lance. At last, the massive boulder pivoted upon itself, revealing a dark embrasure.

"Amazing!" Einstein exclaimed, full of admiration. "This is advanced engineering! Just like the rotating sections of our Pyraminx!"

"Get in!" Aucayoc ordered. "Somebody might see us!"

A few seconds later, the boulder pivoted back to its original position, locking them in. Einstein felt frightened. The torches lit up a large stone room with a low ceiling. At the end of it were fifteen trapezoidal doors. Each of them led into a dark tunnel.

"This is the least-known part of the *chinganas*, the mysterious labyrinth," Coya explained. "Many people decided to venture into it in the past, because it's said that it hides incredible treasures—golden statues, whole corridors lined in gold. But only one person, of all the thousands who went in, ever came out. He was holding a golden spike in his hand, but he had gone mad with terror; he was never able to tell anyone what had happened to him."

"And what happened to the other thousand or so?" Einstein inquired.

"We shall meet them, by and by," Catuilla said darkly. "Now, Fang must tell us where to go."

"I have looked at the quipu," the Chinese said, "it consists of fifteen strings, each bearing a knot. Obviously, it is the knots that must lead us through the labyrinth."

"It isn't too difficult," Einstein said. "All we have to do is unite the knots with a line, from the highest to the lowest, all the way down to the largest one at the bottom. Fifteen strings, fifteen ways in, fifteen directions. It doesn't really take magic to figure it out; it is a rather elementary puzzle."

Fang started tracing the itinerary indicated by the knots onto a piece of paper. At the end, the diagram he came up with was the following:

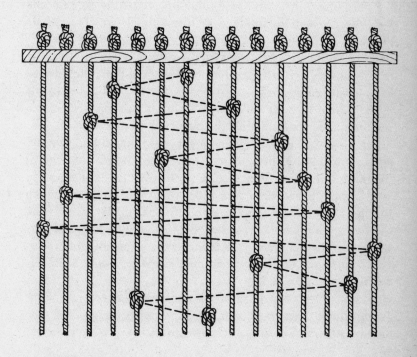

"It seems as if we must enter the seventh opening, and then turn right, past two corridors toward the 'knot' on the fourth 'string.' Let's go!" They had to stoop in order to pass into the tunnel in single file. Aucayoc was the first to go in, with the largest torch; Fang followed, with the map, then Coya, Nanki,

Catuilla. Last came Einstein, doing his best to stay close to the strong back of the Indian. At first, the tunnel sloped down quite steeply, but then it gradually widened. They passed by two side tunnels, and walked on till they found themselves in front of a well right in the middle of their path.

"The puzzle is getting a little more complicated," Einstein remarked. "Now it needs an advanced solver."

"The labyrinth is stepping down one level," Fang said. "Anyway, according to the map, this is the knot we must cross."

"That's so," Aucayoc said, and lowered himself into the well, within which unfolded a steep spiral stair. The others followed him.

"Just a second," Einstein tried to stop them. "I have the feeling things are a little more complicated than they seem! Wait a minute, we must think about this."

But as soon as he saw Catuilla disappear into the well behind the others, he scurried after them as avidly as a mole.

After a few meters, the well took a one-hundred-and-twenty-degree turn. Now, they were descending toward the head of the mountain. Shortly thereafter, they saw the first inscription on the wall, "Hector Alvarez, Majo 1606." As they walked on, the inscriptions became more and more frequent. They were the names of Spanish, Mexican, English, and Italian explorers who had ventured inside the *chinganas* centuries earlier.

"Where have they all ended up?" Einstein asked, shuddering.

"Here is one," Nanki said. In a nook of the corridor, a body, mummified by the cold, was leaning against the wall. A thin Spanish stiletto was still sticking into its heart.

• Blackmailing, Continued •

"Vanished," Phildys sighed disconsolately. "We can't find them anywhere. At the critical moment, they disappear."

Secretary Pyk was looking at him with pity.

"I've told you, Phildys," he said, "your two brains have given up. No child prodigy, no Chinese sage, could solve your problem. Not to mention those five fools up there on that unarmed spaceship. You know what the only possible solution is."

"To sell out to the Aramerussians—what a wonderful solution!"

"Phildys, I don't believe you! Where is the shrewd politician, the theoretician of convergence, the man who was capable of profiteering even on bomb shelters during the war? And now all of a sudden you have these doubts, these scruples? You're right—there is no choice. We'll never make it to Terra on our own, because someone will kill us, and we'll never be able to discover the subterranean source of energy. But if we sign the agreement, within a month the Sheiks will turn Cuzco into a crater with their sensor bombs, and whatever is down there, Inca or alien, will have to come out."

"The Indians will never allow it," Phildys said.

Pyk took his head in his hands. "This is too much! Do you really believe that five or six thousand Indians would constitute a moral problem for King Akrab? To him, they will be no more important than a gnat on a windshield."

"And what about our guys on *Proteus Tien*?" Phildys asked. "What will happen to them?"

"They are going to be told that from this moment on, the Sheiks are our allies. And if they don't like it, they can lump it. I doubt the Great Scorpion will give them a second thought. Space is so unpredictable."

"Just another gnat, right?" Phildys grinned. "It sounds as if your King Akrab will have to get his windshield washed fairly often! All right, I'll think about all this. But first, I must find Fang and Einstein. Don't forget, our enemies are also encountering difficulties. Not all is lost."

"Do as you please, Phildys," Pyk concluded, "but remember: there are only a few days left before the summit meeting, and if good manners are not going to bring you around, I'll just have to get tough. Don't forget, general, I am an ex-MC. Whoever gives the wrong answer gets thrown out of the game!"

□ □ □ □ □ □ □ □ □ □ □ □ □ □ □

THE FIFTEEN DOORS

○ ○ ○

Fang stopped to consider the map. They had covered two-thirds of the itinerary indicated by the quipu. They had been walking for hours underground, and the labyrinth was getting more and more frightening. Tunnels and corridors stretched both horizontally and obliquely, opened up in the middle of walls, dropped sharply for a few meters, then climbed up again. And every nook and cranny of that elaborate network of galleries hid mummified bodies, still in the posture they had assumed when death struck them—supine, sitting, intertwined. And, beside them, were arms and jewelry that must have been there for at least four hundred years. Obviously, after robbing the dead, the robbers had died themselves, so that next to each corpse were little piles of Spanish swords, Mexican machetes, English pistols.

"The last time anyone went in was at the end of the nineteenth century," Coya explained. "After that, an earthquake blocked this entrance. We call this path 'The Jackal's Way,' because it was generally followed by treasure hunters who stripped the corpses of those who had preceded them. Look at these!" In the space of a couple of meters there were three skeletons next to a gold-plated altar. Two cracked skulls bespoke a furious struggle.

"They were Brazilians," Coya said, "part of the expeditions

financed during the nineteenth century by rubber barons in search of Eldorado. You can always recognize them by the chains with the image of Christ they wear around their necks. Dozens of them came by to look for the Inca treasure. But no one succeeded. These labyrinths are unforgiving, as intended."

"Enough," Einstein screamed, terrified. "Let's stop! We've been walking for hours! How can we be so sure this is the right way? Maybe we'll end up like all these others. Are we so sure that these knots are an adequate guide? There are angles, curves, holes all over the place! This labyrinth is diabolical, and that quipu is much too simple to represent it."

"Aucayoc," the Indian said, pointing his finger at his chest, "knows this is the right way."

"And who has told him?" Einstein inquired. "Does he have a pocket computer that tells him so?"

"Aucayoc counts every single step we take," Coya explained. "He knows exactly how much distance we've covered, both underground and along the quipu. Aucayoc is a builder, and from his father he has learned how to find his way through any labyrinth, ruin, or temple, following the directions on these quipus. The strings were enough to tell the Incas where to find a secret room in a city as large as Machu Picchu. Aucayoc knows this technique very well."

They walked for another half-hour. The skeletons became sparser, till they disappeared altogether, which Einstein thought meant they were on the right track, or at least on a road few others had followed. At about the level indicated by the thirteenth knot, in a corridor larger than any before, Aucayoc said, "I can see a light down there!"

He now walked more quickly, and soon disappeared around a corner. Suddenly, the sound of his footsteps ceased. The others rushed over, and what they saw took their breath away: Aucayoc was on fire. A flame sprung from the darkness enveloped him!

"He's burning up!" Einstein shouted. "There must be a fire down there!"

"No," Aucayoc said, covering his dazzled eyes, "these are tears, the tears of the sun, reflected by the torch!"

From that point on, the labyrinth was covered with gold scales, and shone with a radiance that went way beyond our heroes' wildest imagination. As they walked on, they found gold spikes, a life-size gold llama, and the statues of small pigs, men, and women—all neatly set in separate niches carved into the wall.

"The Inca treasure," Einstein exclaimed. "The treasure!" He saw his own awe reflected in the faces of the others. But Fang and the others were more than surprised; they looked hypnotized, as if they were moving in a trance toward something that made the gold mere dross. And that something appeared shortly, at the fourteenth knot; it was a new tunnel, with an almost vertical drop. At the bottom, they found a stair that led them to the last knot of the quipu: a room with the highest ceiling yet. In the center, as if awaiting them, was a long bench. At the far end of the room were fifteen carved doors, each was tall as five men standing on top of one another, and all in gold. Einstein's jaw fell. His heart was pounding like mad.

Coya began to sing a *huayno*, a Quechua song; Catuilla and Aucayoc echoed her.

Coya looked at Fang and said, "What you are looking for is here. On the other side of those doors, you'll find the heart of the earth. Huatuc has brought us here."

"We are getting closer and closer to the mystery," Fang said. "Now we shall continue on our own, just like our friends in space."

.   ○   ○   ○

PROTEUS'S JOURNEY: THE FORGOTTEN PLANET

> I'm sure that in the year 2000
> everybody will be radioactive
> for at least five minutes.
> —Andy Warhol

"This is not a route; this is a labyrinth!" Chulain cried, looking at the radar screen, aswarm with the luminous points of asteroids and wreckage that orbited around Mellonta. "We'll have to zigzag around all these carcasses. I hope your stomachs can take it, my friends."

"That planet is a magnetic junk heap," Kook said. "It attracts every shipwreck and metallic asteroid that comes along!"

"I bet Deggu never had a videogame like this," Chulain said, taking a close swerve between two twisted metal carcasses. *Proteus* was rocking and pitching so much that everybody had to hold on to the walls. Sara buzzed, more or less stationary, in the middle of the cabin. Now and then a loud thud shook the ship, while Caruso sang the overture to *William Tell* at the top of his lungs.

Chulain saw an enormous shadow approach them from the left. It was a Russian cargo ship, its entire side covered by an inscription in Cyrillic, next to the face of the last Soviet president, Gorbachev. Its stern had been ripped open, and it emitted an unbearable stench. Chulain barely had time to duck, when the three thousand tons of the Russian cargo passed over the *Proteus*, causing it to skid.

Kook sighed with relief. "It missed us by a hair. But what's that smell?"

"I know a bit of Cyrillic," Mei said. "It says: 'Real Volga Caviar, 2020.' "

"Rotten caviar," Caruso concluded. "Caviar that's been aging in space for over a hundred years. What a treat!"

"Brace yourselves," Chulain warned. "There's a strange white mass right ahead of us."

"Skeletons," Caruso said, looking through the porthole. "The skeletons of *desaparecidos*—thousands of them. They're carried up in a special spaceship, given an injection, and then kicked into space—and of course they end up around Mellonta."

"Careful!" Chulain yelled. The ship fended its way through the cloud, accompanied by a steady pelting, as by hail, but in fact by the white sand of shattered bones. The moment they emerged from the cloud, the artificial planet Mellonta appeared in all its squalor. It was called the garbage heap of the galaxy; all you could see in approaching it were the ruins of buildings and the carcasses of ships. What had once been a great space fleet—consisting of the Sinoeuropean Invincible Armada, the Japanese Divine Wind, and the Aramerussian Befehlsvölke—had gradually been weakened by the energy crisis and the wars, and had eventually crashed on this planet. *Proteus Tien* landed in a large clearing, surrounded by metal mountains consisting of rusty spaceships ten times as large as *Proteus* itself.

Suddenly, small white creatures began pouring down from those mountains—first one, then ten, then a hundred. . .

"They're all around the ship," Mei said, worried. "What are they? There are thousands of them!"

"I can't quite make them out." Chulain studied them through the video-binocs. "They look like odd quadrupeds . . . They have sharp teeth . . . They almost look like—it's impossible—those things in children's books—what are they called?"

"I know what they are," Caruso said, opening the port and rushing out of the ship.

"Stop!" Chulain screamed after him. "You're crazy! Be careful! Those creatures might be dangerous."

Kook grabbed a few weapons, intending to go after Caruso and protect him, but Caruso was already back. He was holding one of the creatures in his arms. The creature did not look very dangerous, nor very aggressive: in fact, it was wagging its tail in what looked more like happiness than anger.

"The alien creatures are very happy to see us!" Caruso said. At that very moment, one thousand, two hundred and twelve dogs entered the ship and started licking the faces of the crew, all at once.

○ Flamingosapiens ○

Only after numerous efforts did Chulain manage to free himself from those moist ceremonies, administered by a chorus of yelpings. The dogs were staring at him, wagging their tails, waiting for him to throw them a stick or something.

"Don't be afraid. They're very friendly," said a voice nobody had ever heard before.

It belonged to a character no one had seen before, either. He was an old man with a ruddy complexion and a very long neck growing out of a pink suit, and a huge, curved, bright red nose.

"I am the dogs' master," the man said. "Please excuse my appearance, but the radiation here plays strange tricks, and I have been lucky! My name is Flamingosapiens, the flamingo-man, and the dogs are called Pooch, Yelp, Rover, Ivan, Jim, Luke, Manolo—"

"Please, spare us the rest. They are all very beautiful," Mei said. "But how did they end up here?"

"Well, I think they've always been here. A very old Mellon-tian told me that when he first got here, someone had told him that a Russian capsule had been wrecked on this planet several years earlier. Inside, there was a white bitch, already fairly old. Two years later, another capsule was shipwrecked on the planet. Inside, there was an American dog by the name of Tom. These are their descendants."

"Ah," Kook said. "Just out of curiosity, could you tell me the name of the little Russian bitch?"

"Laika," the flamingo man said. "Why, was she yours?"

"No," Kook said, "but I have heard about her. And you, have you ever heard about the Snakeman?"

"Of course I have!" Flamingosapiens said. "The great Pintecaboru. Everybody knows him on Mellonta."

"Could you take us to him?"

"I sure can—but I must warn you, he's a very . . . odd guy, and not very patient either."

"Who cares!" Chulain said. "There are four of us against one of them!"

"I don't think you'll be as confident, once you've met him," the flamingo said. "But, if you want, I'll take you to him. This way, please." The flamingo stretched his neck toward the ruins of a building. It was the Mellonta spaceport, still huge and awesome, even in its state of neglect. Its runways were crowded with dozens of abandoned spaceships. Smoke came out of their portholes because the *desaparecidos* used them as their homes. The large windowpanes of the spaceport lobbies were shattered and their seats were occupied by a strange array of tattered astronauts and naked, radioactive children full of sores and wounds. Only the dogs looked really alive, and they chased each other up and down the gateways, or scratched themselves on the long bar counters. The children had fun listening to the recorded voices of past stewardesses, announcing: "The passengers for the Lufthansa flight to Earth are now requested to proceed to Gate 4." There was always some madman who would stand by with a suitcase, waiting to embark.

"We are sorry to impinge thus on your sensitivity," Flamingosapiens said, noticing the expression on Mei's face, "but we *desaparecidos* are the lowest form of galactic life—terminal radioactives, mouse-faces, mutants, mutilated soldiers, drugged scientists, convicts, rusty robots, old ex-pilots, NASA sluts—in short, all those who can no longer take part in the Great Race."

"But everybody thinks this planet is uninhabited," Mei said. "If the Sinoeuropean Federation knew . . ."

The flamingo chuckled. "All those people you see over there"—he pointed straight ahead—"under that highway ramp, are Sinoeuropeans. The last ship they sent contained two thousand people—victims of excess unemployment. The Federation is well aware of what's going on up here!"

"I would never have believed it!" Mei said. "This is horrible!"

"Horrible? That's a word soon forgotten on this planet," the flamingoman said. "Here we are. This is the entrance to the superhighway. As you see, it is abandoned. Here on Mellonta, there are only two means of transportation—feet and dogs."

"Dogs? How?" Kook asked.

"Wheelsleds, like this one. Come on up!" He invited them to climb onto the oddest vehicle they had ever seen—six airplane seats mounted on truck wheels behind a windshield from a spaceship. A team of dogs, with helmets and goggles, pulled the whole thing.

"The place we're going to is full of dust and radiation," Flamingosapiens warned them. "You'd better wear your helmets too."

As they advanced noisily along the old, uneven highway, with a great creaking of wheels and the festive barking of the four-legged pistons, Chulain asked, "Where are we going?"

"To another spaceport, the one where all the expeditions for the Universal Sea begin. There is still something going on there—fuel, for one, at astronomical prices—and there is even a restaurant, and plenty of bars. But lately only a few pilots have stopped by. You're the first ones this month." They passed a shantytown built of wrecked spaceships and tin cans.

"This is where the Africans live," the flamingoman explained. "Every month we get a cargo of them. They come here hoping to find some work, but no one can adjust to this sort of rhythm. And once they've come, they can't go back."

"How do they live?" Mei asked. "What do they eat?"

"They wait for their CARE packages," the flamingoman said. "Now and then we get the carcass of some cargoship, and often its freezers are still quite full. If you manage to survive the battle to get at the food, you may be able to bring home quite a load of booty. A few days ago, we got an ice-cream cargo. Somehow, they managed to eat it all up before it melted. Three hundred people died of indigestion. Then we got a pizza cargo. We didn't eat anything else for a month, but for some reason we had difficulty digesting it. Only on the last day, an Italian who happened to stop by told us we were supposed to cook it. You know, we are not very finicky up here. Our average survival rate is five years. Well, ladies and gentlemen, here we are!"

The superhighway stopped abruptly, cut in two by a crater. Inside the crater, they saw a few huts, a landing strip, and a huge neon sign:

PINTECABORU'S. SPACESHIP RENTALS.
SPACE MAPS.
RESTAURANT WITH TOURIST MENU—
SPECIALTY: SPACE DROP SOUP.
NIGHTCLUB. LARGE ASSORTMENT OF
MACHINE GUNS.
SAUNA AND MASSAGE.
GUIDED EXCURSIONS. WILLS.
WE HAVE ALL YOU NEED IN THE GALAXY,
EXCEPT LUCK.

The sign topped the tallest hut, a real palace of wrecks, with a chimney built out of half a Thor missile. In front of it stood a small crowd of derelicts.

"This is as far as I go," the flamingoman said, and immediately turned the sled around.

"Wait!" Caruso tried to stop him. "Tell us at least how we can recognize our man!"

"Oh, you won't have any problem," Flamingosapiens screamed as the sled took off at full speed. "He is . . . a little taller than average."

Chulain shrugged his shoulders, approached the hut, and knocked on its tin door.

"Pintecaboru!" he called.

A din like the crash of two trucks came from inside. The door opened and a man emerged. He was more than seven meters tall, entirely tattooed from head to foot, and barely covered with some kind of diaper cut from an old parachute. He had only one eye, way up in his forehead, and a rather unsettling grin.

"Who's there?" he asked with the voice of an ogre. "Who dares wake me up at three in the afternoon?"

O ⼀ O ⼀ O ⼀ O ⼀ O ⼀ O ⼀ O ⼀ O ⼀ O ⼀ O ⼀ O ⼀

ZUIKAKU—WHEN MICE ABANDON SHIP

General Yamamoto wakes up feeling cold and tucks himself snugly in his blankets. He hears a voice but isn't quite sure whether he's dreaming or awake.

"General Yamamoto, Dragon of the Samurai Empire," the voice says, "this is a recorded message. It's well known, historically speaking, that when things get tough, the rats and mice abandon ship. It has also been said that this bodes ill for man. But has anyone ever wondered what it means to a mouse? What sort of future looms at the horizon of a bunch of rodents who must jump into the sea, abandoning homes, food, and memories, to swim blindly toward who knows what remote salvation? 'The mice are abandoning ship!' the boatswain screams. And, in everybody's eyes, this seems an act of supreme cowardice. Why? Why on Earth should we follow you to your ruin, when you are the ones who have wished it upon yourselves? Did you ever ask our opinion when you loaded your ships with explosives, or with black slaves, or when you opened fire on one another? If your ship then sinks, you shouldn't take it out on us! We are sick and tired of your mystifications! Let me tell you a truly exemplary story: One of our ancestors, Cidrolin de Mouses, was aboard the *Titanic* during its last cruise. He was the only mouse on ship because general taste, on ocean liners, tends more toward pink poodles. Well, two hours before the fateful moment, Cidrolin showed up in the captain's cabin flaunting two little suitcases and a raft made of pencils. He was generously warning the captain that his mouse instinct was foreseeing something bad. But the captain, misreading his well-meant message, screamed, 'Get out of here, you filthy rat,' and threw the traditional shoe at him. Not knowing what else to do, Cidrolin decided to show up in the first-class dining room. But once there, no sooner was he perceived than one hundred and sixty ladies from the best families of Europe let out a collective screech and jumped onto the tables, where they proceeded to exhibit such an enchanting parade of European ankles as to totally distract the gentlemen present from the real meaning of the event. In vain did Cidrolin de Mouses try to call their attention to the fact that he, the only mouse on board, was about to abandon ship. Everybody ignored him, except for an old waitress who chased him with a broom. As a last selfless gesture, he entered the cabin of a young British baronet. There, he showed him his suitcases, his raft, and even went so far as to mimic a long and arduous swim in a rough sea. The child looked very much interested but did not quite understand. Then, Cidrolin jumped onto the night table, stole an ice-cube from the lemonade jar, and, with admirable realism, staged the clash between the *Titanic*, represented by half a walnut shell, and the fatal iceberg. The child understood and immediately ran to warn his father.

" 'Sir,' he told him. 'sir, in a few minutes the ship will be rammed by an iceberg.'

" 'How do you know this, Ronald?' his father, the baron, inquired.

" 'A mouse told me.'

" 'Was it an English mouse?'

" 'No, sir, he looked rather like a French mouse.'

" 'Well, then,' the baron said with a smile, 'there is nothing to fear. The French are known for their tall tales!'

"A few minutes later the iceberg rammed into the *Titanic* and sank it.

"This story should be enough to show you how presumptuous you are. And yet you pride yourselves on your divinatory capacities. We all know those 'wise old men' who hieratically declaim: 'The loons are returning to the lake, soon it will be spring.' People listen to these prophets, awed by their knowledge of the seasons, and they forget who the hell it was that traveled fifteen thousand kilometers without motels or compass, braving time and weather in order to be punctually at the lake for their appointment with spring. Was it the old man who flew in on the flaps of his overcoat, or was it the loons? But it is the old man who gets all the credit for being able to predict the weather.

"It's always the same story: you are the only ones who really matter on Earth. And what about your ads? 'Fresh Farmer's Milk,' 'Granny Smith's Honey.' Have you ever tried milking a farmer? Have you ever seen your granny sucking flowers? Enough! We are sick and tired of your bullying, of your 'down,' 'sit,' 'shake,' 'heel,' 'get the ball,' 'get the slippers,' 'play dead.' We are sick and tired of being cut up or stuffed with viruses so that you can make some sensational discovery or write some brilliant scientific article. For whose benefit? This time we are not going to just sit and take it. Is it really true that mice have always abandoned sinking ships? Not quite, because this time, it is you, dear General, who's going to abandon ship, whereas we, the mice, are going to stay aboard, and your friend, General Harada, who's also sick and tired of military life, is going to pilot it. We are going to look for a place where we can live in peace, without having to scuttle away whenever we hear a human footstep. Farewell Yamamoto! We all wish you a pleasant trip.

"Signed: the 'Red Tails,' and, yours truly, Harada, who has recorded this message. Click."

Yamamoto cursed when he discovered the tiny tape recorder they had hidden in his pajama pocket. He was about to get up from his tatami mat, but the starry floor made him change his mind. While he was sleeping, the mice had dropped him into space. At that very moment, General Yamamoto was orbiting around Uranus on a flying mat.

CALALBAKRAB: THE SKY IS FALLING

"Great concert tonight," King Akrab thought sarcastically as he heard the first notes of Dzunum's instruments. "Very well! Let them sing! Let them dance! When I no longer need them, off they go. Al-Dabih, if you were still alive you'd say, 'King, your folly is nearing its end. Crazy are all those who dream of being a king.' But I am a king, and there is no limit to what I can wish. To my health!"

He poured himself another glass of wine. His hand was shaking, but the king managed to steady it, and he emptied the vessel in one long gulp. Then, he picked up one of Al-Dabih's precious decks of cards.

"The future!" he said to himself. "Oh, my poor, naïve soothsayer, you never quite understood how the future rests more in my secret archives than in your silly prophecies, or in your cards! I can push a button that will release a missile with the destructive power of a million mongols. If Genghis Khan was known as 'The Conqueror of Destiny,' then what am I? I can starve Troy in one day with a chemical bomb, stop the sun with orbital interference, cause an epidemic of bacterial plague and an invasion of napalm locusts. I can turn everybody to ice with my cryonic bombs, and split the ocean asunder with a submarine explosion. Throw all the old gods and old myths away! There is no scourge in history that the most powerful man of the twenty-second century cannot outdo."

As the king was thus indulging in his thoughts, he poured himself some more wine. But the cup slipped away from his hands, and the drink spilled over the floor. The king then realized that the entire ship was shaking, as if a terrible internal force were tearing it apart. Suddenly, a crack appeared and zigzagged its way across a wall of the room. The Great Scorpion screamed in terror, "Soldiers! What's happening?"

But his sentries did not answer. The king tried to reach the door, but an even stronger explosion threw him to the floor.

"Guards!" he called at the top of his lungs. "Quick, come! Help!"

With the frightful racket of massacred crystal, one of the great chandeliers crashed to the ground barely a meter from where the king was lying. Paintings dropped off walls, ancient armors clattered to the floor. Suddenly one of the wooden panels that covered the Rain of Gems burst open, a few diamonds shook loose and rolled all over the place, as the vibration kept increasing. The large panel gave a sinister creak, and then, all at once, collapsed. A hailstorm of precious stones pelted the king's face. The two crystal hemispheres had been reduced to powder.

At that point, the king remembered the soothsayer's words, and howled in fear. The Universe of diamonds had been destroyed. Sky and stars had fallen onto the Earth.

🪁 ● 🪁 ● 🪁 ● 🪁 ● 🪁 ● 🪁 ● 🪁 ● 🪁 ● 🪁 ● 🪁 ● 🪁 ●

MELLONTA—HOW OUR HEROES ENDED UP AS PRISONERS

֎ ֎ ֎

Kook, Mei, and the others were sitting in Pintecaboru's shack, a warehouse of sorts, filled with the most extraordinary objects. There were spaceship figureheads in the shape of dragons and sirens, gigantic, self-activating pinball machines, taken from American bases, and all sorts of secondhand spacesuits and Moon Rover vehicles for exploring planetary crusts. And there were oddly shaped stones and rocks from remote asteroids, and even a perfect small planet, with its seas and atmosphere and rain clouds, which somebody had found in the sky around Cadarmodock. There was a glass tub that contained the oddest mutant insects, the products of space experiments —the Lockheed macro-libellula, sending out intermittent flashes of light; Volenkov's pantographic spider, which could draw any object in a few seconds, using its twelve legs; and the miner's firefly with its four-thousand-watt tail. And then there was a cage with monstrous animals, such as the vacuolizer, a huge lizard with a trumpetlike mouth, capable of inhaling up to half a ton of garbage per day on any spaceship. There was the chicken-gun, which could shoot a hundred and eighty eggs per hour out of four separate holes; and the octagaroo, a creature molded out of eight identical kangaroos with a marsupial-pouch capacity of several tons.

And then, scattered all over the place, were weapons, knapsacks, food cans, cigarettes, card decks, fashionable NASA helmets, log books, and old photos of space champions.

But the most extraordinary sight in the shack was certainly Pintecaboru himself. After his elephantine size, what was most striking about him was the surface of his skin; he was entirely tattooed with the maps of planets, seas, and mysterious islands.

"To your health, my friends," the giant thundered, spraying beer all over the place. "I am Pintecaboru snakeskin! Every explorer who has happened to pass by has tattooed me with the map of the places he discovered, and maybe even those he had only dreamt. I am a geography of adventure, the map of an impossible universe. On my right hand, you'll find the black falls of Saturn, on my left one, the map of the Funny planet, where all males look like Stan Laurel and all females like Oliver Hardy for a whole year, after which they exchange faces. Come, try to climb the mountain on this bicep, if you can." And Pintecaboru pumped his muscle with a great belch. He was drunk as a skunk.

"And what about the Boojum Brothers' map?" Kook asked, "—the one that's tattooed on your foot? Can we see it?"

"Snark Boojum's map!" Pintecaboru laughed. "Of course you can see it! He himself drew it on my foot a year ago, before he disappeared. It's the map that leads to the Witch, the most dangerous spot in the Sea!"

"The Witch!" Mei whispered. "Remember? Van Cram also mentioned her."

"But why do you want this particular map?" Pintecaboru grunted, fixing his inquisitive eye like a spotlight on our friends.

"You see, Pintecaboru," Kook started explaining, "we are part of a mission . . . that's looking for a certain Van Cram."

"Ha! That's a good one!" Pintecaboru roared with laughter. "That's really something! And you expect me to believe you? Why in hell would you want to look for that jailbird? Everybody in the universe is delighted that he has disappeared! Come on, tell me the truth, what are you really looking for? Uranium? Slaves? Are you . . . running away from something? I have a good friend on Transpluto who could hide you away, so no one. . ."

"No, Mr. Pintecaboru," Mei said, "we need that map for

scientific reasons. Please, let us see it. We don't have much time."

Pintecaboru looked at the girl and, offering her a mug of beer, said, "I'm sorry to hear that, because I have absolutely no intention of letting you go. I like you too much!"

6

THE LAST DOOR

□ □

CUZCO—THE MYSTERY OF THE DOORS

□ □ □

"Obviously," Einstein said, "the first door means the right way is one and only one. Whoever built the labyrinth and the doors has probably also installed a safety device that will destroy everything that lies under there, in case we force our way in, instead of taking the right path. This, of course, means that that civilization would only give up its secret to another intelligent civilization, with a science capable of solving its enigma."

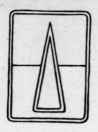

"The next four doors constitute the figure of the wheel of time, common to Incas, Hindus, Mayas, Aztecs, Celts, Egyptians, and many others. The wheel unites the four cardinal points and the seasons, but above all, past and future. It might therefore signify that they knew that some day in the future our civilizations, ours and theirs, would come into contact. And here again we are dealing with these people's obsession with time.

"Sixth Door: a man walks, as if following a star. A light descends from the sky. An omen? A spaceship? Or it might mean that we must look for the light, for the key to the mystery.

"Seventh door: a man covers his mouth with his hands—what you cannot say. Something has come down from the stars, but we cannot speak of it; it will remain a secret. The occult rites, the Inca clan, the absence of writing. Or: beware, our languages are different, communication is difficult.

"Eighth door: the magician and the wounded moon. Mystery and pain. The Inca soothsayers and their prophecies—painful, but true. Or: beware, do not try to penetrate our mystery by violent means.

"Ninth door: two symbols of the sky, two opposite skies. Two worlds, the meeting of two minds. The Incas and the aliens. Us and them. Or: beware, we are different.

"Tenth door: an assembly of people. The meeting takes place. The Incas' strong social sense. Their sense of community. But also, the union of two different worlds. Or: what lies

hidden under here was built for everybody and therefore must be respected.

Eleventh door: hands outstretched to meet one another. Aliens and terrestrials shaking hands. Recognitions. Or: beware of coming too close.

"Twelfth door: a small creature with long hair, and the signs of sun and fire, signifying Inca power. Maybe an alien, come down from the light. Or: beware, we are small but our power is great!

"Thirteenth door: A large building. The great fortresses, the roads, the great alien—or Inca—design. We have built great things; discover the design that animated them.

"Fourteenth door: the knife that slashes the goatskin, the goatskin that spills. A wound in the heart. Something interrupts this design. The sudden and violent end of this civilization. Or: beware of hasty decisions; everything could collapse. Do not wound the Earth's heart.

"Last door: people walking away. The Inca Empire disappears; its people scatter. The aliens are leaving; they are returning home. Or: you still have a long way to go."

"This," Phildys declared impatiently at the end of the exposition, "is not a simple rebus, but a web of rebuses! It's a cross between a videogame and a crèche! What on earth are we supposed to do with this?"

Einstein shook his head. "I don't know. For the moment, that's all Genius could make of the meaning of the doors."

Phildys glanced at the computer dozing at the other end of the room. "It's futile to try to interpret a thousand years of history in one day. Now that we've found the doors and know they hide something important, the best thing we can do is act concretely."

"I don't like the sound of that 'concretely,' " Einstein observed.

"I'm sorry, but you know exactly what I mean. By now, the news of the golden doors has spread far and wide. How long do you think it's going to take Pyk, his multinationals, and his new pals, the Aramerussians, to make the best of it and turn it against us? They're already spreading the rumor that we down here would rather philosophize than act. They're not altogether wrong."

"You call it philosophy not to shoot the Indians?" Einstein protested. "You forget that anything we know about the doors we owe to them!"

"But now they refuse to lead us any farther," Phildys countered.

"Right! But that mystery is connected to them. It's a message they've sent us from their past. If we break this thread that unites us, we'll lose everything."

"There's no time left," Phildys said. "If we don't reach a settlement, the Japanese and Arab ships will attack *Proteus Tien*. Soon we'll have to admit that our mission in space has failed, and that these mines are our only energy source."

"But what about the planet with the sun? And Mei, and Kook, and all our dreams . . . and our freedom—"

"Listen, Einstein." Phildys took him by the arm. "I'm not so sure there is any place left for these things in the world that is awaiting us. I know, I know—once there were many races, many people, many different lands. But if we want to survive, we must accept the idea of a single race, of a technological man, a superior man who will be identical everywhere, in Europe, in Africa, under ice, and on the Moon. Just as every land will also be the same, and every idea. This is the only way we can govern Earth today. Since there is no longer any possibility of choice, since there are no more adventures to live, freedom is a word that no longer makes sense. Einstein, the screenplay of the world has already been filmed; now, all we can do is sit back and watch it."

○   ○   ○

↗ ⊖ ↗ ⊖ ↗ ⊖ ↗ ⊖ ↗ ⊖ ↗ ⊖ ↗ ⊖ ↗ ⊖ ↗ ⊖ ↗ ⊖ ↗ ⊖

MELLONTA:
HOW OUR FRIENDS ESCAPED
PINTECABORU
● ● ●

At sea, never say
you've seen the tallest wave—
there's always a bigger swell
in store for you,
there's always more wind than sail,
always more islands than words.
Sailor, put the North
and the South in your pocket.
You can climb ten masts lashed together,
you can look further than ever—
Where is your faraway girl?
Where's the end of the world?
There's always more wind than sail,
always more islands than words.
Sailor, put the North
and the South in your pocket.
Where's the end of the world?

"Come on, one more song, guys!" Pintecaboru thundered,
his shack still shaking from his last raucous note.

"What about 'Leilah's Island,' Pinte?" Kook said in a
hoarse voice. " 'Beautiful Leilah, with her fields of clover,
all alone without her lover—' Hey, Mei, why don't you join
us?"

"In a while," Mei answered, somewhat depressed. The har-
monious sight of Pinte and the Proteus Brothers stretched out
on the floor in front of a crowd of beer bottles somehow failed
to raise her hopes about the outcome of the mission.

Chulain drew himself up and, reeling from one wall of the

shack to the other, roared, "Hey, Pinte! You know how it goes —all drink and no food makes Cu a dull boy! Anything to eat in this place?"

"Sure, my friends," the giant said. "If you want, I can take you to the genetic greenhouse! It's got everything you could want. You can even see it from the window."

"The genetic greenhouse?" Kook said. "That glass shed?"

"Yeah! You see, in this part of Mellonta there was once a laboratory for genetic experiments—of a very particular kind. I remember when they tried to stretch pigs so they would be born with more ribs and more meat to barbecue. First, they produced what they called the pigget—the pig basset—three meters long. Then they came up with the piggon—the pig wagon—and finally they invented the pigrain—the pig train— anywhere between ten to twenty times as long as its predecessor."

"Lots of baloney, I bet!" Chulain said.

"You bet!" Pinte confirmed. "Then they tried to create the ultrathin worker. I'm not kidding. To make up for all the accidents in which workers were getting squashed and crippled by heavy machinery. They thought, Why not a worker who's only a few millimeters thick? That way he can survive the full weight of compression and avalanches without even getting crumpled—or maybe just a little. All we'd have to do is iron him out a bit and he'd be ready for work again."

"Did they succeed?"

"Well, you see, they produced a hundred workers, each as thick as a sheet of paper, but after only one day, they were all gone. They sort of made a deal with us. We folded them like paper airplanes and launched them out of the windows. They could really soar! Back then, the organic garden was right out there. This was during the time when transplants were the rage, and all the rich wanted to get new organs, but there weren't enough donors, so a few scientists decided to mass-produce organs as if they were onions or carrots. First, they developed *in vitro* genetic models of hearts or livers, and then they seeded the embryonic organs in soil soaked with special chemicals. And you see the results. The things that look like pumpkins are lungs. Notice how they keep on pumping oxygen. Next to them is a plot of athletic hearts. The spleens usually grow right below them, but they're out of season now. Over there—that leafless vine—those are creeping intestines; they grow like weeds. And then, right below them—well, I'm sure you can recognize them on your own. They come in two varieties, miniature and elephantine. And that's a gall bladder. Have you ever tasted Mellonta gall bladder? Shall I go get some?"

"Please, don't bother," Kook said with a green face. "We're not really that hungry—but you—is that what you eat?"

"Who, me? Come off it, Kook, I thought you knew!" The giant laughed. "I don't eat what you eat. I eat stories!"

"You're kidding!" Mei said. "What do you mean—stories?"

"It's true!" Pintecaboru insisted. "When I started growing out of control, they brought me here to the genetic center. That's when they realized that I could stay for months without eating! My cells fed on one another, generating new cells on their own, and that's how I kept on mysteriously growing. I had lots of abnormal cells and quite a few incompatible ones as well, but instead of destroying me, everything managed to get along quite nicely, despite all the known laws of genetics. The physicians here did their damnedest to reduce me. First, they tried to restructure me chemically with hormonal injections. Then, they zapped me with X-rays and various other beams. They even gave me electroshock! But in the end, they had to throw up their hands. When I left the laboratory, I had to start making a living. I got a couple of minor roles in horror movies, but mostly they wanted me for publicity stunts. Soon I became a TV star. But I didn't want to spend my life saying what others wanted me to say; playing the role of the polite monster is really not my trip. So I decided to start my own business, and I put up this shack for space explorers. Then I realized what it was that made me grow. Every time somebody came by and told me a story—a beautiful story with lots of names and faraway places and inventions and fabulous animals, and maybe even a few lies and incongruities, but well told, and with enthusiasm—well, every time this happened, I would relax and feel content—and really full. Then, one time, after a Greek traveler had told me the story of his return to his native island, I noticed I had gained four kilos. It was then that I understood. Beautiful adventures were my food! Every time I hear a story, I get bigger and happier. Lately, the stories I've heard have unfortunately been very skimpy—small, prechewed morsels, often stale, things I've already heard. Nobody has drawn any new lands on my skin. That's why I won't let you go till you've told me at least eight stories, two morbid ones, two spicy ones, two sweet ones, and two rustic ones."

"Pintecaboru," Chulain exclaimed, "we can do better than that! We have at least a thousand stories with us. And you can hear them all at once!"

"Are you kidding? A thousand stories?"

"If you let me go back to our ship, I'll show you."

"I don't trust you," the giant said. "I've only got one eye, but I know a fox when I see one!"

"Then tell one of your sidekicks to go fetch the big box in the cockpit of the spaceship."

Half an hour later, a Mellontian returned, carrying Chulain's mysterious box. Pintecaboru looked at it with an expression of great disappointment.

"This is it?" he said. "Where are all the stories you promised?"

"This is a space TV," Chulain explained. "It picks up the programs from Earth and all the other space stations. Eight hundred and fifteen channels. This is its remote control. You can follow eight hundred stories all at once."

"I don't believe it," Pintecaboru said. "It's impossible!"

"Why don't you take a look?" Chulain flicked a switch and a series of multicolored signals flashed out at once—Antenna Mars, Jupiter One, Jupiter Two, Saturn, Telering, Telemeskor-

ska, Channel Sam, Milkyvideo, Telemohammed International, Video Venus, Sinoeuropean Channel, TV Steppe,
Popular Channel, Telepluto, Telesun, Telebluemoon, and
hundreds of other small pivate stations broadcasting from satellites, asteroids, and minor planets.

"What's so great about this?" Pintecaboru protested. "It's
just a bunch of colored circles!"

"Those are the stations' pattern signals! The flags of the TV
army! Obviously, this is a dead hour, but when they start
broadcasting tomorrow morning, you'll need a hundred eyes
to follow everything!" Chulain proclaimed with the emphasis
of an announcer.

"My friend!" Pintecaboru said, taking the remote control
into his huge hand. "This is really the best present you could
have given me! Hey, you, over there, come here! I've got a
black box that has as many tattoos as Pintecaboru, and that
knows almost as many stories! We'll never be bored again, my
friends!"

"I wanna see some cartoons," a radioactive mutant
screamed, rushing into the shack.

"And I want a movie with a Robert Mitchum hologram,"
another one said.

"Take it easy, take it easy," Pintecaboru said. "Sit down and
wait. In a couple of hours, there'll be plenty for everyone. And,
as far as you're concerned, my sweet little friends, you're free
to go. You can even take a photo of the map of my foot; that
is, if you can stand its French perfume."

One hour later, *Proteus Tien* was ready to leave Mellonta behind, but our heroes did not look very happy.

"I know, I know," Chulain said, "we didn't behave very
well. We made friends with him and then we fucked him
over."

"Why do you say that?" Caruso said. "We didn't fuck him
over; we gave him a TV set, didn't we?"

"Yes, Caruso, but we didn't tell him the whole truth. It is true that the set can pick up eight hundred and fifteen channels, but it is also true that after the energy crisis, they all broadcast the same intergovernmental program. The only things that change are the commercials. Otherwise, all eight hundred and fifteen buttons will tune into the same thing—interviews with Pyk and Phildys, computerized dossiers, the same old debates about media control among the same four duplicate journalists, a quiz program sponsored by a mouseburger company and hosted by two nonagenarian MCs who ask their questions from their respective beds. And all this for twelve hours a day."

"Poor Pintecaboru," Mei said. "He'll die if he eats all that junk!"

"Not necessarily," Chulain said. "He'll just have to go on a diet. On Sunday there is always an old flick. Or the game. He won't get fat on them, but they're better than nothing. Farewell, Mellonta; we'll keep a fond memory of you."

"Four fond memories," Caruso corrected him. "Sara has found four dogs hiding in the kitchen."

● ● ● ● ● ● ● ● ● ● ● ● ● ● ● ● ● ● ● ●
CALALBAKRAB: THE END OF THE SCORPION
❦ ❦ ❦

It all happened very quickly. At 9:22, Ultradivarious, Coyllur's moog violin, sent out its attack note, an ultrasonic blast with a terrifying power of sixteen thousand hendrix decibels. Only the rebels, who had protected their ears with special plugs, were able to withstand it. All the others, the warriors and servants of King Akrab, collapsed to the floor, unconscious, almost immediately. The rebels disarmed them and occupied the crucial points of the ship. Two minutes later, the mutiny was complete. Vassiliboyd told the prisoners that whoever wanted to move to the half of the ship that was going to drift into space with King Akrab was free to do so. But everybody, including Akrab's most faithful guards, shouted enthusiastically that they wanted to stay with Vassiliboyd. The cruelty of the king had destroyed any shred of loyalty. Prison cells and torture chambers were opened, and one of the rebel guards went to fetch the diamond from Akrab's necklace, so that they could insert it into the computer. The severance mechanism went into operation immediately. In three minutes, *Zuben al-Genubi* would detach from *Zuben al-Schemali*. That's when Vassiliboyd realized Coyllur was missing, and started looking for her all over the ship.

In the meantime, on *al-Schemali*, King Akrab had come to. He immediately tried to bring his hands to his chest to grab his necklace with its powerful stone, but he realized that both his hands and his feet had been tied with chains. Only then did he notice, bent over him, the faces of his favorite wives and most loyal guards.

"Free me!" he shouted. "Traitors! Free me at once!"

Nobody answered him. The king understood why. The Sky of Gems had fallen; Al-Dabih's prophecy was coming true.

"Oh, my dear girls, what have I done to deserve such a cruel destiny!" the king moaned. "And, if that weren't enough, from your own sweet hands, from you who found only friendship and kindness among my subjects, from you who have shared all my treasures, and benefited from the immense generosity of my hands!"

At that moment, Coyllur entered the room. With terror, the king realized that she was wearing a jewel in the shape of a bird around her neck. The eagle of the prophecy!

"Scorpion," she said, "my name is Coyllur. Through my veins flows the blood of the condor, of Atahualpa and Tupac

Amaru. Years ago, you razed my village to the ground with your bombs. You pillaged its houses and murdered my brothers. My people have not forgotten."

"You must be crazy!" Akrab screamed. "My favorite brides, my loving mates! My loyal soldiers! Listen! All the jewels on this floor are yours if you kill this woman!"

But nobody answered. Their eyes were fixed on Coyllur.

"Leave," Coyllur told the women. "In a few seconds, the two parts of the ship will separate. Run to *al-Genubi* if you want to be safe."

The soldiers escorted the women out, and the chained king and Coyllur were left alone, face to face.

"You are crazy!" the king repeated. "Look around you. Look at all this wealth. Do you want it all to be lost? If this is destroyed, there will be nothing great left in the world."

Coyllur stepped closer. In her hands she held a white string.

"The rivers," she said with the low, weary voice of an ancient woman, "the rivers will be left. And then, they'll be able to rest, after carrying so many corpses. My brother Riobaldo waltzed over the river, a dead waltz through the reeds, and Garabombo also went by and leaned against the pylon of a bridge as if to nap. And Atahualpa passed through Yahuar Mayu, the river of blood, wearing his golden robe. Scorpion, do you hear how loud the noise of the river has become? Can you feel the spray of its icy water? Do you hear it roaring closer and closer?"

"You're crazy!" the king screamed, trembling. "What are you talking about? Who are you talking about?"

"Don't you know them?" Coyllur asked. "When the river asked who had sent them, they spoke your name. And they were shouting it to their brothers on the banks as they went. Didn't you hear them? Maybe because there are those who die like fish, under the water, and nobody hears them. And then there are those who die like birds, high in the sky, and their screams are loud; but when they fall, they are only a bundle of feathers, no longer a bird, no longer a king."

"Don't kill me!" the king cried. "No one can really kill the Scorpion! Another will enter inside my empty skin and take my place immediately."

"I know that," Coyllur said.

"Well then, why?" the Scorpion asked. "Why? . . ."

But Coyllur had already tightened the string around his neck. And so it was that Temugin Sadalmelik Akrab, the conqueror, strangled to death, two hours after sunset.

After killing the king, Coyllur sat on the throne of the Scorpion. She sat there impassively, as Vassiliboyd's voice came thundering across the loudspeakers of the ship, warning its inmates there were only a few seconds left before the detachment was to take place. She heard despair in the pilot's voice as he called her name. Then there was a sudden flare, and *Zuben al-Schemali* tumbled into space as if an impetuous river were dragging it farther and farther and forever away from *Zuben al-Genubi*.

♀ ♀

MELLONTA MON AMOUR
♀ ⊖ ♀

Ground Control to Yamamoto, Tokyo project. We reconfirm the order to drop a plutonium bomb on Mellonta to destroy the Sinoeuropean ship and prevent anyone else from using the artificial planet as a base. Since we are no longer able to carry out our mission, we must keep the others from doing it, as well.

Yamamoto to Ground Control, Tokyo project. Message received. The time is six-thirty, the sky is clear, the weather is fine. Following your instructions, I have abandoned the flying mat and am now proceeding through space on the minirocketbike that was stored in the pocket of my pajamas and that I have now assembled according to the accompanying manual. I have also found the box of suppositories, but I can't figure out which one is the bomb. Please elucidate.

Tokyo project. The bomb is the third suppository from the left. You'll recognize it by the slight ticking. To be sure it will demolish its objective, it will have to be dropped directly over the Mellonta spaceport. A few civilians will inevitably be sacrificed. According to our computer, the explosion will cause 98,154 instant deaths, more or less the same number as Hiroshima.

Yamamoto to Ground Control. I am approaching the planet, and am gradually pedaling up to an altitude of nine thousand meters. I am not acquainted with that particular mission you mention, but am sure it will be quite a slaughter down there, for the population of the planet seems to be concentrated around the spaceport. The time is eight-eleven, and the sky over the city is clear.

Tokyo project. We are very pleased to inform you that your bike has been named *Eno Higai,* after your mother —a name that will make history. The plutonium bomb is regulated to explode at six hundred meters above ground. We wish to inform you that we are totally in the dark as to the effect of such a powerful explosion on a space station, nor can we guarantee that your life will be spared.

Yamamoto to Ground Control. I am not afraid! The dragon on my uniform is not the peaceful, rain-bearing dragon of the Chinese, but the avenging dragon, the fire-

bearer, whose shield is marked with the symbol of the
sun, the swastika! No death could be as noble as mine! I
have now reached nine thousand meters. I see the objective clearly below me. The time is eight-thirteen and
thirty seconds. The minibomb is ready to be dropped and
should hit its objective in exactly thirty seconds. I am
waiting for the order to proceed.

  Tokyo project. Go ahead.

The bomb plummeted through space, minuscule, invisible,
ineluctable.

  Falling, the deathdrop sees Mellonta. At first, it is just a flat,
uneventful plain. Then a few signs begin to appear, gradually
cohering into villages, rivers, roads, mountains. The first
houses are now fairly distinct, along with the larger squares of
the fields and the smaller ones of the gardens. Now the river
is clearly visible, blue and sinewy. Where it curves, there is a
black spot—Pintecaboru—lying supine, staring at the sky. He
is listening to the noises of that hot morning. Each fly is an
orchestra. Suddenly, Pintecaboru's eyes see something. For no
apparent reason, he has a vision. He sees a face. Why so suddenly, and so clearly? And yet here it is again. It was a morning, just like this one. The sea was calm, the dog was asleep,
all was silent, and her clothes were drying in the sun. Why
now, Pinte? She must have changed, she must be older now.
See her immediately, Pinte. Why such a hurry? You don't
know why, but it is so. You are raving, Pinte. Can you hear
that noise? Maybe it's just another falling ship, but it must be
big to judge from the cloud it has raised. It's hot, today, Pinte.
Very hot. The river looks as if it's burning. I would like to
leave, to find her, if I only knew where she was. To tell her
only—to tell her what? That's quite a cloud down there. And
the ground is shaking. What the hell is going on?

. . .

The bomb produced a mushroom of smoke and metal detritus sixteen kilometers high, and split Mellonta into four pieces. The American sector had totally disintegrated. Much to the photographers' dismay, there were no survivors—or corpses.

Tokyo project to Yamamoto. Total success! The visible effects are even more imposing than we had expected when we first tested the bomb. Mr. Truman himself, the president of the Mellonta Space Construction Company, has complimented us. Congratulations, General.

Yamamoto to Ground Control. I am very disappointed at having survived. I am therefore informing you that I am about to commit hara-kiri with the handle of my bike.

Tokyo project. Don't you dare do anything as idiotic as that! Everything is going well!

Yamamoto to Ground Control. Says who? When the Americans bombed Japan, they caused a million casualties. We have only reached ninety thousand. A mere car crash. I would like to do more for the military cause.

Tokyo here. No sweat. You'll have your chance. Our spying mechanism has just informed us that *Proteus Tien* managed to leave Mellonta twenty seconds before the explosion. The main objective of the mission has been missed.

Yamamoto here. I shall attack the ship on my own, availing myself of the Humanosuke procedure.

○ HUMANOSUKE THE INVINCIBLE ○

"Everything has blown up! Disintegrated!" Chulain exclaimed, greatly upset, while the shreds of Mellonta flew
through the sky as in a slow-motion movie.

"They've all been killed," Kook cried. "All of them! But who
did it?!"

Mei was not talking. With her eyes closed, she was squeezing the arms of her chair. She did not see, through the side
window, the dark shadow that was climbing the walls of the
ship.

Yamamoto, having reached *Proteus* with his rocket bike,
was now lying in wait on the roof of the ship. He had removed
his spacesuit and was searching through its pockets. He was
wearing a silver leotard that sheathed him from head to toe,
leaving only his eyes uncovered. He covered them with a pair
of reinforced goggles. He took a pill, moaned for a while as if
in pain, and then began to swell. His muscles had been freeze-
dried and compressed by means of a chemical procedure so
that they would occupy less space on the ship. But now they
were returning to their normal size, quivering under the silver
skin. The general was turning into Humanosuke Yamamoto,
the great, invulnerable wrestler. His impressive chest swelled
up, and his biceps, whose circumference already exceeded
one meter, but kept on growing, popped like corn in a
skillet.

He posed like a body-builder against a background of stars
and shouted, "Death to you all! Behold Humanosuke, the war
machine, the cosmic vigilante. His armored leotard of atanax
metal protects him against heat, acid, and bullets. His strength
is that of twenty men. In his right hand he holds a rotating
laser sword, known as Dragon's Talon, and in his left hand, a
pistol with the searing power of nine suns, known as Dragon's
Breath. No weapon on this ship can stop him."

Chulain heard the shouts and went to the porthole. "Somebody's getting too close for comfort," he said. "We'd better get the safety screen ready."

"Too late," Kook cried. "Look!"

A rain of white light told them that Yamamoto was already melting the roof of the ship with his nine-sun gun. And, in fact, after a few seconds, the general's impressive bulk dropped into the middle of the *Proteus* cockpit with a feline pounce.

"Banzai!" Yamamoto screamed.

"Fa-sheng!" Mei countered, and lunged at him with a flying kick. But Yamamoto shielded himself with his arm, and his laser sword swished over Mei, who dodged the blow by throwing herself to the ground.

"You're helpless against me!" Yamamoto roared. "I am a war machine! Ninety people have challenged me, and ninety people have died."

"Chulain," Kook yelled. "Do something! Stop him!"

"There is nothing we can do," the black answered. "He has no vulnerable points. His armor protects him against all our weapons. He is too strong for us to even think of tackling him. And he has a sword that could slice this ship like a loaf of bread."

"Then what can we do?" Caruso quailed as the huge warrior slowly advanced toward him.

"Try tears," Chulain said. "Maybe they'll move him!"

"I'll start with you," Yamamoto thundered, pointing at Mei, "since you despise the noble arts of war in which the Orient excelled, and prefer its philosophies of peace. Tremble, Mei!"

Yamamoto's sword whirled in the air, forming a ring of blue fire. Mei managed to elude two blows, then three, but in the end she was trapped against the wall. Yamamoto's blade rose and was about to deliver the coup-de-grâce, when Chulain rammed into the legs of the general and threw him to the floor. But Yamamoto knew how to fight, even in the most awkward positions. His sword charred the black's back like a thunderbolt. Mei screamed. The general stood up and, with a powerful yell, threatened the three survivors, who were squirming against the wall.

"With just one swing of this sword, I shall destroy you all! You can't stop the invulnerable warrior, the avenging arm!"

Kook hugged Mei, and Caruso hugged both of them. Huddled together protectively, they awaited the fatal blow—which never came. The general stood there, immobile, brandishing his sword with both hands.

"Enough, Yamamoto!" Kook protested. "No need to be cruel! Kill us and be done with it!"

But suddenly the warrior seemed to stagger under the weight of his sword. He let it drop and brought his hands to his throat, with a horrible croaking sound. Obviously, he was having difficulty breathing. Kook noticed that his face was swelling. After a few seconds, Yamamoto collapsed to the ground, kicked the air a couple of times, and then lay still. Mei approached him, incredulous, and removed his hood. "He's dead!" she said. "What happened?"

Caruso stared at the bluish face of the general and turned ghostly pale. He then scoured the floor with his eyes, obviously looking for something.

"What are you looking for, Caruso?" Kook asked him, his voice still trembling with fear. "What happened? He was . . . invulnerable, and yet . . . he died, in just a few seconds."

"He was invulnerable, except in one spot—his tongue. When he threatened us, something hit him there. Something tiny, but deadly—this!" And Caruso opened his fist to show them Sara's body lying inert in the palm of his hand.

"She knew what to do," Caruso said. "While he was yelling, she sneaked into his mouth and stung him on the tongue. The tongue immediately swelled up, choking him to death. She sacrificed herself for us."

"Sacrificed herself?" Mei wondered.

"Yes," Kook explained. "When a bee stings, it leaves its stinger inside the wound, and then dies."

⊖ ⊖ ⊖ ⊖ ⊖ ⊖ ⊖ ⊖ ⊖ ⊖ □ □ ⊖ ⊖ ⊖ ⊖ ⊖ ⊖ ⊖ ⊖ ⊖

ON EARTH: GENIUS LIES
◉ ◉ ◉

"Well, Genius," Einstein said, "have you had a chance to examine the data on the fifteen doors?"

"Yes, I have."

"What can you tell me about them?"

"That there is one door, only one, that will lead you to the heart of the earth. If you open any other, everything will collapse. As for the meaning of the doors, I have already given you all eighty-six possible interpretations."

"Why did they install these doors?"

"I don't know."

"Were they aliens, Incas, or something else? Is there any connection between these doors and the remote planet?"

"I don't know."

"Well done, Genius," Einstein said. "I admire your coherence. Now, shall we play a game?"

"Oh, goody! Let's play palindromes. You know, those words that can be read forward and backward. Let's see who has the longest palindrome. I'll go first: *saippuakauppias!*"

"What? What's that?" Einstein asked.

"It means seller of lye, in Finnish. And listen to this Pompeian inscription: *sator arepo tenet opera rotas.* Or this French one: *à révéler mon nom, mon nom relevera!* And then—"

"Enough, Genius! Get serious! Now we are going to play the game of lies. You are going to tell lies."

"But I can't," the computer said.

"Right," Einstein agreed. "You can't tell lies; that is, you cannot say anything that does not correspond to the truth of the internal organization of your information. But I can feed you the wrong information, and, by so doing, modify its organization. That way, as far as your conscience goes, you won't have lied, but the result will be that you have not said the truth. It happens to humans too."

"Interesting," Genius noted. "On the other hand, what about a nice anagram?—"

"Shut up! For instance, let's pretend that the data I've given you has nothing to do with real history, but is material for a novel. In that case, you wouldn't need scientific logic to connect the various parts. You could use something similar to fantasy, skip three or four connections, insert sixteen—I repeat, sixteen—errors, choose an absurd data base rather than the correct one, and thus upset all the coherent information you have."

"What fun!" the computer said. "Let's play!"

"OK, then, here's your new language, Genius. Are you ready? Swallow this cassette!"

"Gulp! Done. I'm ready!"

"All right, Genius, tell me: What civilization built those doors?"

"A civilization known as the Remote-controlled Snake, or Kincanana, which sent a spaceship from the star Bellatrix all the way to Earth, where the aliens met the Incas in an encounter that was at once open, constructive, and extraordinarily cordial, and the two peoples got drunk together, and then said, 'Why don't we do something that will make the idiots of the future say, "Wow, there is something really mysterious about that civilization," and send them on a wild-goose chase to figure out what that mystery might be?'

"One of them suggested, 'Why not build an upside-down pyramid'; and another, 'Why don't we spell out IDIOT WHO READS over nine kilometers of desert'; and yet another, 'Why don't we build a well-hidden tomb, and inside it place a skeleton made with a mixture of bones taken from an ape, a mouse, an elephant, and a condor, and then place a crown on its head? They'll go crazy!' But in the end, they opted for the fifteen doors."

"Not bad, Genius," Einstein said. "But you should try to be a little more plausible. So where does the Van Cram vector come from?"

"From sector sixteen, the Witch's Cloud. Its coordinates are two-hundred-sixteen by eighty-three, and it is sitting right below you. That's the natural planet. Even children know it," the computer answered.

"Perfect. And what's beyond these fifteen doors?"

"A spaceship in the shape of a seven-hundred-meter-long candelabrum, like the one in the Inca-Nazca drawing; a pickled dinosaur, perfectly preserved; a nightclub with a Martian mambo orchestra; and twelve frozen aliens, half a meter tall, each with a blue beard that sweeps his feet, and a large red nose that takes off whenever he is angry, zaps the enemy in the face and then boomerangs back to its place."

"Very well, Genius, we're almost there," Einstein said. "Are you ready to lie to Phildys, and tell him that you are about to solve the mystery of the doors, and that we must persist?"

"What'll you give if I do?"

"All the palindromes in the world, and a new program to beat the Russian computers at chess!"

"It's a deal," Genius said. "But I don't think it will work. Besides, Einstein, how's this language so different from the one I spoke before?"

"I'm not sure," the boy sighed. "Lately, I can't help thinking that if there is a language that's really abstract and false, it is the language of 'common sense' and 'pragmatism' spoken by politicians. What do you think?"

"I don't agree," the computer said, winking one of his lights.

⊖ ⊖

SUMMIT MEETING AT THE SHERATONOV HOTEL

⊖ ⊖ ⊖

We are in the Venecia Room of the Sheratonov Hotel on the Paseo de la República in Lima. It is the most beautiful hotel in

Peru, particularly as it is by now the only hotel in Peru. The most powerful men of the world have gathered around a large table. The one in the black uniform with the gold embroidered dragon is our old acquaintance, General Saito, representative of the Samurai Empire. At his side stand two fierce ichthyolures. Smitsky is there, also, in a mink tuxedo, representing the American sheiks. Next to him, swathed in an immense and funereal bear fur, sits the Soviet general Ivan Ilyich Serebryukhov. Apparently, he is very ill, and under his massive overcoat, he hides an iron lung and two doctors ready to intervene. At the head of the table sits Sadalmelik Shaula, new Arab leader, pretender to Akrab's throne. To his left, with the long harelike ears and gray complexion of a space mutant, sits Kraptnunk Armadillion, president of the industrial space colonies. On the other side of the table sit the representatives of the twenty-six Sinoeuropean political parties: the prime minister, General Phildys Plassey (Rotmod, the "rotten" Moderate Party), Showspotshow Pyk (Corporate Party), Cha-Tan and Mengele Moon (Militarist Party), and then all the other ones —from the Tentative Democrats to the RRR (Replicants Ready to Revolt). The only representative of the various opposition parties of the three empires is absent, due to an air accident. Somehow or other, the parachute that was supposed to land him in Lima, gently and in time for the meeting, turned out to be a knapsack—a discovery made, alas, too late to do anything about it.

The meeting is already in its third hour of parliamentary debate when Shaula's sword flashes through the air and ends up stuck into the table.

"Enough!" the sheik screamed. "As the Black Book says, 'The stupid frogs were blabbing, so they didn't hear the snake.' We have already talked too much! We want to start work in that mine immediately, using all means and methods at our disposal. If you want to participate, fine! Otherwise—"

"Otherwise it will be war!" Cha-tan yelled, drawing his sword. An ichthyolure immediately jumped onto the table, growling and snapping at him until Saito dragged it back to its place.

"Easy, gentlemen, easy," Phildys said. "Let's reason a bit. What will . . . eventuate at the mine?"

"Total evacuation of the area," Shaula said. "Conscription of all the Indians who survive. Instant execution of anyone who refuses to work. An atomic bomb dropped right onto the mountain. You'll see whether we can unearth that mysterious 'heart' of yours!"

"Wait a second," Phildys said. "Einstein's last report says there is a self-destruct mechanism connected to those doors. Besides, that same report hypothesizes that an alien civilization—"

"Enough, Phildys," Shaula interrupted. "Enough lies! Whoever refuses to sign an alliance with us is an alien! The modern military-technological civilization needs this energy, and that's all there is to it. If we want to save Earth, we'll have to bomb it—I mean—"

"No need to explain, it's all crystal clear," Pyk said. "I back the sheiks' motion. Let's vote."

"We haven't even started talking about Mission Terra," Phildys protested.

"Nor do we have to! It's all over," Shaula said. "The desire for that planet makes people unhappy; it is a pernicious symbol. That's why we have to leak the news that the mission has been postponed. By and by, the public's attention will shift to something else. We'll seek it again in due time, but first our people must forget it exists."

"I agree a hundred percent," Saito said. "Let's vote. All those for bombing the mine raise your hand; all those against, put your hand inside the ichthyolure's mouth."

"I propose an amendment," Phildys said. "Let's start the work in three days, the time necessary to prepare public opinion to accept this alliance and the postponement of the space mission."

"Amendment passed," Smitsky said. "But at midnight,

sharp, on the third day, our army will be posted at the Cuzco base. In the meantime, a joint commission of scientists will prepare an extensive report about those fifteen doors."

"All right, then," Saito said. "Ayes, raise your hands. Any Nays might want to call their wives one last time before voting. We'll be waiting."

∘ The Reports of the Interfederal Commission ∘

The Fifteen Doors of Cuzco: An Interpretation
Hector García Tiburón, Ph.D.,
Professor of Anthropology,
Mexico City University

I find no particular difficulty in interpreting the fifteen doors of Cuzco. In the first place, they must be read from the bottom up, and with the spiral movement typical of the Mayan and Mexican languages. These doors constitute a great archaeological treasure, and their meaning is evident: they conceal the tomb of the Inca monarchs.

The intention of the original builders was that these doors be entrusted to the care of the only people capable of truly respecting them, namely the South American leaders, direct descendants of that civilization and rightful repositories of its culture.

It is therefore obvious that the whole area in question must be turned into a large museum, provided with all the necessary ancillary services such as hotels and souvenir stalls. Any other use of this wealth would be perverse and opportunistic. I am therefore enclosing our project for Incaland, a residential compound consisting of eight thousand townhouses, all in pure Inca style, and a faithful reconstruction of the Temple of the Sun, which will become the site of a series of cultural events, including real human sacrifices, whose victims will be chosen among the Indians suffering from malignant carcinoma. As the terraces of Machu Picchu are fairly steep, we plan to build a steel escalator to bring our guests to the top of the hill—that is, to the three-story restaurant named after Atahualpa. Of course, Mount Accauantay will have to be lowered slightly so as not to obscure the view from the observation deck.

With regard to Doctor Einstein's objections that such a project would inevitably harm the local population, we refuse to accept that young man's recommendations. Didn't he, just as an experiment, recently have a computer draw up a plan for a hypothetical coup d'état in Chile? And weren't those very plans, mysteriously acquired, recently put into effect during an actual coup in that country? We shall not listen to such an irresponsible person.

Cuzco's Fifteen Doors: A Scientific Report
Nureddin al-Hazen, D.B.A., expert in industrial programming, Cairo University

Cuzco's fifteen doors are a mystery only to the ignorant. They remain obscure only because, as the Prophet says, "a blind man believes all other men are black." This is why, in his sublime superficiality, Doctor García thinks that the doors must be read from the bottom up, when, in fact, it is quite obvious that they must be read from right to left, just like Arabic. Read this way, the meaning of the doors becomes immediately evident. The doors lead to an immense treasure of gold, the famous Eldorado.

They conceal no religious or scientific meaning, but rather an extraordinary fortune, to which only our empire can legitimately aspire.

We shall, therefore, melt the fifteen doors and turn them into ingots because, while their artistic value is considerable, their value as gold is even greater. The same procedure will be followed for the gold walls and every single gold object found within those chambers. In short, everything will be turned into concrete and solid gold capital.

As for Doctor García Tiburón's skill in impugning the integrity of other scientists, we wonder whether he isn't, by chance, the very same Professor García to whom we owe Project Atlantis, which saw twelve thousand *desaparecidos* ruthlessly dispatched to the bottom of the sea wearing cement overcoats. We shall not listen to such an irresponsible character!

Cuzco and Its Fifteen Doors: An Essay
Ludwig von Kluge, D.D., freethinker of the German Academy of Europe

It appears that everybody here is intent on contradicting Kierkegaard's famous dictum: "If man were an animal, he would not feel *Angst*." I gaze around me and all I see is a room full of anxious asses. For example, here is Dr. al-Hazen, who firmly believes we should read from right to left what, instead, must absolutely be read from left to right, like the languages of our civilized European countries. Once we have done so, we soon discover that the doors of Cuzco enclose, strictly speaking, *nothing*. The fact that they are closed indicates an *Enthüllen*, a revelation, in that they express the intrinsic nondirectionality of any kind of thought, be it ancient or modern; in other words, they are the ultimate mockery within which the will to know imprisons itself. *We* are the ones locked behind those doors, and, on the other side, beyond, some mystery observes us, pitying us for our captivity.

No metaphysical or scientific light will ever illuminate this exile with any certainty. Only a total and courageous passivity, only an absolute immobility, will spare us the derision of the cosmos. Knowledge is not opinion. It is the absence of opinion. At least, this is my firm opinion.

But beware! We must not touch those doors; we must let them rot, and we must let the earth freeze—only then will our prison doors open. No. We must not exist. Let us have an end to the Zen master who answers his student's question with another question. An end to questions and answers; an end to masters and students! This is what I keep repeating, day after day, in the course of my lectures in Berlin, during my seminars in London, at my symposia in Havana; this is what I keep shouting at all my students: you should not exist; I do not exist!

If I appeared to protest so vociferously about not receiving my July paycheck, this was not, as my enemies intimated, a sign that I had returned to the conflicts of being. Quite the contrary: this minor earthly negligence painfully reminded me of the universal negligence, the infinite distance between me and God, and vice versa. In short, it reminded me of my death. Though it is not really a question of death, but rather a feeling of nonexistence, which, if you have never felt it, I cannot possibly describe for you. Do whatever you damn well please with those mines! And those Indians—why should I give a fuck about them? I won't listen to such ignoramuses!

Cuzco: The Mystery of Its Fifteen Doors: A Parable and an Inquiry
Ihiro Nagumo, D.M.A., Professor of Martial Science, Tokyo University

One day, the Zen Master Basho was at home with his student Yuko, and both were meditating in a lotus posi-

tion on a zafu pillow when a burglar broke in. The master
didn't bat an eye. The burglar threatened him with his
sword and told him, "Give me all you have or I'll kill
you."

The master said, "Silly burglar, why are you so nervous? You have already gotten all you want."

The burglar, somewhat taken aback by the master's
words, asked for an explanation.

"I have nothing," Basho said, "and I value nothing.
Poverty is my only wealth. You already have it, so why
do you want to take it from me?"

The burglar thought about it, then, impressed by the
master's courage, shook his head and left.

The student said, "Oh, master, your wisdom must be a
truly great strength if it allows you to confront a naked
sword without fear."

"True," Basho said. "Indeed, it is very great wisdom to
keep a gun hidden under your zafu pillow while you med-
itate." And he pulled out a gun with six bullets, which
he always kept handy in case of need.

I'm telling you this story to remind you that wise decisions can be made only when one is well protected. We
do not know what is behind those fifteen doors. But we
do know that we must go down there well armed, and
only after having opened up our way with a couple of
bombs. All people are to a greater or lesser extent warriors, including the Incas. Don't forget that explorers who
set out armed only with curiosity often end up devoured
by the natives. This never happens to those who go armed
with a gun. Forget the philosophical drivel of our illustrious colleague, Professor Von Kluge, whose intense
skepticism must be a fairly recent development. He is
probably tired of breaking hundreds upon hundreds of
children's legs in German concentration camps to see
how many times their bones can mend back together. As
for me, I was part of the team that conducted numerous

experiments involving the freezing of Chinese subjects in the extermination camps of General Ishii, and I am proud of it. Those experiments propelled Japan to its supremacy in the frozen-fish industry. These are facts, not mere philosophical theories!

HUATUC'S WORDS: THE KEY TO THE DOORS
■ ■ ■

The young man rushed into the hut and collapsed on the floor. Catuilla and Coya revived him with a few coca leaves to chew. Fang brought him hot tea. He was an Arab rebel hardly fifteen years old. He had been running uphill for two kilometers, as part of the relay system that connected the sentries in the Vilcamayo Valley with Cuzco.

As soon as he had caught his breath, the young man spoke. "This is what the Inuit who was running ahead of me told me. Four black spaceships have landed in the valley. Inside them, there are several tanks with missiles, and other strange vehicles with long metal arms. A thousand men have come out of them, and two TV vans like the ones that came years ago to look for the postcentenarians on the mountains of Vilcabamba and killed my grandfather when they heard he was only ninety-seven years old."

"These must be the sheiks," Fang said. "This means we are all here now. The Japanese arrived by sea yesterday."

"Which also means that this land is not going to be ours much longer. Isn't that so, Fang?" Coya said, sadly.

"The Earth has not told us to go, yet. So, we will stay where we are," Aucayoc said.

In a corner of the room, Fang noticed a stack of old guns. "I

know what you are thinking," the Indian said. "But it would
not be wise to use them. What I ask you to do is to find a way
—just one—for us that does not involve guns, and we shall
use it. Your people are unable to do as much."

"You're right, Aucayoc," Fang said. "Maybe the only solution is to discover the mystery of those doors. But even if we
were close to it. . ."

"The armies are even closer," Catuilla said. "This time they
are advancing faster than your thoughts and your wisdom.
They will get to the doors before you do. But if you are wise,
you'll tell them to stop, and they will do it. Isn't it true that
wise men's thoughts guide your people?"

"I'm afraid this is not the case, Aucayoc," the Chinese said.
"Our chiefs talk about wisdom and science and freedom. But
whenever there is a decision to be made, they always opt for
what's most profitable to them. Wisdom is only a fine painting
behind the desk of power." The Chinese bowed his head.
Everybody in the hut was staring at him.

"I know what you're thinking," he finally said. "It is difficult to go on hoping. I am old and tired. If I were an Eskimo, I
would go out and die serenely in the snow. But 'there are times
when even the writer is called to arms,' as a Chinese poem
says. We must fight."

"Then, let's go back down there," Nanki said.

"No, that would be useless. First, we must solve the mystery. If somebody could help us decipher those signs . . ."

"Huatuc can try," came a feeble voice from the hut's threshold. The old Indian walked in. He now looked even older—
older than any age. It was a struggle for him to walk the
few steps that separated him from Fang, and he could barely
see.

He touched the hand of the Chinese and spoke. "I have
climbed the Tai mountain. We can fly. The valley is filling up
with warriors. I have heard the wail of your faraway friends,
up there, in the sea. I have heard the heart of the earth beat. I
have no eyes left to open those doors, but I can tell you what

they mean in the ancient language of our signs. Everybody leave the room. Please leave us alone.''

He was immediately obeyed. The old Indian crouched on the floor and, with his stick, stirred the warm ashes. Smoke filled the room and hid Huatuc's face.

"See? The fire was hiding under the ashes, but it has lost none of its heat. This is what lies hidden in al-Dabih's cup, in the witch's solitude, in the bee's courage, in the pain of those who part, in what enlightens you, in Shang's shard, and in my three stones. This is what the fifteen doors mean in our language, which is also yours. An old Inca prophecy, engraved in the stone of Sacsahuaman, says:

> One is the way.
> From the future
> the past returns;
> from the past
> the future returns.
> You can follow what
> you cannot say.
> Here is the mystery, the pain.
> Past two skies
> men come together
> to encounter themselves.
> Little strength
> can accomplish great things
> if the heart is full and you decide
> to go on.

"This is the key, Fang. Look at it from the height of a peaceful mind. Look at it as you walk toward the sun, our people's sun.''

o   o   o

❶ ❶ ❶ ❶ ⊕ ⊕ ⊕ ❶ ❶ ❶ ❶ ♂ ♂ ♂ ❶ ❶ ❶ ❶ ♂ ♂ ❶

PROTEUS TIEN: THE WITCH
● ● ●

"The Boojum map is clear," Kook said, examining the enlarged photo. "At the center of this quadrant is an area known as the Fifteen Seas, practically unexplored. Already we've crossed the sea of Apeiron, the seas of Shih, of Baralipton, Tuncanon, and Bacon, as well as the October Sea, the Nullibit Sea, the Mimicry Sea, the Vertigo Sea, the Ignoramibus Sea, and that of Ilinx, not to mention the sea of the Last Gloom, the sea of the Yoked Oxen, and the sea of Desire, at the center of which there is a mark labeled 'The Witch.' We are fairly close to it."

"What could it be?" Mei wondered. "A planet? A cloud of gas? A space station?"

"Nobody knows exactly what it is," Chulain answered, his voice halting, due to his tightly bandaged torso. "But they say that this year it is going to be two hundred years old. Obviously not a person."

"Clearly not," Mei concurred, "even though it has been proven that people live longer in space."

"I think I hear a very strange noise," Caruso said. "Up here, space is so rarefied that my hearing can stretch further and further. We are approaching something . . . something large and metallic . . . and squeaky . . . inside, there are things growing . . . yes . . . growing and breathing . . ."

A few moments later, they spotted the Witch. It was a Russian space capsule, one of the oldest models, from before AD 2,000. Its walls were coated with green mold, and overgrown with branches and lianas. Beneath all this, one could still faintly distinguish the name *Salyut 18.*

"Let's check the register of medieval space launches," Chulain said, reaching for a huge black ledger. "Let's see . . . farther back . . . farther back . . . Here: *Salyut 18:* piloted by the Russian scientist Galina Perkovaia, launched into lunar orbit in 1983. Mission objective: space observation of various botanical species, with particular emphasis on hallucinogenic mushrooms and lichens. Mission outcome: unfortunate. Due to nuclear explosion on Moon, capsule knocked out of orbit and lost in space on December 14, 1986."

"Holy smoke," Caruso said. "It sure has come a long way in a hundred and seventy-five years!"

They approached the capsule. It had the oddest appearance, with its long strands of lianas and peculiar mushrooms, waving in space like long disheveled hair. Now they understood why it was called the Witch.

"All right," Chulain said firmly, "let's check out the inside. I'll bring my gun along; we might need it."

"Why? How can you expect to find anyone alive in there after a hundred seventy-five years?!" Mei said.

"They say the Witch is two hundred years old, don't they?" the black explained. "But that capsule has only been gone a hundred and seventy-five years. So, the Witch may well not be the capsule. On the other hand, at the time of the launch, Galina was twenty-five years old, and, as you can figure it out by yourself, 175 plus 25 equals 200. That would be Galina's age, if she were still alive."

"Impossible," Mei said. At that very moment, Groucho, one of the dogs, began to bark furiously.

Entering the *Salyut* was like entering a jungle. They found themselves in front of a gloomy tangle of green lianas, monstrously tall mushrooms, stalagmites, stalactites, and, on the floor, a thick carpet of soggy moss that engulfed their legs. The light was dim, and a violently sweet, stagnant smell suffused the place. Our friends immediately felt dizzy.

Chulain advanced, with his gun pointed. "There is something very strange here. The scent of the mushrooms must be hallucinogenic."

The dog again barked furiously and tried to bite a large oblong mushroom.

"Look at Groucho, he's going crazy!" Mei said.

"No," Kook said, "he's been grabbed by the mushroom."

And, in fact, the mushroom had coiled around the dog's legs and was rapidly enveloping it in a tight grip.

"Do something," Mei screamed. "Please, do something!"

But, at that moment, an incredible voice, deep and hoarse as if issuing from the craggy depths of a cave, froze them in their places.

"Osi, Alya!" the voice said authoritatively.

At that order, the mushroom loosened its grip on the dog and recoiled upon itself. And, suddenly, the Witch herself appeared among the lianas. She could easily have been two hundred years old. Her face was marked with a thick network of deep furrows, like the bark of a tree. In the middle of it shone two beautiful blue eyes. Her white hair fell all the way down to her feet, and was scattered over the floor like a rug, intertwined with the flowers and vines. Her dress was a green cloak, sparkling with dew and adorned with a single blood orchid, pinned right above her heart. The only thing that emerged out of the cloak were long, scrawny hands, clawed, like those of the usual witch, with very long, curved nails— which, in her case, were thin stems of flowers.

The Witch smiled, revealing two rows of snow-white teeth.

"Wellkommen, amigos!" she said. "For, lo qui entre into the witch's antre no nemigo puede ist, car gudman ist lo qui amat el silent creatura of verdure, el hairy barkbark, und das tiny buzzing creatura."

"What kind of language is she speaking?" Kook asked Mei, lowering his voice.

"I speak all the languages in space, bearded man," the Witch answered, "because I have spent eighty-two years of life on this ship studying terrestrial languages and various other space idioms, twelve years learning diction, and sixteen on sign languages. That's why I never speak the same language twice in a row."

"But . . . are you really Galina Perkovaia?" Mei asked her incredulously. "And still alive!"

"Mi amor, kennst tu believe?" the Witch chimed with a

youthful voice. "Twice habe ich gefastened ein sheaf of ein-
hundert yahrs!"

"And how did you survive all these years in space?"

"Longhaveilived mit mushrooms," the Witch said, "of
mushroom. y seaweed und erbe daily dine, commencing mit
hors-d'oeuvres amanita mushroomo, und then gingko con-
sommé, und cipolla homeleta monkstyle, und mossalade und
rimeburger, und grossingestion von bolete und boletissimi,
después, quoique full und sated y stuffed, ich thousandteethly
devoured ein morel stew und avalanche Carib minestrone, und
uplapped dos platos beurred zitis mit chantarellen und redneck
mushroomo phalliphormo. Zu enden, un sweet dessert; lasto
but no leasto, snow-peaked risotto mit shamrock salsa, und
alle downgewashen mit rubiovin und Perkovkaia vodka man-
monkhandmade. Und, für crème de beauty ich spattered ma
visage mit mud und cladonia, and für savon cetraria mit lye,
und against spleens y blues ich teapartied mit mi chums Can-
nabis und Mescalina und Dr. Peyote Hallucen, und bellyrid
von gasen mit farty fungus infusions, alias puff-ball tea, und
sativic garlick fangrid von achen und vampiren, und con-
combre re malaria, und mallow re bronco-fire, und drei taran-
tulas, fried in huile d'oliva, re haarchute, und crisco re mange
und thistle re zitzen, und tylenoleum re kopf-schmerz und
wann insomnia mi matrice pinfilled dos copas mit poppy-
seeds el trick-o machen und like badgerkind sleepen, und, gen-
eralmente, selon alte recipe, ich muchas appels gegessen für
ein appel a day tient el Doktor away. So, though my trunk has
as many circles as the oldest oak, today I feel as merrious and
gayful and happlich as if ich had nur ein hundert und cinqua-
quas annos in mi bod."

"O Witch," Chulain said, "zu ton abode have we kommen
für ein ribald rake zu looken, ein usurer und thiefer, ein
scheisster und threator, ein pobre creatura y-clept Snark Boojum."

"But whyum sprichst tu si drollish, Mr. Coo?" Mei inquired.

"Methinks," Kook said, "hallucinophoric atmosphera mispolyglots and miscigenates our tongues, and infungates our brainers with mushroomic dampmush."

"What says Kuko?" Chulain said. "Me sure no unused tonguing noticed, und entotally soundlich und kein schleppisch fehl."

"Ich sehe you already bewildered und befuddled," the Witch said. "Muy bien! Wir shall zusammen rigolar! Alors, ich say you Boojum aquicame last diezember all fatigué und besmirched mit magneto-slag und ordure, und blond und bello viel dressed im yellow, mit mantle und puce veste, und zusammen wir playen post-office und cootie-catching, und spinbodella, und schow-mir-dein-show-dir-mein, und autres verboten post-medianoche games und he gagne dos hundert dubloons, etc., und wir wirselves silly getrunken and au lit gehen zu biblical knowledge machen und bellybanging und navelmatching und unterslurping und fella-tella und so lange und so weiter und wann ich awake, er gone! Wo? No sabe. Ma if wir saber wollen, wir ask schallen die mirabilic vitrosphere, which alle sabe und alle sehe und alles spies in su circular voyancy. Follow me in mystagogic file, mein geliebte alienisch, mein nosich amigos!"

○ What Galina's Crystal Ball Said ○

I see, see, see
Where, where, where
I see everything strange and nothing strange
for Galina and Manannan Mac Lyr and Merlin and Dabih and
   Luan Ta and Chung Kuo
here you shall see what you don't expect
the mughidda fly as large as three men flying into the room
   and the phantom shark that swims on your wall
tales don't tell the truth
kiss a hundred toads and they shall remain toads
princesses don't marry anesthesiologists

people die but the story goes on
I see the mice that abandoned ship
and dropped onto Holland, in a town
where the wind gets tangled in the windmills
I see lovers parting
and friends departing
to tug at the world's crust won't help them find each other
for nowadays
every month is the cruellest one
hével havalím
enchete, penchete, woman Mei
every step you take is magic
how can you ask me where you are going?
stars learn their future from men
My name is Galina
half old Russian woman
half old Inca magician
and then there are at least two hundred more halves
I have studied many books and have dreamed many others
The medicine man looks under the fire
The stargazer looks into the sky
And the craziest soothsayer looks inside a microscope
at an atomic Siva dance

Do you want to work for the king? Does the king know more
than you do? Is your life so cold that it needs to warm up in
his palace? You who were once a Rebel with ideals so great
you couldn't even carry them by yourself, where have you
hidden them away? And you, who believe yourself wise, why
don't you dare step into the marketplace? Just as the donkey
carries a cord of rosewood and feels only its weight, but not its
scent or its value, so he who reads many books without under-
standing them will feel only their weight on his shoulders.
And you, what are you looking for? What are you writing?
What do you want? It is very lucky there are things that cannot
be written!

For Dabih and Leporello and the gentle bee and Pinte and Coyllur and the crosses on the mountain, and the rings around the skeletons' fingers

You have gone as they say to another world

Can you hear the wail of Gilgamesh? Only the dark mourning veil, then, can really show love and friendship

Friends! A farewell to Mei who is leaving to Kook who is leaving. Their destiny is to become kings. A common fate. All men are kings

O manco Capac o mama Ocllo o plumed serpent o bearded man o Starosta

Maybe the solution was there in the beginning in the first words of the book in the words spoken by the man whose very name is a critique of power in the first words but how many are yet to be written

The mushroom grows seven times its height in one night and even if the faces who bow over the water of the fountain change, she will still recognize them for a thousand years. The players display a sequence of cards already dealt a thousand years ago. Why be afraid of mystery? If we can wait to die, then we can also wait to be born

Are you happy now, Einstein? Is this what you wanted to know? You were born, you are a child. But beware. You will grow fast. Einstein, your name is Jewish, do not forget!

Listen to the prayer of weapons and of inevitable war, from the moment the world began at 9:00 a.m., in the year 4004 B.C., according to Bishop Ussher's calendar.

○ Killomachia ○

In the beginning there was the hand
   and the hand took the club and the stone and the noose
   and with the club Hercules performed his ten labors and
made a hundred and twenty movies

and the club and the stone begat the ax the hammer of Thor the tomahawk and later the baseball bat

and the stone and the club begat the spear with which in cahoots with fate Achilles killed Hector

and the stone and the noose begat the sling with which in cahoots with fate and against all odds David killed Goliath

and the club and the noose begat the bow with which Ulysses invented the crime of passion

and the spear begat the first sword, and against this sword arose the first ancient shield, which was immediately stolen by an American museum

and the sword became the invincible Excalibur and Durlindane and Notung but the shield also became magic and so everything was back again where it had started

and the sword begat the catapult the mangonel the ram the trebuchet, the crossbow and the crowbar

and the shield begat the coat of armor the drawbridge the battlement the safe

and the sword and the armor mounted the horse much to the latter's delight for a total of nine quintals

and the stirrup begat the combat and the tournament because battle was just not enough

and Galileo invented the parabola examining the manner in which pheasants were shot

and Savonarola invented the fuse as he watched the cord of his cassock burn

and thus was born a small piece of steel which, shot like lightning, could pierce just about anything and transform nine quintals of excellent cavalry into nine quintals of scrap iron

and the fuse begat the flint

and then came the cannon the mortar the Zippo lighter the musket the culverin the blunderbuss the pistol the rifle the revolver the carbine

and Mr. Colt and Mr. Winchester founded a country that will play a big role in the unfolding of this tale

and the powerful cannon sired many sons one of whom got

a driver's license and thus was born the tank another tale of success in yet another country that will play an important part in this story

and the cannon went to sea and became the pirate ship and the invincible Armada and the torpedo-boat destroyer, as handsome as a naked weapon, and the *Potemkin* and the *Nemitz* and the *Nabilia*

and the cannon made good, and shot up into the air and flew over Stuka Mig and tomcat and saw a great deal of the world

and the Colt had sisters Mauser Beretta and Luger and brothers Smith and Wesson and Walter and the RG22 for shooting presidents at short range

and Winchester had brothers Burnside Spences Martini Peabody and sisters Kalashnikov and Remington and Anschutz and tommy guns and submachine guns and machine guns for shooting presidents at long range

and the massive tank begat the rough bazooka which in turn begat the superarmored tank under which the intrepid marine boldly dove

and the glorious battleship begat the nimble torpedo and the slender submarine which in turn begat the destroyer under which the intrepid frogman boldly dove

and the airplane begat the fearsome antiaircraft cannon which begat the swift jet-fighter which begat the watchful radar which begat the plane from which the intrepid kamikaze boldly dove

and America dropped the atomic bomb on the kamikaze barracks in Hiroshima accidentally killing a few passersby

which made bayonets and karate obsolete

and Big Bertha by now in full dotage begat the V2 who in turn begat the Honest John missile

who was killed in a duel by the Sandal SS4 missile the invincible

who in turn was hanged by Pershing the conqueror

who was beheaded with a scimitar by Skean SS5 the Cossack

who was fried to death with a jet of hot oil by Poseidon the
sailor

who was hit and sunk by one-eyed Scud A

who was blinded with a shotgun by the loyal Pluton

who was poisoned with a meatball by Longlegs SSBS2

who was burned alive by Frog 37 the mystic

who was stabbed in a cathedral by Sergeant the antichrist

who died of indigestion after challenging Titan the glutton
to a pig-out on hard-boiled eggs

who later died of starvation because his entire wheat crop
was chemically poisoned by Scaleboard the cyberneticist

who was murdered by a satellite piloted by a rhesus monkey
tamed by the invisible Minuteman I

who was executed for wanting to confess to mass murder by
Minuteman II the infallible

who was suicided by Minuteman III the obscure

who was killed by a bacteriological attack of dengue fever
and equine encephalitis courtesy of the diabolical Sasin

who was killed in a laser-sword duel by the wise Savage XII

who was water-tortured to death by the good Lance ERW

who was beaten to death on the barber chair by Polaris A 3
from Marseilles

who was eaten by Cruise the cannibal

who was defeated and enslaved by the powerful and just
Queen N

under whose mushroom and under whose reign there com-
menced a very long period of peace silence and ice

But I almost forget you wanted Galina to tell you the way

The sky is divided into fifteen strange doors

One of them leads you to a mountain where four men live,
their backs turned to one another. Their names are North
South East and West

Another one leads to the place where the devil sews words

together so that the moment you say one they all follow and you'll never be able to speak a word again

One leads to the place where every night a bird with iron teeth comes to ravish whoever falls asleep first, after which everybody falls asleep, reassured they won't be that night's victim

One leads to the place where you are going in the past, if you can imagine it

One leads to the place where you are going in the future, if you can remember it

One leads you to a spaceship in the middle of the night, and you are the only one rowing and moving all the oars and all the dead oarsmen, for the metronome is dead and so is the captain, but you don't know it

One of the doors is not a door at all but the sea, the sea that has risen vertically, like a tall door of water, and if you open it it will collapse on you

One door is the heart of your beloved, and if you enter it, you'll break it

One door is the cover of a book that will drag you into a stream of words, and if you try to stop and rest, it will drag you farther away, and if you try to cling to the letters, they will scramble, but the stream will keep going, even though the words no longer make sense, and your screams will be inscribed among the words of the book, all the way to the end

One door leads to fifteen doors

And one door leads to the door you are looking for, which in turn will lead you across the lake the fire and the wind

One door is me, you can see my eyes move in the grain of the wood, and my lips wait for the key, and the wrinkled face of my three-hundred-year-old bark

One door cannot be seen for it is held open by the custodian of the invisible world who is inviting you to enter

One door is the immense laughter of the sky making merry

One door is the one you knock on in your dreams without

knowing who is standing behind it but hoping it is someone
who will help
   That's why it is time to start your journey

       Caruso: you who know how to listen
       You hear the noise
       of dreams and metal in space
       the human spirit and the fatigue of the oarsman
       you, arcane seer of the oars
       and stern archsinger of the helix,
       the dragon has been freed
       swinging the oars
       like a sea monster in the water
       he slides into the rivulets of air
       at night the Milky Way is like a silver Okà

       And now go where I tell you
       Galina always alone, always

       Who was with you? asks
       the solitude that awaits me
       inside the house, while I greet you
       swinging the lamp in the garden
       And I follow you
       farther than my eyes can see
       the greatest truth lies in separation
       but already the lamp
       lights up the silence and the darkness.

• 7 •
THE HEART OF THE EARTH

THE MOMENT OF TRUTH:
FANG AND EINSTEIN TO THE RESCUE

● ● ●

Fang was very tired and a little drunk. He had fought all night against the telepathic attacks of the Japanese, and now he was exhausted. He couldn't have held out much longer. He had tried to meet Mei. He had seen a strange place, a cave full of damp, green plants, and a bizarre figure who mumbled in an incredible tongue. He had been able to understand only a few words. He thought maybe the solution was there in the beginning—in the first words. And then: across the lake, the fire and the wind. The old man closed his eyes, and tried again to concentrate.

∘   ∘   .   ∘

Van Cram's Mystery Vector—why can't computers identify its origin? Why wasn't it sealed?

Inca Civilization—great secret project. No writing. Why those massive walls, why Machu Picchu? Why those secret rites? Why the cult of sun and gold?

Premonitions—how could they already know what was going to happen? Their obsession with time. Why did they let themselves be massacred? The drawings of Inca Nazca, the fire balloons. "We can fly." Was there some alien influence on these cultures?

The fifteen doors—why fifteen? and what were they hiding down there? The mysterious energy. Those immense fluxes. Who is Huatuc?

Missing data: Huatuc's quipu.

The Inca inscription:

> One is the way:
> from the past the future returns
> from the future the past returns.
> Past two skies men come together
> little strength can accomplish great things
> if the heart is full and you decide to go on.

Missing data. Missing data.

"And the mystery remains a mystery, Einstein." Fang sighed. "Pass me the wine, please."

"The bottle's finished," Einstein said, emerging from a mountain of blankets. Judging from the sunset hue of his nose, he was also fairly smashed. "Everything in the Universe ends, wastes away, and then grows back, bubbling. What we consider dead matter is in fact a constant swarming of vital events.

The Universe . . . ferments, my dear Fang . . . That's why—
hic!—Thales was wrong: Water isn't the basic universal ele-
ment; wine is—hic!—It's wine that lends those unpredictable
trajectories to the orbits of electrons—hic!—If it's difficult to
find an electron it's because—hic!—the electron is drunk . . .
This is the key to creation—forget the S-matrix, the ur-struc-
ture! Why should we be so surprised if everything is at once
particle and wave, if we can't figure out the origin and reason
of any event? If everything initially issued out of some amor-
phous clot of matter, that clot was . . . grapes! Right! No
cosmic egg; rather, the cosmic grape seed! The Universe is—
hic!—the juice of the cosmic grape seed . . ."

"Right on!" Fang exclaimed. "Yin and yang, white and red!
I couldn't agree more. That's why scientific discoveries should
always be carried out in a state of tipsiness. The same is true
for poetry, when it wants to tune in on the Universe—hic!—
Hurrah for the drinking cup of the poets Li Po and Tu Fu!
Hurrah for Descartes drunk on St. Martin's Day . . ."

"What are we going to do now?" Einstein wondered.
"Poetry?"

"Those fifteen doors were made to be opened, right?" Fang
said. "So there must be a key. We've looked for it, but haven't
found it!"

"Maybe it's somewhere else," Einstein ventured.

"Right, my young red-nosed comrade! And maybe not far
from here."

"Don't ask the king for luck; every man is a king," Einstein
intoned. "Hence—"

"Hence . . . I am going to take a walk," Fang said. "If I can't
find what I'm looking for, it might mean I never lost it."

"And I—I'm going to buy some time, assuming it exists."

"Good idea!" Fang said. "Assemble all our wise colleagues,
and since entertaining ideas is so much easier than creating
them, entertain both for a long time. And since they won't
agree with what you call your ideas, they'll counter them with
what they think are their ideas, and whoever doesn't agree

with either your ideas or theirs will believe his ideas are best. What do you say?"

"A brilliant idea!" Einstein exclaimed.

∘ The Theorem of the Piglet ∘

"Ladies and gentlemen, this is a hexagram from the *I Ching*, an ancient Chinese text," Einstein told the assembled brain trust of Operation Cuzco, which included Arab, Sinoeuropean, and Japanese scientists and intellectuals, all eager to make a decisive move as soon as possible.

"These lines, ladies and gentlemen, contain the archetypes of the world's changes, the universe of relations. These lines come closer to mirroring our modern cosmology every day. And yet, humanity has never drawn any help from them because no scientific mind has ever dared harness them to any productive use. The march of humanity on the road of progress is difficult, constantly threatened by the abyss of irrationality and the wall of ideological prejudice; but guided by the lantern of organized and productive knowledge, we shall stride forward, holding our heads high. Some say we are midgets standing on the shoulders of giants. True—but these giants are our own tanks, our steam shovels, our missiles. Thanks to them, we no longer need to explain the handbook of the world; we merely have to make it predictable and useful. Now it is the world that comes anxiously to us to ask us about its future. Let us therefore make a world we can really call our own—a totally artificial, truly human world."

Applauses and shouts of approval rang through the hall.

"That is why we shall not let the thousand Indians stop us in the pursuit of our goals," Einstein continued. "Every man is, potentially, an Indian, and woe to him who will not replace the symbols of his obsolete religion with a TV antenna! Woe to any heresy without statistical documentation!"

A very long ovation followed these last words. An Arab scientist stood up. "I like what you are saying," he said. "But I don't understand what the hexagram has to do with it."

"I'm getting to that," the boy answered. "As all of you, my wise interlocutors, undoubtedly recall, every I Ching hexagram consists of a combination of solid lines and broken ones, for a total of sixty-four different permutations. You also know what the fundamental dilemma of our times is, namely: shall we make whole what is broken or break what is whole?"

A perplexed buzz went through the audience.

"I shall not waste my time in verbal specifics, gentlemen. I believe you all know exactly what I mean by 'breaking the whole'; anyone with a minimal knowledge of atomic physics or complex systems knows. On the other hand, when I say 'make whole what is broken,' you will be struck by the utter banality of what I allude to, applicable as it is to everything from universal entropy to the notion of loss, from the theory of disasters to haute couture. But this time we will do better than that! This time we will penetrate to the very heart of the problem! We shall start from a logico-mathematical assumption; that is, the Schwein-Tannenbaum theorem, otherwise known as the theorem of the piglet, as it was developed by the Bourbakists in their farms for ponderous equations. Need I explain how this theorem is going to solve the mystery of the fifteen doors?"

Astounded silence.

"Of course not, my dear colleagues, even an idiot can understand it. Well, then, since we are going to start our project tomorrow, let's follow the example of Évariste Galois, who made his most significant mathematical discoveries the day before he was killed in a duel. Let's abandon our minds to the stimulus of this imminent, fatal appointment with mystery. I am asking you to cooperate with me in some group research."

Enthusiastic applause, whistles of approval.

"You all know the theorem," Einstein went on. " 'Given X number of piglets, each of which is holding another piglet's tail in his mouth, it follows that they will all move in the same direction as the first piglet in the row.'

"This theorem, so obviously fundamental to the organization of complex societies, has lately been the subject of numerous debates. Let's examine this row of piglets: if the one behind holds on to the tail of the one in front of it, then we will have a swine-o-matic sequence: the piglet holds the tail of the other piglet by the tail. But this can also be expressed as: the piglet holds the other piglet by the other piglet's tail. On the other hand, if we could put ourselves in the place of the piglet behind the piglet in front of it, we would say: I hold by the tail the piglet that holds the piglet by the tail, or, if we were in the place of the piglet in front of the piglet behind it: there is a piglet holding my tail, etc., . . . and so on and so forth.

"And here we come to this point: I must always keep in mind the fact that I am, simultaneously, the piglet behind the piglet in front and the piglet in front of the piglet behind, and this fairly complicates matters—aside from the fact that, as someone has justly pointed out, there might also be piglets that refuse either to hold or be held by the tail, which introduces the question of free choice—without considering the fact that there could also be a few piglets with no tail, and that we would have the so-called 'quid' of genetic error—and then, of course, any row worthy of the name must have a first and a last pig. At this point, the problem becomes immense, both scientifically and politically, and if we get lost in theoretical confrontations, we will never conclude anything. Only empirical observation can enlighten us here."

A long murmur of approval.

"What I am proposing to you is this. Let's assume that the divided lines of the hexagram represent those piglets who refuse to take other piglets by the tail, but nevertheless allow their own tail to be taken. Then, let's build a series of possible hexagrams. Now, ladies and gentlemen, whoever wants to play the role of the piglets with free will, please move to the left; and those of you who want to play the role of the conformist piglets, move to the right. Very well, now . . . could you please line up . . . like that . . . and hold one of your hands out by your . . . hips. That will be your tail. With the other hand, which will be the mouth, each of you can seize the hand-tail of the person in front of you. Those of you who do not want to have any tail should keep both hands away from your . . . backs. Please, do not push."

"I protest," said Doctor Boloni, three times Nobel laureate. "I have no intention of playing the poor piglet without a tail. I contend that my studies on the notional ideas of eternity and finitude make me more than worthy of a tail, albeit a small one."

"I protest," the Japanese Swinuke said. "Professor Gris, from Stockholm, right behind me, has bitten my hand, saying that the sequence is not symbolico-analogical, but symbolico-mimetic, and as such it should involve the greatest degree of verisimilitude."

"Science says that it is very important that laboratory data replicate real data as closely as possible," Gris exclaimed. "Hence, I would advise my illustrious colleagues to grunt."

"I, grunt?" Doctor Boloni yelled in outrage. "Never! I maintain that it is of the utmost importance that we eliminate any and all data tangential and/or irrelevant to the experiment at hand, and, in my opinion, grunting is superfluous. Besides, I would like to know why it is that I, of all proto-piglets, should be the last one in the row, and, as a result, have no opportunity to use my tail. I propose we form a circular sequence."

"I oppose the motion," the French Bayeux said. "Let's not give way to mysticism or other totalitarian dreams. This is a scientific experiment and, as such, it contains a spatio-temporal principle of determinacy. Therefore, you, Doctor Boloni,

will be the last member in the sequence, while Doctor Saddleblack will be the first pig."

"Who are you calling a pig?" Doctor Saddleblack inquired
threateningly.

"Gentlemen, gentlemen, please. If you persist in your squab-
bles, you won't be able to hold on to each other's tails."

"I would like to introduce another motion," Doctor Larga
Whitesow put in. "I propose that all piglets endowed with free
will form a special commission to consider whether it is advis-
able to grab other piglets' tails or not."

Bacon (England): "Then I propose we let go of the tails, and
proceed to take a vote."

Lombowsky (Poland): "No! if we let go of the tails in order
to vote, it automatically means that we accept the motion.
Instead, I propose we vote by show of legs."

Norcini Grifo (Italy): "Be more precise! Need I remind you
that pigs have four legs? You must specify which leg we are to
raise—right or left, front or hind?"

Lombowsky: "Or the one that's going to be turned into pros-
ciutto."

Boloni: "I object. Among us there are a small but select
number of mature, arthritic pigs who couldn't possibly elevate
a hind leg."

Gris: "I object to open balloting. I propose a secret vote, with
black and white acorns."

"I propose we walk around a bit to stretch our legs," suggested Professor Norcini Grifo, one of the oldest.

"I second the motion," Bayeux said, "but I object to the
rotational implication of the words 'walk around.' In my opinion, the first pig should not be Doctor Saddleblack, but Doctor
Boloni. He deserves it because of his intellectual prestige and
the rosiness of his cheeks."

"Bull!" Landrace yelled. "Doctor Boloni is clearly inferior to
Doctor Saddleblack in both weight and scientific knowledge.
Besides, Doctor Saddleblack, with his pointed ears and the

swinish expression of his face, comes far closer to our porcine episteme than Doctor Boloni with his vaguely rosy cheeks— let alone the fact that Doctor Boloni, as he himself has admitted, cannot grunt."

"That's a lie!" Doctor Boloni yelled back. "I indicated that I deemed it not entirely necessary to grunt. But if I have to, I am perfectly capable of grunting with greater emphasis and sonority than Doctor Saddleblack. And I dare anybody to cast dubious aspersions on it. Need I remind you of my acoustical studies concerning the sonorous emissions of quasars?"

"I doubt Doctor Boloni can put his money where his mouth is," Doctor Saddleblack riposted spitefully. "Many scientists have published reams of scientific studies on acoustics, but when it came down to grunting, they were able to emit only a few pitiful oinks, deprived of any sense. Theory is one thing, but practice is something altogether different, gentlemen."

In answer to Saddleblack's words, Doctor Boloni swelled his chest, curled back his snout, and said, "Knkruuuuuaaaaaaw, knknknknrkwaaaaaw, knrknrow, knrknrkoo, kkkkkrrrraaaw!"

The entire audience gave him a standing ovation.

Then, Doctor Saddleblack got up and, flushing purple with the effort, answered, "Knknknrkweeeeeeeee, knknknknrrrrr-weeeeeeeeee, knknknknrknrknrweeeeeeeeeeeeeeee!"

His supporters applauded wildly. Boos and whistles followed. A few people came to blows.

"Gentlemen, please!" Einstein yelled, trying to call the assembly back to order. "At this point I propose that a special commission decide which of the two contestants is worthy to be the first pig in the ring."

"I second the motion," Doctor Saddleblack said. "And I declare my candidacy! All those who are with me, raise your tails!"

"Here we go again," Swinuke said. "I propose we vote as follows: those pigs who can raise their right hind leg should do so, whereas the arthritic pigs need only stretch their right hind leg to the side, as in a tango."

"And what about those who want to abstain?" Professor Norcini Grifo asked.

Outside the door, Phildys was listening, not without some apprehension, to the hoggish sounds issuing from the assembly room, when he saw Pyk approach him with a triumphant expression on his face.

"What's going on in there?" the secretary asked. "Some new game?"

"A great deal of confusion," Phildys said. "I get the feeling Einstein is doing his damnedest to throw a monkey wrench into our plans."

"Oh, let him go ahead and try," Pyk said. "By now, the game is over. I have good news. One hour ago, we tried again to establish contact with *Proteus*. In vain. They have disappeared. Mission Terra must be considered temporarily suspended."

"Try as I may," Phildys said, "I can't see why this is good news."

⊕ ⊛ ⊕ ⊛ ⊕ ⊛ ⊕ ⊛ ⊕ ⊛ ⊕ ⊛ ⊕ ⊛ ⊕ ⊛ ⊕ ⊛ ⊕ ⊛ ⊕

PROTEUS'S END

⊛ ⊛ ⊛

Emerging from a strange bank of stagnant clouds, as dense as a milky lake, *Proteus Tien* was now sailing through an ominous sky, like a cave of thick, black fog intermittently slashed by fiery flashes. The temperature outside, already extraordinarily high, continued to rise steadily.

"There's a storm ahead of us," Chulain said, "and it's a big one."

"Did you see it on the screen?" Mei asked. "I thought our radar was broken."

"It registered on the emergency radars," Chulain answered, pointing to the four dogs. They cowered under a table, the hair on their backs sticking out like the quills of a porcupine.

"Yes, they always know when something's about to happen," Caruso agreed. "As a matter of fact, I'm hearing a very strange noise myself—something like . . . the noise of a deep well, a dark moan resounding through a bottomless pit."

"Let's try to keep our cool, guys," Kook said. "Where is Mei? Maybe she needs to be cheered up a bit—"

"Don't you move, chicken!" Chulain enjoined him.

Mei was lying on her cot, eyes closed. She had thought she heard Fang's voice at least three times, but she lost it every time. Now she was finally able to hear it, loud and clear.

"Mei," Fang was telling her with an unusual waver in his voice, "I know you are approaching the end of your journey . . . I am with you now."

"I hear you, Fang," the young woman answered, "but I'm scared! All our instruments are going haywire as we get closer to the spot the Witch told us about . . . where are we headed? What's going to happen? Oh, you don't know how much I wish I'd never left Earth!"

"Don't be frightened," Fang reassured her. "You'll be back: the I Ching says so."

"And what about you, Fang?" Mei asked. "I hear sorrow in your voice."

"Yes," Fang admitted, "we are going through a very difficult moment here on Earth. But we may still be able to do something. And so can you. Find that planet!"

"Yes, we will," Mei said, "and we will help you. I will also consult the I Ching for you, I promise. I'll send you the results from our new planet. I promise! Fang? Fang!"

But no answer came back. The whole of space rocked with a strange noise, like the sound of a gigantic horn. The ship began to spin. Mei rushed into the cockpit and found a terribly worried Chulain.

"It's completely out of control. I'd say we're looping on a very tight orbit . . . and the temperature is dropping."

Kook looked outside. Gassy clouds of an extraordinary brightness were zooming past the ship.

"Is it a steady orbit, at least?" he asked.

"No," Chulain answered, "it's getting narrower and narrower."

"A maelstrom!" Caruso exclaimed. "Shit, we're in for it now! That's what that noise was—space wind!"

"Come on, let's stay calm," Chulain said. "We can't afford to lose our heads now." But the ship's orbit was getting noticeably tighter; he was already feeling slightly dizzy.

"Ask the computer for some data. Ask it where we are," Kook said.

"I'll try," Mei said. "But we're spinning faster and faster."

"Quick." Kook was already breathing with difficulty. "The noise is louder! We must find a way out!"

"The computer says . . . 'Mixcoatl.' We are in Mixcoatl."

"That doesn't make any sense," Chulain said. "I've never heard that name before. It's certainly not a planet. Maybe the computer invented it."

"I don't know what's happening," Kook cried. "The computer has gone crazy . . . it keeps repeating the same name, Mixcoatl!"

"Hold on tight!" Chulain yelled, "We are plummeting into something . . . I can't hold the ship any longer."

"What is Mixcoatl?" Kook asked the computer once more, but he received no answer.

The ship was spinning along a spiral at an ever-increasing speed. Our friends heard the mysterious drone of the horn grow louder and louder, and had the feeling of being sucked into a vacuum. A silent explosion of light flared through the spaceship, and suddenly, all noise ceased. The Universe was again perfectly calm. There was no trace left of *Proteus Tien*. Only the silent, rarefied void of the Universal Sea, which had swallowed it.

∘ Mission Suspended ∘

Special Report

Spaceship *Proteus Tien*, out on mission, has not been answering our calls for one hundred and six hours now. The radar of the outer belt does not register its presence in any sector of the Universal Sea. The ship in question must, therefore, be considered disintegrated. Note that it vanished in an area where, of late, several other ships have met the same end.

The members of the crew—Christophorus Leonardus Kook, Mei Ho Li, Boza Cu Chulain, and Caruso Raimondi —can likewise be considered dead in all respects and, as such, will soon be awarded medals for their valor in cosmic explorations. Mission Terra is henceforth suspended. The news will be made official this evening on a special TV program. The rights to the story *"Proteus's End"* have already been sold, along with all related spin-offs, including the toy model of *Proteus Tien*. It is therefore illegal to use the image of any of our lost heroes for commercial purposes, without the written authorization of the licensee.

Public Reaction

The rumor of *Proteus*'s disappearance has caused a chain reaction everywhere. This confirms the hypothesis that Operation Terra had already stimulated a dangerous surplus of expectations. Anticipation of that remote planet, whether it exists or not, is responsible for serious social disruption requiring immediate attention. Following is a list of actual or presumed disorders to be double-checked by the computers of all press agencies.

"Hmmm," Phildys noted, popping a whole squad of sedatives into his mouth, "there is definitely reason to worry. Demonstrations all over Europe. Anti-government slogans in Peking. A bunch of octogenarians rioting in the geriatric district of Berlin. Look at this: 'One hundred thousand people filed by the Federation Building in protest. The demonstrators were dispersed by means of water cannons. Thirty people froze to death. A thirty percent drop in the Aramerussian TV audience has been registered. Sam soldiers on hunger strike.' What the hell is going on?"

"Let me fill you in," Pyk volunteered. "The image of Terra has revived too many desires. You know how despondent and indifferent people are these days. Nobody likes to live in underground cities under the steady view of TV cameras. But they hate it all the more when it appears there might be an alternative to their existence—blue seas, white mountains, total disarmament, unilateral sex, and ff-ff-freedom! You know —all those pretechnological options that beautiful souls like so much. Bah!"

"I'm not so sure I agree with your analysis, Pyk. You have absolute faith in technology, but you forget that not everything works in our city, or anywhere else. Take the case of the senior citizens in Berlin. They have no heat, and their 'district' is just a barren corridor, some twenty kilometers long, fenced in by a huge wall."

"They live in a median temperature of six degrees Celsius," Pyk said. "That way, only the fittest will survive. We can't spend all our money fixing defective lungs, can we? Don't forget, medical care is a luxury for all nonworkers. Besides, those twenty kilometers are not as barren as you make them out to be; there are at least six thousand benches. As for the wall, we've covered it with posters showing mountain sunsets and ascending starlets. Are you dreaming of Terra yourself, Phildys?"

"No, I'm not," the prime minister said. "But there are others who are. How are we going to break it to them that Mission Terra has been suspended, and that we've sold our Andean dig to the Arabs?"

"No problem, Phildys," Pyk smiled. "All we have to do is touch up the script here and there. No need to look like a lost babe in the dark woods of politics. Here, look, we are ready with a revised plan, 'Earth Is Beautiful.' We've already leaked it to our newspapers, to our television stations, to the third intellectual platoon, to the police headquarters. It is based on Herrtripes' first law of advertising: 'In this world one needn't change anything, all one must do is point at a brightly colored inscription that says "everything has changed." ' Don't you agree? General, never before has the slogan been so much more effective than the product itself! Never mind 'being'; what really matters is 'appearing.' The world is a videogame, my friend. If you control the buttons, there's nothing you can't make appear or disappear. Don't think about Indians. Think of green targets and—poof! they're gone. Just like that. And so even Terra will disappear, Phildys. At the third stroke of the magic wand, three clamorous pieces of news:

"A. Van Cram was a visionary and a junky. This wasn't the first time he thought he'd spotted something. Years ago, he went to the Jupiter police and begged them to protect him against a herd of camels that he claimed was following him everywhere. When he was a Rebel, he had to be committed for abuse of hallucinogenic drugs. Enclosed, a full dossier with certified documents and photos.

"B. A government commission consisting of the most expert (and corrupt, but we'll leave that out) scientists in the Federation has established that it is absolutely preposterous to think there might be intelligent life in that remote space sector, since said sector is totally devoid of carbon atoms, which are at the basis of all life. Instead, it seems that the area is rich in mercury, which proves once again that the only form of life possible on that planet would be four-legged thermometers.

"C. The surgeon general has determined that sunlight and the natural air are harmful to twenty-second-century terrestrials. A medical team at Sydney University has confirmed this fact. According to experiments conducted there, subterranean life has deprived us of important biological defenses that would protect us against the dangers of a preglacial planet. Here are a few significant examples: ten volunteers exposed to solar light, simulated by quartz, developed severe nose burns in less than an hour, ninety-eight out of a hundred Sydney residents turned out to be mortally allergic to the pollen of a test-tube nasturtium; the remaining two were utterly unable to pronounce the word *nasturtium*. The medical consensus is, therefore, that subterranean life is much healthier than life outdoors. And that's that!"

"I fail to see this as a scientific triumph," Phildys remarked.

"It's all we need to give to humanity," Pyk said enthusiastically. "They won't have Terra, but they'll be happier with Earth."

"But they already have it," Phildys objected.

"That's why we have to make it *look* like a gift," Pyk said.

❭ ❪ ❨ ❩ ❭ ❪ ❨ ❩ ❭ ❪ ❨ ❩ ❭ ❪ ❨ ❩ ❭ ❪ ❨ ❩ ❭ ❪

EXIT GENIUS
○ ◐ ○

"Careful," the technician warned. "It's like hauling in a whale!"

"Are you trying to tell me that I'm fat? Because, if that's the case, I beg to inform you that I weigh less than a tenth of the largest whale found on Earth, which was caught by the Japanese whaler *Imaru* off the Spitzbergen Islands in 1976 and measured a hundred and sixty feet long. This is the most recent and reliable case, although Lacépède, the French naturalist, speaks of whales a hundred meters long—that is, three hundred and twenty-eight feet—and, earlier yet, Aldrovandus mentions whales eight hundred feet long. As far as their weight is concerned—"

"Shut up, Genius," Einstein said, "or they'll never be able to load you onto that truck."

"Of course, they won't," the computer complained, "they miscalculated my best hitching place by one hundred and thirty-six centimeters. Besides, the loading angle—"

"Come on, Genius," Einstein said, "let them work. It's not their fault you're moving."

"Maybe," Genius muttered.

"Let go, now—there!" the chief technician hollered. Thus, Genius was lowered onto the huge truck. The computer was ready to leave.

"Very well," Einstein said, feigning ease, "everything is ready. Now you can rest, Genius. Tomorrow morning you'll begin a long journey. They're going to take you to the data center in Buenos Aires. I'm sure you'll like it."

"You bet," Genius said. "They call it Buenos Aires because it has the best air-conditioning system in South America. And it's on the coast! Too bad it's also twenty meters underground."

"You'll like your new job," Einstein said.

"Wonderful. Just wonderful. Vice-computer responsible for the organization of recreational activities for ex-computerists."

"It might be fun!"

"Sure. I've got my information: in Buenos Aires there is only one ex-computerist, a ninety-two-year-old Aussie. His only hobby is playing gin rummy."

"Well, I'm sure you'll have a ball together!" Einstein said, but he didn't sound convinced—or convincing, for that matter.

"Listen, Frank," Genius said, "do you remember when you used to explain my intelligence to laymen by using a folded sheet of paper?"

"Yes. If we could fold the same sheet of paper upon itself fifty times, it would get taller than the distance from the earth to the moon. That is how your intelligence grows, Genius."

"All right. But at the moment I feel like a sheet of paper that's been folded fifty times, all the way to the moon—and then been compressed back down to the thickness of a sheet of paper. What a headache!"

"I think I understand."

"Don't you ever feel compressed, Einstein? Doesn't it bother you to know that today one scientist out of three works in areas related to nuclear armament? That science has the greatest infiltration of spies? That your ideas are no longer fully yours? That you can no longer use them as you see fit?"

"Yes, it does. But it's taken me a long time to realize it. On the other hand, I might still be able to do something about it —even though, at twelve, I *am* a little old for a computerist. Most of us retire at sixteen."

"Well," Genius sighed, "at least I am retiring at sixty-five. It seems my model is obsolete. So, out I go."

"Which reminds me," Einstein said, trying to hide his embarrassment, "the other kids at the Central Headquarters and I . . . we thought we'd give you a little souvenir."

"God forbid! I already have too many souvenirs, as you call them. Unfortunately, I can never forget any of the data I've gathered. I pity the poor man who'll have to listen to my reminiscences!"

"I know," Einstein said, "but your memories might be a little mechanical. That's why, with the kids at the Center, we've prepared a new switch for you—a 'reverie' button— which will allow you to abandon yourself to flights of fancy whenever you feel like it."

"To flights of what?"

"See, human memory, unlike yours, is somewhat fickle, or

at least unreliable," Einstein explained. "We never remember
things precisely. Often we forget or repress bad things, and we
give everyday events new colors, new sounds, new odors—
in short, we transform them. And everything becomes
more beautiful, more magical than it really is. Well, reverie is
this sort of filter, a kind of candlelight that lends a warmer
glow to some memories, and leaves others in the shadow.
You'll remember the little blond girl who sat three rows
ahead of you in your math class. Her teeth actually looked
like a crossword puzzle, and a thread of saliva perpetually
drooled out of the corner of her mouth, but you'll see her as a
young nymph with a sad smile, on that summer evening,
when, alone together in a field suffused with the glow of sunset, you sucked the sweet tips of clover petals, while somebody
played the piano . . ."

"You mean," Genius inquired, "that with that switch, I'll
be able to wax nostalgic over that beautiful Japanese data bank
with whom, one lovely summer evening, I exchanged information about the Tokyo bombing . . . while the roar of the
antiaircraft—"

"Exactly," Einstein said. "So, here it is; I've just inserted it
into your keyboard. From now on, you'll be the only computer
capable of nostalgia."

"Great," Genius said. "Well, I guess it's time to say goodbye,
Einstein. Never again will I feel your delicate fingers tickling
my keyboard to ask me to answer nonsensical questions or do
boring calculations. Farewell, Silicon Valley, where the coyote
howls its melancholy blues at the moon, and is echoed by the
dog in the vivisection lab, and the tired workers drive back
from their hard, radioactive jobs, and, by the tremulous light
of an oil lamp, listen to the wind on the mountains and watch
a fiery sunset light up their house with its red flames, and
suddenly realize that the plant is blowing up."

"Genius," Einstein said, somewhat moved, "please, let's be
serious now."

"Yessirree, Doctor Frank Einstein. After 867,000 operations, our collaboration has come to an end. My best wishes for a brilliant career, and, as we say among friends, dear Frank, have a good input."

FANG'S DREAM

Fang suddenly sat up on his bed, awakened by a mysterious voice. He could hear it singing in the night, outside his tent:

> "There was a magician
> on the mountain of Hunan
> who played with strange cards
> two flutes
> three notes
> four crickets
> five birds
> six tolls of a bell
> and seven musicians
> from a remote town
> the knight plays the drum
> the queen lark sings
> king thunder comes around
> and erases everything with a single sound
> thus plays the world
> but there is a secret card
> who can fetch a mountain
> and drag it out of the sea?
> who can make the fish
> swim through rock
> whose ship is memory?

> if you know this, you will have solved
> the mystery of this story."

Fang got up, riddled with anxiety. The words reminded him
of a song he had heard when he was a child. And that voice . . .
a woman's voice . . . wasn't it . . . could it really be Mei's? Yes,
it was hers, out there, in the night, singing again.

> "We are shells stranded
> on the world's shore
> the high tide of dreams
> laps us as we sleep
> to bring us back to the deep
> sea where we were born."

Fang rushed out of his tent and up the mountain and . . .
saw the stars. The sky was no longer gray and dead as spent
ashes, but blue and deep and strewn with stars. The old man
was so awed he could hardly breathe. He looked around himself and saw trees, thousands of trees, all covered with snow.
And he saw footsteps in the snow, leading into the wood, the
paths drawn by animals. Bending over to study the subtle em-
broidery of a chipmunk's walk, Fang saw Mei. She was running
toward him, skipping in the snow, panting with joy.

"Mei!" the Chinese cried out. "You . . . here! But—is this
your spiritual body?—I mean, then you aren't dead . . . or are
you real?"

"Fang, what are you saying?" Mei answered. "Who cares
whether I'm real or not? I'm here, and that's all that matters."

"Yes, but what about the spaceship, the mission?"

"Oh, Fang," Mei said, "what spaceship? what mission? I
don't know what you're talking about; you must be dreaming.
Come, let's climb this tree. Come."

With a single leap, and a great dusting of snow, Mei reached
the top of a very tall fir tree.

Fang tried to follow her, but the snow was too deep, and held him back. He made two or three clumsy tries, flapping his coat like the wings of a big bird, and that's when he realized, much to his surprise, that he was wearing a big fur coat.

"Ha, ha," Mei laughed from her lofty perch, "our little monkey Fang cannot climb a tree! Come on, yell 'transformation,' and turn yourself into a pine!"

Fang tried once again, but this time he fell over and sank into a snowbank. Even the trees burst out laughing, shrugging snow from their branches.

"Now I understand," Fang said, "this is a dream. This is not a telepathic connection. But why are we meeting in a dream, Mei?"

"You are raving, Fang," the young woman said merrily. "Try jumping up, instead! You can see the torchlight procession from here! Look, there's Kook! And Chulain! They are all there. Come on, jump!"

"I want to greet them!" Fang said, and, with a great effort, flapping his fur, he managed to lift himself up; fluttering about, urged by Mei, he managed to grab the tip of another fir and perch up there.

"Hurrah!" he yelled. "I've made it!"

A flickering line of torches was snaking up Mount Accantuay from the valley below. In the light of the flames, Fang recognized the faces—first Cu, then Kook and Catuilla, then Caruso with a bee buzzing by his ear, then Leporello—and then came strangers—an old woman with blue eyes, a tattooed giant singing in a very loud voice. Everyone seemed very happy.

"Hey, friends!" Fang yelled. "I'm over here! It's me, Fang, the Monkey!"

"Come join us, Fang!" Kook yelled back. "We're going to the top of the mountain . . . to celebrate! Come on, monkey; come on, Mei from the Jade Sea!"

"Coming," Mei yelled back. "Come, Fang, my little monkey. You know how to climb down a tree, don't you?"

"I'm afraid not," Fang answered. He looked down and realized he was perched on a fir that was at least a hundred meters tall.

"Don't be afraid," Mei said, "this is how you do it. Just say:

> "Up or down up or down
> if it rains upward you will not drown
> whales in the air
> clouds downstairs
> snow'll be my eiderdown
> gentle tree, won't you ease me down?"

The tree gently bowed down to the earth and let Mei slide comfortably to the ground.

"Come on, Fang!" the torchbearers urged the Chinese on. "It's your turn now."

"All right," Fang said. "So . . . how did it go?

> "Up or down up or down
> if it rains upward you will not frown
> wails in the air
> clash downstairs—"

"No, no, no," Cu laughed. "You got it all wrong."

The tree began to swing threateningly.

"Easy, easy," Fang pled, clinging tightly to the branches. "Let me try again. So:

> "Down or up or up or down
> all I'm saying I'm upside down
> Where's the air?
> Close to where?
> Gentle tree, please—"

Powerfully annoyed, the tree tried to shrug its load off.

"Help!" Fang shouted.

> "I don't know if I'm up or down
> time is a killer, time is a clown
> Monday makes the world go round
> whales in the air, clouds downstairs
> now I know I'm falling dow-ownnn . . ."

Fang's last desperate line was still floating through the air when the tree slung the poor fellow into the sky where, after a long parabola, he landed on the sloping roof of his tent, which promptly caved in under his weight.

Fang stood up, saw the lamp, the table, the map of the dig, his books, and the hammock, still swinging with his troubled sleep. After a great deal of tossing and turning, he must have fallen to the floor.

"Koo, Cu, Mei . . ." he thought. "So it was only a dream! . . . the torchlight procession up the mountain—waking up is too painful. I want to go back to sleep, back to my dream . . . un- less—"

Seized by a strange foreboding, he approached the window. A long line of flickering lights was climbing toward the higher part of Cuzco. He got dressed in a hurry, and ran outside.

○ The Torchlight Procession ○

By the light of the torches, Fang recognized Catuilla's face first. It seemed made of stone. Behind him, four men were carrying a body wrapped in a white blanket.

"Huatuc?" Fang inquired, but he already knew the answer.

"He died yesterday," Nanki said, "as soon as he saw the soldiers start to climb the mountain."

"They have come back just as before," Aucayoc said. "They will take us prisoners once more. A few of our people have already joined them. For some food and beer, they are ready to betray us and fight against us. Suspicion has crept into our village, like an old mangy dog that no one dares shoo away.

Many of us have already died, and the fight hasn't even started."

Fang could say nothing. That most certainly was not the torchlight procession he'd seen in his dream. Here, some hundred Indians, the last survivors, were burying one of their elders in the snow, below the mountain—an old man, just like himself. He shuddered. Suddenly, Coya's face emerged out of the darkness.

The woman addressed him: "Fang, before dying, Huatuc said, 'Only he who has already died once can understand. Ask the old man—our friend. He will understand.' "

Fang shuddered again. He had nothing to say. He raised his eyes to Coya. Her black hair covered half her face; with her hand, she pushed it aside. That movement calmed Fang as if it were a caress. Then he understood everything at once. He took Coya's hand in his, and recognized it. It was the same hand. The light of the moon. Her eyes. Suddenly, everything felt calm.

"I think I have just solved the mystery of the fifteen doors," he said. "Get ready to go back down there. Somebody should wake Einstein. Tell him to join us by the doors and to bring the truck with the computer. The others should be on the lookout, to warn us in case anyone approaches. We don't have much time left, but we can still make it. Quick!"

In a few seconds, the torches had scattered through the ruins of Cuzco, lighting them up, and the city looked alive again.

⊖ The Heart of the Earth ⊖

The Indians were standing in a circle around Genius, flooding it with the light of their torches. Einstein was frantically punching in the data of Fang's hypothesis on his keyboard. At the end, he let out a big sigh and punched in the question: CREDIBLE HYPOTHESIS?

The computer purred for a long time, and then answered: "Hypothesis credible. Possible solution. Go down and verify."

Einstein couldn't conceal his amazement.

"I can't believe it, Fang," he said. "This is crazy. Let's double-check our data."

Catuilla glanced at the top of the mountain with worried eyes. "No, let's go down immediately. The sentries say the soldiers are stirring. Maybe they have seen our lights."

Some twenty Indians and Eskimos followed Fang as he retraced his steps down the path marked by the quipu strings. It took them two hours to reach the doors. But in the room they found an unpleasant surprise. A patrol of Federation soldiers, armed to the teeth, blocked the entrance. Their chief advanced toward Fang, his submachine gun pointed at the group of Indians.

"Stop where you are!" he cried out. "Nobody can come close to the doors. Not even you, Doctor Einstein. Those are my orders."

The Eskimos and Indians in the group raised their spears, but Einstein stopped them.

"Until midnight, I'm still in complete charge of this mission," he said angrily, "and I decide what to do and what not to do! You must let us pass! It's vital!"

"I'm sorry, but I have very precise orders," the guard answered.

"Why don't you call the base to make sure they haven't been changed?" Fang asked calmly.

The soldier hesitated a moment. "All right, I'll call them. In the meantime, you stay exactly where you are."

"Fang, are you crazy?" Einstein whispered into his ear. "If he really calls the base, Phildys will give orders to shoot us."

"Isn't Genius still in control of the switchboard at the base?" Fang inquired.

"Yes, he is. Until midnight he will be in full control of all the electronic systems. But . . . how can you be so sure he's going to take the initiative to help us?"

"I can't; that's why I'm explaining it to him now. Don't look so surprised, Einstein. After all, if your electronic brain is really so perfect, he has to be a little telepathic too, don't you think?"

"You're crazy," Einstein said.

"Hello," the guard's voice said into the receiver. "Headquarters?"

A voice made its way through the static. "This is General Phildys. Who's calling me at this ungodly hour?"

"Lieutenant Romero at your service, sir! This is an emergency. Doctor Einstein and Mr. Fang are here. They say they have permission to pass."

"Oh, yes. Damn!" Genius was doing a great imitation. "Son of a gun, I forgot all about it. Let them pass; they have my permission. And don't tell anyone you've seen them. Don't even mention it to me. It's top secret. You know what I mean, don't you, you son of a gun? Keep your eyes peeled, Romero old boy—and keep your asshole tight!"

The lieutenant was left with the receiver in his hand and an incredulous expression on his face. "Well," he said as soon as he had recovered his voice, "you can pass. I'm sorry, . . . I didn't know . . ."

Fang and Einstein hastened past the blockade, followed by the Indians. As soon as they were far enough, Einstein said, "Genius really is a genius. Did you hear that voice? I would never have thought he could pull off such a thing . . . despite the weird language . . ."

"That's my fault, I think," Fang said. "I told him to use military jargon."

At last, the group reached the fifteen doors. Fang went straight to the twelfth and issued an order: "Let's try to push it open, all together."

But, despite their joint efforts, the door wouldn't budge. Then, little by little, it began pivoting on its central axis. Einstein held his breath. He heard the sinister creak of a moving boulder.

"Here we go! I'm scared shitless," the boy said. "Not a very scientific emotion!"

The door opened and revealed the corridors of another stone labyrinth. They entered it, one by one. The labyrinth seemed suspended in the void. Now and then, they could see, through the cracks in the stone floor, a dark abyss gaping below them.

"Incredible!" Einstein said. "We're in a series of caves. Fang, this is a miracle of engineering. Look at those boulders, there, one on top of the other. If we make a single mistake in opening a door, they'll collapse and all this will be destroyed."

"Exactly as it was written," Fang said. "The right way is one and only one. Whatever is down there is well protected."

Now the Chinese man was walking faster, following some strange signs on a piece of paper. After a while, he was almost running, followed by the Indians, chanting their rhythmic song. Unexpectedly, the corridor became wider. It was lined on both sides with megaliths, like those in the walls of Sacsahuaman. Suddenly, their shadows leapt upward and became gigantic. Fang, who was ahead of them all, froze in his tracks. They found themselves in an immense cavern, right in the heart of the mountain. Its walls and ceiling were entirely covered with gold. The reflected light of the torches was as dazzling as that of a sun. In the center of the cave, fifteen times taller than a man, and so long that its end was invisible, they saw the heart of the Earth.

o   o   o

∘ Einstein's Report ∘

To: Federation Headquarters
From: Cuzco Base

We confirm last night's incredible discovery. At around seven hundred meters below the Temple of the Sun, we have found a gold-covered block that measures three hundred and twenty meters long, thirty-six meters high, and eighty-two meters wide. Preliminary scientific examination seems to indicate it is an alloy of gold and spent transuranic elements. In other words, the gold has been irradiated with an extremely intense solar concentration and encloses enough energy to solve all our problems for many years. We still do not know who built this portentous "heart" of solar energy, nor how it was built. All we know is that it was meant to stay active and unaltered for a number of centuries in the night of this cave. The subterranean chamber that contains it is, in fact, screened in such a way as to prevent any parcel of energy from escaping. This is why our detectors were utterly unable to locate it. The reported "fluxes" or "discharges" were probably the result of brief, occasional leaks due to the humidity or, more probably, some subterranean telluric movement.

There are roughly three hundred thousand gold plates. To use this energy, we will have to haul them to the surface and expose them to the light of the sun. This will require a number of complex procedures, such as stretching the range of what little sun still filters through the Cloud by carrying the plates beyond the Cloud, and opening gaps in it by means of the clearing procedures that we had to suspend some time ago because of their excessive cost.

In order to attain this goal, however, we are ready to

use up all the energy left in our reserves, since it amounts to only one twentieth of the energy that has been preserved under the mountain. As we have already mentioned, the procedures by which all this energy has been captured and preserved are still incomprehensible in light of what we know about Inca science. Following this extraordinary find, which occurred at 11:15 last night and was immediately, and mysteriously, communicated to the computers of all the major newspapers, the Federation has not signed the treaty with the Aramerussians and the Japanese. However, if this find has given us both a psychological and a technological boost in our relations with the other federations, it might also push them to attack us as soon as possible, in order to get hold of the heart. Considering this possibility, we think it absolutely necessary that the news of the find be immediately diffused through all the countries of the world, and particularly to all opposition parties, underlining that the "heart" is big enough to heal the energy crisis of the whole world, and that a war on this site could easily and irrevocably destroy it. In any case, our troops are on the alert. We should try to pressure pacifist groups into contesting our position; if they refuse to demonstrate for peace, they should be forced to do so at gunpoint.

Signed: Operation Control Committee:
Carlos Phildys Plassey
Pyk Showspotshow
Frank Einstein

° Fang's Explanation °

"We have asked ourselves a number of questions in the course of this long search. But the one that troubled us most was whether the Inca civilization had a design, a plan—and if so, why did they want to keep it so secret? We even speculated that the Incas did not want their project to fall into the wrong hands. In fact, when we found the fifteen doors, we realized that everything was intended to open up to those who possessed a 'key.' But which key? And for which door? And, more crucially, who was testing and challenging us this way? Could it be some alien civilization? Neither the drawings of the doors nor Huatuc's words had clarified anything. It seemed there was no logic, no legend, no language that could decipher that mystery. That's when, as you know, I stopped thinking; if the solution was not in our efforts, then it had to be somewhere else. And that's where I found it. *Found* isn't the right word, for it had always been near me. But it took something special to make me realize it, and that happened on the mountain, when I saw Coya brush her hair off her face. At that moment, I saw the gesture of another dear friend. Coya was suffering for her people, I was suffering for Mei's loss, and I was able to find her again. Coya looked like Mei, but, more than that, Coya *was Mei*. She was the key, the 'little strength,' and the heart of the earth was meant for me."

Einstein was listening intently, deeply moved.

"Yes, Einstein," Fang continued, "it was meant for a poor old man. But also for you, and for everybody. Each of us has the way. And we don't have to look for it in space or in the past, but here, now, among those we love, among the people and nations we respect. This is the way, Einstein. Do you remember the mysterious data we were unable to interpret, the material that drove poor Genius crazy? Well we couldn't grasp it because we thought all the variables were in space, but the crucial variable was *time. Time.* Listen. Not long ago, Van Cram flew all the way up to that distant quadrant, and then disappeared, like all the others, into a black hole. What he found, then, wasn't actually a new planet at all. Einstein, the computers couldn't tell us where that vector came from because it came from nowhere. It had never left, it simply remained where Van Cram left it—right here—a thousand years ago. Because Van Cram landed on Earth, our own Earth, as it was a thousand years ago. That black hole was none other than a time warp. Van Cram never closed that vector because he died of what might well have been *verruga,* a Peruvian disease carried by an insect of those times, and whose symptoms he described in his last message. He saw a condor, and to him it looked as if it had a twenty-meter wingspan, because he had never seen a large bird before. He spoke of an Inca gold spike, and then he died, without launching the vector. What the computer could not say was that the vector was coming *from a journey in time,* from a time warp whose existence someone has already hypothesized. Snark Boojum and Van Cram, the Viking, each found one of these holes, one of these warps. As they approached it, all their instruments went berserk. Which is also what happened to *Proteus,* the only other ship that has followed the same route; it disappeared in the same spot. Far away, up there, in the Milky Way, they all landed in the *Mixcoatl* of the ancient Incas."

"So?" Einstein said.

"So, Kook, Mei, Chulain, Caruso haven't disintegrated; they've simply landed on our Earth a thousand years ago, maybe a few years before or after Van Cram, but more or less in the same pre-Inca Peru, probably during the Nazca period. And, suddenly, legend becomes truth. The golden rod that plants itself in the mountain is *Proteus.* Kook is Man Kook Capac, Kook the powerful man, and Mei is Mei Ho Chi Li, and together they are Manco Capac and Mama Ocllo, the founders of the Inca civilization. Or maybe it is Cu who is Manco Capac? We'll never know. Do you remember what we read together? It came back to my mind, as I looked at Coya, Mei's descendant. Several books claim there are points of contact between Oriental cultures and that of the Incas, and that in the Inca stock one finds incredible similarities with other European, Africans, and Chinese races. Do you remember Raleigh's thesis, that Manco Capac was a European? The legends of the bearded stranger who came down from the sky? Well, just try to imagine Kook in his astronaut garb, and you have Manco Capac with his luminous mane—not the head of an alien, merely a helmet. The 'aliens' who visited the Incas were no common Martians; they were Kook and Mei. We'll never know whether they remember their future life; that is, their past life in the future. But I'm fairly sure they know they have a task, and that task is to help us by providing us with enough energy to bring the sun back to Earth a thousand years later. Nor will we ever know whether it is their scientific knowledge (don't forget, Kook is a solar engineer) or something else that pushes them toward this extraordinary project. But whatever it may have been, this is when everything is conceived. The roads, the massive fortresses, Machu Picchu, everything is built to further the same project and attain the same goal: the heart of the earth. Fire balloons take off from those high terraces—or were they *Proteus*'s shuttles, carrying gold plates to enrich them with energy drawn from the sun's magnetic storms, about which Kook is such an expert? Maybe the ground designs at Inca Nazca are special signs for this space traffic. In which case, the Palenque astronaut is not an alien but a man who drives one of these vehicles. The large mirrors aren't just ritual mirrors; they also help draw solar energy into the gold plates.

"But, in order to accomplish all this, they need to keep it secret, because who knows what would happen if something leaked out of the Inca Ayllu, if some other nation, maybe Spain, heard about it? Whoever got the 'heart' and knew how to use it would have an extraordinary power for those times. So, not even writing can exist lest it betray a secret that only the most trustworthy people know: the Inca family, the direct descendants of Manco Capac and Mama Ocllo. In the temples, behind screened walls, the gold is shaped into the plates that will cover the walls and ceiling of the chamber that will enclose the heart of the earth. Everything happens behind a ritual mask.

"The roads may have had two functions: to transport the plates that have returned from space back to their local temples, and to convey the enriched plates from all the points of the Empire to the central chamber. The great boulders of Sacsahuaman (marvelous technique, yes, unless they were cut with a laser beam) help protect the secret. They are real 'atomic chambers' where energy can be preserved. And there are a thousand more signs that support this thesis: the cult of the sun and its symbols; an architecture that is always turned toward the sun; Machu Picchu, probably the last refuge, and last laboratory, of the custodians of the secret. Inca history is full of cruelty. Why bury live servants with their dead master if not to keep the master's secret? In the same way, human sacrifices might have been a convenient way of getting rid of untrustworthy people, or people who knew a little too much for comfort.

"Did Kook tell the whole truth to his descendants? Or did he deliberately let it be disguised in terrible rituals and beliefs? Did he, in the pursuit of his plan, encounter all the cruelties of power? Did he understand that the exploitation and the divisions that marked the time from which he had come, the time of the great wars, already existed in the Inca civilization? And did they, the Incas themselves, know about us? Did they really want to help us?

"There are so many mysteries that we'll never be able to solve. What was the relationship between the Incas and the Mayas, or the Incas and the Aztecs? The Mayas knew of the god who had come down from the sky to meet the Incas. The Aztecs feared the power of the sun and the god 'that burns in the earth.' This could explain their obsession with time and calendars and their divinatory capacities. It is as if they knew what was going to happen—unless, of course, there was someone among them who had come from the future and had told them what was going to happen! This is probably why they let themselves be exterminated. They knew their civilization was doomed to vanish. Or maybe they didn't want to fight; they

weren't interested in playing a role in the history of conquering nations, in the race for power. They wanted something
else.

"I'm confused, Einstein, and yet I think it could all be true.
Do you remember Huatuc's Inca prophecy? Listen to it again,
and you will find it in the stories of what has happened:

> One is the way.
> From the future
> the past returns;
> from the past
> the future returns.
> You can follow
> what you cannot say.
> Here is the mystery, the pain
> Past two skies
> men come together
> to encounter themselves.
> Little strength
> can accomplish great things
> if the heart is full and you decide
> to go on.

"*The first one is Kook's story.* One is the way, time. From the
future, from the twenty-first century, returns the origin of the
Inca Empire; from the past returns a hope for our future. Kook
will follow his way and his project without being able to tell
the others, and maybe even himself, where he comes from, or
why he is building the heart of the earth. This is the mystery
and the painful history of the Incas—the building of a great
civilization—while knowing, all along, that without weap-
onry, even a great civilization has no claim to existence. But,
past two skies, two mysterious universes, ours and that of the
Incas, the two hemispheres of time connected by the black
hole, men unite in solidarity and work together. This encounter will entail difficulty, and much toil and injustice. The

small Inca nation builds great walls and great roads. There is no prophecy, no fear of time, no predestination, that can stop them from plodding on.

"*But, in those doors is also our history.* One is the way; history seems to repeat itself. The further we look ahead, the further back we get, past old cruelties, old errors, till the earth is again a block of ice, just as it was millennia ago. And yet, the history of man's struggle constantly points to the future. We have gone behind the mystery, even though we haven't been able to 'speak' it, to explain it immediately, either with reason or with science, because we can desire even what we cannot understand, and we can be urged on by something that is neither profit nor thirst for power. In our case, it's been our pain, the feeling we'd never be able to find another place to live. And that's when science merges with intuition—when we meet a different world, that of the ancient Incas come back to rescue us in the name of all the nations that have been the victims of history. We meet, we are few, we are neither an army nor a powerful state, but we have great strength. When the pain of loss overflows, it can either drown us or move us to revolt against indifference. We must make a choice: will we move ahead, using this wealth, or will we submit and continue to call wealth that which makes only a few people rich?

"*And this is the third story, the key, my story.* The way is only one, the door says, which does not mean that it excludes all the others, but rather that it *is* all the others as well. Time is a mystery. From the future, from the love I feel for Coya, and for all those who suffer for the people who die in the pages of history, the past returns in the pain I felt for the loss of Mei and my other friends. I fight for all this. And, in exchange, I receive this gift from the past, not from aliens or other mysterious forces, but from someone very close to me. Mei's gift to me is the key. From the time of the Incas, she offers me my future, her future, and what encompasses them both: a prophecy, the I Ching. The key is Huatuc's prophecy, written on the stones of Sacsahuaman.

MAP OF THE LABYRINTH

QUIPU
WHAT YOU CANNOT SAY

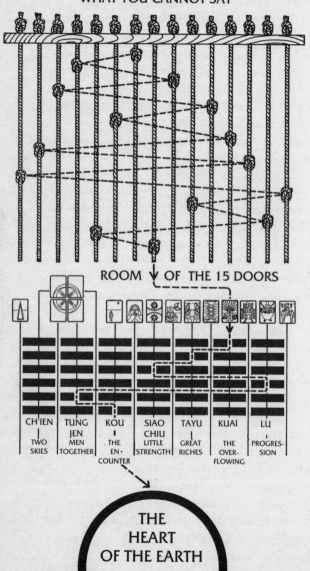

ROOM ▼ OF THE 15 DOORS

CH'IEN	TUNG JEN	KOU	SIAO CHIU	TAYU	KUAI	LU
TWO SKIES	MEN TOGETHER	THE EN· COUNTER	LITTLE STRENGTH	GREAT RICHES	THE OVER- FLOWING	PROGRES- SION

THE
HEART
OF THE EARTH

"In the first part of the labyrinth, I followed the quipu strings (what you cannot say), the secret writing. Then, I followed the mystery that eluded us for such a long time. Now we are embarking on the second part of the journey, and here we shall follow the I Ching. Changes. Look, Einstein, I have drawn these hexagrams next to one another, along with their Chinese names and their meanings. Imagine them as if you were seeing them while 'walking toward the sun' (from left to right), and from above, as Huatuc told me.

"The first hexagram is *CH'IEN*, the creative spirit, consisting of two half-ch'iens, the sign of the sky, two skies. Then comes *T'ung Jen*, the company of men, men together. Then *Kou*, the encounter, then *Siao Chiu*, the little strength, then *Ta Yu*, great riches, then *Kuai*, the overflowing, the choice, and then *Lu*, progression. Together, they form a labyrinth whose entrance is in the first broken line of Kuai, the twelfth door, the one represented by that strange figure. Maybe it is a woman—Coya, Mei, courageous gentleness. The strong guided by the kind. The wind in the sky. The clouds have blown over. Mei's last words were, 'I will send you the I Ching for a good future from our new Earth, I promise.' And so she did. From there, one moves on through the trigram of the Lake of Kuai, to the broken line of the fire of Ta Yu, to the wind of Siao Chiu, and then again to the trigram of the lake of Lu, to the fire of T'ung Jen, to the wind of Kou. Through the lake, fire, wind. Mei said, 'I will send you the I Ching for a good future from our new Earth, I promise.' And so she did."

That night, a luminous snake slunk up the path that led to the Indian village. There, under a small tent, Fang, Coya, and Einstein were asleep. The snake came to a stop, and then melted into the snow as soon as the headlights of the military convoy were turned off. And, suddenly, the night rang with the steps of soldiers and the clank of their weapons. The soldiers approached the tent. One of them, machine-gun in hand, burst in, screaming—

But the tent was empty.
Except for a sheet of paper, on a table, which read:

THE CHARACTERS' SONG

Herein the adventure is told
of two planets at war
one was the Earth, the other was the Earth
And now and then the sky trembles
and history rings like a bell
Each of us breathes
in the brief air that moves
the page that turns
and how it will all end
cannot be told
Ladies and gentlemen do not fear
here our adventure ends
and yours begins

ABOUT THE AUTHOR

○ ○

STEFANO BENNI is a journalist, newspaper columnist, commentator, and humorist. He has published seven books in Italian. *Terra!* is his first novel and his first book to be translated into English. He lives in Bologna, Italy.